The Jaguar Mask

This is a work of fiction. All characters, organizations, and events portrayed in this novel are either products of the author's imagination or are reproduced as fiction.

The Jaguar Mask

Cover art by Julia Louise Pereira
https://julialouisepereira.com

Edited by Selena Middleton

Published by Stelliform Press
Hamilton, Ontario, Canada
https://stelliform.press

Library and Archives Canada Cataloguing in Publication
Title: The jaguar mask / Michael J. DeLuca.
Names: DeLuca, Michael J., 1979- author.
Identifiers: Canadiana (print) 20240311116 | Canadiana (ebook) 20240311124
| ISBN 9781778092602 (softcover) | ISBN 9781778092619 (EPUB)
Subjects: LCGFT: Novels. Classification: LCC PS3604.E5487 J34 2024 |
DDC 813/.6—dc23

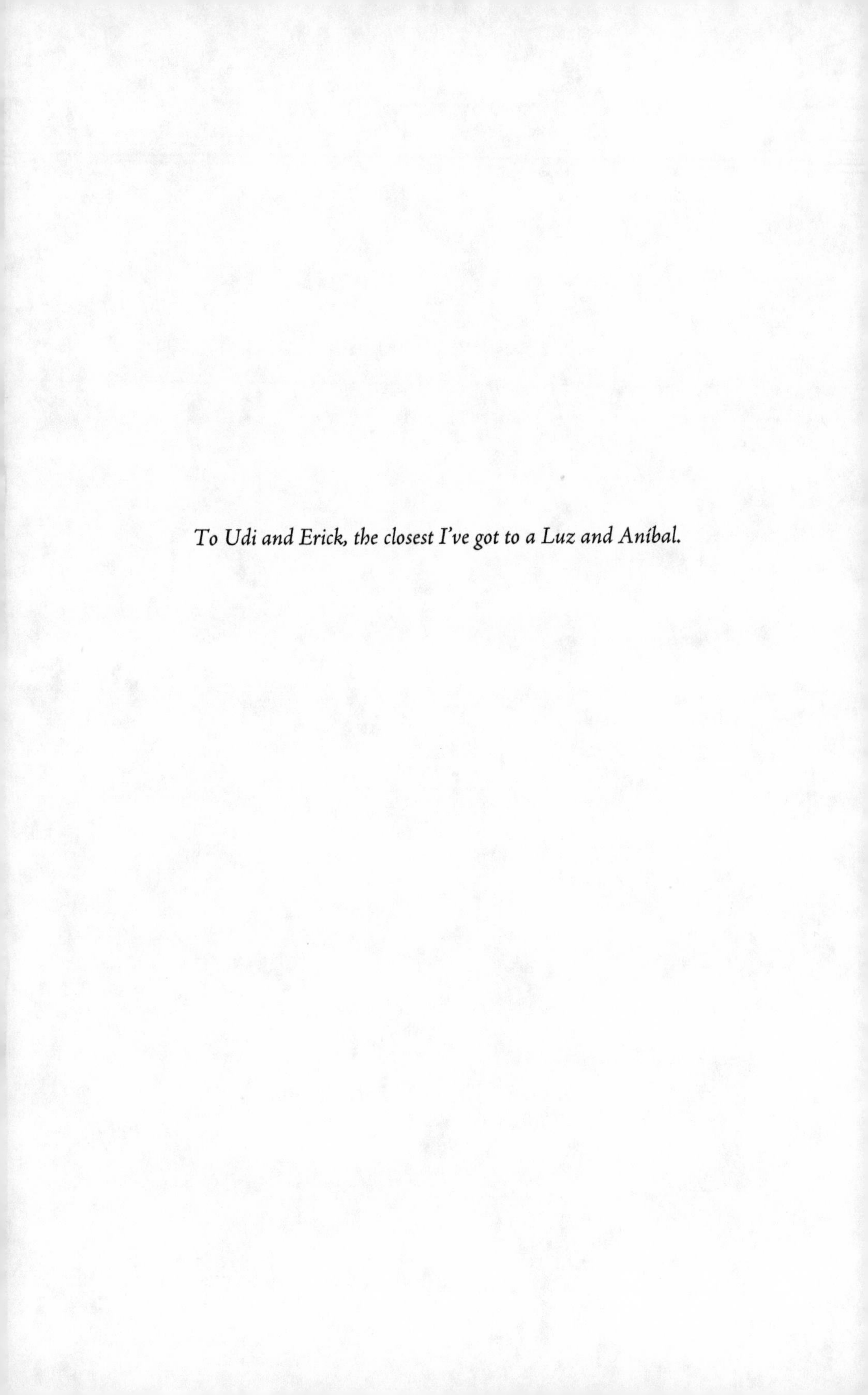

To Udi and Erick, the closest I've got to a Luz and Aníbal.

THE JAGUAR MASK

Michael J. DeLuca

Stelliform Press
Hamilton, Ontario

Table of Contents

Cristina's Dream

Four angels of death in the colorful plumage of trogons hunted the crowded city market, wearing the gang-tattooed, barely-pubescent bodies of mareros, carrying machine pistols painted the pale of maize husks burned to ash. Though the mareros mugged warrior faces and joked, contesting as if under duress to parrot devil-may-care vulgarities, the angels' gazes never wavered, eyes fixed in their sockets like the eyes of owls. People fled from them or didn't. A man lying discarded under a jagged-toothed awning raised a hand — a ring, dull gold and emerald in shadow — and whispered something to the one with the half-skull face tattoo whose angel's tail-feathers were barred volcanic blue and white. He repeated it. The one in the Santa Muerte shirt touched the faint fuzz of boy-moustache above his lip with a powder-burned finger. They didn't make any more jokes.

Down the street of stalls where men in mirrored glasses tried to sell your stolen cellphone back to you, through close-hung canyons of cooking implements, past shit-smelling bundles of live turkeys trussed in mesh sacks, past a pair of uniformed policemen who looked the other way, the angels proceeded to a comedor at the end of a row. The Comedor Santa Rosa de Lima was distin-guished from the others only by its glowing coat of saffron paint and the small crowd of people in line at the lunch counter, who at the angels' approach scattered in a burst like sparrows.

Above the narrow eat-in table by the kitchen hung two of Cristina's framed paintings — of the Virgin and Antigua in a hurricane — and a string of paper letters that once said "HAPPY BIRTHDAY" cut and reassembled to read "PRAY FOR US." Beneath them, a pair of government employees sat with an absurdly tall, distinguished foreign diplomat folded double over plates of fried chicken and rice. Cristina's mother emerged from the kitchen, brushing flour from her hands onto her grease-transparent apron, shouting a warning drowned by the chainsaw-running-on-empty rattle of bullets that painted them, all four, in red against the saffron-colored wall.

It came as something like a dream, on the bus with the death-harbinger newspaper twisted in her lap under the baby and her phone crushed in her fist, buzzing: her Tía Constancia this time, or again — she'd lost track. But it couldn't be a dream, because nobody could dream aboard a crowded, rickety bus careening around the sides of mountains except babies and old women who'd been practicing all their lives. So not a dream. A vision.

The phone quit buzzing, then started again. "Don't answer it," said Lencho sleepily, his slim hips twisted sideways on the bench seat to accommodate a bulky stranger.

But Cristina was Mama's oldest, her favorite, as agreed by everyone but Cristina, making her chief among the bereaved as well as the one they all would come to, from now on, about everything. She didn't know how to get out of it. She didn't know who to anoint in her place or how to be cruel enough to visit it on anybody else. She didn't know how the family would change, and it scared her.

"Tell me," she said into the phone, a finger in her other ear against the bus loudspeaker blasting a tin ranchera.

"There's a girl at the door," said Tía Constancia's voice, high and panicky, intercut by the mountain's shadow. "At your mother's house, a girl. She says she worked there, at the comedor. She's crying."

"Let her in!" said Cristina.

The driver, barely visible past a topography of heads, bags and babies, hunched into the brake and cut wide around teethmarks where the ravine was eating the road. Everybody leaned left. A rust-and-blue hatchback bound in the other direction screeched to a halt, honking like an angry jay.

"What? Sorry, Tía." Cristina worried for the bundle of colorful, meaningless canvases on the roof of the bus. They represented weeks of work, potential months of groceries and phone bills, and not one shred of emotional investment. Let them fly.

"What if she's lying?" Constancia repeated. "This is the city, it's dangerous. She could have read it in the news. She could be a thief."

Cristina's Tía Constancia cherished worry as a basic element of human interaction, like smiling or physical touch. Mama considered it a form of procrastination. How they'd developed these opposed but complimentary traits was something their children would never be permitted to understand.

Now Constancia was the eldest.

But the city *was* dangerous. A necessary evil to making a living, according to Mama. Cristina preferred the highlands, where the balance of their enormous family remained, so scattered across mountain hamlets they never got together anymore. They'd get together now.

"Would you rather leave an innocent girl who just survived a terrible trauma crying on the doorstep," said Cristina, "or maybe risk letting a thief in to steal Mama's saints? What would the saints say?" What Mama would say she didn't have to guess.

"San Gregorio forgive us — the saints can speak for themselves, Colocha." A pause, some muffled argument — who else was at the house? "I'm letting her in," said Tía in a tone of warning. *It's on your head now, Colocha.*

She hung up, or the call faded. Already they were lurching down out of clouds into sprawling outskirts that leapt and shivered past the windows: vehicle chop-shops, tiéndas, pandering political billboards, concrete-block buildings haloed in rebar, drifts of offal in the armpits of switchbacks. The baby coughed and spat up, restless in sleep. Cristina wiped him with her shawl.

"Let me," said Lencho. "He likes me better."

She was so tired already. She squirmed to lay Miguel Ángel on his brother's shoulder, then took the twisted-up copy of the *Diary* with its tabloid headline and forced it out through the crack in the window, where the wind tore it open and disseminated the sheets fluttering into the valley. She pressed her forehead against the skin-textured brown plastic of the seat in front of her and closed her eyes.

Under the Mask

Artisans Market Massacre! Four Disemboweled by Bullets. A blurry image occupied most of the screen: a woman in a flowered blouse and a man in a fedora sobbed in each other's arms surrounded by cops half-smiling with the flush of fame; the rest was logo.

The fucking *Diary*. Must be the third time at least they'd recycled that photo. Felipe flipped back to the music player on his fancy, new, probably stolen phone and cranked a dubstep hook that rattled Baby's mirrors, a bubble of bass isolating him from the world. He rested one maze-patterned paw on the wooden conquistador mask on the seat beside him and went back to watching through the cracked, tinted glass.

City traffic merged by inches onto the eastbound Pan American Highway, striped by late afternoon in orange bars that shifted with the locust branches. Block glass glimmered dully from fortified apartment buildings. In the overgrown shadow of the ruined aqueduct, a knot of sparrows rippled like a stereo visualizer. Two teenagers on the median waiting for the light expressed mutual devotion in a snarl of arms and legs. In a rare moment, in the right mood, the city could be transformed. But it was all still predators and prey.

On the sidewalk, recent arrivals hollow-eyed with culture shock dragged toward the airport bus stop. He never bothered with the terminal itself anymore: too much security, and to the purse-clutching foreigner an unlicensed cab looked like a disappearing waiting to happen. Here, though, a hundred meters from the exit, the slightly more intrepid traveler otherwise too cheap for a taxi found themself surrounded by sullen brown locals. Inevitably they'd get desperate, and Felipe would be waiting.

Aníbal's ringtone was incongruously chill: acoustic guitar, the intro to a protest song. He stabbed at the screen. "What? Kind of in the middle of something."

"Felipe, what up, 'mano." His roommate played macho like she'd been born to it — her Spanish was flawless, her voice a smoke-aged growl. "Wondering if you're coming out with us tonight."

Back in Santa Catarina, he'd never have passed up a life-threatening ride in a pickup truck bed down the volcano's flanks to the clubs in Antigua. In the city, he tried to do without: too much risk. It was easier, cheaper, safer just working until his eyes crossed and he couldn't help passing out despite sobriety. He growled non-committally. "Like I said, if I'm free. For real though, what? Need a ride? Word from your mama?"

Aníbal laughed ruefully. Her parents had cut off her allowance; she and Luz owed him their part of the rent. "The protest, remember?"

He winced. "Ah, yeah. That today?"

The calendars taped under the stereo display — one Christian, the other the concentric and interlocking gears of the Long Count — had a special highlighter color just for Luz and Aníbal and their shoestring human rights agenda, chartreuse for fucking crazy. He'd heard it all over a week of breakfasts, though there'd been nothing in the news: police had supposedly massacred twenty-two campesinos in Totonicapán, in some mountain village he'd never heard of and now would never hear the end, probably not so different from where he grew up, only farther from the city, poorer, and to its citizens' greater sorrow, on top of some silver deposits the government could not be stopped from selling off to foreign interests, like everything else. For this, poor farmers were simultaneously poisoned and relocated — or would have been if the police hadn't murdered them for complaining. Just like in the old days. And just like in the old days, there were people who thought they could fight it. Only now it was his two best friends in the world.

The further you got from the city, the further back you went in time. Out there, the internet, phone cameras, and therefore objective reality hadn't been invented. Not that he didn't believe completely real oppression was being visited on somebody somewhere who deserved better than a handful of penniless idealists agitating on their behalf.

"Tomorrow. Tons of people coming in by bus, we could really use the help ... but also now. Right now."

It was always now, right now. "Listen —"

"A friend, a supporter, needs to get out of the city. No questions asked. I'm dealing with permits. Luz has to meet some people in Antigua." A government that required daily civil rights demonstrations as a reminder not to murder its own citizens was the same government they expected to treat demonstrators fairly when they came looking for permission. "You're the most 'no questions asked' person I know ..."

Heavy knuckles against the window by his ear — Felipe jumped half out of his skin. The side mirror showed him the middle third of a squat man in a cheap suit, a cheaper windbreaker zipped over it. He fumbled the mask up over his face, tightening the ribbon that suddenly fit over human ears. Had they seen? Of course not; that was what the tinted glass was for.

"Ninth Ave," said the suit, through the narrowest of window slits Felipe cracked open to afford it. "Artisans' market." Then, louder, angry, into a flip phone: "I don't work for you, remember? Consider it a favor, to be called in at the least convenient moment."

"What?" said Aníbal.

This was not someone in the market for Indigenous handicrafts. Felipe muffled the receiver. "Sorry, man. I try not to get involved."

The thick lips quirked. "Relax, I'm not the police. Tell you what: get me there while it's light, you name your price."

"Hello?" said Aníbal.

Felipe hesitated only briefly. Chances were Aníbal's phantom fare couldn't pay — not a lot of money in justice. It seemed he was going to be solely responsible for the rent. He could manage, if he knuckled down. But it would mean no more sending money home, keeping his parents' cable on, his nephew in plastic army men. He hadn't been home in a year, though Santa Catarina was just the other side of the volcano.

And there was always something else. Gas. Bribes for the cops. Someday that crack in the windshield would open up and cut him to pieces, unless he got it fixed. Not today.

He named a ridiculous price — the kind he usually reserved for foreigners.

"Come on, man," Aníbal was saying in his ear. "You know how rare it is for NGOs and locals to get together. We've got a chance at real, international attention. And — ah — my friend is in a lot of trouble. Play tough all you want, I know you care about this stuff."

The suit propped the phone against a shoulder, arguing inaudibly with someone on the other end, and plunged hands into windbreaker pockets. Felipe, who drove an illegal cab in one of the deadliest cities in the world, flinched. He'd learned to expect guns. The suit barked a laugh and thumbed a large bill against the black glass.

"Felipe? You there?"

"I'm here," he told her, looking at the money.

Then the suit jammed something else through the crack in the window: the muzzle of a cheap pistol. A throat-clearing sound, like the start of a landslide. "Have I mentioned I'm in a hurry?"

Felipe's own revolver, a pawnshop impulse buy, was buried in the glove box behind the tire gauge and a handful of fake IDs. Stupid thing had never helped him, not once. "I can't," he told Aníbal. He didn't want to worry her. More than she already was. "I already got a fare ... a big one. But I'll see you at Forty Doors, okay?"

A small growl. "Yeah, bullshit. Fine. Listen, can you just call me when you're —"

He cut off the call, checked himself in the mirror. For whatever reason, his mind translated this mask — a rosy-cheeked, beatific caricature of a sixteenth-century Spanish conqueror — to a handsome, jade-eyed Argentine. Some days he hated the moustache; for the moment it would do fine.

In the world of her tourist-bait paintings, there was no city. All the roads wound tranquilly down to the lake between jacarandas blooming out of season and quaint old houses made from adobe and red tile instead of concrete and tin, the kind of houses not even rich people built anymore because of earthquakes. It was always morning or sunset, just before the rains rolled in or after they'd broken. Far-eyed women wore dresses woven yesterday, and there was no violence and no pain.

A curving ribbon of red trailed along the painted gutter, unmistakably a trickle of blood. The thin black slash on the painted street — a piece of dirt, a fleck of blackened cornhusk blown from somebody's griddle? It looked like a gun. Like the cheap semiautomatic rifle carried by everyone from police to grocery store security. Stiff wind and the goose-pimpled skin under her arms made her suddenly glad of the baby sleeping in his bundle against her back despite the penetrating highland sun. Cristina laid aside palette and brush and grabbed a rag to blot away her mistake. When she reached for the brush again, the heel was angry red with bougainvillea dye, but the tip had been dipped in black.

With an explosive hiss of brakes, the noon bus from Chimal pulled up teetering beneath its rooftop burden of trussed poultry, textiles and maize sacks, and the shouted advertisements began anew from the crowd of vendors the bus stop accumulated like river flotsam. Two foreigners stepped off, looking decidedly green — poor things — and Cristina did her best to shake off the chill. She levered herself and little Miguel Ángelito up off the stool to make a show of it. Foreigners — tourists — it was their shallow romanticism that determined what kind of art could earn a living, what kind of artist Cristina could be. Though she also had to be able to make a sale. Attracting attention was her nephew Lencho's area of expertise, so handsome with his big eyes and soft lashes. He was more than sufficiently full-of-himself to shout at the top of his lungs at perfect strangers, but he'd taken some money and run off downhill to get a chocobanana and flirt. He was thirteen. She couldn't blame him. The trouble was, she was shy, or lost in her own head — whichever the last person who depended on that money to live said the last time she'd failed them.

Hugo was last off the bus, his broad shoulders and chest turned sideways to fit down the steps past the ayudante, the buttons of his too-small jacket scraping the doorframe. She hadn't been expecting him. He waved away an offered newspaper, frowning slightly as he indicated the one tucked under his arm. A few bundles remained atop the bus bound for Huehuetenango, but he'd brought nothing else, not even an easel. Hugo couldn't sell his work here.

The wind placed a giant hand in the small of his back and shoved him toward Cristina. The paintings rattled, secure in their places.

"This is lovely," he said of a painting depicting a church facade to the green-eyed foreign couple as they passed. The Iglésia San Martín in Sacatepéquez, famous for its brilliant blue facade and reliefs of angels earthbound by armloads of fruit, here surreally lit by sunset, framed by mountains closer and darker than the mountains could possibly be, and with no sign anywhere of the zombie drunk who perpetually wandered the church square drooling on tourists for money. It wasn't as bad as the lake scenes, at least the contrasts gave a hint of drama. But Hugo didn't think so. Hugo wouldn't paint anything of the kind.

The foreign couple hadn't understood a word, or pretended not to. Bemused, they plunged downhill, clutching hats and wallets, lost moths drawn to the lake's ethereal glow.

"You should concentrate more on your own work," Hugo said to Cristina.

He always said that. "You know I can't. I need the money." Nobody paid for truth. Cristina was first to pull away, but not before his warm, rough embrace had woken the baby. "Hugo, what are you doing here?"

"I'm here when you need me," he said. "Take some time to yourself. I can sell art." *Terrible* art, she heard. "I can change diapers. Here, let me take him."

Lencho — Francisco now, he kept insisting — waved coming uphill past street vendors and pastel-painted storefronts, his chocolate-stained lips unpuckering into a contagious smile as he caught sight of Hugo. "Tío! What did you bring me?"

"I'm not your tío," Hugo said, with less than his usual humor. Shoving hands in his pockets, searching, he produced a dull coin.

He'd come all the way from Comalapa, left his studio, his students. "What are you doing here?" she repeated.

"Let me hold Miguel Ángel." Confused, she relented. The baby stopped fussing and opened his eyes, and she couldn't help smiling. Mama said he was barely old enough to recognize faces, let alone the world — but he seemed so astonished by everything.

Then Hugo passed her the paper, and she remembered the painted blood, the painted gun.

Comedor Santa Rosa de Lima

He'd expected to find Ninth Ave choked with green-and-yellow-striped police vehicles, tires on curbs, rubber burns on pavement, jackboots, yellow tape, submachine guns. Instead, just two official vehicles blocked the alley: a police pickup and a black SUV. Traffic crawled. Well-heeled shoppers filtered through the long shadows of buildings, while tiny women in huipíles woven in colors the blinding-on-black of malfunctioning LED displays scurried under heavy burdens from their path. Felipe wondered if they were here under duress; everybody but the tourists had to know what had happened.

The snores from the backseat were like a needle slipped past the edge of a turntable. Felipe cranked up the dubstep, and his fare coughed awake and waved the gun. "Turn that shit off." Toad eyes darted in the rearview as Baby crawled close enough to the SUV to reveal the government prefix on the plates. "Don't stop here. Circle around, find another alley."

Felipe picked an appropriately narrow side street and wedged Baby between a Datsun pickup older than he was and a heap of trash. He glanced at the dash clock before he cut the engine: eighteen minutes. Not a record; not bad for rush hour. "Five hundred," Felipe told the mirror.

The suit dragged a finger across each of the bags under his eyes in turn. "Barely gave me a chance to wink. Think I deserve a little more of your time."

This was why Felipe liked the airport; foreigners didn't know how to argue. "Want me to wait? Half now, or I'm gone."

"Half now, and you're coming with me for the rest." Sliding into the middle seat and leaning intimately forward, the suit gave Felipe a generous faceful of alcoholic coffee breath and a glance at a fat wallet, open to the inevitable ID card with its bad photo and official seal, impossibly beautiful green bird perched atop crossed rifles.

Special Inspector of National Civil Police Rodrigo Francisco Cuerva Zamora.

Felipe suppressed a groan. "You said you weren't a cop."

A shrug. "I'm not — anymore." The ID held steady long enough for him to catch that it expired in February, eight months ago. He glanced, out of nervous habit, at the calendars. Four Road according to the Maya sacred calendar, the feast of San Gregorio in the Christian. Saint's days in Santa Catarina, Felipe had always felt safe with the jaguar mask, the one his parents had given him at birth. In the city there were no sure things.

"Inspector Zamora to my former boss. Or my wife, who you won't have occasion to meet. You call me El Bufo like everybody else. I want us to understand each other. You drive an illegal cab, I used to be a police inspector. Simpático." He grinned yellow, and to Felipe's surprise, leaned back and put the gun away behind his stained lapel. "You want to show me some ID?"

"Not if I can help it?"

Ex-police Inspector El Bufo didn't insist. "Then get out of the fucking car."

Felipe thought about the revolver in the glove box, thought better of it.

The ultramodern, angular colonnade of the artisans' market rose incongruous amid the rotting Belle Epoque masonry of the old city, moss and creepers digging between casements absent only where fresh paint covered expired political graffiti. Concrete reliefs framing the entrance depicted heroic workers laboring in abundant fields beneath temples restored to ancient glory. Something resembling an evening rush was underway. Government workers, foreign diplomats and mining company execs with their spouses and servants, even a priest or two circled past stalls offering — at tourist markup — tamales, dulces, hot milk with rice, hot punch with rum-infused pineapple and chirimoya, woven and embroidered cloth, shoes, hammocks, figurines of gods and angels, hyperbolic paintings of a kind with the reliefs at the entrance. All of it fake, an illusion. Aníbal would say the government needed places like this to justify itself. Hard as Molinero tried to convince everyone his authority extended seamlessly from those ancient temples, they would still be in ruins. The real city market, where Luz and Aníbal shopped on Sundays, assembled itself overnight in a trash-strewn empty lot behind the bus terminal, then disappeared just as quickly. The food was the best anywhere, and cheap, if you knew how to deal. Felipe preferred the megamart, where the masks were obvious.

One market aisle leading back toward Eighth had been partitioned with chainlink and orange plastic. The stalls were dark, sluggish flies spiraling. Kids peeked through gaps in the fence. El Bufo brushed them off like flies, and like flies they swarmed back. He kicked at the fence until a uniformed cop with a submachine gun dragged it aside, and the kids fled.

"My assistant," El Bufo grunted, when the cop waved the gun at Felipe — who would have been happier joining the kids.

He'd waited out a hijacker once, sat staring at nothing in the rearview until the would-be thief got nervous and bolted. Of course, the kid only had a knife. And he hadn't paid his fare. And he'd looked so skinny and pathetic running off into the Zone Three midnight Felipe almost regretted not giving in so he wouldn't have to feel guilty when he saw the corpse in the morning news.

"Would you shut up and play along?" El Bufo murmured, though Felipe hadn't said a word.

The crime scene was the last stall in the row. It smelled like a combination slaughterhouse and fried chicken shack and looked like something had chewed it in half. Broken tile and bullet casings lay in drifts. Beyond another chainlink-and-orange-plastic screen, the police pickup and the black SUV waited in the alley.

El Bufo took a long look, a shallow breath, and started to laugh.

"What's so funny?" asked another cop with a submachine gun slung over his belly.

"Where's the blood?" El Bufo said. "I mean the rest of it. Ought to be running in the gutters."

There was blood — everywhere but the floor. Blood transformed the yellow wall from desperately to delusionally cheery, spattered the counter, the cheap tablecloth, the cheap landscape hung above the table, even the plastic flowers.

"Don't look at me," said the cop. "Mopped up after they took the bodies. Didn't want it scaring the shoppers?"

"And they left you to make sure nobody else disturbs the evidence now they got it disturbed just how they wanted."

"Didn't want to make it easy for you," said a voice behind them among market shadows.

"Gilberto," said El Bufo, shooting Felipe a look. Felipe had known him half an hour and already he was speaking in glances?

"And who's this?" said Gilberto, all false friendliness. He was thin-featured with a permanent sneer, no uniform — just another cheap suit — clipboard under one arm and a styrofoam cup steaming in his hand. "Your chauffeur. Looks like something you scraped off the floor of a nightclub."

"This is Félix," said El Bufo, putting an arm around Felipe, a momentary, leering caricature of intimacy. "Distract him," he mouthed theatrically into his ear, then stepped past him, over a pile of rubble into the kitchen.

Félix? Like the cat.

The rooster-necked Gilberto — El Gallo, Felipe decided, laughing inwardly with desperation — sniffed, then slurped from his cup. "Get him out of here," he told the uniforms, gesturing to Felipe, never taking his eyes from El Bufo's back.

Two black-clad cops heaved bonelessly forward, with square-billed caps and pants tucked into boots, submachine guns pointed at him, expressions as bloody and blank as the walls. Like all such cops, to Felipe they resembled nothing so much as bad Che impersonators. He raised his hands very carefully. They were younger than Felipe. Reasonably good-looking. What would make someone like that join the police? Did it get them girls? What girls?

"Let's see some ID."

They weren't going to shoot him, not in the middle of the market. El Bufo was holding onto serious money, money he could use. "I, ah, left it in the car?"

While they searched him, only nominally invasively, El Bufo puttered in the kitchen. He tipped the landscape and a painting of the Virgin away from the wall. He picked up a neatly decapitated porcelain figurine of San Antonio from the blood-spattered table, put it down again. He ran a finger around the rim of a saucepan and tasted it.

"No ID," one of the cops said unnecessarily.

"My name is Félix Orellano," Felipe lied. "I'm nobody, I swear. I drive a cab."

"So search his cab," snapped El Gallo, not in the least distracted from El Bufo's smallest movements. He waved a hand. "Just get him out of here."

El Bufo shot Felipe a martyred look, then disappeared under the counter.

One of the cops prodded Felipe with a muzzle. The other grabbed his arm, twisted it painfully behind him and pushed him back toward the chainlink fence.

"Hey, I'm cooperating! Come on, he basically hijacked me here. He still owes me half the fare."

El Gallo laughed. "Get in line."

They'd know he wasn't licensed as soon as they saw Baby. They wouldn't care. They certainly had better things they could be doing. But cops — these cops, he was sure — were assholes. The glove box was stuffed with fake IDs, none of which said his name was Félix.

As they dragged the chainlink aside, El Bufo reappeared from beneath the counter, took the headless saint statuette from the bloody table and hurled it to the floor, where it exploded like a shot.

The cops wheeled, guns at the ready, but El Bufo had disappeared again. Felipe wished he'd had the presence of mind to buy coffee or atol from one of the solicitous old campesinas so he could beg her to hide him now. He should have taken his chances with Aníbal. He should have dumped El Bufo at the curb.

"Don't get jumpy," called El Bufo. "Just making sure you're paying attention."

"Stand down!" El Gallo waved away their weapons impatiently. "I never pegged you for suicide by cop, Rigo. Is civilian life so bad? Not enough people to manipulate, eh? You don't want the job, say so. I can see a ripe future for you as a radio preacher."

El Bufo came up again, smirked performatively, and picked his way out from behind the counter. "What exactly led you to believe I'd want this job? No bodies, no blood. Bunch of media noise. And I get what?"

El Gallo coughed. "You get to work again, Rigo. How long has it been?"

They scowled at each other.

"My last case working with my friend Gilberto," El Bufo told Felipe, "he let me take the fall for a 'record-keeping error.' The usual kind. Allowed a dangerous man of prominent station to walk free. I got fired — disgraced — and my friend gained a not insignificant promotion. Now he throws me this gristly bone dressed up as an apology, figures he's left me no choice but to accept."

El Gallo sipped coffee. There was, obviously, more going on here.

"You want my help," ventured El Bufo, "how about a little respect? This man —" El Bufo indicated Felipe. "— is my highly trained assistant. His opinion is invaluable to me."

El Gallo lifted his pronounced adams-apple, drawing attention to the repeatedly whitewashed, then re-graffitied wall above the alley. Like so many others across the city, here in the gathering dusk the blue fist of Molinero's Reform party all but obscured the open red hand of the previous, nominally less repressive administration. "I'm trying to help you, former Inspector Zamora. High-profile case, this. A matter of international attention, maybe. National, certainly. The president knows it. Sonriente knows it, you can be sure. I think you'll be surprised how easily they can forgive."

"Guess we'll find out," El Bufo grunted.

El Gallo held out the clipboard, the top sheet covered in handwritten scrawl. "Witnesses, such as there were. Names and numbers. 'Nobody saw anything.'"

El Bufo frowned. He took the clipboard and went over the cover pages cursorily, turning on his heel so that Felipe could look over his shoulder. He pulled one of the manila folders, flipped it open. "And the victims? Who were they really?"

"Autopsies pending." El Gallo narrated while El Bufo flipped the files open and shut. They acted like cops in a telenovela, all the while shooting each other the most uncomfortable looks. Felipe couldn't decide if they were serious about any of it. "Like it said in the news. Mynor Parrales, Dario Chanax, couple of mid-level bureaucrats, might as well have been you or — ahem, me, anyway." Their government ID headshots showed two middle-aged men, one sullen, the other dazed. Next, an older woman, hard-eyed, in a corté embroidered with quetzales. "Eufemia Yochi Ramos, grandmother, proprietress of this rat-haven. Collateral damage. Wasn't carrying ID —" He eyed Felipe. "But around here at least, she's famous."

Last, El Gallo fingered a photocopied foreign passport, spotted with what had to be more blood. A foreigner, athletic, with salt-and-pepper stubble. "David Alden Antonellis." Even Felipe could tell he was mangling the name. "Human rights lobbyist, former Ambassador from somewhere — not here. Your typical, rich, good-hearted-past-the-point-of-reckless fool, whose entire fault it is you or I have anything to do with this case. Tried to leverage his connections someplace leverage wouldn't reach. Remind you of anyone we know?"

"What a tragedy. That woman's cooking was worth three lawyers any day." El Bufo shoved the clipboard under his arm. "And you figured you'd help me out by telling all this to the media first."

"I didn't say a word. Not exactly airtight chain of custody in this department, you remember."

"How could I forget?"

If they were trying to outcompete each other at sarcasm, El Bufo had maybe the thinnest edge.

"Want to let me in on your plan?" said El Gallo.

El Bufo produced a cigarrita from somewhere, which he shoved between his lips and lit while he talked around it. "Got a few ideas. Let you know what they turn up. Time to go, Félix."

El Gallo clapped El Bufo lingeringly on the back between the shoulder blades. He leaned close to Felipe, his coffee breath condensing on the conquistador mask. No alcohol, at least. He liked his coffee sweet. "Don't trust this cabrón, understand?"

Dropping into Baby's passenger seat beside Felipe, El Bufo pulled out a crumpled, greasy fist of cash that made the whole car stink like the crime scene, burned fryer oil and death — thousands, not hundreds. "Old lady had it stashed inside San Antonio," he said, winking, in answer to Felipe's stare. "Figure she'd want it disbursed bringing her killers to justice." He plucked five large, worn bills and stuffed them in Felipe's hoodie pocket, then made the rest disappear as a pair of punks strolled out of the alley, mohawks glistening. "Not that you earned it — but you'll learn."

"I can't take this," Felipe said, making no move to give it back. Luz and Aníbal would kill him if they knew. Since they didn't, he could use it to pay rent.

Streetlights buzzed to life overhead. Bats flitted from their roosts under the eaves of the cathedral. Traffic crawled along Ninth. It wouldn't be easy getting out of here.

El Bufo opened the topmost of the evidence folders, revealing the face of Eufemia Yochi Ramos, mother of three, famous for her fried chicken. He read out the home address, a row house in Mixco.

"What — now?"

"The trail," pronounced El Bufo, feeling under the seat for the lever to recline the seat back, "is already getting cold."

Felipe shook his head. "I can't."

"You can't what?"

"I can call you another cab." He'd had three guns pointed at him in the last hour. He needed a minute. At least. And a drink. Preferably several. Luz and Aníbal would be waiting. "Someone else you can trust."

"Trust?" El Bufo laughed. "You're telling me you want to end this partnership before it's begun? You know there's more where that came from. A lot more. You can't pretend that wasn't fun, putting one over on old Gilberto."

He gave an odd, wistful sigh, nostalgic for old times with his corrupt asshole cop partner.

It had been more life-threatening, terrifying 'fun' than he'd had in a year. But El Bufo had called him "Félix," and now Felipe needed to know what El Bufo knew about anthropomorphic cats in conquistador masks. The last conversation he'd had on the subject — the only one in his entire adult life — had been with his half-brother Rubén; it had consisted of twelve words, and ended with Felipe quitting his job on Rubén's bus and lighting out for the city alone.

"When it comes to hanging onto his job," El Bufo was saying, "making love to the powers that be, Gilberto's the master.

Doctoring a crime scene, he's not exactly Lonnrot. Figures he doesn't have to be. He left a lead hanging, thinks I'm not stupid enough to pull it before it gets disappeared. If it hasn't been already. You're too young to remember; this shit used to be commonplace. Still is — they're tired of talking about it. Nobody *investigates* a murder like this. You put on a show. Which is where I come in."

"What lead?"

"A witness." El Bufo drew a pinched thumb and forefinger from his windbreaker pocket; Felipe's eyes focused on a few long, dark strands of human hair. "Girl who worked in the kitchen hid in the cupboards. The old story, country cousin sent to the city to live with her Tía Eufemia, learn to cook and clean, send money back home. She wasn't sharp enough to know about her boss's stash, but easy odds she robbed the body — she needed bus fare to get home. Question is, does she go home, back to the highlands? Or does she go to Eufemia's?"

Felipe checked his phone: another text from Luz. Hours yet before he was supposed to be at Forty Doors. It was going to take forever to get across the beltway.

He put Baby in gear. "What did he do to you, really? Gilberto."

El Bufo closed a thick fist over the evidence folders and lay back in his seat. "Tell you some other time."

Felipe hadn't come to the city to get away from his family, but for their sake, though sometimes the two were hard to keep straight.

"Don't do this, please." Rubén said when it happened, keeping his eyes on the road. "These people can't handle it. Neither can we."

The mask hadn't slipped. But everybody on the bus had seen. A lapse of concentration, a crack in his self-control? He didn't know how it worked. He never had; there'd been no one to teach him, not even one thin thread of connection from their Evangelical parents back past war and conquest to a pre-colonized past. But there was no mistaking it in the wide eyes of old women, the farmworkers' masks of indifference suddenly lifted from under straw hats and behind dusty collars.

At home in Santa Catarina, a shitty, dusty plantation village just far enough outside the city to be nowhere, people had forgotten, if they'd ever known; they'd had twenty years to let go of the rumors and accept him for what he appeared to be. The people aboard Rubén's bus were strangers, alike only in that they'd gotten on between Xela and the city sometime before dawn on a weekday. They had their own problems, their own faith, suspicions, superstitions. Just like everyone in Santa Catarina and everywhere else, they'd had a lot of practice at forgetting, letting go of loved ones disappeared. It kept happening, even an entire generation since the war. Rubén was right, they didn't need this any more than he did.

Standing in the aisle, rocking with the switchbacks, imagining the eyes of everyone aboard boring into the maze-patterned fur at the nape of his neck, the gangsta Bugs Bunny decal above the stairs glaring back at him with eloquent, paternal skepticism from under the words "HE DIED FOR US" in head-high blackletter, it took a minute to accept that this was the kind of moment people died of — and for. Nobody talked about the war — nobody who'd suffered through it, which was everyone above a certain age, half the people on that bus. It was too painful, his parents would say. They'd seen things, done things, but who'd admit that? He didn't even know what had happened to his father's arm, though he'd heard the story more often than he could count, the only speck of truth the stump itself. But you couldn't spend twenty years sharing a village with a loud, invisible silence and not make guesses as to its shape. He heard it as parable, a moral lesson. Keep your head down, don't get involved.

He sank down into the stairwell, out of everyone's sight but his brother's. As if that could undo what they'd seen. He'd had another brother once, a full brother. Martín had died before Felipe was even born. Felipe wondered sometimes, was he like me? Was that why he was dead?

He waited for a relatively safe stretch of highway, pulled the lever to fold open the door, then with practiced care climbed out, up the ladder and into the roof racks where only the vultures could see. Clinging between repurposed masa sacks and a pink plastic Dora-knockoff suitcase, he felt sick, lightheaded. Just the exhaust. Just the thin air. The brittle colors of the dry season clawed their way up out of the mountain gorges sharper and deadlier than before, and the vultures' ellipses shifted focus to his own vulnerable head.

Rubén was right, but it wasn't only that: Felipe wanted to get away. From Santa Catarina and its heartbreak, from his parents, his friends, even from Rubén. From the specter of what they knew, what they might remember.

At the next route crossing, Rubén paid him and hired a new ayudante, easy as that, and Felipe was on his own.

It so happened he'd been saving for a car, meticulously and at no small hardship. Nominal friends had begun to think him miserly. Girls, he'd once determined, would take an interest when he owned a car. In the time it had taken to afford one, girls in Santa Catarina had given up on him completely.

After years watching Rubén tinker with bus engines on the sides of highways, he knew how to pick out a jewel among lemons. The red '91 Corolla with the brown racing stripe didn't look like much; that was half the point. The crack in the windshield brought the price down, and he blew everything he had left on the stereo. He tinkered with names, called it Luz for awhile. That felt wrong. He settled on Baby.

The city presented itself by inevitability rather than any plan. Rolling down from the volcano on a wave of reggae into that wasps' nest of streets, he couldn't help thinking of Babylon. It was sprawling, complex, corrupt, it made his mother worry and his father shake his head, until he stopped calling to reassure them.

A recipe for anonymity, perfect and unrepeatable: a change of clothes; a change of face; a cracked windshield of tinted glass; half a million people afraid of themselves, of everyone around them, of the city itself, its haze, its leaf-shadow textures and unfathomable concrete; another half million out to prey on them. Nobody in the city wanted to know what anybody else was hiding.

Her Mother's House

Her mother's row house was as she remembered: windworn, weeds fissuring concrete into postvolcanic wastes. Behind the fence across the street, the ravine plunged away overgrown with junkyards and shanty hamlets, a forbidden river at its bottom. Herding Lencho out of Tío Juan's pickup to the big steel sliding door, Miguel Ángel slung wriggling under her breasts, she looked up beyond bougainvillea-wrapped barbwire for the stained-plastic figures superglued in the upstairs window — a crafts project she and her sister Corísa did when they were little, twenty years ago now. Mama punished them with washing every window in the house, but she let the figures stay. The windows hadn't been cleaned since.

Tía Constancia wore one of Mama's grease-colored aprons; she enveloped Cristina in such a hug Lencho had to intervene on behalf of the baby. "How could this happen?" she asked. "Who could be so awful?"

There wasn't anything to say.

A couple of Tío Juan's workers unloaded Cristina's stack of canvases from the truck bed and piled them by the door, careful to touch only the edges of the frames with their rough hands. Tío Juan leaned a sunburned elbow out the passenger window, awkward, frowning. He'd hover forever making them all late trying to think what to say, so she went back and kissed him.

Inside, it was warm, full of good smells and voices, comforts turned on their heads. The door clanged closed.

The stew smelled different from Mama's. In the kitchen, a gaggle of cousins assembled tamalitos. From the courtyard beyond came uncharacteristic silence — someone doing laundry the canaries didn't recognize? Six children and two dogs ran past underfoot, giving her no chance to register which ones. In the school graduation photos by the door, Cristina's smile looked strained.

"She's on the back balcony," Constancia said, getting something like a hold of herself, however briefly. "The girl from the comedor. She ran up there the minute I opened the door."

Tío Pancho, Mama's younger brother, sat at the big pedestal table off the kitchen. Cristina slid into a seat across from him, and he looked up from a cup of agua de Jamaica, the prayer plain on his face for the curio-case saints to transform it into something stronger. He might be six or seven years sober, a thousand, or none. A copy of the paper lay face-down between them.

"Heard from Teresa?"

Cristina hadn't. Not since Teresa left, without her newborn baby son, to try the border crossing months ago. She cast a glance around in case anybody knew different. Majo laid by her elbow a warm mug and a platter of pan dulce. Cristina's stomach churned, then changed its mind. She tore a piece off a yawning caiman and stuffed it into her mouth: a crumbly, anise-flavored cottonball that forestalled the need for conversation for the moments until she swallowed. The mug said "San Lúis Obispo Intramural Youth Football." Her father had been gone long enough — since before Pancho had last had a drink, she hoped — it was just another part of the house that had been Mama's. Of the five members of her family rendered in the upstairs window, three remained. Two, if you didn't count Teresa.

"God be with Eufemia, and Teresa too," said a voice from nowhere, from the house itself: Abuela Nina, her mother's mother, needlepointing in the claw-footed chair under the skylight. "And with all of us." The faded complexity of her embroidered corte blended with the afghan, rendering visible only her puckered face and quick hands, their rhythmic twitch and pull with the needle automatic, like they belonged to someone else. Cristina got up to kiss her cheek and look over her shoulder. Flowers framed the inescapable lake, the volcano crowned by sunrise, an old, old pattern. In the center of the frame, two women would appear, turned from the viewer, their dresses richer than Abuela's, bright as if they'd been sewn yesterday. Who they were, what they felt — Cristina used to ask herself that; today it was too deep to plumb.

"I love you, Abuelita."

She nodded, her lips moving in silence. Saying rosaries. For someone as old as Abuelita, Cristina supposed, it must become routine: the deaths, the faceless women. Like they were lined up waiting at a door. For a moment she envied that.

"Cristina, please, we need you." Majo hovering at her elbow. In the kitchen, the assembly line for tamalitos was backing up before the pot, inexpertly-tied cornhusks full of beans and stewed masa spilling over onto the floor.

She elbowed in to replace Pilar, retying bundles rapidly before passing them to Cele to cook. "You can start on the salsa," she told Pilar, who had worked at the comedor too, her first respectable job. Without Mama, none of them would know how to function.

"Something's missing," Constancia was saying, slurping broth from a ladle.

Cristina could tell by the smell. "Did you remember the achiote?" There had been none at the market. That sort of thing happened more and more.

Bustling in the cramped, bright kitchen, spilled masa stirred by slippered feet made angel-clouds in the light above the sink. Tío Pancho found Papa's record collection, and they shuffle-danced to Cuban jazz. Sneezing, the little dogs barking, in the middle of it Cristina found she could cry.

"It's good," Constancia told her, holding onto her from behind like always, crying too.

They ate, too many for the table even with all its leaves. Tío said an awkward grace; what was there to be thankful for? That anyone was left. Everybody had watery instant coffee with dulces and dipped extra tamalitos to soak up the last broth from around the bones. The spices still weren't right; it didn't matter, and it was everything.

It was eerie and familiar, that they weren't all talking about it — Mama's murder — at once. It felt wrong, not healthy, and also the easiest thing. Routine. Lencho helped his little cousins cut their food. With effort, she formulated an innocuous question for Majo and Pilar about school, friends; they chattered obligingly until that topic ran down. Pancho interviewed them about their plans for the future, received the predictable teenage equivocations, and turned to Cristina. She steeled herself for the inevitable questions. How is your "art?" Is it still selling? Had you thought about coming back to help your mother? Will you take over at the comedor?

The questions didn't come. Pancho let out his breath. Canary voices filled in the quiet.

The girl on the back balcony hadn't eaten a thing. Cristina grasped at this fact as an escape. "I'll make her a plate," she said, as if saying it could make it true. Constancia sat up, startled from a daze. Cristina had to prod her only gently before she began clearing the table.

When the front door chimed, she was on the balcony stairs, hand on the chilly metal railing, watching the girl from Mama's comedor pick at her supper by the fern-patterned light from the kitchen window.

Everyone she'd expected to be here was here. Tío Juan would work late, making up for all those trips to the bus station. More would come for the funeral in Zunil, but not everyone could pick up and take work with them like Cristina. Or abandon it and not care.

The neighborhood was full of strangers now. People got richer and moved out of the city, got old and passed on, got poor, got evicted. People disappeared. The new people who moved in stayed behind locked doors and barb wire.

So who could it be? Who else would the colony guards let past the gate? A muffled shriek from Tía Constancia brought the answer.

A game show chattered from the TV; her uncle and cousins had abandoned a game of conquian, hands and faces reflected indistinct between cards scattered on the glass-top table like they were sitting with the shadows of their dead. Abuela had gone to bed, leaving her needlepoint unfinished. Cristina headed off a stream of little cousins and nieces and herded them upstairs. She spent an indecisive moment fretting outside Mama's bedroom. "You can sleep in my room," she told them.

The door chimed again, was supplemented by pounding and the barking of the dogs.

Cristina chased the dogs into the garage and shut them in. The peephole's fisheye showed a squat figure, the face broad-mouthed and bulging-eyed. Another man stood beyond the angle of the porch light, taller, his stance a startled cat's. Vividly, she imagined the city night a swamp, full of insect noises and things hungering; bulb eyes, tongues and toothy smiles leaning in from beyond the edges of the frame. If she painted it, nobody would buy it.

She opened the door as far as the chain would allow.

"Inspector Zamora," said the toadlike man, flashing an official seal. "I have bad news."

"We read about it in the paper," said Cristina.

The article had been all about the foreign lawyer, who worked for the kind of big aid organization that accepted untold millions in guilt money from other foreigners whenever there was an earthquake, a hurricane, a ruptured oil pipeline, a civil war, a genocide — and distributed some fraction of that, after expenses, taxes, bribes, the salaries of lobbyists and handsome foreign lawyers, to those it decided were in need. Mention of Mama had come almost as an afterthought.

"You couldn't have called?" Tía Constancia demanded shrilly, hiding behind Cristina. "It's been more than a day!"

Cristina, suddenly relieved not to have learned of her mother's death from this batrachian Inspector, couldn't help experiencing this as an attack. *Why couldn't you have been here sooner, Colocha? Why didn't you know in your heart the moment the bullets struck?*

"Ignorance," pronounced the Inspector, "is bliss." The other one in the darkness seemed to flinch. "Someone here may be able to identify your mother's killers. May we come in?"

Cristina closed the door. She fiddled with the chain and tried to compose herself, looking with despair at the adults and near-adults remaining in the room.

"They can't think we had anything to do with it!" Constancia said, shrunk against the wall of portraits as though she could fade into it.

"They will, if we don't let them in."

Tío Pancho pushed back his chair. His hands rested briefly on his niece Pilar's shoulders as he maneuvered between her and the curio cabinet overstuffed with precarious saints. "Upstairs," he said to his nieces. Pilar paused to clean up the cards; he intervened as though taking charge — but he wouldn't. At least he stayed. Lencho protested; Cristina lifted the sleeping baby from a bassinet and placed him in his brother's arms, and he went meekly after the others.

The knock came again.

There was never a moment when Mama presented Cristina with her permanently cumin-flavored wooden spoon and said, "You will become me." At her quinceañera — the stupidest memory she could be having right now — Cristina had danced when it was necessary, laughed and whispered about the boys with her friends. The boy who'd overheard — she couldn't remember his name. Her father hadn't yet disappeared. Papi carried himself well enough through the party; he said the right things at the right times. And Cristina adored him, and resented Mama, who held her tongue but couldn't hide that she hated the entire production of quinces from start to finish and always had. Encased in a quetzal-colored dress so thick with ruffles nobody would have known if she'd been mounted on wheels, wearing makeup to match and clashing with every other thing in the room, Cristina decided she'd clash with Mama too. She chose that moment to announce, now that she was an adult, that she wouldn't be working at the comedor, but instead would go to art school in a foreign city. And Mama calmly explained that despite Papi's eloquent toast, Cristina wasn't an adult or anything like it.

That lesson in humility continued through Corísa's quinces, Teresa's, and on through her younger sisters' weddings, their first and second children. Papi disappeared, and it was never determined, or even discussed, whether it had anything to do with his drinking. Somewhere in there — long before learning to change diapers for Teresa's baby abandoned in all but name and lug him around on her back while pursuing her own much-mitigated dreams of art — she'd grown up. Mama knew that. She must have. Otherwise, why was everybody, including Cristina, waiting for her to answer the door?

The daughter didn't look like her mother — her face was soft where Eufemia's was hard, round where her mother's was angular beneath the same unruly curls. But Felipe didn't doubt El Bufo's guess.

When he stepped out of the shadows, her face went pale. When he followed El Bufo over the threshold, her red eyes widened. Her hand trembled on the latch.

To an older man and woman, both of whom bore much more family resemblance, El Bufo introduced himself again as Inspector Zamora. Felipe wondered what secrets those toadeyes gleaned darting from their anxious faces to the room beyond — but he couldn't escape the daughter's gaze. The money his fingers crushed S-shaped in his pocket belonged to her.

"Félix Orellano," he told her, as if a lie could dissipate it. "I'm his assistant." His reflection in the line of graduation photos on the wall showed only a vaguely handsome Argentine, hair slick black, eyes striking blue-green. Maybe she'd never seen blue eyes.

She reached for him — an odd gesture, not seeking a handshake but exploratory, like a doctor trying to find where it hurt. He took a step away, a small one, to stop her reaching inside his hoodie pocket for his hand. She drew back like she'd been stung. She knew. How could she? El Bufo knew. Did he? What did he know? He knew Felipe wore a mask. He might not know why. He might not see what lay beneath. So what did she know?

Twice in one day.

The mask — the conquistador mask — it must be broken. It was just a wooden mask. It had worked since Rubén had bought it for him when he was six. It wasn't even the same one — on the bus a year ago, he'd been wearing the jaguar mask. He could have switched in the car on the way here. The caiman, the jaguar: both made it easier to blend, in different situations. But then El Bufo would have known he had more than one. If he didn't already.

The masks weren't the problem. They were just masks, inert. That made it worse. His instinct was to run, hide. Everyone was staring — but not the way she was. El Bufo was shaking his head, don't. The other two, her aunt and uncle, were staring at her! She'd been crying. She would again — her mother was dead. Had he imagined it?

"What's the matter, Colocha?"

"Can we sit?" said El Bufo.

Across from Cristina at the table where she'd eaten breakfast before school every day for fifteen years, in board shorts and a Bob Marley sweatshirt, sat a jaguar in a man mask. Pilar's conquian hand lay face-up before him — an imperfect flush. She'd never seen eyes so big, so slow to blink, such a bright blue-green so little like the sea. Alone, maybe the eyes wouldn't scare her. The ears were flattened, velveteen. The zipped hoodie exposed a strip of throat, dense with fur patterned tawny and black, rippling smooth and as richly muscled as a bullfighter's, a football forward's leaping huge on one of those giant TVs at the mall.

Tía offered tea. The Inspector refused. The jaguar kept looking for the exits.

What was the polite response to a jaguar refusing hospitality? Why were they looking at her, when there was a jaguar in the room? She stood up as abruptly as she'd sat down, rattling the table, and started clearing teacups. Chipped, mismatched, their plainness under any circumstance but these would have faded to transparency. With a jaguar in a man mask and a detective whose demeanor hinted accusation sitting at Mama's table, they shamed her — that for everything Mama had done with her life, Cristina could present only these worn things. She found an apron and washed dishes, watching in the window glass the thin reflections of the inspector and his terrible assistant.

She'd had visions before: the laughing San Simón, idol of the lake people, who sometimes appeared unbidden on windowsills or in tree shadows in a peasant scene. Sometimes she painted him out, sometimes she let him stay. Or the painted gun in the gutter the day she heard of Mama's death. But those had been in paint, not the real world. And there the jaguar still sat, looking supremely uncomfortable, or so she'd have thought if she had the slightest idea how to read the body language of a jaguar trying to occupy a dining room chair.

"I'll come to the point," said Police Inspector Bullfrog, who was not a bullfrog, just an ugly, cursorily respectful man with a croak of a voice. "We're looking for someone who would have been at the comedor at the Artisans' Market yesterday afternoon. A girl — fifteen and petite, or perhaps younger. Perhaps with cooking grease in her hair."

"Do you mean someone who worked there?" asked Tío Pancho. "'Femia always had one or two helping out ..."

"There must be fifty girls working here in the city who learned from my sister. You think one of them could be involved?"

"We don't know enough to say. But I'm almost certain a girl fitting that description was present during the shooting. For now, we only want to speak to her."

"Then you don't have any suspects?" shrilled Constancia before Tío could speak.

Inspector Bullfrog's huge mouth conferred on his frown a sense of absurdity. "Not at this time."

"Can you at least tell us why they did it? Eufemia was such a good person. She didn't care about politics at all. She was innocent, hardworking —"

"I'm afraid we don't know," cut in the Inspector, coughing.

"The author of the *Diary* article seems sure it was some sort of political assassination," Tía insisted. She reached past her brother, clutching his arm, lifted the paper and slapped it down in front of the Inspector. "Maybe you should be questioning this reporter instead!"

Inspector Bullfrog made a show of studying the paper. "The *Diary's* views don't reflect the official position. In fact, I wouldn't be surprised if this reporter soon found himself out of a job. You're certain about Sra. Ramos's political affiliations?"

"'Political affiliations?' Eufemia hated politics!"

"She never even voted," Pancho confirmed.

"What was it she used to say, when the party solicitor knocked at dinnertime? She nearly closed the door on his nose!"

"'I'll vote when the Lord runs for office, not before.'" Pancho smiled, with what seemed a great effort.

"He wouldn't, of course. God works through people."

Cristina scrubbed at a soup ladle. The more nervous Tía Constancia got, the more manic. If Mama were here, Tía wouldn't be talking this way now. The government had been hard on Catholics after the war, Cristina was barely old enough to remember. But Mama's answer to all of it — the scrutiny, the "fees," the deliberate, inconvenient police presence or lack thereof outside church services depending on the occasion, even up to the Bishop's assassination, which Cristina did remember — had been not to dignify it with a response.

Focus on what's important.

Mama, this is *important.*

Focus on what you can control.

The Inspector leaned back in his chair. "You're suggesting Eufemia Ramos was murdered by agents of Satan? Doesn't narrow it down, I'm afraid." The jaguar shifted uncomfortably, though his human face maintained its wooden joviality. "Now about this girl, the eyewitness —"

Tía Constancia pushed back her chair. "You must see pictures of my sister. How can you possibly expect to find her killer when you don't understand her? I know you'd never believe her capable of this political scheming if you'd met her even once. But how can you know who she was when all you've seen of her is ... Cristina, please, you must show me where to find the albums." And she stuffed Cristina's apron into her dripping hands and dragged her toward the stairs.

The police Inspector rose as if to follow, gazing — rather distractedly, Cristina thought — at her parents' wedding photo. Tío Pancho hastily moved in front of him. "They'll only be a moment. Take some tea and pan dulce. We're in mourning," he added, without a hint of reproach.

The jaguar just sat there. If he wasn't a jaguar, Cristina might have guessed he was dying of embarrassment.

On the landing, Pilar clung to the railing as if the house were a sinking ship, Lencho and six children behind her. "I couldn't stop them," she stage-whispered. "I tried to keep them quiet — they don't understand!"

Lencho understood. He looked like a ghost.

"They're children," Cristina told Pilar gently. So was Pilar. "Everyone, back to your rooms please, this is serious."

Constancia chhhed them both, pulled Cristina into Mama's room and closed the door.

"Tía, what are you doing?" Cristina whispered. "He'll know we're hiding something."

"He'll ransack the house whether we're hiding something or not! Did you notice the other man hasn't said a word? He's the muscle! If we don't give them what they want, they'll take it by force!"

She imagined the jaguar leaping out of the mask and those ridiculous clothes onto the table, claws cutting through playing cards into glass.

No. The Inspector was distracted, his focus elsewhere. The jaguar was mortified. Constancia was panicking — it was what she did best. She needed Mama to be stern with her, practical. Which meant Cristina. "Why shouldn't we give them what they want, Tía? They just want to ask questions."

"What did the girl say? When you talked to her."

Cristina frowned. "I — nothing. I've never seen her before." Nothing strange about that. "I brought her some food. She was crying, then she was eating. Then the doorbell rang. But … she must know something."

"I don't know. You heard him: this is about *politics* somehow. I'm afraid what could happen. When the Bishop was killed — but you're too young. We don't know what side this Inspector is on. If what that poor girl saw doesn't fit what he decides is true … Witnesses die."

Two hours ago you thought she was a thief. But Constancia knew. She was of Mama's generation, she knew what "politics" could mean, and Cristina blissfully — thanks to Mama — didn't.

"Then we'll hide her," said Cristina. "If they don't know she's here ... if Tío Pancho hasn't told them ... then they'll leave us alone?"

"Oh, I'm so glad you're here, Colocha," said Tía. "I'll help Pancho distract him, you find some way to hide her. Does she still keep the albums in the wardrobe?"

Cristina climbed up on the bed and helped clear the accumulation of debris from the top of her mother's wardrobe to get at the albums, untouched since one of her sisters had last desired that escape, turning moisture-stuck pages past lives unremembered that cycled into their descendants' lives nevertheless. The spines were fake leather, cracked at the seams: five full, three empty. She didn't know where Papi's camera had got to.

Tía took two of the albums downstairs. Despite everything, Cristina felt sorry for the Inspector.

She found Miguel Ángel by the sound of his crying on the bed in his mother's old room. She changed him, refrained from hunting Lencho down to scold him, instead dragged Pilar in to soothe the baby and Pilar both. Then she navigated past the laundry and detritus into her parents' bathroom, to the high, square window that opened onto the balcony. She fought the lever to crank the glass outward, letting in the night, city smog, jasmine, rust, and a little shriek of surprise.

The girl sat in the dark where Cristina had left her: petite, as the Inspector had said, slightly plump, which happened with girls new to Mama's kitchen, in sandals and a butterfly-patterned huipil, its colors dulled by darkness. The plate of food and the soup bowl she'd licked clean. She wasn't crying anymore — but now she was even more dangerous.

"It's just me," Cristina whispered. "Someone's here asking questions. We need to hide you."

The gap had been big enough to squeeze through when she was thirteen. She ran skeptical hands down her hips. She stepped onto the back of the toilet, used a towel to wipe away the worst grime, then stuffed herself through. Her breasts had to be squashed and scraped to fit, and the hips were worse. Folded in half, kicking in midair, the window frame digging into her stomach while she struggled to squeeze her ass into a rectangle, she whispered, "Help."

And the girl who'd seen Mama's killers got up, took Cristina by the wrists and tugged, while Cristina wriggled and entreated her to be gentle, until she figured out the right angle for her hip bones, and they both collapsed in a tangle on the hard, sharp stairs. The metal clanged like cymbals, and Cristina imagined the jaguar's head whipping round, black nostrils quivering beneath that awful mask.

"We have to get you out of here," she told the girl, whose cheeks reflected citylight. But the only way out was past the jaguar.

They sat against the parapet, between the satellite dish and a fountain of rebar that in its heart sheltered an abandoned bird's nest. Cristina's knee pulsed hotly where she'd skinned it against the wall getting up here, blood she couldn't see trickling down her calf. She was grateful for the heat of the day's sun emanating from the concrete rooftop. No telling how long they'd have to wait. Long enough, she supposed, that she'd better get over her fear of this poor girl and what she knew.

"What's your name?"

"María Elena." She hugged her knees. Cristina had to strain to hear her over the city, though they sat shoulder to shoulder.

"You've been working for my mother. Living here, at the house." *You were there when the angels came for Mama.* "Where did you stay?"

"The first room at the top of the stairs."

"My room," said Cristina. She'd shared it with Corísa, then Teresa. By the end, both her sisters were married and Cristina had it to herself again. She remembered how huge it had seemed when Corísa moved out. Later, unoccupied, it had filled up with debris, canvases propped a dozen deep against the walls, corners and closets taking on shared storage duties for yet another cousin or aunt gone back to the highlands or abroad. "Sorry about the mess."

María Elena didn't answer. She might have smiled a very small, strained smile in the dark.

"Was that why you asked for me before?" Cristina prompted. It felt like an interrogation. "On the phone, my aunt said …"

"I had to say something. She wouldn't leave me alone!"

Was she frightened of Constancia? After working for Mama? "How long have you been here?"

"Three weeks."

Three weeks wasn't enough. Two decades hadn't done it.

"But she talked about me. Mama. What — what did she say?" What a terrible thing to ask.

In the dark, María Elena's was nothing like the indignant reaction of a normal, untraumatized teenager, Majo or Pilar. "You weren't perfect, you weren't the most obedient, but you stayed. You didn't run away."

Toughening them up. That's how Mama would put it, if any-one dared ask. There was money to be made in the city, opportunity, if you were lucky. Rich ladinos lived in the city. Ladinos needed cooks, maids, nurses. But you had to be ready to be treated the way a ladino treats a maid. The city was dangerous; you had to learn how to get around, where not to go, what not to say. You had to be ready to get bullied, groped, pinched, humiliated. Robbed, on the buses or in the streets. Or worse.

Mama found her girls through word of mouth — friends' daughters, friends of friends of girls she'd trained. They came from all over, but mostly from the highlands, little villages in the mountains like the one Mama had grown up in. Usually the girls were poor. Often they needed to learn Spanish. They knew nothing about the world. Mama was harsh with them at the beginning. She also rarely let them out of her sight.

Cristina realized suddenly how much time had passed. Hugo had showed up in Los Encuentros early this afternoon. She and Lencho caught the first bus they could. They were almost to the city by the time Tía called thinking some strange girl wanted to steal the silverware. But according to the paper, the murder had taken place at lunchtime yesterday.

So it had taken María Elena more than a day just to get from the Comedor Santa Rosa de Lima to this house in Colonía San Bartolomeo.

Now she sat hugging her knees even tighter, hair in her eyes. Before dusk had faded away, Cristina hadn't noticed bruises. The girl hadn't looked hurt, aside from the dried tears. Tía Constancia hadn't said anything. Of course, she and Tía had both been preoccupied.

"How did you get back here?" asked Cristina. "From the market. After —"

A tiny shrug. "The bus."

"Did something happen? Are you all right?"

María Elena didn't speak.

She could hear Mama saying it under her breath, standing over the sink as teenage Cristina slunk in after a late night. *Selfish.*

"You don't have to say anything. You've had a terrible day as it is. But you're ... you're safe now. We just have to keep quiet." Cristina scootched closer, held out a hand.

After a long minute, María Elena took it. Her palm was sweaty, her grip tight.

Crickets screeched from the ravine, canaries chirped sleepily from the courtyard. Muffled voices, contentious, came from inside the house. Traffic hummed beyond the colony gate. The lonely lights of hillside villages on the far side of the valley shone clear above trapped pollution; the parapet hid the rest of the city. They might be sitting on a rooftop in Los Encuentros, or in one of the bigger towns around the lake, if it weren't for noise, and the sky: solid cloud pregnant with reflected light, harsh white, pale blue, halogen pink.

Cristina hated the city.

Corísa had been quick to move away to Xela as soon as she got married. For Teresa it had taken longer, but by the end she'd been so desperate to get away she was ready to risk a journey of five thousand kilometers, coyotes and narcos and border patrols. Maybe she was cleaning rich foreigners' toilets, maybe she was lying in a ditch in the desert. At least she wasn't here. Cristina, who'd been the first to want out, had never quite found the momentum. She got as far as Hugo's art school in Comalapa. Then the city pulled her back.

After Papi disappeared, Mama's daughters tried to convince her to pack up and move away. She refused. The sisters speculated endlessly: did she expect Papi to return? Would she take him back? Could there be another woman, or had something else broken them up, like money? But their parents only talked about money when one of their daughters came begging for help. Corísa thought Mama could have done just as well with a bigger, nicer restaurant in Xela, but Corísa had married young; she'd barely worked at the comedor. She didn't understand Mama's rapport with her clientele, the respect she commanded. Corísa's husband had a good job, working for the power company in Xela. She didn't know what money trouble was like. Teresa hated money, hated talking about it, hated thinking about it. Eventually, desperate to achieve what Corísa had, refusing to account for what had happened with Papi, she wound up with the lazy, duplicitous Mario Ernesto, who relied on her determined obliviousness. When she went chasing after him, leaving her children for Mama and Cristina to worry about, the question of moving away was put to bed for good.

Cristina was being stupid, going over memories she couldn't change. She ought to be painting, channeling anger and grief into art, like Hugo was always telling her. Like Abuela with her needlepoint.

An eerie sound from the courtyard — a lack of sound. The canaries had gone silent. María Elena's fingers stiffened in Cristina's.

"I'll be back in a second." She pulled her hand away. Crawling gingerly across the roof, past the congealed corpse of a lost kite, snarled wires and rusted eruptions of rebar, Cristina thought about the frog Inspector prowling through the rooms below.

She raised her head slowly over the parapet and looked down into the courtyard. A cool wind carried night-blooming jasmine and char. The city sprawl revealed itself between the black thrusts of ridges. Light from squatters' fires flickered in the ravine.

From the courtyard, the jaguar looked straight at her, ears pricked sharp and alert, huge eyes like highway reflectors casting back the kitchen light from behind the ritual mask.

He could smell them, up on the roof, above the clotheslines and the bouganvillea and the avocado tree's crown. Two of them, the daughter and the girl, camomile-scented soap and old grease and fear, and something else he couldn't place, oily, waxy, harsh.

But only the daughter was looking back at him.

Those eyes, that face — he didn't want to be the source of that fear. He didn't want El Bufo's cruelty to pay off. He wanted to know why that look: what was it she saw? But he couldn't have that. He'd made himself these people's enemy just by coming in the door.

He retreated back into the house. Past the mildewed walls of the laundry room, the terrified canaries, past the kitchen and the dead woman's bewildering sister trying to tell a story about dyeing coconut sugar at Christmastime. He paced to the table, where the great pile of money lay, stained and ignored.

The family were too proud and principled to take it. It was theirs, but they didn't know. They thought it was bribe money, beneath them. It was. They didn't need it, with their sprawling house and armed guards at the colony gate and endless supply of little plaster saints. Felipe wasn't a thief. On the other hand, El Bufo had already stolen it. He'd only left it to make a point: he represented the deep-pocketed government and wasn't to be fucked with. Except he didn't represent the government.

Taking it, Felipe concluded, wasn't stealing. It was pragmatism. He could give it back, after he got a chance to explain. After he understood.

He scooped up the money, stuffed it by handfuls into his hoodie pocket, and headed for the door.

El Bufo stood watching him from the top of the stairs.

El Bufo spent the ride swigging from a half-pint of whiskey, speaking only when it became necessary to bark directions. The witness had slipped through his fingers. Felipe made one move for the stereo; El Bufo froze him with a snarl. At first, he wanted to go back downtown — not to the crime scene — something about interrogating drunks at the cathedral stoop. Felipe was tired. He was shaken. There was more cash in his pocket than he'd ever seen. He wanted a drink. He'd needed one an hour ago. Now he needed three. "I'll take you home," he said.

El Bufo slouched down in the passenger seat, brooded at his reflection in the window and seemed to let it slide.

Felipe drove fast, hoping to get rid of him before he changed his mind. From the overpass, the opera house atop its fortified hill lit up blue and sharp, jewel of the city's high culture, surrounded by walled colonies far fancier than the one they'd left behind. The curve of its stylized feline jaw aimed with puffed-up arrogance at the heavens; as they merged south onto Elena Street, it turned as though settling in its sleep. Nobody ever died in hails of bullets at the opera house.

El Bufo directed him abruptly left off Elena into Zone Three; from there, the neighborhoods deteriorated quickly.

As they approached a dark corner by a shuttered laundry, he put away the bottle. "Let me out."

"Seriously?" Felipe kept rolling. This was marero territory. The nearest three streetlights were dead, the fourth flickering.

"What do you think?" snapped El Bufo.

Figures moved in the periphery of Baby's headlights. Shadow-puppet shapes contorted against empty shopfronts where political slogans had been spray-painted over with gang signs. Zone Three was mostly all right in daylight — depressing, but dangerous only to the unwise. Like most of the city. At night, the cemetery that marked its southern border was no place you wanted to be, and a few blocks north, the squats and shanties of the sprawling Barrio El Gallito sprouted from the hillside like a fungal colony; Felipe wouldn't go near that rat's nest at noon with an armed escort. *I can drop you at your door,* he'd been trying to say. But a cop — even an ex-cop — would be crazy to live this close to El Gallito. Felipe watched the shadows.

The mareros were a corporatized drug gang, enforcers and recruiters for the narcos. Rumor was they made you rape and kill your sister to get in. If mareros killed Eufemia, this whole chauffeuring the fake police inspector thing wasn't worth it, no matter how much money was involved, no matter what secrets he knew or how many tinfoil guns he could wave in anyone's face.

"You lost ten minutes back there taking the overpass instead of the San Juan. What you don't know about this place could upholster my coffin." As if to demonstrate, El Bufo popped open the locked glove compartment and drew out Felipe's illegal revolver. He flicked on the dome light and opened the cylinder. "You really ought to keep it loaded. What good is it if it isn't loaded?"

Felipe would have sworn it had been loaded the last time he put it away. He braked gracelessly; a squeal of rubber and the car slammed to a stop. His eyes flicked between mirrors. Phantom mareros strutted from the alleys bearing instruments of torture. "You can only push so far, man."

El Bufo studied him impassively, cradling the gun, turning it in his hands with a look Felipe couldn't read, but he was suddenly glad it wasn't loaded.

"Right here's just fine," El Bufo said, and reached across the e-brake to drop the empty revolver between Felipe's thighs. A lewd grimace. "Tomorrow morning. I'll call, early."

Felipe shrugged noncommittally, shoved the gun under his leg to keep it from sliding under the pedals, and fucked off, fast, as soon as the door closed behind el cerote. In the rearview, El Bufo was small and forlorn, hands buried in windbreaker pockets, no longer the bullish, supremely confident ex-detective Felipe had until an hour ago almost entirely believed him to be.

Forty Doors

Stashing the car in a guarded lot he'd have been too cheap for any other night, Felipe put on the jaguar mask — the face he thought of as his own, the one he showed his parents, his brother, his friends — and a pair of orange-silver mirror shades, and headed for the Forty Doors.

He crossed the plaza under the shadows of locust trees, past the conch-shaped auditorium shell where lovers interthreaded on benches. In the ads along Sixth Ave, plastic-skinned women lounged in two dimensions, while flocks of real girls trying to emulate them twittered over shopping bags and bleeding-edge phones, trailed by lone wolves in polyester shirts. The GPS map on his own probably-stolen phone put him a thousand meters from the site of the shootings. Everybody acted like they didn't know or didn't care. The Presidential Palace glowered across the plaza, ivory-lit, windows black.

He scolded himself: time to relax. Time to party, to dance, to let go. He let himself shiver a little with anticipation.

He was two hours late.

Half a block beyond the inflated rents of the "revitalized" old city, the crowds thinned; the fashions got weird. Police lights traveled the crumbling contours of building facades, mapping moss-creched colonial lintels, wrought-iron remnants of window casements dripping with bromeliads, graffiti murals, modern glass and steel. Outside the Forty Doors, a narrow, five-story vertical gap in the middle of a block was occupied by two ripped guys wielding hand stamps: a star. Cover charge tonight; live music later. Felipe felt a twinge of disappointment at having missed the chance to pay his friends' way in. Still, as he passed this gauntlet unscathed, his muscles unknotted. *Open sesame*, he thought, an old joke.

Three levels of doors filled three sides of a courtyard open to the sky, stairwells at the forward corners. Each door, once an office for some harried government clerk, now concealed a tiny bar, each with different music, a different theme. Worn-pink and green Christmas lights webbed between them.

He texted Luz; she replied. He misunderstood. Or she was playing, leading him astray, payback for making them wait?

Luz, tiny and voluptuous, the first girl to develop in Felipe's class at the Santa Catarina village school as well as the smartest and most ambitious, had occupied his mind from approximately the ages of eleven to twenty. Not that she flaunted it — he thought she'd found the perfect compromise between openness and modesty. He might have said so at the time, if he could find a way to communicate without completely undermining his credibility.

Instead, they were friends. They played football on the gravel pitch behind the school, they shared playlists, stole cigarettes, tried out bad jokes on each other. They developed a secret handshake he'd forgotten, except for the palmed cigarette. Of course it was Luz who'd been the first to quit.

Growing up with a uniquely external perspective on human sexuality, Felipe considered his secret devotion to reflect well on both Luz and himself. But she'd gone to university on a city scholarship and spent half a year abroad on some foreign grant before the idea of leaving home even occurred to him. When he bought the car and moved to the city, an unspoken foundation of that plan had been to find her and tell her how he felt. Hilariously, humblingly, he arrived and found he'd been looking at the whole thing upside down and inside out.

He chased them between bars. There were more than forty; it was just a clever name. They got hard to count after three. As he moved between them, his spine shivered, pulled between competing rhythms. He caught them holed up in a "coffeehouse" on the second floor: a single-seat stage unoccupied in a corner, dramatically lit portraits of tortured poets cragged on flaking walls. They were surrounded by such a crowd of activist friends as could cram in around the bar. Luz and Aníbal could blend with that crowd when they wanted, expressing shared disdain for the status quo that was destined to defeat them through seasonally inappropriate sandals, grungy slogan shirts and general unwashedness. Today, he supposed they'd preferred to look stylish and elite for the officials issuing protest permits. Luz wore a flared skirt patterned in flecks of loud color against black, sharp-toed boots and a battered leather jacket; her evocative figure was wrapped up with Aníbal's in as profound an expression of devotion as the cookie-cutter lovers he'd passed in the plaza could dream. Aníbal was beautiful too: black hair like a Greek god's, tall and broad-shouldered, though slight, easy in slacks, polished loafers and a dress shirt open at the chest to reveal an utter lack of breasts or chest hair. For a foreigner like Aníbal in particular, it was in no way safe to signal queerness, even in a place like this. But she gave herself away a very little with fidgetiness, a subtle femininity in the way she fixed her collar; it had taken Felipe a long time to catch it. Now that he had, he watched for it; it was comforting in ways he couldn't admit. He was proud of them, the most unpretentiously elegant couple behind any one of the Forty Doors — except, of course, for the pretense. But he loved that too.

They'd explained it all to him, together, patiently if not without a heavy shot of snark, when Luz had first introduced him. "In the North," she'd said, "I could say, 'Hey, I'm Aníbal, and my pronouns are they/she/him.' But I know that won't fly here. So now you'll ask, 'Then why would you move here?' Simple. Here I don't have to answer to my fucking family. And here, there's Luz."

Felipe had never heard anything so relatable in his life.

Aníbal finished a drink, stretched and sinuated through her friends to meet him, bumped a fist. "Where you been, man?"

"Long day. Not what I expected. I'm just glad it's over."

Luz and Aníbal shared a look: Luz pissed off and dangerous, Aníbal — if he didn't know better — scared. Felipe was taken aback. But it was brief enough.

"Us too," said Luz. "Talk about it later?"

He let out a breath of relief. Later, when they were alone, safe. For now, they could dance.

The two of them were home for him now, calmer and safer than any home he'd had. He was their third wheel — a wheel, he liked to think, that provided balance. In a fit of magnanimity, he bought a round for the crowd, then regretted it. Using Eufemia's money didn't bother him. He wasn't letting it bother him — that was work, this wasn't. But it got their attention. He dodged suggestions he take the sunglasses off, worried if his reflection looked right in phone screens and beer bottles whenever a lighter flared in the haze. They took turns telling him about today's efforts to raise awareness of the plight of Indigenous peoples. He was one of those, he figured; so was Luz. But it meant something different when they said it. To most people in the city — in the *Diary*, for example — calling someone Indígeno was an insult. But he figured he could afford to shrug it off and be practical — his life didn't depend on the land, but on people. Anyway, they wouldn't be out there protesting for him.

The permits they'd been able to secure for tomorrow covered rigidly delineated areas around the Palace of Justice and Reformer Square, limitations they'd debated at length whether to ignore. Even these permits had been denied at first, until they secured other permits, which could have been avoided only a week prior, if they'd thought to get word to someone who in the intervening time had inconveniently and scandalously been gunned down in broad daylight.

Antonellis: they knew the guy. A foreigner, like Aníbal. An activist, but in a whole other league. Unlike Aníbal, nobody had cut him off from his inherited wealth. Instead, they'd more or less handed him the purse strings to millions on millions in foreign aid money. Not a shred of which had gone to pay Luz and Aníbal's end of the rent.

Felipe finished the rum he'd been trying to savor, started to go for another, was prevented. One of the trust fund activist kids bought the next round, then another. At least it changed the subject. More rum was provided, then beer, enabling him to devote semi-unwilling attention to a decent-looking foreign blonde, already tipsy, as she waxed hyperbolic about the Indigenous vision of the world: its clarity, how untainted, uncorrupt! Luz rolled her eyes at the perfect moment and set him laughing, saving him undoing the points he'd accrued. It ought to be a sign that idealistic strangers from a thousand miles away made more of an effort to change things than most people who lived here.

He declined an offered cigarette and resisted getting pulled back into the ongoing "greed or ignorance" discussion of the new regime's natural resources policy. It wasn't "either/or," more like how many greasy buckets of each. The rich got richer. Those in power among the colonized got to kiss a loafer instead of a boot.

He grew impatient with the music selection, protest songs from another place and time whose eloquent wording everybody had so memorized as to divest them of meaning, when so much glorious variety was only a door away. Through the floor, he could feel the pull of reggaeton.

"Here's one to send chills up your spine." Anibal uncrossed ankles from atop Luz's knee. "Antonellis knew about the protests. It's pretty obvious he was assassinated. He told Luz he met with somebody from Boreal Mining only a few days before Totonícapan. Who's paying off who? What if they killed him because they found out he was involved with us?"

David Alden Antonellis: Felipe remembered the handsome, distracted movie star face from the case file and felt his buzz slipping away.

Luz looked stricken. "No. David dealt with a lot of different people's money, all the time. I'm sure he had all kinds of enemies."

"Exactly!" Aníbal brandished a fist. "I mean, here's a guy whose entire ability to accomplish anything in this country is predicated on being a friend to business. Right? They give him money, he gives them the moral high ground — but it only works if the money ends up supporting projects in line with their 'values.' As long as it's going to build schools on the Pacific slope, repair roads, bribe bureaucrats to actually do their jobs, everything's fine. But if even a sliver of it ends up funding 'radicals,' interfering in their ability to make a profit, and the people holding the purse strings trace it back to him ..."

"They wouldn't have to kill him. If they didn't like what he was doing with their money, all they had to do was get him fired."

"Sure, but we know how those kinds of appointments work. Everybody's in bed with everybody. They figured putting out a hit was their only, best option. Tried and true."

"Now you're just making shit up. It's dangerous — and off-message," Luz said pointedly. "We're not out in the streets tomorrow to dignify violence or make accusations. We've got concrete, achievable demands. All foreign extraction rights suspended until they can be renegotiated with public input. Stakeholders and international courts back at the table. We can't let this sidetrack us now."

Aníbal laughed and raised her hands. "Okay, okay, we know. What do we want?"

"International oversight," everybody but Felipe recited, another old, bad joke.

"When do we want it?"

"Permanently!"

"And justice for Berta Cáceres, no immunity for Monterríos, reparations for extrajudicial killings." Aníbal put out a half-finished cigarette against her thumb, made a few arcane passes, and the stub disappeared. "We're all on the same page. Tomorrow, it'll be just like we planned. Still — I can't help but wonder. You knew him better than I did, Luz — you've got to have a guess, right?"

Luz sipped her drink without leaving so much as a fleck of dark red lipstick on the glass, giving Aníbal a long look he couldn't read. Everyone else shut up except Woody Guthrie, who sang in English about promises defaulted on in the Promised Land. Felipe didn't like that look. It reminded him too much of the way he'd conspired with her when they were twelve, playing different loudmouths off against each other on the football pitch after school. Not so much anymore.

"He's not the only one who died, you know." The words were out of his mouth before he could stop himself. Helping out a corrupt ex-cop, skimming the fruits of that corruption right off the top to buy them drinks — it could look like he was working for the enemy. He was.

Luz put her drink down. "What do you mean?" She gave him her full attention now, which wasn't an improvement.

They were used to him not having an opinion. Every time he tried, it went horribly. Luz and Aníbal spent half their lives in arguments like this — they had degrees in it. He was lucky they still wanted to hang out. He was their third wheel, not their babysitter. Then again, he was about to be paying their rent. "I mean, a couple of justice department bureaucrats, who cares? They were probably corrupt. They might have deserved it? But what about the woman from the comedor? She had nothing to do with any of this."

"Felipe, why are you bringing this up?"

He didn't know Eufemia Ramos. But her face, her picture from the dossier, kept churning with pieces of the day he was supposed to be forgetting: mopped-up blood, swept-up rubble. Her family. Eufemia's daughter recoiling from his presence, her eyes from the rooftop. That little girl, the witness.

He should buy another round, use the occasion to hustle them all out behind a different door with a not so maudlin theme. But now the look on Luz's face said she wasn't letting him brush this off. All he could do was dig himself deeper. "I just mean, if you're going to get all up in arms about farmers in Totonícapan — and now a foreign lobbyist — what about people who die in the city every day? He's the only reason we're talking about this — not because people got gunned down in the street in broad daylight. That's routine."

Aníbal's look was warning now. "But he's not just some foreign lobbyist. He was our friend. Luz's friend, anyway. Right, Luz?"

"We have to pick our battles," said Luz carefully. "We can't help everybody, there's too much. It's overwhelming. People do what they can."

Sometimes nothing. She didn't say it, but she meant it. Felipe looked after himself, his family, his friends. It ought to be enough, but it wasn't.

He yielded like he always did, staring at his hands. "Yeah, okay, you're right. Sorry. Go on."

It was Aníbal who saved him. "Nah, it's my bad. We came here to get away from politics!" She finished a beer and grabbed Luz with a grin. "Come on. This revolution needs a better soundtrack. Can't impassion anyone without a little rage. Something the people can shake their asses to."

He could have kissed her. Instead, he downed somebody else's shot of rum, sweet and intense with vanilla. He shook himself — one of the few feline mannerisms that in the right circumstance translated perfectly — and offered a hand to the blonde. Drunk foreigners were putty before the call to dance, aptitude notwithstanding. He could play the demonstrative lover when he needed to; he'd learned it from his mother's telenovelas almost before he learned to play human.

Still, Aníbal outdid him every time.

Forty Doors was the best in the city for barhopping, easy as walking down the hall. Lights blurred, bass rattled, grooves were sought, settled into, jumped, discarded. One-walled corridors and flaking plaster stairwells tipped and jostled to roll them toward new destinations like marbles in a maze. Discord, between one door and the next: reggaeton behind, salsa ahead. Machismo made sense in the context of hip hop: it was a front, a game. Crackling fields of dubstep ululated through the crowd, electric discordance, utterly engrossing. Outside a hardcore bar, the door torched black and sharp with shrapnel, the air sharp with violence, Felipe crossed paths with a ghoul: a young, skinny guy, clear-eyed, a skull tattooed over half his face. The crowd parted around him. He *can't take it off,* Felipe thought. A marero, or just a pretender.

This was what he'd come for. It had been a reason to stay in the city, after he'd understood about Luz, before he really understood and fell in love with both of them together. Music made everything easier: dealing with people, understanding them, hiding from them. Rhythm was a blueprint for form. While he danced, sometimes he could convince himself he didn't need the mask.

Luz and Aníbal were laughing, in love, asking nothing of him. It was as much as he could have hoped for. But idealism got people killed. They didn't understand how good they had it or how close they were to losing it. An acquaintance of theirs — a coworker, friend? — had been murdered. It might have had nothing to do with them. He hoped not. He'd keep them out of it if he could — keep El Bufo from finding out either of them even existed — though it felt like wishful thinking, given everything El Bufo already knew.

Everywhere they led, the tail of activists got tireder, fewer. It was harder to get mugged moving in packs, but a handful at a time they accepted their limits, abandoned valiant efforts to do like the Romans, kissed goodbye, and flaked off home. The blonde, to her credit, was among the last to go. He hadn't gotten her name. Guys he knew would have killed for that, but he wanted someone he could talk to.

Not necessarily someone for whom he'd be willing to take off the mask.

Long after only the three of them remained, Felipe, Luz, and Aníbal grooved to a standstill at a trip-hop lounge on the top floor.

Hammocks and plastic chairs spilled into the corridor, pursued by woozy turntable scratch and looped vocals sliced from torch songs. Felipe fell into a hammock, pleasantly aware of his pulse, of the weight and shape of human muscle, lazily tempted to kick off shoes, stretch toes, arch spine, discard the mask and blunt his claws against the wall.

Luz rocked the hammock with a bump of her hip. "Time for bed?"

In the sky above the courtyard, clouds vortexed momentarily; a huge green star winked in the absence. He stifled a yawn; a noise of contentment deep in his throat, beyond his control. "Long day."

"Productive day for you, seems like," put in Aníbal, her slim shape folded over the railing, watching the polyrhythmic chaos below. "Since when do you pay for other people's drinks?"

Through the mask's face, Felipe mustered a secretive smile. "Got me a patron."

Aníbal laughed. "What, a sugar mama?"

"I wish." He didn't, really. But Aníbal was so good at the swagger sometimes he couldn't help playing along. "Wants me tomorrow, too. If it keeps up, you guys are going to owe me a lot of rent money."

Luz pushed the hammock playfully. "You're working for us tomorrow, you promised."

Tomorrow. A sick wave of apprehension made him sit up and get his feet on the floor. El Bufo was somewhere in Zone Three right now, maybe getting murdered by mareros. Trash pickers at the dump months later would find his ugly windbreaker and maybe some finger bones. He was dangerous, dishonest. Next time, the money might actually come from the government instead of some poor dead woman's stash. Would that be worse?

"What?" asked Luz. "What's the matter?"

"Nothing," said Felipe. He tried to shake it off. "I mean — we've talked about this. Working for friends is great, until they stop being able to afford it. Then it's bad for everyone."

Luz and Aníbal spoke in the silent language of lovers. Living with the two of them had been awkward at first, then a gift. Now Aníbal's rich, foreign family had stopped sending money. Felipe wasn't about to share about his own family, so he didn't ask — but he wondered if they'd found out how she'd been living. Charity work and activism were one thing. He wondered who'd told them.

"Rum," said Aníbal dully. "We need rum." She spun on the pad of her foot like a dancer. Her hand lingered briefly at Luz's waist as she headed into the bar.

Luz sank into the hammock beside him. He would have been proud if her warm proximity and cinnamon scent didn't turn him on even a little. "I'm sorry," she said. "I know we've been taking advantage. And we can't anymore. The money ran out, and we've been too much in the habit to stop. I know we have to. But we really do need you tomorrow. If there were somebody else we felt safe asking, we would. Some of the families of the victims are coming all the way from Totonícapan. The NGO paid for coach buses to the city, but I need to be able to get the leaders around once they're here, and I can't let them ride city buses. I need them to feel safe."

There was something going on down in the courtyard, near the entrance, disrupting the rhythms of the crowd. A fight? He gave up the hammock to Luz.

She leaned back, black curls dangling. "They're going to start paying Aníbal. They are. I'm helping them find a new revenue source. As soon as that comes through, she'll be on the payroll. Then we'll be able to pay you back."

"Sure," Felipe said. "I'm not worried. I just feel like I need to be taking work where I can get it."

"Of course!" said Luz. "This is just for tomorrow. After that, we won't ask anymore. Or we'll figure out how to pay you."

"Of course," he echoed, without conviction. "Just ... maybe don't expect me to be as impeccably prompt as usual?" He could play clients off each other, use each as an excuse to duck out on the other when things got awkward. He'd done it before.

Then somebody cut the power. A click, a fading buzz, and dark and silence took the place of the frenetic discord as if all the doors had slammed at once. Overhead, the rectangle of sky framed by the roof lines brightened to the color of flesh. Then, near the entrance, flashlights — three of them, harsh, searching. La tira — police. Shadows stretched and swam up the walls. Felipe shrank from the beams along with everybody else. Over the indignant, drunken murmur, one of the cops was shouting a name.

Luz clawed her way out of the hammock. The edge of a spotlight caught her face, stripped it utterly of languor and distorted it into something warlike. She yelled to Felipe. Or maybe she was calling Aníbal; it was hard to tell in the dark among the escalating sounds of fear.

Fucking police were trained to use fear, they defaulted to it. And now he worked for them. Sort of.

Luz grabbed his elbow and started toward a door, the one Aníbal had gone into for rum, the trip-hop bar.

"Stay here," he heard himself saying. "Just stay here — they're not looking for us. Stairways are going to be crazy, they're the only way out. Wait it out, we'll be fine."

"Aníbal!" she called again.

"I'll go," he said, trying to snake out of her grasp, failing.

But there was Aníbal's tall, elegant silhouette, with three shot glasses pressed together clinking, a finger through each. "Lucky everybody else went home," she said, forcing a smile the shadow turned predatory.

"Get *down,*" hissed Luz. Aníbal obeyed, dropping to a knee.

The cops went door to door. The flashlight beams narrowed; darkness encroached, then fled again as they emerged.

Rum sloshed over fingertips as they shared shot glasses around. "Luck," said Luz sarcastically. They drank.

The rum helped Felipe at least momentarily, a wave of artificial calm. For Luz it seemed to have the opposite effect. Squatting over the filthy floor in her fuck-me boots, hugging her skirt to her knees, she looked ready to explode, telltale lines sharpening between her brows. "I guarantee this is about the murders yesterday. It's standard show-of-power bullshit. Even an implied threat to people in control — especially when the people in control are directly responsible — they round up a bunch of undesirables in the richest neighborhoods and lock them up without trial, to make it look like they're doing something." She'd been like this even in the schoolyard, breaking up fights to scold the combatants, infuriated at injustice, however slight. Felipe's strategy had been to stay the hell out of it, maybe later take a little revenge from the shadows. Once in awhile, they'd managed to work together. The difference between them, he figured, was that he'd had no choice but to hide even from the people he loved.

At a door across the courtyard and one level down, the lights lingered. Felipe tried to remember which bar, but it all ran together. People — not cops but partiers — spilled out into the passage toward the stairs. Another cop was waiting for them, turning them back. Inside the bar, the spotlights swung crazily, almost like club lights. Somebody was getting the shit beaten out of them. Felipe's pulse ramped up in his throat. When they made it up here, what would happen? He could run, hide. He could hold his ground in front of a gun. But could Luz? He remembered how she'd been that moment at the beginning of the night, edgy, fragile. Dangerous.

"We've got to go," she said, her voice tight.

The stairwells weren't the only way out, he realized. Not from here. Not for him. He could follow the spotlights, the shadows: up and out. From the ceiling to the roof looked less than a meter, the concrete scored with age and imperfections. Clawholds. A bounding leap, the railing, then the corner, then the roof. Get above it. Up into the night. Like Eufemia's daughter. He could make it. It was dark, nobody would see — just wait for the spotlights to pass.

"Hey," said Aníbal. "Let's not get crazy." Placing her shot glass on the floor, she put a hand on Luz's shoulder, the other on Felipe's. "Even if they were looking for us, how would they know to find us here? They could have arrested us at city hall."

She was right. Someone *would* see: Luz and Aníbal.

"You were the one ranting about murder conspiracies an hour ago!" Luz was saying. "We can't take any chances."

"What do you call trying to sneak past a bunch of police?"

Luz said something else, but it was drowned by gunfire. If not for the muzzle flares — death's heads igniting in the dark — Felipe might have mistaken it for firecrackers, strings of them set off in the streets on saints' days, pop-pop-pop-pop-pop, high-pitched and shrill. They threw themselves to the floor, sticky with spilled beer and cigarette ash. A shotgun boomed. Someone was screaming, then stopped.

A minute, two minutes. Then the power came back on: lights soft pink, green, silver flecks from a disco ball. Then the music, a powerful female voice singing a slow lament to skipping high-hat. Felipe mentally filled in the scratched-vinyl screech as the playhead on the soundtrack of the world was unceremoniously shoved ten minutes back.

"Fuck it," said Luz, getting up. "I have to pee." She walked off, boot heels thocking.

Felipe glanced at Aníbal. *What's going on with her?*

"I don't know, man." Aníbal collected their scattered shot glasses, tipped each to her pointed tongue in succession, catching stray drops. "Two years we've been in love, you'd think we'd know each other. I guess it's the murder, that guy Antonellis. What happened in Totonicapán, that's different, you know? It's a cause, it's government oppression, it fits with what we do. It's not like she doesn't feel for the victims, their families. But she can do something about it, she can organize, agitate. She's great at that. But with Antonellis ..." She trailed off. "I'm talking out of my ass. I'm going to make sure she's okay."

Felipe gathered himself off the floor. The blood rushed to his head; his muscles were jelly. He felt like he'd survived a car crash. With the lights on, he recognized the fire-blackened door where the gunfight had gone down: the hardcore bar. Two cops emerged with a body, a piece of cloth draped over the face. The skull kid. Shooting cops was another way to prove yourself to the mareros, if you were desperate enough. If you could believe the tabloids.

The crowd no longer seemed much in the mood for dancing.

Luz and Aníbal sat in back, Felipe alone in front, averting his eyes from the mirrors as usual so they could mush faces and grope in relative privacy if they wanted, not that they needed privacy. Tonight they barely touched. Something had changed between them; he'd been there the whole time and he didn't know what. Maybe they were just shell-shocked, tired.

He turned up the stereo — hardcore hip-hop angry enough to keep him awake, despite protests from the backseat — and made it safely home through dead streets to Zone Nine. He let the car idle while he unlocked the gate, then pulled into the underground garage, relocked the gate, woke the girls (he dared refer to them as such only in thought) and herded them upstairs.

Their apartment serendipitously provided the minimum possible space they could get along in without killing each other — as long as they respected boundaries. There was a kitchenette/common room, a bathroom, and two tiny bedrooms, each with one window opening on a light-starved ventilation shaft, all at a monthly rate that until recently had been conveniently survivable. Luz and Aníbal went straight to bed, together; whatever was going on between them hadn't interfered that far, at least.

Felipe was dragging, but he went all the way back downstairs again to unload the masks and the gun from the glove box. He'd keep it at home from now on. Unloaded.

He locked the apartment door, then the bedroom door behind him, then flopped onto the bed, letting the masks and everything else fall where they may among the clutter. He arched his spine and yawned. His shoes slipped off of their own accord, and he wriggled out of his clothes as his body ceased to correspond to them. His hind paws stretched past the edge of the bed before he pulled them up, curling around them. He ground the tips of his ears into the pillow and tried not to think while the crickets trapped in the ventilation shaft ticked a countdown to morning.

At the Artisans' Market

Cristina woke from the blue, blood-red and black of night and dreams to the gray of predawn and found herself in her own bed, like old times, though the warm bodies on either side weren't the same and the weight hanging above her was entirely new. Sometime in the night, she'd dragged the sheets from her cousin María José and piled them on María Elena. The clock's red digits told her Mama would be up already, plucking chickens.

She lay there a minute, seeing, remembering, then got up to pluck chickens.

The kitchen lights burned stark against the pale outside; the window was dirty enough to blur the tiredness from her reflection. Mama's purple rubber gloves lay draped over the drying rack. The radio — had Mama ever listened to the radio? The record player had been Papi's. Anyway, it would wake the house. She hummed something under her breath. The kettle barely chirped before she had it off the heat.

The chickens, she realized when she opened the fridge, shouldn't be there. They came whole from the butcher's, six of them delivered to the comedor every afternoon with feathers intact because it was cheaper, and because, Mama said, it helped keep the juices in. Mama lugged them home in a wheeled plastic cooler, and they spent the night in the fridge. In the morning, with help from her girls, she hacked off heads and feet for stew, plucked, cleaned, broke them down for frying, larded, herbed and breaded them. Then back to the comedor they went in the same cooler, to fry or roast in time for lunch.

But Mama had died at lunchtime.

Plucking chickens required no small strength and wore out wrists and shoulders; over years it made Mama's forearms thick as turkey legs, though her hands stayed soft from all the lard. Once, in a festive mood during Holy Week, and to teach him a lesson, Mama challenged one of Teresa's boyfriends to arm wrestle. He refused. He didn't want to hurt her, he claimed. That Mama could be susceptible to the slightest harm from such a preening rooster was so patently absurd that Cristina and Corísa couldn't hold back laughter, and Mama wouldn't let it go. Stung, the boy was spurred to accept. Perhaps to save his dignity, Mama let him struggle a minute, a bored expression on her face. His dignity was not saved. Teresa didn't speak to Mama for days.

Cristina made it through one chicken before her arms were hot and throbbing. She stood flexing her hands, eyes closed, then peeled off the purple gloves and went to wake María Elena, who looked even less rested than Cristina felt. "Sorry. Can you help with the chickens?"

María Elena got out of bed. Cristina rearranged the sheets to better cover Majo and told her to go back to sleep.

Soon they had a rhythm going. That they were together in this was a relief. She'd been alone. Everyone was entitled to miss Mama in their own way; only she and Mael were expected to become her.

"Can I call you Mael?"

María Elena nodded, her narrow lips pressed in that look of permanent uncertainty that had already begun to define her.

They were all but finished when Tía Constancia appeared in the dining room doorway in her nightdress and began to cry. "I almost thought ..."

Not again. Cristina bit her tongue. She wasn't trying to become her mother; she was plucking chickens for something to do to avoid having to hurt. But she didn't want to hurt Tía either, any more than she already hurt. "There's hot water," she said carefully. "We haven't thought about breakfast at all."

Tía touched Cristina's arm and set to work, pulling eggs, milk and leftovers from the fridge, turning on the heat beneath the griddle. She wanted the same thing, Cristina realized: something to do.

"Are you really going?" Tía asked.

Cristina hadn't thought that far ahead. But that she even asked the question made Cristina realize it wasn't Constancia expecting her to become Mama. It was Mama.

She fought her way out of the rubber gloves for good this time and hugged her Tía tight.

By the time Tío Juan's old pickup groaned outside, night had turned the corner into dawn. Cristina and Mael were sitting down to scrambled eggs and refried beans when he came in.

Constancia squeezed her husband's hand over the griddle. She cried some more. Cristina poured too much hot sauce on her eggs and tried to concentrate on eating.

"I only stopped to see how everyone was doing," Tío said, with unusual eloquence. She used to wonder how his workers knew what to do with nothing to go on but his pregnant looks. Now he gave one to Cristina, and she struggled to present him with a face that would tell him all he needed to know.

"Go," said Constancia. "We'll be all right. We haven't even talked about arrangements!"

Cristina abandoned her breakfast. If she stayed, it would mean more uncomfortable pauses begging to be interrupted with hugs and sobbing or more food, more unfulfillable expectations. "Can you drop us in the city, Tío?" She looked at María Elena, who kept eating with the determination of someone who didn't take breakfast for granted. "Someone has to see about the comedor. And we won't be able to make any arrangements without — without a body."

"Of course," said Tío. "But hurry. The men are waiting."

Cristina ran upstairs and tiptoed through rooms until she found Miguel Ángel, awake and curious-eyed in Pilar's arms in Papi's recliner. She gathered him carefully up, at which he yawned and fussed, his big, impossibly clear eyes crinkling dangerously until she dug his empty bottle from under the blankets. Pilar remained in the same position as before, out cold cradling an invisible baby. Cristina kissed her cheek, feeling guilty and grateful at having been allowed to sleep through the night. She tugged the nappy bag out from under Pilar's feet, changed him, went downstairs to mix formula and warm it to refill the bottle. When Miguel Ángel was finished, she bundled him up in a triangle of shawl and slung him, snug and comforting, against her belly.

Tía said, "You don't have to take him. I'm here. Your cousins, his big brother — you have plenty of help."

"I can do it," said Cristina at the door, to herself as well as to the universe. She shouldered the nappy bag, took up the handle of the cooler filled with dismembered chickens, nodded to Mael. Tío's truck rumbled outside. "It's my turn. Mama gave him to me, so I'm taking him. Okay?"

The sun drew dark lines along the creases in Tío Juan's cheeks. He drove with the window cracked despite the morning's chill, wisps from his cigarette spilling down over the bridge into the mist-beset gorge, until the baby cried and he put it away. Cristina sat hugging Miguel Ángel, whispering reassurances she didn't feel. Beside her, Mael leaned against the window. Four workmen joked quietly in the truckbed behind them, squatting on bags of sand and cement. For years, this had been Mama's morning, chicken in a cooler under her feet, taciturn, dependable Juan and a cowed apprentice at either side, the truck's broken ventilation system spilling engine heat over their knees. What had Mama thought about every morning? How her daughters were failing her? Had she prayed? A rosary hung from the mirror, clicking against the faded orange windscreen decal JESUS IS LORD. Maybe Tío Juan was so silent, maybe he seemed so relaxed and patient because he prayed all the time.

In the shuddering old truck, the bumps could bruise your tailbone if you didn't sit just right.

Cristina knew four prayers, for when it was expected: the Pater Noster, the Ave María, the Creed, which she could make it through only if everyone around her was praying along, and a catchall of her own invention for when a priest called for personal reflection. *Lord, please take care of my family and help them get through this.* And then a litany of the names of everyone she loved. God didn't answer prayers. The point was giving the benefit of the doubt to those who thought otherwise. *Mama,* she thought first — but it wasn't as if Eufemia Ramos would be waiting around at the gates for one more mortal endorsement.

For Cristina the limit to human experience of the miraculous was the baby in her arms, hovering between awe and tears and clawing for a nipple through her clothes.

Traffic jostled. The hills poured them down out of the suburbs into the city. Zone One was busy enough and they were late enough Tío had to drop them a block from the market. "Call if you need anything."

The Comedor Santa Rosa de Lima was blocked off with orange plastic hurricane fencing. Peeking through, she saw rubble, shattered tile. "But this is my mother's rented space," she protested to the armed man standing guard in fatigues, guiltily relieved. The man shrugged, stared at her, stared at Mael, and placed a call, a few official-sounding monosyllables. He would not let them pass.

She had last seen this place in dreams.

She couldn't help but see it again in all its supernumerary assault of color and dramatic light: the men wearing angels, human faces masked in painted skulls and gothic scrollwork, human natures obscured by the task to which they'd gone unquestioning. It was as if Mama's beliefs had been sent by God, disguised as reality, to unmake her.

The armed man reached out to steady her. He was talking at her, using the bored voice of authority like that Inspector Toad had used at Mama's house last night, telling her she couldn't linger to process or grieve, she must process through official channels. She turned her back on the impossible labyrinth beyond the fence. She took deep breaths. It was hunger; she hadn't eaten enough. It was thirst. Grief made people forget to eat and drink, everyone knew that. Constancia had failed to play Mama's role just as Cristina had; Mama would have browbeaten her at least into finishing her tea in the car. It was lack of caffeine; there was never anything but decaf in Mama's kitchen, often not even that, nothing but hibiscus and horchata. At home, Cristina refrained out of respect; on windy roadsides in the cold highlands with her canvases, often with two children to look after, she drank coffee.

Miguel Ángel began again to whimper. "Headquarters?" she parroted back to the guard. "I want ... I want my mother's body." The guard's coldness made her feel she was pouting, incoherent beyond reason. "We need to bury her."

He spoke thickly into his phone some more, then gave her a number to call. She thumbed it dizzily into a new contact in her phone, "Mama's Body," while feathery blue things swirled in the space around the screen. She reached for the wheeled cooler's plastic handle, leaned on its flimsy support.

She looked for Mael, her other charge, her other comfort. But Mael had disappeared.

Cristina scanned the market aisles, looking everywhere but behind her. Mael couldn't have gone far; this would be the only part of the city she knew. Had she made friends with other market girls? Too shy, Cristina thought — but she'd only known Mael a day, a terrible day, the worst day, the kind that would change anyone. As a little girl Cristina knew every nook of these aisles, almost every face, but that was long ago and now she recognized only a few of the oldest women. She wondered if Mael missed her own family's local market, once a week along some little cliffside street with a view of distant peaks, where she knew everyone, even the men.

Maybe she'd gone to the cathedral. Did she believe in God? Maybe not, after yesterday.

Cristina stopped at the Comedor of the Annunciation. Mama had never failed to find a word of derision for their overseasoned kaqik and feeble attempts at price undercutting. Once the unfamiliar cook understood, he was happy to accept the cooler and its contents. He hadn't seen Mael. She didn't linger to consider his offer of repayment or his condolences.

Beneath an edge of the market's winglike awnings, a crowd of women huddled hip to hip on low benches around a tin vat of atol big enough for any two of them to curl up inside. They made room. None was Mael. She sipped scalding hot, sweet atol from a styrofoam cup and asked after a thin girl, thirteen or fourteen, who looked like she'd seen a ghost. These women, so different, young, old, each in embroidered traje and shawl not like any of the others', nevertheless formed a brood. If they'd taken Mael in among them, she'd be safe until she wasn't. Cristina saw them, uncharitably, as pigeons, crowding periwinkle against the gray cobbles of the plaza around someone's discarded tortilla. A blue-storm sky, the flags of the Presidential Palace curling, a red-brown angel striding toward them, a hawk-angel or a shrike-angel, single-minded, inattentive to their mortal concerns, to scatter them to the four directions.

Wasn't that how things went between humans and angels?

She had a second helping of atol, a cup of sweet, thin coffee cut with roasted corn, then another. No sign of Mael. Warmed by body heat from the women and the baby and warm food in her stomach, she felt more herself — guiltier because of it. *I'm sorry I made you come,* she rehearsed for when they met again. *I was* selfish, *I forgot you were there, mixing dough or spooning curtidos over rice, in her kitchen when the angels came. For you, it* was *real. No wonder you ran. I should have left you with Constancia and come alone.*

Mael. I should have made you tell me what really happened.

In a corner behind the benches, at the other women's feet, she laid the baby down atop her spread-out shawl to change him. He was hungry again. They watched the crowd together, Cristina recognizing no one, Miguel Ángel seeing only forms, Cristina full of dread, he full of ... of nothing, a vessel to be filled. She was so jealous of him.

What an idiot Teresa had been to leave him.

She wrapped him up snug again and left the market, made a long circuit counterclockwise around the old city center, west along the cold, shadowed side of the cathedral, ducking in a moment through the north transept, looking up and down the pews, feeling tiny, holy and desperate at once. She whispered a hasty Ave María, *Lord help them get through this, Mama, María Elena,* then she ducked out again, along the plaza past the Palace, its pigeons, bulletproof SUVs and flags, then south between the concert shell and the fountain, east past the shuttered posh boutiques and back to the sunny side of the cathedral, a hand against the warm stone, arriving finally at the hurricane fence and the yellow tape around Mama's comedor.

The armed guard frowned.

"The girl who was with me before — she hasn't been back this way?"

He told her no — there had been no girl with her before. Something in his tone or the shotgun pointed at her feet left her unconvinced.

She dug in her satchel past nappies, powdered formula and bottle, found a tube of red acrylic and went to the wall, where she used a stub of pencil for a clumsy palette knife to slash "MAEL," her own name, and her phone number — half of it, before the man with the gun put a hand on her arm.

"This is a crime scene."

She felt like crying, so she indulged it. "Please. She's — my sister, I can't lose her. She doesn't know the city at all." Again into the satchel; she tore a corner from a back page of her ratty spiral sketchbook and scrawled her number on it, graphite edged in red. She pressed it on him, letting her touch linger despite being creeped out by the softness of his hand — she was old for him, and she probably looked a wreck, but she had no choice but to try, even

Mama would have said so. "You could call, if you see her. I don't even know if she has her phone."

"Get out of here."

She would have gone back to the atolera, though she wasn't hungry anymore. But the moment had passed. The women were gone, each off again to their own stalls.

Her feet took her east past the artists' stalls with their familiar visions of volcanic sunsets, old city streets bursting with jacarandas, hillsides made from patterned cloth. The world was a wonderful, one-dimensional place if you could keep your eye inside the frame. Her fingers itched to put just one true face among these masks. She had the notebook, the stubby pencil speared through the spirals. The people seated behind the canvases, half-expectant, half-resigned, were not her family but her kin. They saw visions. She might know one of them, from the roadside or from Hugo's classes in Comalapa. She could retrieve the money for Mama's last chickens from the cook at the Comedor of the Annunciation, trade it for a canvas; someone might let her share their paints. But it would be a waste of time, and also money, and hope.

The thin crowd flowed past her. She got out her phone, found the number labeled "Mama's Body," dialed home instead.

"Tell me."

"I lost her, Tía."

"Is that you, Cristina dear? What did you lose?"

"I lost María Elena. I brought her to the comedor, and of course it was a crime scene, and I don't know what I was thinking but when I looked, she was gone." She was losing control again; people were looking. She walked fast, talking faster, trying to escape the feeling of vertigo.

"You know how Mama was with them. She wanted them to suffer and not complain." Because a servant who complains gets punished. Or fired. "I think Mael must have been hurting, but she couldn't say because that wasn't how Mama taught her. I didn't even ask if she wanted to come. You saw how she was, she wouldn't speak. *She saw it happen,* Tía. She wasn't ready. Now she's ..."

Tía sighed into the phone, and Cristina prepared herself for the response that was coming. Her feet took her out of the market along Eighth.

"We did the right thing taking her in, dear," Tía said. "You were right about that. I was wrong. And you're right to worry for her now, obviously she must be traumatized by what happened, not making good choices. But it's not your fault what happened. We hardly know this girl. Just because she disappeared doesn't mean she's in danger. Maybe she met a boy she knew. Maybe they made a plan to meet and she's off with him now. I'm sorry I didn't see this coming and make you stay. You should come home now, Colocha. Everyone's awake, your uncle is telling the story of how Eufemia met your papa. There's nothing more you can do there."

A rush of false relief. She stepped into the street briefly, around a couple walking hip-to-hip. *Could* Mael have met someone here, a boy? It seemed impossible.

Mama would have given her the hard truth.

She crossed into the plaza, took a seat on one of the low, round retaining walls in a locust tree's shade where she could watch the police on the cathedral corner and see down Eighth. She took a breath, coughed, shielded Miguel Ángel from a passing man's cigar.

Through the phone came canaries singing, kids yelling, a dog barking. "Are you there, Colocha?"

"I'm still here. Tía, the police gave me a number to call. To get Mama back. Could you? Please. I need to keep looking for Mael. She couldn't have a boyfriend — she was too new here, and Mama wouldn't allow it. She has to be around here. Unless ... maybe she got on a bus to go home?" Wherever her home was.

"Maybe that's what happened," Tía said, and Cristina heard immediately how desperate it sounded. But she promised to call the police. Cristina gave her the number, promised to be careful. She spread out her shawl on the locust tree's grimed roots and lay Miguel Ángel on top of it. She brushed his cheek.

She got out the sketchbook and pencil, opened to a blank page.

Worshippers trickled from the cathedral's tall gates. When the last had left, the two policemen swung them closed and chained them.

Dead Ends

When Felipe woke, Luz and Aníbal were gone, and El Bufo was pounding at the door. The jaguar mask lay at the foot of the bed.

The crack of sunlight that was all the apartment ever got didn't penetrate the ventilation shaft until noon, and then it shone in Luz and Aníbal's window, where it rarely did anybody any good. They were morning people. The kitchen smelled of fried plantains and coffee — this was their big day.

The fragment of trash-salvaged mirror he'd nailed by the door showed Felipe's own human face: an honest face, he liked to think, despite its fundamental falsehood, green eyes striking and out of place beneath dark brows.

It was the wrong mask.

Through the peephole, El Bufo looked, if possible, even uglier and more disheveled than the night before — but alive, and no fool. Better safe than sorry. Rubbing agate from his eyes, Felipe went back for the conquistador mask.

"If I rolled that way," El Bufo said when he opened the door, and Felipe realized he'd also forgotten his clothes. "You look like the other luchador. The one about to get beaten to a pulp." His gaze roamed past Felipe into the apartment, and Felipe realized how much trouble he was in.

"Your roommates," said El Bufo. "Do they know?"

The place was tiny, full of their stuff and almost nothing of his own. Maps, pamphlets, nightclub flyers, foreign language and law textbooks piled on the little desk and spilling onto the floor. On the table, surrounded by breakfast dishes and painfully incriminating books of dissident political and economic theory — Luz's massively thumbed university discard copy of *Open Veins of Latin America* alone was something you could get disappeared for — a potted basil reached feebly for artificial light. Masa and green flecks of chiles decorated the messy kitchenette. In the little painting framed above the sink, eerily electric-hued campesinos lurched home through dusklit fields, weighted with machetes, broad-brimmed hats and the yoke of wage slavery. Felipe hated that painting, though he understood why she'd bought it.

Felipe shivered. "Would you please fucking call ahead next time."

"I did," said El Bufo mildly, taking a bottle of aguardiente from the cupboard next to the sink as if he'd known exactly where to find it.

He ducked into his room for clothes — shorts, sandals, an Arsenal football jersey, phone and keys into pockets and a shoebox of masks under his arm. He hesitated over the wad of cash, left it where it was. "How do you know where I live?" He'd never even given his real name.

"Vehicle registration," El Bufo grunted over his shoulder. He cracked the seal on the liquor and swigged, smearing grubby fingerprints on the painting.

"Leave that alone," said Felipe. But El Bufo had already moved on, past the progressively more faded photos of assassinated activists — Berta Cáceres, Juana Raymundo, Telésforo Pivaral, Rigoberta Choc, Gaspar Ilóm — to the map taped above the desk. The map was feathered with color-coded plastic arrows identifying the sites of protest actions, roadblocks — both government security checkpoints and the homegrown kind — deforestation, desertification, the ruinous paths of both pyroclastic mudflows and toxic runoff, foreign mining rights grabs, too much for Felipe to keep track. He was relieved they seemed to have taken the one for today's protests with them — as he recalled, it had the word "PIGS" scrawled on it in black crayon in several places, with arrows for anticipated troop advances like they were strategizing for war.

Luz had been nowhere near this organized as a kid. It was the two of them together, a mutually amplified, incongruous whirlwind of sex and deeply passionate clerical effort. Of course, he kept his own calendars, no doubt not entirely free of Aníbal's influence, but those were different. Practical.

"Okay, enough," he said, physically steering El Bufo away from their open bedroom door. "You already know more than enough to blackmail me into whatever you need. Can we go already? Just let me get coffee."

He filled the kettle from Aníbal's terracotta filtration tank, without which he no longer considered the water safe to drink — though he'd been drinking it most of his life — and turned on the stove.

"Don't bother," said El Bufo. "We'll stop on the way."

The dashboard calendars named today Four Death, the feast of San Teodora Guerín — a martyr. The words were circled and highlighted in lurid yellow: protest day. On Death days, all things being equal, Felipe preferred the caiman mask, which gave his reflection coily hair, a complexion a different shade of Brown, and a clear hint of Garífuna ancestry in the high brow and narrow jaw. As with the conquistador, but in inverse, the caiman mask seemed to cause people either to afford him a little more respect or to let their eyes slide right past him as if he wasn't there — unsettled by otherness? He had a skull mask, but he never wore it; death had meant something different to his ancestors. El Bufo was used to the conquistador mask; today, the conquistador it would be. The rest went in their shoebox into the hollow place under his seat.

"I got rid of the gun," Felipe lied as El Bufo took the passenger seat.

"You're learning."

They got coffee at one of the absurdly upscale chain restaurants crowded among the towering malls and hotels of Zona Viva, where if you could afford the premium, you could order from an overdressed, overpolite stooge suspended above a parking garage exit ramp in a plexiglass box without setting foot out of your car.

Luz and Aníbal had taken him to Zona Viva for the first time back when Aníbal still had her parents' money, to see an awful disaster movie on a giant 3D screen in a mall that looked like a space station. It was like another world. How the Zone Three barrios and this place could exist a kilometer apart was unfathomable until he recognized the obvious: one depended on the other.

"Best coffee in the city," said El Bufo with a sigh. And it was. "Fair" trade, shade-grown, Indígeno-harvested organic Vienna from the foothills outside Antigua, export quality, corporate-roasted, available to ladinos, foreigners and (ex-)cops only, richer than rich and blacker than black, its glossy, grassy, earthy scent filled the car like handfuls of freshly charred volcanic injustice shoved up your nose.

"Now, back to the scene of the crime, please."

Felipe complied, now exquisitely, painfully awake, trying to think how the fuck he was going to get out of this in time to triage the thousands of texts from Luz already lighting up his phone.

"Guess you made it home last night," he ventured. Small talk.

El Bufo watched the traffic, mopeds and black-windowed luxury SUVs. "Didn't go home." That explained the clothes. Though they'd looked that worn-in yesterday. "Nor did I get my balls fed to me by knife-wielding prepubescents, sorry to disappoint. Cultivate a little confidence in me. You *are* trusting me with your secrets."

"Come *on,*" Felipe burst out. "You weren't just looking for a driver." He sucked down more coffee, seeking clarity.

"Hmm?" said El Bufo.

"Yesterday, when we met." *You were waiting for me.*

"An assistant," agreed El Bufo magnanimously.

"How am I supposed to *assist* if you don't tell me anything? You want me to trust you? Give me an excuse."

El Bufo laughed, sloshing coffee on the seat. "Good. Fine. While you were sleeping it off, I made some calls, asked some questions. Did a little reading."

"You're telling me you went to Zone Three in the middle of the night looking for an internet café."

He ignored this. "Our primary victim, Mister Antonellis, was an upstanding man, dedicated, skilled at his job but aware of its limits. Powerful people expected him to go far. They were mistaken. He overstepped similar limits, it seems, in his home country — a calculated political risk. He got burned. He was reassigned here. Wife came over with him — means he had something to lose. But the work wasn't enough for him. So he gets involved with this independent NGO."

"NGO?" Felipe tried to make it sound like ignorance. He already didn't like where this was going.

"Non-government organization," said El Bufo, humoring him. "Notoriously unregulated. Like a nonprofit, a charity. Only they can take donations from whoever they want, use them however they want."

Aníbal complained about other groups competing with theirs for grant money, but Luz considered it counter-productive. Focus on what we can actually do, she was always saying.

"Recently, this group has been protesting a certain police action in Totonícapan province." He waved a dismissive hand. "Eminent domain, a preeminent Canadian mining concern, and poor locals — squatters, really — getting in the way of progress. Lost cause … except somehow, it's getting international attention. Trouble for Molinero's regime." He cleared his throat. "Too many people forget what the war was like. But you're too young to remember."

"I … don't really," Felipe admitted. Even Luz and Aníbal talked around the war rather than about it, though it seemed like they blamed the war — and those who bankrolled and prosecuted it — for everything.

"Consider yourself lucky," said El Bufo. "Didn't make much difference in the city, anyway — war happens in the provinces. Some ways, it's still going on. We just learned how to hide it."

A cold shiver. *We.*

Traffic slowed. Felipe braked, dodged: a bus had broken down in the right lane. "These people remember," said El Bufo darkly. "Look at them."

Passengers picked their way in single file along the shoulder, tottering under bags and bundles. Any other day, he'd be trying to pull a fare. The woman walking in the lead looked like she'd lived through the civil war *and* the revolution. A few steps behind her, a man with a crutch wore the right leg of his pants pinned shut above the knee. His cragged face expressed such eloquent sorrow it could only mean he used it to earn his living. Felipe knew that mask: his father wore it every day. A gap opened; he gunned it.

They entered the s-curve along the Las Torres bluffs. The cardboard shanties and plastic tents of El Gallito cascaded past on the right, then surged up again, crowded on the steep sides of the facing hill like debris on the crest of a wave. Hidden in the ravine, a fork of the river dug canyons through the garbage dunes of the city dump. Beyond that, occluded by the hill, was the cemetery.

"So he helped this NGO —"

"Funneled them shitloads of money probably earmarked for some government pet project, yeah."

"— and you think somebody killed him over it," Felipe finished. Luz hadn't thought so. And she knew the guy, she worked with him. Knowing Luz, she was probably instrumental in winning him over to their cause.

And then he was executed in broad daylight. Who wouldn't freak over something like that? It didn't mean she was involved. It didn't mean she knew who killed him.

El Bufo grunted. "You want to know how many dead foreigners I've investigated in eleven years?"

From the way the ones outside the airport jumped at shadows, you'd think they were endangered. From the way they spent money, you'd think every day was their last. "A lot?"

"This is the first. It doesn't make business sense. Real money comes from foreign aid — hundreds of millions, more every year. Why spoil that?" El Bufo downed the last drops of his coffee and cranked down his window enough to pitch the cup out, where it joined the other trash drifting against the guardrail.

Felipe grimaced behind the mask but kept his mouth shut — he'd done the same, until Aníbal nagged him out of it. "So why kill him? If somebody didn't like what he was doing, why not just get him fired?" Parroting Luz's objection from last night — another small betrayal he immediately regretted. "Who's to say he was even the target? Maybe the killer was some disgruntled customer tired of getting overcharged for Eufemia's — the old lady's greasy chicken?"

"Her chicken was delicious," El Bufo retorted. "And cheap. Used to take Gilberto there, years ago when I was grooming him to pick me for partner." He fell silent, looking out over the ravine.

"The good old times," Felipe ventured.

El Bufo ignored this, scowling, but went on. "And the other two, Parrales and Chanax, were bureaucracy yes-men. Department of Human Rights, but they'd barely been there a month, transfer from Justice after somebody figured out they'd been appointed by the previous administration. Getting rid of them was a bonus. Antonellis was the target. Otherwise, the assassins would have known they had the wrong guy the minute they saw him."

"Yeah. Okay." Felipe merged to catch the Eighth Ave off-ramp. "So who?"

"Somebody who stood to be damaged by publicity as a result of these protests. Mining company. Police. Higher-ups in his own organization. Even somebody from Molinero's regime."

"Police," repeated Felipe, his stomach turning over. He should have asked for a croissant or something.

El Bufo gave a phlegmy snort. "Why do you think they put me on the job?" He held up a thumb, then a finger. "Either old Gilberto's actually still going through the motions, he's got the same suspicions I do and wants somebody from outside to do the dirty work, in which case he's lying about being able to put me back on the payroll ... or the higher-ups need a scapegoat. They appreciate how well I played that role for them the first time, and they assume there's no chance I'll finger the real culprit. In which case Gilberto's just following orders like the whipping boy he's always been. Worst case, I figure out who's actually responsible, somehow rediscover the principles I gave up in exchange for the badge, and refuse to cut a deal. They let me hang myself in my prior indiscretions."

"That's if it's the police." Felipe breathed deep as he cut north to Seventh to avoid the plaza.

"Oh, they're involved. Believe me."

"That ... would sound pretty crazy to some people," Felipe said carefully. That the police were corrupt was no kind of surprise. They got paid poorly, got murdered not infrequently, and they took bribes and did plenty of their own murdering to make up for the former and avoid the latter. More surprising that one of Aníbal's conspiracy theories might turn out to be right.

El Bufo laughed. "You're not some people."

I'm not any *people.*

But there was no point calling him on it. Not until Felipe figured out what to do. This time had to be different. The last time he'd let down his guard, let the mask slip somehow, seventy strangers went home with a fleeting impression their grandmothers' bedtime stories had come momentarily true. None of them knew him. None of them would see him again. Running from El Bufo would be something else entirely.

For the moment, he put Eufémia's daughter out of his head.

"Got to understand how the system works," El Bufo was saying. "You don't know the first thing about power, do you, 'Félix?' The system got me where I am today. Once, I was a fresh-faced cabrón with a uniform and a hand-me-down AK like the boys at the crime scene. I moved up because I learned. I played the game. Lost my badge because I didn't play smart enough. You know what the trick is, the object of the game? Money unites people, unites interests. The mining company, the bank, the government, the narcos. Even the charities. You want power, you go where the money is, you do what the money wants. Turn here."

It took Felipe a moment to recognize the change of subject. "What, here?"

"Here," croaked El Bufo ominously. "You're going to miss it."

"This is Fifth," Felipe protested, but he took the turn. "It dead-ends at the plaza. I know what I'm doing — this is tourist territory, I spend half my time here. You want Seventh."

"Not going to the market. Not yet. Need to make a stop."

Fifth was one-way along the west wall of the Presidential Palace, a stately belle epoque edifice built, like most of the old city, from imported marble in the early days of the fruit companies, but distinct in its long sight lines, the absence of epiphytes digging roots into its cornices, not to mention the electrified fence and manned gates. Statues of dead robber barons adorned the upper floors. Cars lined the curb, all of them black and gleaming. One was parked at a deliberate angle, blocking the way forward.

"Pull up at the gate and wait. Won't take a minute."

"What the fuck is this?"

"SAAS headquarters," said El Bufo, incomprehensibly calm.

The Secretariat of Administrative Affairs and Security, Felipe knew from his occasional indulgence of Aníbal-induced paranoia on internet conspiracy message boards, was nothing but a rebranding of the old Presidential Guard. The Guard had ostensibly been tasked with providing security for the head of state, but was actually an independent, paramilitary intelligence agency answering only to President Molinero, who had himself belonged to the Guard back in the nineties before he entered politics.

Feeling the universe dropping out from under him, Felipe inched forward, trying to look inconspicuous despite the obvious impossibility: Baby was the only non-bulletproof vehicle in sight. Everybody was staring at them. "What the fuck are we doing here? Are you crazy? There's cameras everywhere." He slouched in his seat, certain they could see him even through the glare, the smoked glass, and the mask.

El Bufo shrugged, looking uncomfortable. "Seeing if Gilberto got me reinstated. Picking up my check if he did. So I know how far I can trust him."

"You were SAAS? I thought you were civil police. Your badge said you were civil police."

"Yeah, that one's fake."

"This is an unlicensed cab," Felipe yelled. "They'll confiscate my car. Some senator's kid will end up driving it from his walled compound to the beach and back. This car is my living."

"I took care of that."

"What?"

"Changed your plates."

It took a moment for this to sink in. His plates: El Bufo had run his license plates through some official database to find out where he lived. And his legal name, and who knew what else. Then — had he edited the database? Or had he gone down to the garage ahead of him and switched Baby's plates with someone else's? "You're telling me this *now*?"

The street swarmed with uniforms. Two soldiers stepped from the barred gate and moved to either side of the car, assault rifles aimed at the pavement. A third — an officer, judging by the quetzal pin and beret and his flat action hero expression — strolled up to the driver's side window.

"Where the fuck is Gilberto," El Bufo muttered.

"What?"

"Focus on the task at hand," snapped El Bufo. "Stay calm, sit still, don't do anything stupid. Open the fucking window. Open it all the way, like you've got nothing to hide."

"Nothing to hide? What about my face? I don't want to be associated with you. I don't want anything to do with you, don't you get it?"

"Your face." El Bufo laughed. "Open the window, or I'm not going to be responsible for scraping your brains off the upholstery. Assuming you've got any."

The angle of sunlight and the window's tint cast a sharp line of shade across the face under the beret, lending an impression of coldness. A hand rested atop a holster. Felipe tried and failed to make the Argentine's face in the mirror anything like that cold and serene. He wrapped his human thumb and forefinger around the glass drawer-pull he'd used to replace the broken-off window crank and turned it three smooth revolutions counterclockwise.

He'd never understood the most fundamental aspect of his survival. How, for all those years, had he been able to avoid being seen for what he was?

"If it works, don't fix it," said his half-brother Rubén, primarily of chop-shop bus engines, but by extension of all things. Then, on the bus during Huehuetenango rush hour, it stopped working. Why? When would it happen again? Had it happened already? Was that how El Bufo knew?

"In the northern city where I used to live," Aníbal told Felipe when they first met, and then again occasionally when she was asked to account for herself to a new crop of NGO interns, "there's a polluted river. Just like here. Decades ago, people realized what we were doing to ourselves, and we passed a bunch of laws to stop corporations dumping toxic chemicals in it. And it got better. Birds came back, fish. One day when I was in college, they told us it was safe to swim in. We celebrated, and we swam. But nobody swims anymore. Because they never actually cleaned up the pollution — they just stopped adding more, and left what was already there to get covered over with leaves and silt for thirty years. As a story of redemption we tell ourselves about how we're enlightened, progressive, how we own our mistakes and see ourselves for who we really are, it works. But nobody's looking too closely. Because really cleaning it up would have cost more than we're willing to pay. And now, because of rising seas and half the city built on a swamp, they have to start dredging again. Digging up all that poison."

"Burying our horrors is how we survive," Luz would say on a bad day, like after another national election installed the richest fascist bureaucrat with the biggest smile who could tell the most populist jokes. "This city's been in the top five for murders per capita in the world for as long as we've been alive. You'd think people would be afraid to go to work, to go to the park. Instead, people are happier here than almost anywhere in the developed world."

And yet both of them spent every day of their lives digging into toxic horrors, up to their elbows in it, fighting to find a way to make it clean.

For a little while, he settled into life with Luz and Aníbal, feeling cultured and cosmopolitan, idly discussing revolution over breakfast tacos, drinking better coffee than he ever had. Smoking an unfiltered cigarette on a rooftop against a city sunset, he'd been able to regard what had happened on the bus as an unconscious signal to himself. Time to grow up. He'd saved enough, he'd had enough of his parents and his hometown; Luz had done what he should have years ago.

An attempted carjacking in the streets of Babylon reminded him life wasn't that simple, and the fear came flooding back. What if growing up heralded some inevitable, irreversible transition? The masks, the transformations the masks enabled, might stop working altogether. Or what if something inside him had gone fatally wrong? A cancer. He'd never known what killed his older brother Martín.

Through long hours alone hunting fares, more far-fetched, desperate possibilities occurred to him. Had there been some external actor in the mask's failure on the bus that day, a crazed cultist or supernumary being out of ancient tradition like himself? What if the mask failed again? What if he were found out and cult-sacrificed to dead gods, or named some kind of surrogate god just in time to prove definitively otherwise by getting shot or crucified?

These terrors he was mostly able to dismiss by lack of faith. His father's conviction of the Savior's benevolence had been born out of necessity. After losing an arm and his livelihood, God had presented him with another: charity. But God had done nothing to lift Rubén's son, Felipe's nephew Juan Martín, from the family's ensuing and persistent poverty.

And dismissing supernatural intervention brought Felipe back to the simple explanation for what had happened on the bus: he'd gotten complacent, been lulled by routine. He'd gotten bored. Twenty-five years was a long time to be looking over one's shoulder, and with Luz gone, there'd been nobody left to impress.

He wasn't bored now.

But how well did reason apply to masked jaguars posing as men anyway?

The cut-jawed, actually-human face of the SAAS officer remained stony under the fold of his beret as he bent to the open window. Stoneface was probably in the job requirements. The cops yesterday hadn't had it, but they were rookies. Beret, on the other hand, killed people, had been killing people for years. Black sunglasses covered the only thing about him that might have conveyed a little humanity.

Felipe, suppressing the reflexive motions required to start the car, throw the transmission in reverse and GTFO, instead attempted to match him, to look like a bored taxi driver just waiting to get his pay. He wondered how much Beret got paid. He wondered how many people Beret had killed. He wondered the same about El Bufo.

Beret's eyes moved past Felipe to El Bufo in the passenger seat. El Bufo smiled, a caricature of politeness, and encountering that smile, Beret was pushed back from the window as though propelled by a gust of wind. In an instant, he collected himself. "F*ormer* Inspector Zamora. I had understood you were —"

"Funny," said El Bufo, cutting him off. "That's just what I'm here about. Is he in?"

If the payscale at the SAAS increased by body count — and surely the pecking order went accordingly — El Bufo had been way ahead of this guy. The officer touched his sunglasses, looked away, nodded.

El Bufo got out of the car, made a show of getting out his wallet, then came around to the driver's side and leaned in the window just as Beret had. "I can't believe that fucker wasn't waiting for me. I told him to be waiting outside. I could be forgiven for thinking he didn't even care." An assortment of insultingly small bills fluttered into Felipe's lap. "You're doing fine," he said in Felipe's ear. "Word of advice? After today, you might want to start using a different face. I'll be ten minutes."

Hands in the pockets of that ugly windbreaker, El Bufo strolled past Beret and the gauntlet of guards into the palace. For a moment, everybody watched him, even the guys with the assault rifles.

Felipe gunned the engine, slammed the car into reverse and peeled out backwards up the street, hunched so low over the wheel he could barely see. Only a wedge of the driver's side mirror made him reasonably confident no secret service assassins had been so foolish as to step into Baby's path. He couldn't see Beret. The ones he could see raised rifles to their shoulders and pivoted at the hip like clockwork, tracking him. But they didn't fire.

Then he was careening into traffic, horns honking, tires squealing as he cut across Seventh Ave onto the opposite side street. Would they follow? They hadn't shot him. Maybe they didn't care.

They thought he was just some taxi driver.

Laughing, he turned on the stereo, found something angry, fucking angry, dark and loud. A Mexican prog metal band — lyrics supposedly penned by a demon never more relevant. There was nobody behind him — no flashing lights, no bullets. He did some evasive driving anyway, zigzagging through blocks progressing north and east toward the football stadium. He pulled up under the cover of a bougainvillea knotted and swollen with purple blossoms like a lurid wound overhanging the street, kept the engine running and in gear while he got out the box of masks. The caiman's old wooden brow was chipped green, eyes tiny, dark, long mouthful of laughing teeth. With a different face, sharp Garífuna features in the mirror, he felt calmer.

He got out quickly, walked around the car to look at the plates. They were different plates. He got back in.

He was, without a doubt, being toyed with and manipulated by a murderer-spy who could see through masks to his true nature, not for any crime or political action he'd committed but *because* of that nature, for purposes he didn't understand. What Eufemia's murder had to do with it he didn't know; maybe nothing. Maybe it had just been an excuse to get close, test him, find out his secrets.

What now? Go home and get back Baby's license plates. If the car they'd been swapped to was still there. The palace had cameras, which meant the SAAS knew these plates. Whoever's they were was fucked too now, the poor bastard. They could track him if they wanted. How could they not, after the way he'd peeled out of there? Stupid. This wasn't Santa Catarina, it wasn't the highlands. Everywhere had cameras: petrol stations, residential colonies, banks, government buildings, malls, hotels. The grand anonymity of the city only worked if you flew under the radar.

Maybe Baby needed a mask. There had to be hundreds of Corollas in the city. He could find one, follow it home, trade plates, get Baby repainted to match. A mask no one could see through. He smiled at his sharp Garífuna face in the mirror, winked at his own cleverness, then watched his brow furrow as he realized he had only Eufemia's money for a paint job.

Eufemia was dead, her family didn't need it, they could always sell that nice, big house of theirs.

If he really wanted to be safe, he could ditch Baby, sell her. He loved this car; she'd saved his life, she was his life. But material things weren't important.

There were other cities. He could run. He'd have a hard time getting across any border except illegally; getting a car across would be worse. But he could go to Xela, the hazy, cold city among the high volcanoes hours to the west. He'd never been — he'd never been to any city but this one.

A ring interrupted the chalkboard-scratch roar of guitars through the stereo, his phone lighting up in the ashtray.

Luz. He let it go to voicemail, waited for her to finish leaving a message and the infernal catharsis-fest to resume — then angrily stabbed pause. You couldn't ever start again, not really. Because how could you do that to the people who needed you?

Like his parents, his brother, his nephew Martín, a year older than when Felipe had last seen him.

He listened to the message.

"It's getting crazy —" she said, then swelling noise drowned her words, then fell, then rose again: a chant, a burst of bullhorn static, a siren, a chorus of shouts, a clatter like breaking glass. "We started at the Palace of Justice, and the turnout was already — Then Dr. Ixchel spoke, our keynote, you were supposed to — — this morning. Whatever. Fuck you. She's amazing, Felipe! You should have been there. She's had such a hard life, like — — doesn't even know how old she is — — but even after going away for an education, she's able to keep — — without letting it — Anyway, she gave this speech — — all these other Indigenous leaders around the world, what they'd done right and how they'd — — by their own governments — — David's murder and the mining company and Molinero. It was powerful and inciteful and simple, and the way the crowd reacted —"

It cut off. He'd never heard her so fired up. Not when the millions in new funding had come in through Antonellis. Not when the news first came in about Totonícapan. None of the times Monterríos was indicted or escaped trial on a technicality. Not when the UN first agreed to extend judicial oversight over the restoration process, not when the oversight was withdrawn. The worst was how obviously she wanted him to care.

And he did care. He cared about Luz. And Aníbal. He remembered the rows of black arrows carefully inked on the city map in the kitchen, and the ranks of soldiers armed with assault rifles mustering outside the Palace.

He couldn't possibly slouch any lower in his seat than he already was without changing shape. Nervously, he pulled Baby back into the circuit of streets, keeping an eye out for doppelgänger Corollas.

The phone rang again. He picked up. "Luz? Are you there?"

More murmur and crowd noise, then her voice got close again. "— better? Listen, we just need support. Everybody's moving toward the Plaza, we're at … Eleventh and Fifth Ave. We're stopping traffic! We're way outside our permits, I think the police are going to try something. We may need to get people out. Can you just try and get close? I've got —"

"I can't hear you," he said, braking at a crossing for a line of Indigenous women with children in tow. A vinyl banner dragged between them, block-lettered in red, black and green matching their huipíles. What made them think, this time, that their presence, that banner, was worth the risk of leaving their jobs, bringing their kids?

Luz was gone. Going back to the plaza would put him within sight of the Palace again. Cameras. Dread. He'd figure a long way around.

The light changed. The line of women stretched into motion. *OUR LAND, OUR LIVELIHOOD, OUR LIVES*, said the banner. It was frayed at the edges, the colors faded. This wasn't these women's first protest, or their last.

The next call was from El Bufo. He silenced it, then hit unpause on the demon-haunted rage.

The Protest

The colors came to her bright, startling in contrasts and transitions, as they had since she was a child; she shoved them down and poured her focus into graphite gray and wax red shifting with the paper's skinlike texture. There was always so much detail in her head she could never get onto the page. The day, the city, went on around her, big, anonymous, smelly and loud. She never let the baby out of the corner of her eye, but she needed this.

She drew María Elena, small at first, small enough to fit the page, working at the comedor alone against a void of white in her worn but still-bright huipil the pencil's grays couldn't touch, her hair tied back, her arms pale to the elbows in masa. But the expression wasn't right; she couldn't express it so small. So she turned over a new page and sketched just the face, captured resignation in the ways the too-young skin around her eyes bunched and folded, big and intense enough that by the time she'd rendered the slight tightness of pressure in the upper lip she had run out of space. The eyes were wide and glossed with daylight, and in that light reflected, twice, four winged outlines, flaring. And off in the periphery, Mama, falling, dissolving into bare white.

Still not enough. She needed a canvas, a creamy expanse as wide as this section of cold wall she was sitting on with the baby beside her in the locust's thin shade, the sun growing hot, with an over-interested man perched on the other side in mustache and derby hat. All kinds of people passed all around, none of them Mael. Maybe she needed a wall, like the walls that bore those transcendental murals on the vacant buildings west of Sixth Ave, the murals that had stolen her breath when they'd appeared there last time she'd been home, when Mama had been alive and impatient with her for not coming sooner, not staying longer, wasting her life making beautiful things with paint instead of food. Mama never put it that way, but it was a way Cristina could understand her: food nourished people in ways art couldn't, and Mama, a pragmatist, could never quite manage to see the reverse.

She turned the page and drew Mael's eye, the left eye, huge, each lash a curving lance, iris patterns like peering into lake depths for fish schools just escaping. This time the reflection in the pupil was all Mama, distorted, broad in belly and breast and heavy forearm holding a mallet for pounding flat carne de rez, head and shoulders and skirted legs small and receding, as if Mama were enormous, blown up like a balloon.

Tía called, and Cristina kept sketching, the phone clamped uncomfortably between shoulder and ear as her aunt equivocated, vented and eventually revealed the location of the morgue. Cristina scrawled the address in a margin, put the phone down, turned the page.

She drew Mama as a giant, titanic, like the gods she'd seen in codices at the national museum, hair voluminous and thousand-threaded with wind, in one hand a roast turkey the size of a bus, in the other a tree-trunk ear of grilled corn steaming in its husk, an expression of irked disapproval as she waded among high-rises, searching in vain for the people she was supposed to feed, oblivious to those she was stomping on.

She turned the page — a leap like the leap of contrast between opposites on the color wheel that somehow balanced each other so nicely, new-green leaf and hot red hibiscus flower — and drew the masked jaguar. He wore no clothes but his spotted coat, the pattern transitioning across shoulder and haunch like the patterns in a map, mountains and rivers cut with roads. The tail wrapped round the jaguar's paws, concealing the talons, and the mask was finer than the ugly one he'd worn at Mama's house, more like the noble faces of the masks dancers wore on carnival day in Rabinal, like the stone faces of kings.

Her hand ached. Miguel Ángel fussed. She picked him up, and they stared at what she'd made.

The man in the fedora stared too. And a girl — not Mael — who sat on the adjacent section of wall offering hands full of beaded necklaces to passersby. And another woman, older, who sat behind Cristina under the tree — the girl's mother, using her daughter's adorableness as a lure to sell crafts. These strangers looking over her shoulder made her self-conscious, though there wasn't much she could do.

"What does it mean?" said the man.

With the sketches of Mama and Mael, it was obvious. But the jaguar? Had he said one word to her? His name. Had he been there at all, or was he like the laughing San Simón idol, some kind of half-conscious memory or dream intruding on her life? But San Simón appeared to Cristina only as a painted figure, never in the real world. Except once.

Once a year when they were little, Papi took the girls to the zoo, always on the Sunday after Mama's birthday, after church, so Mama could have the house to herself for an afternoon. The jaguar was always asleep. Impatient for it to prance and pounce and impress them like the occasional gum-eyed, emaciated, half-feral kitten they'd been allowed to feed, they hammered on the mesh walls of its cage. It just lay there, curled on its high shelf, eyes crinkled shut in pained inattention. As she grew older, she pitied it.

"It's a demon," declared the mother of the girl with the necklaces, loudly in Cristina's ear. "Blasphemy!" Frowning, she took her daughter by the elbow, drew her away, and was immediately replaced by others looking for rest, shade, and now demons, craning their necks to see.

This was why Cristina went on painting cheery falsehoods despite what Hugo kept repeating. Risks had consequences. She slapped the sketchbook shut and stood up.

The man in the fedora gave a murmur of regret and reached out to squeeze her behind.

Cristina caught her breath, biting back a scream, holding back a slap that would only make things worse, much worse. She didn't look at him. She never knew what to do when it happened, on the bus or at the comedor, a casual gesture of possession from a complete stranger. She bundled Miguel Ángel into his sling against his protests and wriggling, his unfathomably clear eyes crinkling at the corners, his hands grasping at what no one else could see. "Such a good baby," she whispered, aspirationally trying to soothe the baby and herself.

She looked up and realized how the crowd had grown. More flowed in from the surrounding streets. They had signs and banners, and some of the men wore black t-shirts with orange lettering reading, *WE ARE ALL TOTONÍCAPAN*. Another protest. A big one. Totonícapan?

She'd never find Mael.

She waded against the current of the crowd, away from the Palace, toward the southwest corner of the plaza where the flow was thinner. She looked for Mael in the faces she passed, but there were so many their features ran together. She might not recognize Mael even if she saw her. Posters lifted above the crowd bore memorial portraits of the disappeared, the dead, photoshopped with coronae and holy personages crowded, beckoning them welcome to Paradise. Crucifixes dangled against bright fabric. The individual, the personal, piled up by thousands into overwhelming, murmuring loss. She made for another of the walled-in locust trees, thinking to step up and get a better view, find a way free.

The warning rattle of shaken spray-paint cans pulled her to a stop for a trio of young men in backpacks, hoodies and handkerchief face-masks. Graffiti! The idea of it had always thrilled her: the anonymity, the scale, the chance to take something ugly and lifeless seen by thousands every day and not only turn it beautiful but instill it with meaning. The world their canvas. But the risks.

On her toes she waited, cradling the baby, listening to his murmurs over those of the crowd, dancing to avoid knots of protesters. In the murals that covered the lower floors of the tenements off Sixth Ave, babies became birds, giant bikes piloted by tiny people threatened to flatten cars, ceiba trees sprouted musicians sprouting music. On all those highway medians outside Xela, one artist or hundreds had in a few strokes caught quetzals stylized in flight, long tails curling for meters and meters before they faded into exhaust.

But this was broad daylight, in the middle of a protest, no time for revelations. The boys moved furtively, crouched low, paint cans hissing. One snapped a picture with his phone. They ran, leaving only a few bright, bitter slogans, white and red. *MOLINERO = MURDERER. RISE UP PEOPLE. CHE LIVES.*

Cristina rolled her eyes and clambered over the wall, careful of the paint. She placed a hand with care against the locust trunk, a smooth spot between thorns.

The size of the crowd made moot all hope of finding Mael. It was dizzying; she was glad of the tree under her hand, keeping her rooted. All these people. What did they want? What everyone wanted, she supposed. A sense of control. She knew that was why people came to protests, though she'd never had the courage herself. How many of them would see those few scrawled words of graffiti? How would it make them feel? Seen?

She wanted that and was simultaneously terrified, imagining an entire crowd like this seeing a piece of her art, judging it, the way that woman had.

Cristina wasn't cut out for this. Her school friend, Nati, had gone to a protest once during Holy Week, carried a sign — was that the first time the genocide charges against Monterríos were dropped? She'd met them after at the comedor, all rosy-cheeked with excitement; Mama had given her dinner. To Cristina, sheltered and mothered nearly to death, shouting in the face of authority had seemed childish. And dangerous. Mama lost no time making that clear.

Others had climbed up around Cristina, finding handholds on the same locust tree, craning their necks trying to get a sense of what was happening. But there was no taking it all in. Competing bullhorns blared, and she couldn't see who held them, words echoing back from buildings distorted so she could barely recognize the languages spoken even when she knew them, much of it in the Native tongues so simultaneously incomprehensible and achingly familiar, K'iche', Tz'utujil. "... *Everything that gives the government its power over us, it has stolen / our land, our culture, our food, our water, our knowledge, our wealth, even our people, our lives! / Without us, they would be nothing ...*" There was music. Drums. Marimba. Chanting, clapping.

National flags twitched from the upper floors of the Palace. Figures moved on the roof.

Following the gazes and exclamations of those around her, she noticed lines of police in plastic masks, with clubs and shields, filing into double ranks on the north side of the plaza, before the Palace. She thought she could see more uniformed men massed behind the locked cathedral gate.

Something was about to happen.

But people kept streaming in from the south. Where had they all come from?

Then a series of ringing, metallic thunks cut through the music and roar. A volley of small black objects arced from somewhere behind the line of police, beautiful, leisurely, like birds, trailing expanding plumes of white smoke. Someone beside her pointed, shouting. Others took up the cry. The realization moved through the plaza just ahead of the cloud. The waves of people shifted.

No. She shouldn't be here. Miguel Ángel: the gas could blind him. Those beautiful, clear eyes. For the moment, they were far from the smoke, but the wind was against them. Jolted from paralysis, she stepped down from the wall, covering his face.

She'd never find Mael.

Walking fast, trying to focus on the cobbles in front of her feet and the warm fragility of her nephew's head under her hand, still she saw the crowd from a thousand vantages at once: faces angry, fearful, hopeful, sad, lost, numb, banners, signs, slogan shirts, huipiles, suits, straw hats, shawls, sunglasses, masks, badges, plastic shields, helmets, truncheons, bruises, blood.

She ran into someone tall and sat down hard on the concrete, curling herself instinctively around the baby, who was screaming in earnest now, though barely audible above the crowd.

Hands pulled her up. "I'm sorry — are you all right?" A tall man, narrow at the hip and shoulder, with a smooth, foreign face, bent over her, shouting to be heard.

The woman with him had glossy curls and red lips and wore a too-small, v-cut version of the t-shirt she'd seen all over the plaza, apparently modified by hand. "Cristina?" yelled the woman. "Cristina … Ramos, right? It's Luz Villalobos! We met in Comalapa, at the Indigenous arts fair. Your friend Hugo wanted me to interview you for *Waking Dream*."

"I think I remember," said Cristina dully, a conversational reflex entirely out of place, trying futilely to calm the baby. "You're all right, you're all right." But she did remember. She hadn't exactly refused, just kept putting it off — mostly out of embarrassment. Hugo's expectations could be hard to live up to. *Waking Dream* was a tiny, progressive newsletter for intellectuals and foreigners, with some articles in English and even sometimes K'iche' or Kakchiquel. What did you say to an audience like that?

"Are you here for the protest?" Luz was asking, slightly incredulous.

Miguel Ángel screamed. It was surreal, a polite conversation in the middle of a war. Gas clouds superimposed eerie landscapes over reality. People kept shoving into her, she couldn't get her balance. A collective roar washed over them, a huge, living entity formed out of emotion in chaos, reminding Cristina of that one arena football match she'd attended, last year with Lencho when Mixco's team made the national cup.

"You need to come with us," yelled the man, letting go of Luz's arm, taking Cristina's. "Now!"

"We've got to get out of the wind!" One hand raised in the air, signaling, a clipboard of curling papers jammed in her armpit, a phone to her ear, Luz led the way across the street.

A tiny, very old woman was revealed behind her as though from eclipse, older than Abuela Nina, though livelier, hunched and fragile in a storm-colored shawl. The skin around her eyes was like droughted soil. The crowd parted around her.

For a moment Cristina saw herself, awkward, afraid, a smudge of graphite on her cheek, holding Miguel Ángel far too tight. It was startling, disorienting, different from her visions of the crowd. She loosened her grip, but he kept screaming.

Then the old woman and the man were moving, crossing the street of blaring horns. Cristina let herself be pulled along with them.

They moved past shops hastily shuttered, others still open, shoppers and employees peeping out from behind posh mannequins. Traffic was at a standstill. People were running, overtaking them. Cristina risked a glance back, and through breaks in the fragmenting crowd, caught flashes of plastic visors and truncheons — the police were advancing. She started singing to Miguel Ángel, trying to drown out the bullhorns, car horns, the wind-thrown screams. She was crying freely now. They passed the concert shell and the empty playground, the equipment draped with slogans.

At the plaza's southwest corner, a red sedan with a brown racing stripe was waiting, one tire on the curb, the engine running. The passenger door opened as they approached. "Get in!" the driver shouted. "Hurry up, we need to get out while we can!"

It was the jaguar in the mask.

She blinked, rubbed at her eyes, immediately regretting it as they were stabbed with fire. Now she could barely see at all. The jaguar blurred but didn't disappear, shrinking back into his seat. Forepaws on the wheel, he thrummed the gas absurdly with a hind foot, tail lashing. The man yanked open the rear passenger door. Luz got in and slid to the far side, behind the driver. The old woman followed — just an old woman now, no longer some strange, self-pitying mirror of herself. The kind man waited with impeccable politeness for Cristina, an arm thrown over nose and mouth.

"You're letting in the fucking tear gas," growled the jaguar impatiently.

"It's all right," the kind man yelled. "He's a friend!" Meaning the jaguar.

Cristina got in. The tiny old woman squeezed her knees together obligingly to make room, though she was so small their hips barely touched.

The kind man got in front and shut the doors. The blur and pain in Cristina's vision receded a little. She touched a soft curl of Miguel Ángel's hair. It didn't soothe him.

They couldn't go anywhere. A boxy Chevrolet that could have been Tío Juan's but wasn't had pulled so close the jaguar couldn't even back up off the curb. Everybody made sure the windows were closed tight. The jaguar twisted the ventilation knob to 'recirculate' and turned down the stereo — some kind of music that sounded like cats being electrocuted. "Should be okay," the jaguar said, the doubt plain in his voice, but in perfectly human tones. He craned round, his long, supple neck letting him survey each of passengers in turn. "Until we suffocate."

This jaguar wore a different mask. The other had been woodenly handsome, with high cheekbones and movie star teeth. This one — hilariously — was a jaguar mask. It made his human face rounder, more lifelike, with a strong K'iche' nose. The patterns in his coat, so rich and complex — they changed as she looked.

The sketchbook — she didn't even need to look. The human face the jaguar wore and the mask he'd been wearing in her drawing were the same.

Miguel Ángel cried hysterically, and nothing Cristina could do would avail until she undid his wrappings, lifted her shirt and let him nurse at her dry nipple. It wasn't a comfortable feeling, but she was used to it. They all did it: Cristina, Corísa, even Pilar. The baby loved it. Mama had taught them. "Sorry," she said, folding one leg under to twist against the door for the illusion of modesty and so she wouldn't have to look anyone in the eye. The jaguar faced forward.

"Don't apologize," said Luz quickly. "I'm sorry you got caught up in this. We're lucky we found you."

Gradually, the baby quieted. She kissed his head, carefully wiped his wet face with the inside of her sleeve, then her own.

Luz made introductions. The kind man, Aníbal, was a woman in disguise whose mask it seemed only Cristina had been unable to perceive. Cristina had heard about gender fluidity, of course, and all the horrible things politicians and radio preachers said against people who didn't conform. She knew what they said was wrong. But it was going to take her a moment to adjust.

No one else in the car was struck at all that in the driver's seat, tail trapped beneath the seat-belt strap, sat an endangered jungle cat. This jaguar was their roommate "Felipe" — not the name he'd given when he came to Mama's house.

And the tiny old woman, with whom Luz was obviously head-over-heels in awe, was Dr. Amparo Ixchel, holder of PhDs earned and honorary in international relations, ethnography and linguistics, last native speaker of the ethnic Qu'cab dialect of K'iche', native of the no-longer-extant San Rafael Uxun, survivor of one of the most notorious genocidal massacres of the civil war Cristina had never heard of.

The doctor smiled at Cristina, glowing softly in her corte and huipil embroidered with shining green quetzals, apparently unfazed by the torrent of praise. Cristina wondered how many other such massacres she knew nothing about, and if any of the others had produced magical beings.

Luz's biographic statement highlighted the doctor's weekly address in K'iche' on a guerilla radio station out of Chichi, her humanitarian work in the poorest areas of the highlands, training activists to recognize and counter the deceptive tactics of the foreign extractive concerns, which relied on ignorance and the government looking the other way. "Totonícapan would have been so much worse without her! The Canadians weren't telling people the water was contaminated, except in English, until she —"

"You don't want her with me," the jaguar growled, his eyes on Cristina in the rearview. "Cops have my plates on file now. I could get stopped any time."

"In the middle of all this?" said Aníbal, fidgeting, glued to the window. "What the hell did you do?"

"They wouldn't touch her," Luz said. "They wouldn't dare. She's been on the Nobel Peace Prize committee. She —"

"Thank you for this," said Dr. Ixchel, in a voice small as she was, firm and spice-sweet like dried tamarind, her Spanish inflection ever so slightly different than anyone else's Cristina had ever heard. The car and its occupants seemed to distort inward, the doctor as its focal point. Even Miguel Ángel's toothless gums on her dry nipple couldn't keep her attention away.

"No — thank you," Luz said in a rush. "I'm so sorry. I know you didn't sign up for this." She gestured with the battered clipboard at the windows, the crowd still streaming past. "We knew some kind of elevated response was a possibility, we had contingencies prepared! But it's too soon. We couldn't have anticipated this. They didn't even let us *get* to the band shell, we had musicians planned — this amazing dance troupe from Santiago Atítlan. Thankfully they've already canceled. They're out of harm's way. It was permitted, officially sanctioned! It's the murders. The authorities are obviously on edge. Like at Forty Doors last night — they have to demonstrate they're still in control by hurting as many people as they can."

Aníbal thrust a long arm behind her from the front seat, reaching blindly. Luz dropped the clipboard to the floor at their feet, and her fingers found Aníbal's, gripping. Red fingernails against black. "You did so much," Aníbal said quietly, not for a moment taking her eyes from the crowd outside.

Luz hiccuped, grimaced, and hanging on to Aníbal, turned back to the doctor. "But the turnout was amazing, and we have you to thank for that. Your words were so powerful. We couldn't have done this without you, I'm so glad we could get you away safe. If Felipe hadn't found us —"

"We're not safe yet," growled the jaguar.

Luz gave the jaguar a look Cristina couldn't read. "We're just so grateful," she finished awkwardly, with another ragged breath. "You didn't have to put yourself at risk like this for us."

"I do have to," the doctor corrected gently.

It got quiet inside the car. The protest was over, the crowd routed. Banners, tattered from years of use, fluttered to the ground and were trampled and vomited upon. The police line advanced. They sat watching from the car, trapped.

Cristina hoped everyone she'd met in the crowd, the intolerant woman and her daughter, the lascivious man in the fedora, the lovers she'd passed on the sidewalk, the graffiti artists, and Mael, had gotten somewhere safe, where they could breathe. She went so far as to pray. The ritual words mushed in her mind and fell away.

Someone fell against the hood of the car with a thud. It was one of the masked men in the graffiti backpacks — or another like him. He laid an open palm feebly on the windshield, his eyes and the unprotected part of his face capsaicin red.

"Fuck, no," the jaguar told him mercilessly through the glass. "There's no room."

The graffiti kid slithered down the hood and curled into fetal position on the ground.

Aníbal slid her hand out of Luz's. She unlocked the door.

"Are you crazy?" said the jaguar.

"Don't," said Luz. "Please don't."

"We — I can't just sit here," said Aníbal, the woman disguised as a man with a man's name, the tendons standing out against her slender throat. "This is — don't you see what's happening? It's never been like this. Not for as long as I've been here. Not for years. Ask the doctor." The doctor, who exuded patience and control, for a moment looked like a deer in headlights. "This is real. I'm not talking about just the protest, I mean the unrest. The murders, this reaction. It's historic, and we helped make it happen. Somehow. It's Antonellis. And me."

"Aníbal, you are starting to sound dangerously close to a savior complex here —" said Luz.

"That's what I'm talking about! He thought he could swoop in with all that money, and we let him. If anybody dies today, if cops bash in somebody's skull or this guy right outside asphyxiates from the gas, from allergies, that's on us. It's our fault. Understand? I need to be able to say I did something to make up for it. This is what we've been fighting for."

"They could revoke your visa," said Luz, desperation plain in her voice.

"I have to," said Aníbal.

She drew a pair of swim goggles out of a blazer pocket and put them on. Pulling out a phone, she tapped it until a red star lit in its upper corner, then panned the camera solemnly around the car. The jaguar looked ready to lunge for it — then only interposed a paw between himself and the light. Luz pleaded. Ixchel seemed to retreat into herself. Cristina just stared. Then Aníbal opened the door — barely enough to permit her slim form to pass, and shut it again as soon as she was out. But an acridness whispered into the car, like breathing uncarefully after dropping a handful of diced chiles into a scalding pan, only devoid of invigorating vegetal aromas, all stinging, chemical harshness. Cristina covered Miguel Ángel's face. "It will pass," she whispered, a more honest prayer.

Outside, Aníbal drew her collar up over her nose and mouth. She grabbed the graffiti kid under the armpits and dragged him a few steps to a sewer, arranging him so his ravaged face lay close to the opening. She knelt there, breathing what had to be only marginally less toxic air, pulling a bottle of water and a scrap of típico from her shoulder bag. She soaked the bright cloth, plastered it over her nose and mouth, then rose. Her left eye clenched shut, the other barely cracked, Aníbal moved at a low, crouching run, back across the plaza toward the ragged lines of protesters and police, holding the phone over her head like a torch.

Cristina felt shamed despite the tiny presence of life in her arms who depended on her. To lack that courage, to lack even an understanding of the motivations that underlay it: she squinted around at the others, seeking some confirmation she wasn't alone in this.

Luz clutched at the jaguar's shoulder. "Please help her. Bring her back."

The jaguar sat rigid.

Dr. Ixchel placed a hand over one of Luz's. The spotted scars on her knuckles were the kind worn by the soap-selling women who sat astride the ancient steps in Chichicastenango's Sunday market: lye burns.

Some protesters were pushing back against police, swinging protest signs and fists. What did they expect to accomplish? Why didn't they run? A gesture, like Aníbal's. Stupid, arrogant, insane?

Cristina supposed she'd stood on principle before. Yesterday, she'd helped shelter Mael. She'd taken risks. Not for any great cause, but out of compassion, one grieving human being for another. Even Mama had stood for those principles. But politics — protest, radicalism — it was trying to apply that same goodness, Christian goodness Mama would have said, too broadly. It was taking on too much. It was recklessness, arrogance. Because it invited violence. Because it put people at risk besides yourself.

The little car's engine thrummed. A hole had opened in traffic.

"What the hell are you doing?" said Luz. "We have to wait for her!"

The jaguar shifted, pumped the gas again, and the car leapt away from the curb, dropping back onto the pavement with a shudder, then jerked to a stop, wedged into a narrow opening where an impossibly sharp left turn might just squeeze them free. "This could be our only chance," the jaguar said. His tail twitched, pinned against the seat. "I can get out. Now. If I don't, we'll be here till who knows. Cops will get to us eventually. I told you, I'm a threat to you, a liability. I'm going to need to disappear awhile — but first, *we need to get away.*"

"What happened to you, Felipe? You didn't used to be like this. Those times you stood up for me in school. What happened to make you such a coward?"

Something passed between the two of them, Luz and the jaguar, something dangerous. They watched each other in the mirror, and Dr. Ixchel pursed her lips into wrinkles like volcanoes' flanks.

"She would want you to be safe," the jaguar said.

"Fuck you." Luz wrenched her hand free of the doctor's. Then she was out the door, slamming it and running blindly into the smoke of the plaza, black hair spiraling behind her.

The jaguar hesitated only a moment, watching her go.

Then he wrapped a paw around the little knob that protruded from the steering wheel like an arcade game joystick, spinning it to the left with a frenetic gesture and gunning the engine. The car shot across two lanes of stopped traffic, ran up two wheels onto the opposite curb and along the sidewalk for a few dozen meters, scattering protesters, before swerving back into the street. The Corolla peeled up Fifth Ave away from the plaza, acceleration like a hand pressing Cristina against the seat. He rolled down the window. Fresh air rushed in, and Cristina inhaled gratefully, guiltily, crying with relief.

The jaguar spoke not a word but drove Cristina and the tiny, ancient doctor at a breakneck pace, avoiding protesters, accidents and anyone looking even vaguely official, to the bus station/mall complex north of the city, a huge building like a Uaxactun temple times ten the color of overripe apricot flesh, where no one was being poisoned, clubbed with protest signs or with truncheons and everything was incomprehensibly bright and clean. Iridescent buses waited, glittering and flexing gills, impatient for the rivers of roads. Official city taxis like glossy-shelled beetles, green and white, buzzed past out of the overwhelming sun, hovered in the thin band of the building's shade, then buzzed away again.

Papi had taken his girls shopping at this mall since not long after it opened. The bus route from Comalapa ended here. After attending Hugo's workshop, she'd stood in this same taxi stand, overwhelmed, doubting her place in her family and the world, stuffing canvases too carefully into Papi's tiny hatchback.

Dr. Ixchel tried to pay the jaguar for the ride; he refused. "A pleasure to meet you," she said to Cristina, the formal words eerie in that distinct accent, and Cristina wished to hear her speak her native tongue.

"Be safe," the doctor said instead. "Keep an open mind. Until we meet again." She squeezed Cristina's hand in the worldwise way of a gentleman narcotrafficante inviting a woman to dance, then seemed to think better of it and hugged her around the exhausted, unconscious baby, inhaling deeply until Cristina did the same. Through the raw aftermath of tear gas came the warm, inimitable, slightly sour scent of old woman. From Dr. Amparo Ixchel, somehow even this was astonishing.

Ixchel stepped to the curb, but turned back. "Talk to him. You need to speak, to know each other." Amid her evocative wrinkles, a doubt — a dread? Then she was gone into the bus station's monumental shadows.

The jaguar's eyes, the green of wet-season jungle, watched Cristina in the mirror.

Alone with him, she ought to be afraid. She felt drained, only tangentially in control, like she was dreaming.

"Do you … know her?" asked the jaguar awkwardly.

"I just met her today."

Cristina felt the urge to jump out of the car and run after her, away from the jaguar, get on whatever bus she was getting on, go to Totonícapan or wherever else, leave Mama's body on the cold slab where it lay, leave Mael, leave her family in grief with no one to lead them, sit in a cramped bus seat beside the tiny, ancient doctor and just be.

"Anyplace you need to go, I'll take you."

He'd just left them there in the plaza, a toxic war zone. Luz, Aníbal, that poor graffiti artist.

She didn't know what else she'd have done.

She didn't have to ask anything of him. She could take a bus, a cab, or call her uncle. This jaguar, posing as a detective, had invaded her mother's house. But Ixchel had wanted her to talk to him. She remembered Aníbal running off into the poison fog, Luz after her, and the first time she'd met Luz, when she'd dodged even doing an interview. Maybe now she could do something just a little bit brave.

She knew where she had to go.

"The city morgue," she told him, then waited for the wind that followed on the heels of the specter of death to blow past through the open windows, smelling of too-ripe bananas and urine. She made herself look him full in the mask, those green eyes terrified.

She thought he might hide, raise a paw to shield himself, like he had with Aníbal's camera. "I don't know where that is."

She got out the sketchbook, angling it so he wouldn't see himself depicted there, and found the drawing of Mama floating godlike in Mael's eye. Mama would have hated it, too weird, and not exactly flattering. She read off the address from the margin.

"Okay," said the jaguar, in an outflow of breath, obviously regretting his offer. But he must have felt spurred too. He copied it into his phone.

She leaned back in the seat and closed her eyes.

That harsh music came searing out of the speakers again, then was cut off, replaced by a rising swell of ticking percussion, woodwinds, delicate horns. She knew this music, remembered it: something from Papi's record collection. He laid the phone on the storage console where she could reach it, tethered by its cable to the stereo. "Pick whatever."

The car hummed into motion. Soon they were on the highway back the way they'd come, a broad, high curve, the city sprawled on their left, the volcano behind them.

A brand-new smartphone, unfamiliar, unlocked. She weighed it in her hand. The background image showed a fat toddler walking on a jungle trail, the pause button hovering over his head. She let it play.

"My nephew," said the jaguar uncomfortably. "He's ... probably a lot bigger now."

She resisted laughing at the absurdity of it, all of it. The jaguar wore board shorts and a football jersey. What a waste, to hide any of that beautiful coat, so rich and textured. She couldn't understand how the clothes stayed in place, how his feet reached the pedals. He was so close. She could almost reach and stroke his paw where it rested on the gearshift knob. Certain pariah housecats she'd met long ago would sometimes permit this once you'd fed them and found them a sunbeam and scratched awhile behind their ears. She knew this as an irrational impulse; she'd experienced it with the ocelots and margays and jaguarundi and even the real, always sleeping jaguar at the zoo. Strange what that impulse would mean if the jaguar were also a man. Her skin prickled.

"You were at my mother's house," she said. "It *was* you."

The car picked up speed.

"Does he know? The detective."

"Know what?"

She was going about this the wrong way. It was impossible trying to read him through the mask, imagining the face underneath, lips pulling back from canines. Other people — Luz, the detective, even Tía Constancia and Tío Pancho — seemed to have no problem pretending he was human. Why couldn't she?

"You see me," he said, like cloudbreak, like the lightning that heralds rain. "I knew it."

She nodded unhappily.

"How?"

"I don't know." She wondered if anyone knew. The doctor — according to Luz the most educated person she'd ever met — had known something. If not her, who? Some pagan shaman wreathed in alcohol fumes, copal and tobacco smoke, perched on a ruin? Jaguars in masks were the stuff of the devil. "What about you? I mean, how do you ..."

He shrugged.

Again, the temptation to touch him, to pull at the mask, pull it away and lay the lie bare.

She gave in and started to laugh, quietly, then with less control, louder as he, bewilderingly, joined in. Her eyes teared up again, still stinging from the tear gas, and she dabbed at them with a corner of Miguel Ángel's drool-stained wrap.

Nobody knew anything. Nobody talked about anything. The civil war, the disappeared, all the wars before that. They went around shooting each other's mothers, laying down their lives to protect complete strangers, for no reason at all. If there had been a reason, some mother five hundred years ago had forgotten to mention it to her daughter before she threw herself on the blade of a foreign mining company exec who was only obeying orders, absolutely convinced he was serving God's will without understanding it in the slightest. And the child her daughter bore by that soldier, and all their descendants, everyone alive today, would be bereft forever.

Across the gulf of time bridged by the miracle of digital sound, flamenco dancers paused dramatically, cupped hands raised as if to catch the rain, flared skirts fluttering pearly pink and black. And she remembered: *Sketches of Spain.*

The baby slept, lulled by the engine's vibrations and the exhaustion of grief and pain, a warm lump against her belly. In Miguel Ángel's dreams, she was Teresa, his mother. Meanwhile, in Cristina's nightmare, her own Mama was dead, her Papi gone, and she'd grown up overnight, too soon, forced to shoulder all their responsibilities at once. It could only be by the wild logic of dreams that an ancient, mythic, terrifying trickster being in board shorts had appeared in the midst of her torment to threaten her family, then protect her, then cringe from her in turn.

She was immensely grateful when he changed the subject.

"Luz — who was with you at the protest — with the lipstick. How do you know her?"

"I don't," Cristina admitted. "I mean I met her, she came to my art school in Comalapa, interviewing people for a fundraiser. But she remembered me, even though it's been years."

"You're an artist?"

"Not really. I mean, I just paint copies." She stuffed the sketchbook into her bag. "Luz, she's … a good person. And her friend …"

"Her girlfriend," the jaguar said. "Aníbal."

"Aníbal. How do you know them?"

"They're my roommates."

Two women and a jaguar sharing an apartment. He seemed to take pleasure in her confusion.

"So … I mean … aren't you worried?"

It was the wrong thing to say.

The jaguar cut too fast and close around a slow-moving van to make his exit. Cristina cradled Miguel Ángel with one hand and gripped the door handle with the other. The car jerked to a stop a moment later at the light at the bottom of the ramp.

He wrapped a hand unnecessarily tight around that joystick knob thing on the steering wheel. "Yes, I'm fucking worried! I'm sorry, but — Aníbal, maybe she has an excuse, but Luz? All that bullshit like they didn't mean for it to happen. They know what they're doing. They've been planning for months! They were *trying* to get people arrested, to make a point, like they don't know what jail means. Well, they're going to find out now. And I don't know what I'm supposed to do about it."

The light changed. The streets were busy. Some of the people might have been protesters.

"The morgue," said the jaguar. "You know it's only a couple blocks south of where we just were?"

"Then don't risk it," she said quickly, remembering his terror. "Drop us anywhere, we'll walk."

"Us." He seemed to register the baby in his bundle for the first time. But she remembered the show he'd made of turning away when she'd given Miguel Ángel her nipple. "He's not mine," she said awkwardly. "He's my sister's."

He kept driving, returning his eyes to the road.

Why was he helping her? To make up for leaving Luz and Aníbal? Or for yesterday at the house? He felt guilty. Not, Cristina decided, for deceiving her — after all, he deceived everyone. He hid behind that mask every moment.

She didn't want to owe him anything.

"We hid her from you, you know. Last night. *I* hid her."

"What?" A shrill of trumpets from the stereo. It *had* been him at the house last night. She waited for him to deny it.

Instead he said, "It's good. That you hid her. El Bufo — the detective — he's an asshole."

Whose side was he on? She hated this. She looked away, trying not to cry again as the dream flashed before her, angels, bright feathers, blood. The angels' faces, coldly beatific: she thought she understood that part. If God existed, the only influence He exerted on the world was through those who tried to live up to His example. Had it really been like that? Mael knew. "Anyway, it doesn't matter. She's gone."

"What do you mean? What happened?"

"I lost her. I don't want to talk about it."

The Tower of the Reformer rose. They circled it and left it behind: a rusty, neglected iron memorial to good intentions, aiming its rickety, accusing finger at the angels and the saints and God.

The jaguar fidgeted. He shifted lanes, couldn't find an opening, shifted back. He picked up his phone and put it down again.

"Listen," he said finally. "It's not really about your mother at all. I'm not saying I understand it. But the other victim, Antonellis — he was the real target. Of course, it's all politics. And now, if you believe El Bufo — the inspector — everybody who wanted him dead is in a race to cover their asses. What just happened, breaking up the protest — it's all part of it. A distraction."

She knuckled her eyes with the backs of her hands. Politics. A word she'd forever associate with red-edged blindness, acrid tears burning down her cheeks. "You think Luz and Aníbal are involved?" The way they'd run into that caustic fog together, one after the other. The fingers of Cristina's left hand throbbed with the familiar cramp of holding the pencil, which she knew could only be relieved by taking it up again, working through it.

He shrugged. "They knew him — Luz did, maybe Aníbal too? You heard them. They were working with him — funneling foreign money. Maybe illegally? I don't know." He drove, furiously.

Meanwhile, the music had been building toward a moment she remembered. She sat back to listen as everything fell away except the trumpet, blowing a long, repeating trill Papi had told his girls was the call of a night bird singing at the balcony window of a Spanish infanta. They listened on the record player in the cold evening before bed, sipping hot camomile with honey and milk, the canaries contributing a sleepy chirp. Cristina and her sisters agreed the infanta must be pining for a lover, a prince. Maybe he'd gone off to war, as princes tended to. Maybe he was imprisoned, dead. At the end of each measure, just before dying away, the trumpet let out a deliberate, discordant squeal of grief. Teresa, she remembered, hated this sound, couldn't stand it; she covered her ears and screamed to drown it out. But Papi wanted them to listen.

"Here we are," the jaguar said dully, pulling up at a congested corner.

The sidewalks were full of people. There were no protest signs or shirts reading *WE ARE ALL TOTONÍCAPAN*. Nobody was crying. How could it have gone back to normal?

Across the intersection, another colonial palace: bright yellow stucco, broad white steps. She recognized it from the news: the police headquarters. Stupid. Where else would they autopsy the victim of a political murder conspiracy?

Suddenly she wasn't so eager to get out of the car. Mentally, she drew a tiny sketch, a cartoon. Mama floated over the city like a kite, up among the clouds. A long, wind-slack string led from her wrist to Cristina's own hand, tiptop of the needle at the Tower of the Reformer, holding Mama to earth. Time to cut the string. She dug in her bag, searching for the money the man at the market had given her for Mama's chickens.

"There's no way I'm taking your money," said the jaguar. He plucked a stickynote from the dashboard, produced a marker from the cubby and blacked out whatever had been on it. "In case you ever need a ride." He scribbled a number, and she wondered distantly how he could hold a pen.

The baby slept.

El Bufo

The album wound down to silence as he sat watching the police headquarters in his sideview mirror, waiting to see if she'd come out.

He felt dazed — like he'd been in a fistfight. She knew his secret; so did El Bufo. If the two people in the world the masks didn't work on both turned out to be assholes, he'd be an idiot not to abandon hope for the human race. She could have tortured him with questions, fucked with his head, tried to get something out of him.

Felipe had no experience with death. Not really. His brother Martín had died before he was born. Two kids from school got killed in a motorcycle accident when he was eleven. "What a shame," said his mother, and made everyone pray, but the service fell on a weekday, and the idea of taking off work or school didn't even come up. Years later, one of Santa Catarina's town drunks was discovered not to be merely sleeping it off in the park, the cloud-eyed zombie stare by which people knew him at last permanently fixed. Lots of dead people lay in pastel-colored tombs and under scorched ground in the cemetery at the top of the hill; he visited on death day, dropped candles in offering fires for people his parents said they knew, even helped eat the dead's sweets — but he didn't know them.

He tried to imagine his parents dying. The house, with its saggy couch, ancient tube television and grimy kitchen, would be that much more depressing without them to justify it. Their cluttered bedroom resembled an undersea grotto filled with embarrassing sunken wreckage he'd spent his adult life trying to look at as little as possible. All that would need cleaned out. Rubén could handle it. He'd be the one to inherit the house, he was oldest. Rubén's life would be easier with their parents gone, permanently freed from that resigned stare he put on whenever their father boarded his bus to flash his stump and preach God's mercy. Felipe's own life would be easier: less money to send home, less guilt to carry with him. That would come later. When it happened, when he found out, when he had to stand up in a suit — one of his father's, too big at the waist, too short in the seam, with safety pins in both sleeves — beside Rubén and watch them go behind a stone door, he'd be devastated. Of course he would. Just because he wasn't human didn't mean —

But all that was fantasy.

Luz's phone rang twice, then shunted him to voicemail — she'd seen the call and ignored it. Fine — she wasn't in jail. Anibal's rang six times before the machine picked up.

Which didn't mean she'd been arrested, necessarily. She might be home, waiting to ream him out. They both might, drinking tea and laughing, not calling just to make him sweat. Or else fucking. He checked: no new calls except El Bufo's. All his regular fares by now had taken the hint.

He thought about calling the police. He could switch out the simcard on his phone, lie, ask if they had her in custody. He could offer Eufémia's money as a bribe.

Except Aníbal wasn't her name any more than Félix was his. It was something she used only in-country, only when she was posing as a boy. He'd seen her real name on her passport, but she'd only ever used it at the bank. Then the money had stopped coming. There'd been no reason to remember. Her name wasn't on the lease.

Had she even been carrying ID? Could she be that committed to defending her adopted country, enough to give up the privileges that came with the one she'd been born to?

As far as he knew, neither of them had ever been arrested before. Not even Luz, for all her talk, their whole lives since they'd been kids. She was always careful, always going through official channels, getting permits, filling out forms. There was even a lecture she gave before every protest about what to expect, how to act, what to say, what not to say, how not to get your fingers broken when they put the cuffs on. Sit tight, don't argue, and wait to get bailed out. It sounded legit, world-wise and savvy. It sobered the NGO kids right up, like it was supposed to.

He loved when she took charge like that. Even if it was all bullshit. And he loved how Aníbal lent it credence by body language alone, lounging long and nonchalant, maybe tipping back a chair.

Why now? Why would either of them risk this? Unless they felt guilty, responsible. Because they were involved.

Fuck.

Jail wasn't like in the movies. He'd heard the real story from a school friend who'd stolen the wrong car. It wasn't about who could do the most push-ups, who dropped the soap. It was who you knew, outside and in, who'd put up the money to keep you there or get you out, who'd have your back, bribe the guards and smuggle in food that wasn't full of weevils.

Would they make the obvious mistake and put Aníbal in with the men? Would Aníbal's rich family get over themselves and pull strings to get her released? If they did, she'd never come back.

He couldn't just sit here panicking. Especially not here.

Clean simcards: never a bad idea. He put on the caiman mask, headphones and some Burning Spear, checked his Garífuna kinks in the mirror, locked the car and walked to the wire-encased corner tienda. He paid cash for two cheap cards with eight hours between them, plus a styrofoam cup of thin, burned coffee that made him pine for the barista in the box. He stood sipping in the shadow of a corrugated wall where he could keep one eye on Baby — what did it matter if she showed up on more security footage? — and the other eye on the little side-stairwell leading down below police headquarters where Cristina Ramos had disappeared.

Trenchtown: Felipe had never been and never would; Jamaica might as well be the moon. But he'd listened more than hard enough to understand it lay between Babylon and Zion: where often you went to bed hungry, but love and music got you through. Whether you could make it on music alone had never been clear. Felipe hadn't managed so far. Not for not trying.

When she came out, it was clear she'd been crying again. Maybe all she did was cry. No, that was cruel. She had a phone open, her thumb on the button. She walked to the corner, then back. Not looking, she bumped into a cop, who put a hand on her shoulder. Felipe stiffened, spilling burning coffee on his hands — slim chance this was the one cop in the world who thought "serve and protect" actually applied — but Cristina Ramos shook him off and scurried away, hugging the baby, and the cop let her be.

Finally, her back to Felipe, one hand on the baby in his sling, she raised the phone to her ear.

His phone didn't ring.

He didn't know her. She'd understood more about him looking through his mask than he could possibly have learned standing in her mother's doorway examining graduation photos. His ears burned hot, and the rush of blood drowned the music. He poured out the terrible coffee in the gutter; for Luz's sake, he resisted tossing the cup in the street.

The apartment was as he'd left it: empty, his bedroom door locked, theirs ajar, breakfast congealing, potted herbs dying on the table beside the bottle of aguardiente.

He dumped their plates in the sink and ran the water, looking up at the painting of tenant farmers plodding home through sunset fields, eyes only for the ground in front of them because they had nothing left. These were the people Luz devoted her life to helping, who'd shown up to protest by the thousands because she'd found the money to give them the chance. Stolen it, maybe, with David Antonellis's help, from a bunch of rich foreigners. Like Aníbal's family.

A lot of those exhausted workers would be in jail right now. They couldn't hold them all.

But they could hold Aníbal.

Her mistake lay in believing that if she saw something she hated in the world, if she worked at it, she could change it. The trouble was, everything that made her believe this also made her admirable, lovable, someone whose respect it was impossible to help wanting to earn.

He took a slug of aguardiente: burning, spicy-sweet, like-yet-unlike a faceful of tear gas. He fried up some leftover beans with onion and chile and ate them with half a bag of the handmade tortillas Luz brought home once a week from Sunday market, pale blue, soft with lard and delicious. He wondered if there'd be tortillas next week.

He imagined the scene: Aníbal in custody, heroically accepting responsibility for whatever guilt she felt for her part in taking the money that led to Antonellis's murder and all the rest of it: Eufemia's death, and Mynor Parrales and Dario Chanax too, and by extension, every one of the arrests at the protest. She was the furthest thing from a fool; she'd clench her wrists and keep her palms turned down so the restraints wouldn't cut off circulation no matter how badly they'd gassed her. Unless she was unconscious. She'd sign nothing, say nothing. She'd take advantage of the chaos during processing if she could, maybe smudge her fingerprints, mess up the intake photo just enough. But that would be later. First, she'd be facedown on the pavement. And Luz would come pelting up behind her out of the gas cloud, barefoot and beautiful despite swollen eyes and smeared makeup, spiky heels in hand — no, that was insane, she owned sneakers, she'd be wearing sneakers — skid to a stop, realize what was happening, realize she could not let herself be arrested too, because someone had to be free to try to get these people out. So she wouldn't fight, wouldn't resist. She'd drop to her knees among the grimy cobblestones. Hands behind her head, fingers curled so the truncheons wouldn't break them. They'd pass her by. She wasn't a threat. Surely they'd see that.

There was no point in digging through their reams of notes, plans, the maps, the revolutionary texts, looking for clues to their involvement, their guilt. There was too much. Even if they were responsible for the murders somehow, caught up in conspiracy — what did it matter? It wasn't important. Not now.

He called them both again and got nothing. He texted and got nothing.

Then he stepped carefully across the invisible, unspoken line of personal privacy and mutual respect the existence of which had enabled him to live in harmony with his former crush and her new lover, into their room, looking for something with Aníbal's name on it. He tried to ignore the unmade, slept-in bed, the wire mobile of painted quetzals dangling from the window, the purple patterned tapestry, the bottles on the dresser, the stale scent of copal incense failing to cover that of sex.

He dug through the drawers and found, to his astonishment, a passport and a temporary work visa, renewable after six months, both in the name of Annabelle Jane Trieste. She had different hair in the picture — long, feminine. But it was her. What a name. A princess's name. Further down, in an envelope marked in cursive English "when you're ready," an expired, first-class plane ticket voucher.

He'd been in love with Luz for a long time, the kind of romantic, passionate, stupid love he'd thought could stave off hunger and make life worth living, the kind song lyrics weren't so great at preparing you for. Luz and Aníbal were the ones who'd shown him what love really meant. They were so good at it. They worked together, lived together, slept together. They'd be arguing over the wording of some boring petition, arguing hotly, angrily, then then half an hour later they'd be dancing salsa letting a pan of eggs overcook. He regretted not having been present for the beginning, to see them set eyes on each other. If he'd been less caught up in his own shit, resentful of her ambition, more willing to let go of childhood — he'd have what, followed her to college? Met some foreign lover of his own?

He shoved Aníbal's life back into the drawer and locked the room behind him.

He got the heap of money from his own room, shuffled it together until it was lined up right and his hands were greasy, and he counted: three thousand, one hundred and thirteen. Enough for next month's rent, a paint job for Baby and then some. Running away money. It wasn't his. What could he tell Cristina Ramos? He could try to make it up to her. Solve her mother's murder. Sure.

He stuffed the twelve hundred for the rent between the pages of a novel — *Men of Maize*, a worn university edition, the last place he figured cops would look if they came digging.

He called again. Two rings, voicemail, six rings, voicemail. He texted Luz. *I left the rent with Gaspar Ilóm.*

He switched in a new simcard.

He called the police, waited, was transferred, waited some more. He thought about every cop he'd ever bribed. Once, the first time, to get his father off for panhandling too close to Antigua's touristy central plaza; once trying to get them to actually investigate the theft of the first bicycle he'd been able to afford, a mistake he'd never make again; countless times, using his brother's money, so they'd let his brother's bus through the inter-department security checkpoint without examining the papers of everyone aboard. Countless times to encourage city cops to let him go on operating a taxi without a license. He wondered how much more he'd have to pay off the SAAS, and whether they preferred to be paid in blood.

Finally somebody picked up. "Annabelle Jane Trieste," he said, exactly as he'd been repeating it over and over in his head, mangling the pronunciation, he was sure, so he spelled it. They told him they didn't have anybody by that name and hung up, so he called again, waited again, asked for Aníbal Trieste, no luck, asked for any tall, dark-haired foreign man (or woman) taken into custody in the last eight hours, was hung up on again. He'd never bribed anybody over the phone. He was doing it wrong. He called again. "I have two thousand in cash," he said, "and I want my friend let out of jail."

A pause. "What's your friend's name?"

Oh, for fuck's sake. "Annabelle Jane Trieste."

A longer pause. He could hear phones ringing, people talking, shouting, doors slamming, music, what sounded like an enormous, echoing clock ticking toward the end of the world until he realized it must be the receptionist tapping a pen on the desk. "Call back tomorrow," they said.

He ran a hand over the knobby jaws of the caiman mask. He flung the mask off.

He took another slug of aguardiente. He dialed again, managed to stay on hold for ten minutes, then hung up in frustrated fury.

He knew who he could call. And what it would mean.

If you read the right conspiracy forums — where he'd learned the simcard trick, and then how to proxy his phone so nobody could track him while he was cruising said conspiracy forums — the SAAS were a clandestine extension of the president's will, studiously ignored by every other branch of law enforcement until they showed up to demand something. A fully reinstated SAAS officer, someone who could order around elite security officers without batting an eye, could surely order one lone, nonviolent protester released.

If Felipe could offer something in return.

He paced, claws clicking on the cold tile. He found some hardcore protest rap in a playlist Aníbal had made for him, elaborately foulmouthed takedowns of the rich peppered with shoutouts to dead revolutionaries. He flopped down on his tousled bed, shredding the sheets a little, struggling to laugh as he usually would at the audacity of the lyrics.

If he was really doing this, getting back into it with El Bufo, he could be more careful. Better safe than stupid. Nothing in this apartment would remain safe or private. He got the gun out from under the bed. Selling it would take too much time, draw too much attention. He wiped it again, made sure it was empty, and dropped it into the ventilation shaft. He cleaned up his lunch, his roommates' breakfast and the aguardiente, then stared helpless at the vaguely incriminating hurricane aftermath that was the rest of the apartment. He didn't know what mattered. They were all in trouble with the law now. But he didn't know what Luz might need, what throwing away would make worse, not better. Half-heartedly he collected a few pieces of mail and anything else plainly visible that had his name on it, trashed it, then bagged it all up for the dumpster. He packed a bag.

Down in the garage out of long-established habit, he went the long way around to his car to keep whatever face he happened to be wearing off the security feed. Then he noticed the camera had been turned to the wall. None of the few cars still parked here in the middle of the day wore Baby's old plates. He could switch again with a different one. Sowing chaos, then riding the wave. Like El Bufo. But what was the point, when he was on his way to offer El Bufo his soul? No reason to get a paint job either.

He threw the backpack in the trunk and got in. He changed into the conquistador mask. He switched simcards again. Once he'd psyched himself up enough with reggaeton, he made the call.

No answer. Right: El Bufo wouldn't recognize the number. He hung up, sent a text.

`Pick up.`

`Pick up, it's me F`

-U-C-K-Y-O-U, he was typing when the phone rang.

"Didn't think I'd be hearing from you again," said the voice, thick with conciliatory smarm. "What brought you back? The money? The thrill?"

"I need a favor."

"You're the one owes me a favor. Thanks to me, you're richer *and* wiser." A grunt. A thud, like the sound of a fist to the gut in a badly dubbed kung fu film. "You pussy out like that again, it could cost someone's head. This is dangerous shit. Life and death. Need someone I can rely on."

"Like I can rely on you?"

"If I'd shown you the real badge, you'd have run screaming." An explosion of breath. "You'd have been fine if you'd done what I told you. You're still fine or you wouldn't be talking to me."

"The hell I am. My best friends hate me. All my fares stopped calling." That was as much Luz and Aníbal's fault as El Bufo's. His own as much as anyone's. "How many people you think want a ride from a cab driver on the SAAS payroll?"

"Hey," said El Bufo, suddenly close to the phone. "Shut up about that. Never know who might be listening, right?" More heavy breathing.

Felipe laughed uneasily. "Where are you? What's going on?"

"You want a favor? Be outside the market in let's say twenty minutes."

"No," said Felipe. "No fucking way I'm going near the plaza after all that. Not anytime soon, maybe never. The cops and the ... who knows who else have me on their radar now. Not my plates, but my car. Maybe even my face."

"Your face, right."

"Shut up." Felipe ran a hand over the conquistador's forehead. It wasn't like he had an endless supply.

"Listen, *Félix*: you want my help or not? I'm busy."

"Corner of Eighth and Tenth Ave. Meet me there."

"You expect me to walk? In this sun? What do you think I want a driver for? I'm telling you, kid, you're going to have to grow a backbone."

Felipe scowled and started the car. "That's the deal. Otherwise, I'll disappear. I've got faces you've never seen. You won't see me again." *If you want to see me again, you'll be forced to engage the resources of the country's most powerful spy network to dig me out of whatever hole I find to hide in.* Emptiest threat ever.

"Fine," said El Bufo, and cut off the call, almost as if he'd actually bought it.

El Bufo stood on the corner, thumb extended from a bloody-knuckled fist. He wore a ring on the same hand: a fat, bronze class ring with a green stone. The ring was clean. "Taxi!"

Felipe had the passenger door open before the car even came to a stop. "You're hilarious. Can we get the hell out of here?"

"Kaminal of Tomorrow," grunted El Bufo, settling into the seat. Producing a handkerchief, he proceeded to wipe away the blood — not his own.

"The mall again," said Felipe, studiously not taking the bait. "For what, more coffee?"

"The hotel," El Bufo corrected. "Time we visit Antonellis's wife."

Felipe sank lower in the driver's seat. Another bereaved loved one to torment for information. He concentrated on obeying every traffic law to the letter.

The widow lived in one of the tallest, ugliest buildings in Zona Viva — an 80s-dystopian revision of ancient Kaminaljuyu's lost twinned temples with a posh shopping mall below, and office and hotel towers above joined by a corbeled arch thirty stories high. Official cabs waited twelve deep outside. Felipe never bothered with fares here — the whole of Zona Viva was desert to anybody not awash in first-world glitter. He rolled discreetly past the private guards, waved off the valet, then couldn't find a space in the garage until they were six stories underground.

With its gleaming surfaces, frigid climate control, elevated moving walkways and absurd crisscrossing escalators plodding past minimalist ads for golf resorts and top-shelf rum, the mall so little resembled the city outside it felt like being in orbit. As Luz and Aníbal's third wheel, it had been easy to let himself be pulled through spaces like these, protected in the aura of their combined sophistication and swagger. With El Bufo clomping ahead of him instead, Felipe could feel the place sucking his life force. It was all he could do to keep up.

The hotel lobby was worse. Alien planes of concrete and glass, arranged to evoke the inside of a transparent step-pyramid, threw awful echoes. Quadruple staircases led to a balcony where the front desk squatted like a sacrificial altar. By the time they reached it, Felipe was prepared to fling himself at the knees of the receptionist and beg for clemency.

But she cooperated with El Bufo's expired badge as if everything was routine, and then they were riding to the forty-sixth floor in a vertigo-inducing glass elevator operated by a uniformed teenager.

"Pull it together," snapped El Bufo. Scowling, he lit a cigarrito, the foulness of which Felipe appreciated for its reminder of breathable air.

"You didn't get your job back," Felipe said, suddenly registering the still-expired badge.

"The job," corrected El Bufo. "None of the perks. Sonriente's little joke. I'll be back on the payroll as soon as I give them a suspect. Better this way." He breathed sarcasm and black smoke. "Plausible deniability when I pull something that interferes with their plans. Of course that means when they foul things up, they won't have me to blame. Gilberto loses either way. Stupid suckup can't even follow through with a betrayal properly. If he'd let me in on it from the beginning, by now we'd be running the place."

Felipe clung to the chromed handrail, his stomach dropping out from under him. "What I don't get is why anybody believes you."

"You, of all people, Félix, ought to know how to make someone believe you're something you're not. But you don't, do you?"

He tried to focus on the volcano, floating untouchable in the distance to the southwest between the haze of pollution and clouds. It had been there before this city, and the city before that. Once in a long while, it exploded. Never enough to finish the city for good. That was left up to the people. "You going to tell me?"

El Bufo elbowed the elevator operator in the ribs. "Act like you believe your own bullshit."

The operator coughed and focused pointedly on the smog-hazed city.

People and cars shrank into ants and beetles as the elevator rose. Zone Three emerged from occlusion behind the high-rises. At the foot of the hotel, out of sight of the mall, a grassy hill surrounded by trees and barb-topped chainlink marked one of the ancient temples not yet plowed under.

The doors slid open on a windowless hallway curving into infinity. "Floor forty-six," the operator said meekly. El Bufo sucked on the cigarrita and repeated a room number. The operator pointed left.

Maze-patterned carpet silenced their footsteps.

"About that favor."

"What about it?"

"One of my roommates got arrested at the protests," said Felipe, coughing.

El Bufo, nodding sagely, paused to ash the cigarrita and grind it into the carpet. "Inevitably one pays for one's convictions."

Felipe watched the gray smudge recede behind them. "Can you get her out, please? She's a foreigner, here on a temporary visa. Anything goes on her record, she could be deported."

"I suppose this one can't just put on a different mask and walk out."

Felipe struggled to keep himself from spearing claws through his sandals and shredding the carpet — or the fake detective. "She's been operating under an assumed name. And … an assumed gender."

This turned El Bufo's head. He stared a minute, hurricane clouds circling. "You know how to pick them. But I'm sure I can manage."

"Without your badge?"

"You're forgetting the trick. Works on professional liars as well as on hotel clerks and cab drivers."

"Then do it, if it's so easy. Now. Get her out."

"It's not always easy. The finest bullshit takes time. Your friend may spend a night or two inside. Do her good. First, I want to know what I'm getting in exchange for this help."

"I'll help you."

"How?"

Like I've been *helping.* "I'll drive you. I'll — do whatever you want."

At this, El Bufo smiled. It was terrifying. "For how long?"

"Until … you find a suspect." *Until you throw me under the bus.* A sacrifice. He owed it to Luz, and to Aníbal. A guilty weight in his pocket — the roll of cash he'd been too paranoid to leave in the car, even here inside the fortified first world — reminded him he owed Cristina Ramos too.

El Bufo made a show of getting out his phone. "What's the name? Your roommate."

"Aní — Annabelle Jane Trieste. She's Canadian."

He made a call: a few noncommittal words, the name, nothing to indicate what he was asking or of who. He winked at Felipe. He could be talking to dead air. Felipe felt dizzy. He wondered if it could be the altitude, or if that was the feeling that came with no longer owning his soul.

They reached the widow's door. It was like all the others.

El Bufo put away his phone and got out the familiar, battered wallet with its fake badge: Inspector of National Civil Police Rodrigo Francisco Cuerva Zamora. "Hold it like this. Finger over the photo."

"What?"

"Just flash it, like it's routine. Act like you believe it, and she'll believe you."

With effort, Felipe kept his voice low. "Why the fuck would I want her to? I don't know what to ask." He gestured at himself — sandals, board shorts, football jersey. "Look at me — I don't look like a cop."

El Bufo shrugged. "You're in plainclothes. Undercover. Whatever I want, you said. You've been letting your skills go to waste, hiding behind masks and smoked glass. Consider yourself lucky. If I had your talents ... Well. If I have to force you to use them a little, so be it."

Felipe looked from the door to the badge and back. "W*hy?* What good could this possibly do?"

"You're a nice-looking young man, for the moment. Ask whatever you want. She'll like you. Me, she knows. From before. No, no — don't worry. Do this right, she won't even look at me. Go on. Or your friend stays in jail. I'm so glad you asked me for this favor, Félix."

Felipe considered walking away, down the endless corridor back to the smudge and the elevators. He thought about Aníbal, running off into the tear gas fog. He thought of her sitting in a holding cell under the eyes of cops like every cop he'd known. How long could she keep up the facade?

He raised a fist to the heavy, lacquered wood. "Mrs. Antonellis? Could you open up, please? Police."

It took her forever to come to the door: an elegant, too-thin woman almost as tall as Aníbal, the kind of woman you saw styled and photoshopped in ads for shoes or pills on billboards outside the airport, or in the mall downstairs. She was neither styled nor photoshopped now. She wore black pajamas and her hair was gray-streaked and looked slept-in.

"Mrs. Antonellis?"

She barely glanced at the badge Felipe managed to cover with his thumb exactly as El Bufo had only after having practiced twenty times before she came to the door. She left it open, went and slumped at a high table. Something smelled amazing, chocolate and coffee — was she roasting her own? Aerial photos framed on the kitchenette walls depicted other cities from a god's perspective, alien cities as well as Xela, Antigua, Puerto Barrios, Livingston. Behind her, black leather and imported marble, the entire east wall a window. The place was perfect, the woman in it the only thing that showed a crack.

"Mrs. Antonellis," he started again, "I'm Police Inspector Félix Orellano. This is my assistant, Clownface." El Bufo choked on something between laughter and a murderous roar. "We're here to ask a few more questions about your husband."

She studied him briefly. He managed not to run.

"Does it look like I have anything better to do?" Her Spanish was polished, overeducated, rude. "I can't leave the country, you people put me on a no-fly list. To say nothing of the fact that my husband frittered away most of our money on some activist slut before it got him killed. So I'm not leaving this hotel, not to go to any safe house or even the embassy, so please don't bother bringing it up again. You'll have to forgive my not offering you coffee … it's because I know you'll take it anyway."

El Bufo was, in fact, already taking it. He overfilled three white porcelain cups from a steel-and-plexiglass contraption on the stove, set one sloshing in front of Mrs. Antonellis without even glancing in her direction and pressed the other on Felipe. "Pathetic! A tragedy," he said, speaking with a false Kakchiquel lisp that even with the mask made it Felipe's turn to struggle for a straight face. "We grow the best coffee in the world, but nobody from here knows how to drink it." He clinked cups, and with a vulgar slurp of satisfaction lumbered into what must be the bedroom.

Mrs. Antonellis swore halfheartedly in English. Spilled coffee slid down a table leg to the floor.

Felipe put his cup down without drinking. Ask whatever you want, El Bufo had said. Activist slut? He didn't want to ask. He didn't want to hear it. He wanted to leave her alone. Instead, he cleared his throat. "Your husband worked for and donated extensively to an aid organization."

"The LNCF," she said. "But you knew that."

Felipe made a note in the tiny pad El Bufo had given him, an excuse not to look at her. It was an acronym he'd heard before, but he forgot what it stood for. He could ask Luz. That might not go over well. "And ... was it in that capacity that he took an interest in the Totonícapan movement?"

"The what?"

"The organization that was behind today's protests."

"I don't know anything about that. As I said, I haven't left the hotel since." She hunched to sip from the too-full coffee cup without lifting it from the table. Not that she needed any more from the way she was jittering. "Since it happened."

They'd stepped over an untouched copy of the *Diary* outside the door, next to a stack of room service plates. But she had a TV, and a notebook computer lay closed beside her. She was married to a politician, a lobbyist, whatever — who she seemed to assume was cheating on her. With, it was impossible for him not to guess, Luz. He fucking hated this.

"So … he didn't talk much about his work. Is it okay if I sit down?"

She rolled her eyes. "He tried, I suppose. You know how complicated everything is here. I never understood why he was getting all the threats."

"He was threatened?" He kept writing.

"You people know this. We reported it I don't know how many times. They told us everyone in his position gets them, and if we didn't like it, we could go home."

"Why didn't you?"

She sighed. "What he was doing here was important. He wasn't letting anyone bully him. Not even me."

"What were the threats about?"

"Go home or else. We gave you all this. Look it up yourself."

El Bufo could, maybe. Maybe not. Had Luz and Aníbal been threatened? Could they have kept it from him if they had? What would he have done? Nothing. "I mean, why? What did they want him to stop doing?"

"I told you I don't know. They didn't say. I'm sure David knew perfectly, but …" She gave an exasperated shrug.

El Bufo hadn't brought the file, so Felipe had no profile to flip through. But he pictured Antonellis easily. Salt and pepper stubble, cut jaw. Postcolonial first world guilt posterboy heartthrob.

Whatever El Bufo was doing in the other room, he wasn't tearing it apart. Except for the occasional clink of a coffee cup on marble, it was quiet. He was probably in there laughing into the pillow.

Felipe scribbled rage emojis in the notepad. *How did your husband know Luz, and what the hell were they planning? Did Aníbal know? Were they lovers? Was she fucking him in exchange for millions in first world guilt money?*

If she knew, she'd deny it. Whatever he asked, El Bufo would know about it too.

"Was that all?" she said. "Because if you're finished, I'd really like to get back to staring at the wall." And she glanced at the laptop.

"I'm — thinking," he said. If his own wife had been murdered, or his mother, would he look at the news? Maybe not. Would he lie about it to the cops? Probably. She was uncomfortable — in this place, this situation. What could you expect? He tried to visualize. Marriage. An implausible domestic scene, himself and Luz in the apartment, Aníbal awkwardly absent, though he had nothing in his head to replace her stuff with so it was all still there. A frying pan of chorizo and eggs; he tipped half of them onto her plate, leaned in for a kiss with wooden lips. The imaginary Luz arched a neatly-plucked eyebrow.

He tried again, this time with Cristina Ramos in her mother's big, well-stocked kitchen filled with the scents of dulces and pibil. "I'm vegetarian," Cristina said apologetically.

"So, this isn't working," he said, loudly, for the benefit of the other room. No response. "Why don't we ... how about we pretend I'm not a cop? I'm a friend, a sympathetic ear. I just want to know who your husband was, what he believed in. What he did in his time off. Was he ... passionate about his work? Did he like it here?"

She sipped again, balanced the coffee cup between fingertips and regarded him over it. "A friend."

At least he'd had practice being a friend. Not a very good one. "I'm a good listener," he said. Maybe that at least was true. "This must be hard for you."

She got up, got a towel and mopped up the trickle of coffee. She threw it in the gleaming sink, then sat again, sipped again, and stared at him.

He drank some coffee, the last thing he needed. It was amazing. He tasted chocolate, coffee, honey, cinnamon, cardamom. "Really good," he managed.

She seemed to come to a decision. "Fine. Inspector ...?"

"Orellano." Felipe's last name was K'icab. Sandor Orellano had been the fourteen-year-old kid killed on his motorcycle in Santa Catarina, back when Felipe was having wet dreams of Luz and Luz was kicking everybody's ass in primary school. "Call me Félix."

"You want to be my friend, Inspector Félix? You want to know our dirty laundry? If that's what it takes to get you people to leave me alone. I hate it here. And I was beginning to hate him. Yes, of course he cared about his work. He wasn't ecstatic when he got the appointment — he'd been hoping for someplace flashier. Haiti, Sudan. He had to travel, you understand. His career at home was over ... he finished his term 'with distinction,' no black marks, respected by his peers, all that, but he was too ... 'passionate' to gain any real allies, and without allies ..." The words came fast, in that clipped accent. He had a hard time keeping up. He gave up any pretense of taking notes. "We did some soul-searching. Together. We were still 'partners' then, a team. I felt sorry for him. His career had dead-ended and mine hadn't. I was less help than I could have been. My background is business not politics, thank God, or we'd never talk about anything but work. He chose the nonprofit sector, hoping — what everyone hopes of the nonprofit sector, I suppose. The impossible. I tried to be supportive. We agreed he'd go wherever they sent him and I'd follow when I could, when I'd arranged things. I told him I needed time. To get used to the idea. At first, I thought I might get used to not having him around. That didn't happen. The way he wrote about what he was doing, the way he talked ... he convinced me, finally. I was a fool. So I came."

She pushed off the stool and stepped with her cup to the wall of windows. The way she walked was oddly graceful — barefoot but used to heels? One hand made an absent effort to control her wild hair. "This place. I've traveled with him, around to all those destitute villages, as much I could stand. Highlands, lowlands. The coasts. Everywhere in between. I don't see what he sees. The ruins — they're beautiful. But you practically kill yourself getting to the good ones. And on the way, it gets beaten into your head how everything else is in even worse shape. Uglier. Cheaper. Desperate. Nothing's built to last. Everything's ruined or about to be. Even the people."

She glanced back at him, suddenly seeming to remember who she was talking to.

What did he care if she badmouthed "his" country? *Obviously you've never traveled with me,* he could have said, if he'd been feeling macho — but he was a cop now, not a cab driver. He had a real problem lately being attracted to grieving women.

Reflexively, he checked his reflection in the glass of one of the photos, framed above the table. Still the Argentine. Those striking eyes, the strong jaw — the Argentine *was* macho. He never felt real enough to act like it.

Then he recognized the photo — different from the others — an iconic image from the civil war. Seven figures stood arranged execution-style along a drainage ditch at the edge of a dry milpa in grainy black-and-white. Low in the foreground, three soldiers huddled tête-à-tête, two with their backs to the camera. The third, his face shadowed by the brim of his cap and badly out of focus, was agreed by most to be General Manuel Monterríos, alleged genocidal mastermind, who in the twenty years since the war's official end had been tried, acquitted, and elected president. But he'd never been sworn in, because he'd been retried, mistried; he'd run again, been defeated, tried again, been convicted, given more consecutive life sentences than years remaining in his natural life, and at last he'd been released into peaceful retirement on a technicality trumped-up by a supreme court his influence had placed in power.

Whatever that photo meant to Antonellis or his wife, to Felipe there could be no more perfect expression of futility. The caption might as well read *Shut up, keep your head down, nothing you do will change a thing.*

"How can you look at this every day?" he asked, almost as if he'd been talking to Luz. What made people hang their most horrible pictures in the room most responsible for keeping them alive?

"I try not to." She was still at the window, with its long view past high-rises to the city outskirts, eroding cliffs, dirt football pitches, walled estates, slums. "The contrasts are so stark. Between rich and poor. Not that it isn't like that where we came from. But here, it's all right in front of you. You can't get away. I mean, unless you take a helicopter everywhere, one walled compound to another. But who can get used to that?"

This woman came from a world he'd only seen in movies. She was richer than anyone who'd spoken two sentences to him; narcos and robber barons didn't hire cabs.

"I know there's poverty and cruelty everywhere. David came here to help, and I appreciate that. It's why I stayed. He comes from a 'good' family; he's always trying to live that down. A lot of his childhood he spent not knowing what poverty was. That's not his fault. I just can't anymore. Is that so selfish? And now he had to go and do *this* to me."

Felipe felt dizzy again, suffocated — too much time breathing cigar smoke and recycled air. Stumbling past her, he found a part of the glass wall that opened. Smog. Exhaust, fumes, something frying in peanut oil — plantains.

"Could you not?"

He gasped for breath, and even the thick air made him feel better. "How long have you lived here?"

"Two years."

"Tell me again the last time you left this hotel? Not since the murder?"

Her gaze shifted from the window, sharpened. The muscles tightened in her jaw and pale throat, and he realized he'd gone too far.

"Listen, 'friend,'" she said, her tone hardening. "The minute I set foot outside they'll murder me, remember? I don't have to like this awful country just because my husband wanted to save it. And I don't have to talk to you. You know what, why don't you take your creeper hunchback assistant and get the fuck out. I'm done talking to you, understand?"

El Bufo appeared from the other room, wiping hands on his shirt. He finished Felipe's coffee, then grabbed him and pulled him to the door.

Felipe was still fumbling for an apology when she slammed it behind them.

After ten paces down the corridor, El Bufo stopped short, held out an open hand. After a moment, Felipe filled it with the fake badge. "Good. Now shut up, keep low, and do what I do."

He went back to the widow's door, soft steps muffled by carpet. Crouching below the peephole, he placed against the door a drinking glass he must have stolen from the bathroom. Even without it, Felipe could hear her on the phone, in panicked English. His English was gleaned from dozing through bootleg action films

Rubén ran on the bus's little tv-dvd combo on the overnight routes. The thick door and thicker carpet muffled the words, but he caught the word "ring."

The inspector's fingers, cupped around the glass, were unadorned. The green class ring had disappeared from El Bufo's hand. Following Felipe's look, he extended the same, no longer bloody but still scarred-knuckled finger and grinned.

A cleaning cart came squeaking around the curve of the corridor, pushed by a woman in a spotless pinafore. She hesitated, looking like a deer in headlights. Felipe grabbed at El Bufo's coat seam.

El Bufo glanced up and shoved him off, chhed them both theatrically.

The deep breaths were no longer helping. He needed to be out of this artificial atmosphere, away from El Bufo's manipulative bullshit, listen to a little reggae and sweat off some caffeine.

"Fuck this. I'll be in the car."

El Bufo overtook him halfway to the elevator, gripped him painfully by the upper arm and propelled him onward. "Coward. You don't know what that might have cost us."

"No kidding. So *tell* me."

"He's not dead."

"What? Antonellis? What about all the … bullets?" There'd been blood everywhere but the floor, and above the little table where everybody died, a picture. Not of a genocide in progress, but a landscape threatened by storm. Though with climate change, he supposed they amounted to the same thing. Luz would absolutely say it was people like Antonellis and his wife with their imported marble countertops and colonizer coffee, like Aníbal's parents and their trust fund — and Aníbal wouldn't argue — who were, through complacency and tacit acceptance of blood-bathed luxury, responsible for the hurricanes, the droughts, the floods, the fires, the mass dieoffs, even the dead campesinos in the ditches. Which was why this whole thing was so completely fucked.

"Whoever was taking Antonellis's lunch break," El Bufo grunted. "It wasn't Antonellis. They killed a double."

A double? The idea came to him unbidden: *The murdered man was like me.* No reason to jump to conclusions. "How can you know that?"

"My former partner." El Bufo glared at him, waiting for some line Felipe had no idea how to deliver. "Gilberto. Taking me on was the smartest thing he ever did. I don't know what happened, who's got his tatas in a vise over there at the headquarters of 'national civil police.' Now he respects my intelligence just enough to leave critical forensics results lying out on the desk while he tells me off. Remarkable he had the presence of mind to order them at all. Best part, they've had them since this morning at least, and nobody's said anything."

Felipe had seen photos of Antonellis online. And he'd seen the crime scene report, though only for a second. It had looked like the same guy. "So what does that mean?"

El Bufo stabbed the elevator call button. "You're a smart kid. Work it out."

Felipe tried to read El Bufo's impatient movements, the cuts on his knuckles, the bulge under his coat. Was this why El Bufo had gotten him involved?

The elevator dinged. When the doors opened, El Bufo caught the teenaged operator by his starched lapels and dragged him into the hallway. "Push our own buttons, thanks." He pulled Felipe in after him, ignoring the attendant's protests. The doors slid closed, but he left the buttons alone; they just hung there above the city. "Come on. High-profile foreign philanthropist gets murdered, but it turns out he isn't actually dead. Why cover that up? Particularly when the man on the job is a joke you set up to fail. Give you a hint: where'd they get the photo in his file?"

Salt and pepper first world guilt posterboy: it had been a full scan of his passport. With blood on it. Felipe recalled the astonishment of finding Aníbal's in her underwear drawer. When you came to a place like this from a place like that, you kept your identity close — at least you kept it safe. He'd seen it in the way their foreign NGO friends paid for drinks at Forty Doors. Especially the new ones. A foreign passport was a lifeline to a set of rights you could lose in a moment. So how had the double gotten hold of it?

"He knew about the hit," Felipe said out loud.

"Who?"

"Antonellis."

"What did he know?"

"He knew they wanted him dead."

"Obviously."

"He knew who wanted him dead."

"He had an idea. Seems like he must have known how, and when. What else?"

"And he knew … what would happen after. The investigation. What it would expose."

"What would it expose?"

"Corruption? Conspiracy?"

"No shit. He knew what trouble his own death would cause — or he hoped, anyway," said El Bufo. "This is a guy who hopes too much. Terminally, you might say. So he let it happen — but not to him. This country's so fucked, he figures martyring himself is a faster way to what he wants than trying to convince anybody to change. Now that they know he's alive, they don't want to let him know they know. Finding the killers is secondary. It always was. Antonellis is the prize."

"So that phone call ..."

"She was calling to tip him off." He waggled the scarred fingers of his right hand, now conspicuously absent a gold ring with a dull green jewel.

"About the ring?"

El Bufo nodded. "Took it off a drunk outside the market. One of the regulars. Said a telenovela-looking guy in a track suit and sunglasses gave it to him half an hour before the murders. Figure it was Antonellis. The real Antonellis."

"He showed up for his own murder?"

"Funny thing about that. Drunk couldn't tell me what the guy wanted, *why* he gave him the ring. Seems odd, right? Even for a bleeding heart like him. Not a lot of reason to trust a gutter drunk with jewelry — even a cheap piece of glass like that."

"It was some kind of signal."

El Bufo nodded curtly.

"To the fake Antonellis?"

The elevator doors slid open again. The attendant glanced up guiltily from his phone. El Bufo leaned away from the backdrop of the murky city, pushed Close Door, waited. "Guess again. A few important people I know own a ring like that. The only one who actually wears his is my old boss. Faustino Sonriente." He flashed a row of nicotine-yellowed teeth.

The head of the SAAS. It had been Molinero's job, famously, back during the war, when the finest cabal of assassins and spies in the land was still known as the Presidential Guard. That firing squad photo — the conspiracy theorists said Sonriente was one of the two with their backs to the camera. "You think *he* hired the killers?"

El Bufo planted a thumb on the brass button marked B6 for the underworld, peeled it away leaving a perfect fingerprint, then smeared the print out of existence. The elevator began its meteoric descent. "No. Indirectly? Faustino wears that ring to prove he doesn't care what anybody thinks. He doesn't fear the press. He doesn't have to. But a lot of people have a ring they don't flash. When you graduate from a certain elite military academy founded by the CIA, they hand you a glass of whiskey. Everybody toasts your health, and there it is at the bottom, like the worm in the mezcal. A lot of officers get recruited at that ceremony — army, intelligence. The president has a ring just like it."

"How the fuck do you know about it?"

"Me?" El Bufo shook his head. "No, I came up from the trash. Like you. But you hear stories. Rumor. Myth? They're not just proud of the reputation. They rely on it. So it's not some big secret. You can't spread fear with secrecy."

Felipe clung to the handrail as the city rose around them. This was how the world worked, obvious if you paid the slightest attention: bribes, counterbribes, pullers of strings, masks on masks. Luz understood this. So did Antonellis, and his wife. But there was always the chance that everybody who laughed every time you looked over your shoulder was right, that you were crazy.

"You're telling me Antonellis knew somebody in the government ordered him killed, somebody from this not so secret military cabal. After dozens of threats, he knew this one was real … and he knew where and when. And rather than just … not go, instead he hired a double to die in his place, *then* went out and bought a fake ring, showed up half an hour before what was supposed to be his own murder to leave it as some kind of message for the killers? You know how insane that sounds?"

El Bufo waved a hand; the cuts on his knuckles had opened again. "Guesses that happen to fit. I'd say you can ask Antonellis when we find him, but that doesn't seem likely now, does it."

"You left that ring for her to find. You thought she'd see it and lead us to him."

"It was worthless as evidence. Worse than worthless. That drunk's testimony wouldn't mean spit. She knows he's alive. Maybe she knows where. That was our chance, but it's gone."

"Come on — it's not like she was going to blurt it out. 'What's that, you're hiding from government assassins under a cabana on the Rio Dulce? Lucky you!'"

"There would have been clues. Now there's nothing. All we know is that she knows."

"So what? They didn't hire you to find Antonellis, they hired you to find the killers."

El Bufo's broad mouth pressed flat as a blade. "I *want back in, understand?* You want your friend released, you need me back in. They screwed me when it suited them. I owe them for that. But they're the ones with the power. Without it, you're nothing in this country. I was nothing a long time. I'm not about to just walk away. But to get back in, I have to give them what they want. Antonellis is alive. Now he's in a position to hurt them. They need him dead, for real. They've got people out looking. And they've got me. Insurance. I find who pulled the trigger, they can set up whoever it was to take the fall. I trace the murder back to them, they can blame me instead. But only if they silence Antonellis first. I needed to be the one to find him."

The elevator slowed prematurely. They were still above ground. The doors opened, and El Bufo was suddenly nonchalant as a crowd of rich ladinos filed on in bathing suits, impeccable hair and makeup, designer sunglasses and impossibly soft white towels, laughing at some shared joke. One of the girls smiled at him, flirting obliviously, her head resting easily on a friend's shoulder.

She was smiling at the mask. Avoiding her gaze, Felipe was left with a choice between the ugly truth Antonellis's wife couldn't handle — the smogged city replete with consequences, a city representing his powerlessness — and the uglier El Bufo.

"So what now?" Felipe asked, subdued. El Bufo needed him, or thought he did. As much as he needed El Bufo.

"Now," said El Bufo, scowling, "we go to Zone Three."

Zone Three was even dingier by daylight. Half the buildings lay in ruins, dry weeds bursting from cracks in the stucco, windows barred or boarded with no glass to speak of, everything graffitied with political symbols and gang signs in equal profusion. Reggaeton boomed competing from undead radios unseen in brown shadows. Kids and threadbare dogs raced past the Corolla's fenders.

"Park here," El Bufo ordered, a corner store where heaped brown bananas and crates of cola spilled out past the curb; with desperate optimism, orange paint proclaimed it *The Paradise*.

"Have I mentioned this car is everything I care about in the world?"

El Bufo cranked the window. "Toby," he called, beckoning a skinny kid lounging with one bare foot against the tienda's doorframe. "Watch this car, you come tell me if anybody touches it."

"Of course, El Bufo, sir," said the kid without a hint of irony.

El Bufo thumped Felipe's arm. "Pay him something."

"Seriously?"

"This car's a piece of shit, you ought to be paying him to steal it."

Felipe triple-checked the doors and that he hadn't left anything obviously worth smashing a window for. He fished a bill from the roll of crime scene money, made sure it was smaller than a fifty.

"Go," said the kid, making the money disappear. "I'll take care of it."

Around the corner, down an alley that smelled of incense and piss and steaming tamales, another hand-painted storefront. *Mystic Order of San Francisco of Tecpán.*

"What is this, a fortune teller?"

"A witch," said El Bufo, dead serious. He produced a key and unlocked the storefront's iron grate. "Got a better idea? Figure it's time I capitalized on the one thing I've got that they don't."

"What's that?"

"You."

San Pablo and San Pedro presided over the shrine's two naves, alike as God and Satan robed in pink and purple dyed feathers. Their eyes were glass. A scarred Santa Muerte menaced from the inner wall. The Virgin of Guadalupe was a dozen tower candles scattered on the floor, all but two long since burned black, San Juan Diego in his bird-serpent wings repeated at her feet. A seated figure in red clay, genderless, faceless, pressed a half-shucked ear of corn to its brow. A hook-nosed dragon couched a spiral in umber sand. San Simón — an idol, not a saint — was a wooden doll in a rancher's hat and rags the colors of earth and fire. Wax was everywhere underfoot — wax and flowers withering. Smoke flowed ankle-deep like water churning mud at the foot of a falls, spilling down over the step into the street.

"Lupita," called El Bufo, his voice high and strange.

A woman came around the corner through the beaded curtain. Her knotted hands cupped a wooden carving of a caiman's head, the hollow in the middle smoldering with tobacco and copal. Felipe half-expected her to shriek and drop it at the sight of him, but she set it down before San Pedro, took El Bufo's hand briefly, then sought Felipe's.

"Lupita, this is Félix Orellano."

A witch, a palm reader, a Santera: worker of cathartic curses and love potions for the appeasement of wishful thinking. She was older than El Bufo, but the way she took Felipe's hand in both of hers, spreading the meat of the thumb apart from the heel, was undeniably sexual. A flush of heat surged up his arm, up under the mask.

Until now Felipe would have taken El Bufo for the ultimate rationalist, the ultimate cynic. But it was obvious this woman knew him; he was a regular. More than that: he must have come here the other night.

Did she recognize him? Did she see him through the mask? Sudden, brief panic: which mask was he wearing? Smoke and incense patina dulled the flecks of mirror in the quetzal mosaic by the door; they reflected only forms. El Bufo had brought him here — that should mean the conquistador. He felt with his free hand for the rigid curls of that quixotically upturned moustache.

"I looked forward to this," said the fortune teller, smiling. "Come into the light." And Felipe allowed himself to be drawn into the next room by the wrist, to the only window, where the afternoon sun cast a parallelogram on crumbling tiles, everything else in shadow. The atmosphere was clearer here; he could think.

"Can I get you something? Coffee? Are you hungry?"

He shook his head. She seemed ... kind. What was she doing with El Bufo? She sat at the edge of a withered armchair and bent over his hand, necklaces swinging. Her charcoal hair was sprouting ash-gray at the part.

His eyes adjusted. This wasn't just her office or her shrine; it was her bedroom. A painted screen half-concealed an unmade bed. No toilet, no sink, just a pila with a bucket, a rain barrel, a ceramic filter jug, a charcoal firepit with a kettle warming on the ledge. A jade plant sprawled by the window, huge, spindly, starved for light. Judging from all the shrines and saints and totems, the photographs in weathered frames, the paths deep-worn in the floor tiles and the strata of wax, she'd been doing this a long, long time. There ought to be a little money in catering to belief, if his father was any lesson. It wasn't here.

She released his right hand, reached for his left. He gave it.

"You've been hiding it your whole life?" she said.

A half-question. She knew the answer and didn't. It didn't mean she could see through him. She couldn't: not if she thought she could read palms that weren't even his.

She turned up his left hand, pointing out a crease. "This is your fate. See how thick? And here —" Gesturing again to the right, she looked up into Felipe's face. "Your life lived, your love. It's hardly there at all."

She let him hide his hands behind him. "Félix," she said. "Is that your name?" Her eyes were surrounded by their own dark lines. "I've cast for you it must be fifty times."

"Cast what? Cards, like tarot?" He'd gone to a fortune teller once, a dare from Luz at Santa Catarina's saint's day fair. They'd been thirteen. He'd lied. It wasn't even fun. He'd been terrified. Luz loved it.

He'd let her put him through a lot. You'd think she'd owe him.

Lupita drew open a pouch of woven cloth and poured into an open hand a little heap of blue and yellow dried corn, blood-red seeds, dull chips of crystal. "These are the days," she said.

"What?"

She picked a red seed from the pile and, with whispers, popped it in her mouth. "The sacred calendar. Counting through it helps to see patterns. Each day has its meaning, its nahual. Not so different from the tarot — I use that too, sometimes. Or like a rosary, but without the string. It's the same with the Garífuna gods, the Orisha. They go into hiding. The surface changes, the saints take their place, but the connections are the same. The days correspond to the numbers, to the signs and the movements of the heavens and the ebb and swell of all life: plants, animals, water, winds. You understand?"

He kept his paper copy of the ancient calendar, with its interlocking wheels, taped to the dashboard with the Christian ones for no other reason than that three in ten city dwellers likely to pass him in a day believed in the system of thought it defined, though they'd be crazy to admit it, and nine out of ten foreigners expected it of everyone they met. That calendar had predicted the motions of planets and stars for five thousand years. Just because it had failed to protect its people, just because all its nuance and meaning had been trampled to dust was no reason to stop using it. As long as you didn't try to use it to predict people. Which, he supposed, was in a way what he'd been doing. Himself included. What mask to wear on what day, in what circumstance? He played at relying on a system, because he didn't know how the masks even worked.

"How do you know what I am?" he demanded. "How does *he* know?"

She smiled into her lap. Her fingers kept moving, birdlike, arranging the seeds. He thought she wouldn't answer.

Then it spilled: the words, not the seeds, not yet. "News moves lips to ear among those of my calling. That means slowly. There aren't many of us anymore, and we're tied to the pueblo. Some would say there's no difference between the two. Which is what makes this so complicated. Anyway, word comes around." In her palm, she rolled the seeds in circles. "When it does, you listen. I know an elder woman here in El Gallito. Older than me. There aren't many, but we exist." She laughed. Nervous?

"Months and months ago now, Terrena had a vision. Her daughter married a man from Sacatepequéz, now they only see each other for holy week and the nativity. This year, coming home, she had to travel on the empty days. Dangerous. I've warned her before. She said there was no helping it, but she convinced her son-in-law to go with her. And it turns out, he saw the vision too. Too honest for his own good, that one. When she brought him here, he threatened me. Made me promise I wouldn't take any more of his mother's money. But he wanted so badly to tell me, it got the better of him."

"What did he tell you? What kind of vision?" But he knew. The look she traded with El Bufo.

"On the bus," she said simply, watching him.

Here it was. This was what he'd been dreading. He wanted to laugh. "What does this have to do with the murders? Anything?"

El Bufo shrugged. "You were what I was doing when Gilberto called. I couldn't turn him down, it was too good. It was him. Otherwise I might have taken you straight here. You'd have hated it. You're a stubborn little shit, you know that?"

"How the hell did you even find me? This was all you had, thirdhand from some lady's son-in-law who thought she thought she saw something on the bus, and you found me, but you can't find Antonellis *or* his killers? What kind of detective are you?"

"Oh, I know where the killers are. Visit them presently, this doesn't work out." El Bufo stalked to the bed, stooped, and produced a half-bottle of white rum. Because of course he had some kind of third eye for liquor. "What does it matter how I found you? Legwork. Luck."

"What the fuck do you want from me?"

"What do you think? I want power. All I can get. That's the only way to survive. Yours is different from everybody else's. Can't be taken away. You don't even know how to use it. I wanted to find out. Figured you would too. But no. No, you're too much of a coward. So far you've been more trouble than you're worth. We'll see. Lupita, cast for him."

Felipe shrank from them both, but there was no place to hide, no place to run to. No mask was going to hide him from this. El Bufo didn't understand: his "power" was a weakness, like his father's missing arm, but worse. His earliest memories were of hiding; of course it was what he'd learned to do best. Not well enough. Maybe his parents would have been better off drowning him in an old masa sack like an unwanted kitten, like Martín. He wondered why they hadn't. They had Rubén, a good boy, hard-working, steady. What did they want with a liability?

El Bufo drank. "Pay her, Félix. You have to pay her or it won't work."

"I can't believe you even believe in this shit."

El Bufo struck him, open-handed, hard enough it spun him to the wall, almost dislodging the mask. Felipe put his hands to it by reflex, hunched as he felt his skin for cracks. But he'd deserved it. Because of course El Bufo believed. In magic. In fate and old, dead gods. He'd been stalking a jaguar shapeshifter for months.

"Stop it, Rigo," said Lupita, surprisingly calm. "He also has to want my help."

"Take it off," El Bufo snarled. "Take off the mask and show her. Now."

"Rodrigo, that's enough," she said. "Please wait outside."

El Bufo scowled, but to Felipe's astonishment he complied, taking the bottle. The iron grate outside creaked open, then slammed.

She watched him, expectant. Copal smoke rolled over the floor at her feet, diffuse with light.

Whatever fate she found for him in those seeds would be a lie, at best a self-deception. But he was trapped — cornered. And with the massive, suffocating pressure of El Bufo's presence temporarily removed, he discovered he wasn't about to just curl up and expire of shame. Luz and Aníbal needed him. That had been his motivating force for awhile. Now it was serious, urgent. He needed to be strong enough to help them. Brave enough. He'd already been willing to make a deal with the devil. This ought to be easy, by comparison.

It was different than that time at the carnival fortune teller's with Luz. He wasn't hiding now; he was already exposed. He wanted to know what this woman would say about his life.

Meekly, Felipe passed her a few wrinkled bills. "Does it matter if it isn't mine?"

"This is too much," she said. She frowned. "Stay there." She brought a wooden chair for him, then a table of sorts: a bucket of sand and a piece of plywood pocked with burn marks. She sat again on the edge of the armchair. Placing the money to one side, she began counting seeds and crystals into patterns.

"Who taught you this?" he asked, to fill the silence, after a space of time he could not judge in which he listened for El Bufo out in the alley. He'd heard nothing but faint, competing reggaeton rhythms and the fainter drip of the seeds.

"My mother," she murmured, absorbed.

"Did she live here, in the city?"

The counting paused. Lupita looked up at him, her fingertip aimed at a pile of four. "She brought us here at the end of her life. Because there was money, and to make us safe from war. The city was different then. Easier. No mareros, not so many narcos. The guerillas were far away, and the soldiers had gone to hunt them. Into the lion's den, she called it. Her divination saved our lives. That's why I had to learn."

What about all the others? he wanted to ask. The ones who didn't see. But he had no place accusing anyone. He had no place asking about the war. "Who before that? Who taught her?"

Drip. Drip. Drip, drip. Blue, yellow, blue, dull. "Abuela Tilda."

"Your grandmother?"

"The pueblo's grandmother. Please — I need to concentrate."

He waited, looking around through the copal haze for he didn't know what, a way out, while she whispered in K'iche' and thumbed seeds and crystals onto the scarred wood. Twice more she ate a red seed. The sun rolled in its course; the sunbeam slid tile to broken tile across the floor. Fidgeting, he shifted his chair to follow. Where the sun didn't touch him, he felt cold.

He remembered, in a flash, a certain quality of smoky light from a trip his school had taken to the ruins at Iximche, back when the one mask, the jaguar mask, was still big on him. The light crept along brown stones of temples scored and striated by time, the shadows pulling, pointing, and the foreign guide talked while the kids failed to listen about how every temple had been built such that on a certain day, a certain hour — not every year, but every fifty years, or perhaps only once, ever, two lifetimes distant from the lives of anybody who had worked to build that altar, the light would strike the temple's face, spilling over steps, through crannies into chambers to illuminate some secret. And how much of that was lost because people just like those this foreign guide was talking at, Felipe's people, had come back to these ruins year after year and taken stones away to build their houses. *Don't let yourselves be ignorant,* he seemed to plead, *relearn the past,* while everybody in earshot actively tried to forget that there had been a war, that guerillas had hidden and soldiers hunted them among these very ruins.

And the shadows pulled and pointed them along a wooded path to the east, to where the ashes of offerings cooled on the foundations of an absent altar. The guide said once a great obsidian gemstone had absorbed the last rays of some auspicious day nobody could ever reconstruct because the stone had been taken down and cut square and now belonged to the altar of the church in Tecpán. Then Felipe's teacher had gotten angry and told the guide the stone was part of the church altar because Jesus was Lord, that was part of history too, no matter what else happened, and that trying to tell these children otherwise was irresponsible. After that Felipe wandered off to be alone among the sun-delineated megaliths, and he'd taken off the mask to rest — something he no longer did, ever — and glimpsed himself in a puddle from the recent rain and seen himself shifting through forms, looking first like himself, then the guide, the teacher, his father, his brother.

He ended up missing the bus home and had to take a later local bus, which he had no problem doing; he'd been riding the bus since he could walk, and without the benefit of any great wisdom of the past to guide him.

The day had been like a dream, and he regarded it as such.

Finally, as if waking, the fortune teller let what was left of her handful of seeds fall, rolling and spilling, pattering like rain or a clock gone haywire, till they scattered over the fissured tiles like cities on a map.

"Are you all right?" he asked.

"He won't stop, you know. Rodrigo is a good man — without him I couldn't survive here the way it's become. But he wants what he wants."

"Did the seeds tell you that?"

"They don't need to. The way he talks about you … Maybe I should never have told him, but then we would never have met."

Most people Felipe met, Luz's friends, his fares, looked past him, through him. Of course, he encouraged it. Not this woman. This meant something to her.

"The seeds … they say you're afraid, Félix. Everyone is. Nothing wrong with that if you want to survive. But you're not like everyone else. You let it paralyze you, and you can't. Here, see, this is you, Ajpu, the hunter." She reached for a group of four tokens, red seeds at east and west, corn south, a crystal north.

He waved a hand. "I don't need to know the details." Maybe there was something to the calendar, knowing patterns like those ancient architects. But the important thing was what she thought of him. And she thought he was a coward. The same as El Bufo.

"You do. Because this, here —" Another pile, three blue corn and one red seed. "This is the jaguar. It's confusing, I know. But in this configuration, you're the hunter, and the jaguar signifies death." The way she said it, she might have been telling him this same thing for years. "Félix, it says you have to run. Not forever, but for now. You need to run."

"That's what I've *been* doing."

She shook her head, pointed to another indistinguishable pile of seeds as if it meant everything. "You've been hiding."

Footsteps — not hurried — in the alley outside the window. Pacing. He waited for them to fade.

"It's him, isn't it? He's what I'm running from."

She shrugged.

"Where am I supposed to run to?"

He knew she didn't know. He couldn't stop himself. Suddenly, the illusion that someone might know what he should do was too tempting. He needed help. Even a stopped clock is right sometimes.

"The seeds, the days, they show patterns, not the deviations from them." Again she spoke as if reciting words she'd said a thousand times. "'When the gods, the angels first sat down to make people out of wood, they asked the days, the seeds. And the seeds told them: yes, make people, make someone to keep the calendar and count the days. When the wooden people turned out selfish and thought the world revolved around themselves, the gods had to destroy them and start again.' But that doesn't mean what the seeds said was a lie. It had to be that way: a birth, destruction, birth again. It always is. You have to go. Leave the city. Where, or what you're meant to find, I don't know. But it isn't here."

She got up and brought him a cup of something hot from the stove. Coffee, but sweet and thin, made from roasted corn, not the real thing. He thought of the face El Bufo would make and almost laughed.

"Don't worry," she said, mistaking him. "It's not the same corn."

He drank gratefully anyway.

"Can I ask something else?"

"Of course, yes."

"El Bufo — Rodrigo — you know him."

She nodded.

"He said if I helped him, he could get a friend released from prison. Can he?"

She sat back in the chair. "If he wants. A lot of boys running around El Gallito would be in jail, or worse, if not for him. Though maybe it's worse for everybody that they're not." She smiled another rueful smile, more open this time — and he saw four upper teeth missing from the front of her mouth.

He hunched to hide an involuntary shudder. "Thank you," he said quickly, inadequately, to cover it. "He doesn't deserve you."

"He doesn't want me. It's been thirty years. Now he comes only when his rich wife decides she can't stand the sight of him. Or when he needs something."

Felipe hadn't paid her enough.

He saw what he could do, what it would mean to her. It wasn't something he'd done for anyone but his mother. He didn't know why he wanted to, except that she seemed so kind and long-suffering — what she'd endured from El Bufo over a lifetime he could barely stand after three days — and that she believed so hard in her own self-deception it had worked on him.

The ribbon fit behind his ears — silky, worn and darkened by time, held tight by a simple knot. When the mask slipped off, she saw what was happening and caught it in her hands as it fell. He felt an irreconcilable rush of disappointment that it was the conquistador, not the jaguar mask: she'd read his other hands, been looking at his other face. But perhaps it didn't matter; he was himself now.

Without it he always felt bigger, looser, he took it off so rarely. Not that it was a burden. Despite its rigid, wooden weight, it fit too comfortably. He stretched his shoulders, his spine, dragged claws lightly over the ruined tiles, through scattered seeds and crystals. He yawned.

The cry she let out could have been ecstasy, but it wasn't. In her haste to get away from what he'd shown her, Lupita fell over the side of the chair, and Felipe watched as the conquistador's nose hit the floor with a sickening crack, like an ocote struck by lightning. The mask fell in two pieces, split down the middle.

Then she was against the far wall, whimpering.

Under the distant thud of reggaeton, the grackles' whistles from the roof, his goodwill for her fell away. She'd started this, she'd dragged the truth out of that woman and her son, she'd put El Bufo on his trail. Now she couldn't accept the truth?

El Bufo had appeared in the doorway from the shrine. "My god," he said. "My god." From a windbreaker pocket, he drew that flimsy little pistol.

"Put that away," said Felipe. "Isn't this what you wanted?"

El Bufo stared as if astonished the jaguar could speak.

The other masks were in the car.

He had to move. He moved, circling, his tail lashing with a mind of its own, past the cowering fortune teller, the rumpled bed behind its screen, the charcoal firepit with its comal, the bucket and pila, El Bufo and his gun mantled in copal smoke, the sagging armchair, the window. The window. It was daylight, and out in the street mareros with tattooed faces, masks that could never come off, stalked with switchblades in their waistbands, coke in their blood. They were preferable to this.

The rooftops. The alley was narrow enough. He could hide. He could rest and wait for dark. And if El Bufo followed, he could outrun him. *Run*, she had said, before she'd seen what he was.

He leapt to the sill. It was easy. It was easy to forget, when he suppressed it all day every day, how cordlike his muscles, how quick, how those claws instilled balance and gave purchase even on stone. Across an alley choked with rubble, a ruined terracotta roof sloped upward, dust-brown bromeliads shoving through cracks. As he leapt a second time, a clay figurine, some Nahua bat-demon, slipped from the sill onto the alley's cobbles and shattered.

El Bufo roared something after him. The gun went off like a clap of thunder.

The Funeral

A band of squat men in shiny black shoes, black suits, black fedoras, and quetzal-colored típico ties lurched and swerved up the steep hill behind Mama's hometown of Zunil as if burdened not by tubas, trumpets, trombones, tree-trunk-section tambors and tarnished bells, but rather by drunkenness and sorrow. Behind them came Mama's picture fixed to a pole, her features softened by the mists of memory and photoshop. San Pedro and his choirs waited behind her at the gates, as if she were looking back, looking down — only the old photo ruined the illusion. Behind that came Mama herself, in a black box on her brothers' shoulders. And behind them came Cristina, wailing prayers like Mama would have wanted, leading a crowd of mourners, everyone she'd ever known. The line stretched all the way back to Zunil under a salt-white sun.

The picture on its pole was the Mama-balloon on its string. When the funeral was over, they'd cut it and she'd float away. The picture would become a thing Cristina could save and have ready to wave at the next protest. But what was there to protest? Her mother hadn't been killed to make way for a silver mine because she was poor and in the way of progress. She hadn't died to make anyone richer.

Every time Cristina blinked against the afternoon sun, her artist brain tried to make sense of it, of the whole institution of death. The stony-faced angels scribing themselves in gold and cinnabar against the blood-black canvas of her eyelids were variations on the usual, other people's death scenes haunted by other people's angels. In the highlands, in the city, surrounded by the hungry, tooth-faced, otherworldly monsters of backhoes and bulldozers, by the dull roar of traffic, at the hands of soldiers and mareros and police and the victims' own family members and even priests, everybody took part in a death. Everybody was responsible.

Just a few more hours and Mama would be in her resting place. The past two days had been horrible, confusing, painful and sad, busy with planning, mourning. The days had been overfull with well-wishers, flowers, arbitrating between uncles and cousins who'd carry the casket, mediating between aunts and great aunts over who would cook what for the reception, fighting the cemetery administrator over space in the mausoleum wall near Abuelo Francisco and Mama's ancestors, scrounging and begging for the money to pay for it. But the funeral was happening. It was almost finished. Then she could go back to the ruins of her life.

The funeral procession rollicked through the switchbacks, little kids on the fringes setting firecrackers, women singing, strewing flowers, men sneaking slugs of aguardiente from clear bottles they hid in their coats when the women were looking and passed wet-eyed when they weren't, turning slowly to zombies in Mama's dubious honor. Tía Constancia had been hell-bent on preventing this, had wanted Cristina's help, her influence. Mama would have scolded them sober. Cristina had done what she could stomach. Men were men, they were macho. Though that never seemed to stop Mama. Except with Papi. He'd been drinking again, more openly, just before he disappeared; Mama hated it. Maybe that was why he left. No way to find out now, not ever. Unless Tía knew? But then, of course, she'd have to ask. She'd never mustered courage to ask in ten years. Lost knowledge. Lost time.

Zunil's cemetery had no gate, no fence, just the steep cliff dropping away to the north and west, the steep hill climbing up to the south, the mountain east, and between them a tussock maze of charred altars, marker stones, yellow and pink pastel mausolea maned in moss. The procession narrowed and slowed, stumbling among them. Frankincense and copal smoke threaded between legs and mingled among heads and then was lost to dry sky.

By the slot in the gray wall where Mama's body was to be laid, a skeleton sat folded in on itself in abandon. This was whoever had lain in Mama's slot, struggling to pay the rent, before Cristina arrived with ready money. Space, the cemetery administrator had assured her, was at a premium. People died all the time; there was only so much land. The saving grace, he had not said aloud, was that eventually the people who remembered them died too.

The mourners crammed a semicircle around the crumpled skeleton. The priest cast it a pitying glance. Someone laid a wreath of flowers round its neck. The picture of Mama propped itself against the mausoleum wall. The brass band finished a tune, let their instruments fall from their lips, lingered through prayers, then shuffle-stepped home, still drinking.

The casket was opened, Mama's body exposed, laid out on a thin flower bed under a pale wrap. She'd shrunk again. The last hands to touch Mama — Cristina's, Corísa's — laid rosaries and roses, and then the whole thing slid into the narrow hole it had been designed to fit, whereupon Tío Pancho, Tío Juan and the rest of the bearers collapsed like six inflatable skeletons with their stoppers pulled. Tía Constancia and Pilar and Majo hugged each other and wailed. Corísa hugged her homely, gainfully employed, not-disappeared husband and their two girls and wailed. Cristina hugged herself, all cried out, her face feeling like overworked dough. Lencho held Miguel Ángel in one arm, a firecracker in the other, which he lit off another boy's sparkling fuse, dropped among two others beside a heap of offerings old-burnt and new, and ran, shifting the baby to his other hip. Quick-quick-pause, three flashes, three instants' insurmountable silence. Abuela Nina sat in a splay-footed wicker chair somebody had carried up for her, folded hands shaking slightly as if for want of a needle and thread, her lined face passive as that of the wicker-winged angel who stood over her, sneering.

The priest closed the stone door behind Mama's feet. Cristina let out the longest breath of her life and sank, first to her knees, then lower, getting flecks of dead grass and dust on her black-emerald-blood-and-indigo huipil.

"You were screaming," said Tía Constancia, and Cristina found all the well-wishers surrounding her, offering water, a piece of fruit, a damp cloth for her temples, a seat in Abuela's chair, a slug of aguardiente, a glassy-eyed wink. Through the gaps between the sea of concerned human faces, those spaces like inverted figures, absences sharper and more present than the people themselves, she could see the skeleton folded neatly against the mausoleum wall, his posture so like her own it felt mocking, but no longer wearing the white headdress or the long cloths at wrists and waist, no longer prancing in that slow circle with so many of his brothers, no longer burning like the sun.

"Is it over?"

They'd been reciting something, in their voices like teeth grinding.

Copal — everything stank of copal, resinous and piney, acrid-smoke-sweet. She could still see it glowing, burning in such heaps she had no idea there was so much copal in the world. She could feel a lump of it sticky in her hands, softened by heat. There was nothing in her hands.

But it wasn't what she'd seen or heard or even smelled, it was a feeling. A long, cold, burning feeling, a disjointedness, a collision between belief and truth, a rushing back in, a dam dynamited, a wall crumbling in a flood.

The angels had surrounded her. They came up out of the light and danced in circles holding hands, their hands joining together at the ends of their rigid-robed arms, their wings joining at the tips, the pattern painfully bright. And as she'd seen in the sharp, fixed eyes of every angel, Mama's and the murderers' alike, there was absolutely nothing like ambiguity or equivocation. They were angels *and* they weren't. They were crocodilian preconquista demons, devourers of souls, they *were* souls. They were the unquenchable, ineluctable life force of each entity they haloed, haunted. They were the specter of the past coming out of the future to signify the absolute stoppage of control. They were finality, fatality itself. One thing didn't stop, another thing didn't begin. The wheel could not be slowed, could not be averted. A human being could be an artist and say they weren't an artist, say they were only a painter of copies, say they were an artist not a cook, and it might mean something for a time. Until the angel arrived. The ancients, the dancing angels told her without words, knew this *because* of their antiquity, because of all the time that had passed since they'd lived, all the things they couldn't control. They were like arrows in flight, unstoppable until they were stopped. It wasn't about mercy or the absence of mercy, justice or the absence of justice, it was about endings and going on afterward. Over and over. Forever.

This knowledge, this revelation, they poured into Cristina in cataracts of blinding light. Until it was over and the light went out.

"Please," said a man's voice. "We should give her some space, she's overwhelmed."

Cristina searched for the speaker. It was Hugo, her teacher. Near the back, half a head above the rest, broad-shouldered and dense, round and solemn and concerned. She reached for him, and the well-wishers had no choice but to make way.

"Who is that?" someone said.

"I don't know," said Tía.

"It's Hugo," said Lencho.

"Breathe shallow," said Hugo to Cristina with impossible calm, like a teacher. "Take your time." He made them all step back, even Tía. His form was steady, solid, much bigger than Mama's had been as she was shut behind the wall. Hugo took on focus as the absences lost it; she let his bulk hide her from the skeleton.

The skipping, prolonged bird-whistle screech subsided over minutes in his embrace, sufficient to allow Cristina to hear herself think *what does Hugo think is happening?* Until she could almost believe it had been part of the hallucination, it had never been real.

She released him, and half a moment later Hugo took the hint. She turned her back to him and walked bent toward the edge of the hill with its grass-tufted, grave-markered descent to the tin rooftops of Zunil. The truncated hooks of the trade road, the market road, wheeled over the hump of the next mountain in dusty overripe mango gold.

Hugo took Tía Constancia aside. They spoke. She exclaimed. She held up a hand. He stepped away.

"The reception will be at the market plaza outside San Teodoro in town, starting at sunset," Tía announced. "Everyone is welcome. There's plenty of food."

Above Zunil's market plaza drooped a patchwork roof of yellowed-white and pattern-faded linen, translucent blue plastic sheeting and white gaps of sky Cristina couldn't more than glance past. For all that she wanted to float up there like Mama's balloon, Cristina kept her eyes shaded because the sky's edges sharpened and her mind dizzied trying not to shape them into supernatural beings. Beneath the ragged roof, the shuffling motion of black heads and black-red-blue-green huipiles like bees in a hive made her feel not dizzy but stretched across time. This party, a sending-off for Mama's soul, would be repeated on Death Day in less than a month. It was a continuation of her uncles' drinking jag that had begun before dawn and also of every preparatory tête-à-tête over the last two days, at the church, at the chapel, at Tío Juan's and Great Aunt Crescencia's, at the butcher's, here at the market. It was repetition, continuation, of every Death Day celebration and murdered mother's funeral reception.

Petitioners approached her with sympathies, questions she couldn't answer, requests she couldn't fulfill, as if she wore Mama's soul like a shawl. They were careful of her, some of them, the ones who'd been present at the mausoleum wall. Not careful enough. The place was crowded, but a little space remained around her, an eddy, where she half-crouched on half a plastic chair and wrapped in a blanket shared with Corísa and Miguel Ángel, whose glowing vitality extended to both of them like an IV. She sipped hot rum-and-pineapple punch from a blue tin cup, nursing it, the alcohol fading with the steam that soothed her red eyes, the heat that soothed her throat. No one asked about the murder. No one asked about the vision or her screams. The flowers, they said, were beautiful. Calla lilies, carnations — not Mama's favorites; she liked jonquils. Depending on who was asked — evangelical or Catholic — the service had been perfect, a little long, too old-fashioned, a little improper but what could you expect? None of this was directed at Cristina, not really. For her, it was concerned looks, a squeeze of her hand. But the questions were there. The ones she'd been waiting for, the ones they'd all been asking in her head.

When will you reopen the comedor? And when she tried to deflect, *Who, then?*

In the pit of her stomach, where the punch should have warmed her, the storm surge was strengthening.

She tried to say as much to Corísa.

"You don't have to think about that now," said Corísa. *But you will,* heard Cristina. Comfortable, settled Corísa.

Tío Pancho took her empty blue tin cup, replacing it with a plastic one, steaming full, to which clung a faded upper third of a Virgin of Transition. "It's all right," he said. And *How is your "art?" Is it still selling? Have you thought about coming back to help your mother? Now that she's dead, will you take over at the comedor?* He wandered off. Unsteady. In some recess of her mind, she saw him falling off a cliff, down into a flooded, mud-choked ravine.

She met the man who'd sold Mama her chickens, all the way from the city. She met many men who had loved her mother's cooking, or possibly, in a cloud-obscured past, her mother. Now the two were indistinguishable.

Zunil's mayor, distinguished by the whiteness of his shirt and the wax in his moustache, held a woven grass fedora just beneath the silver cross over his heart and murmured words including "welcome," "condolences," and "justice," their true meaning inscrutable. *When will you be what she was? No one actually said it.*

Food was plentiful, the scents all around her, anís, vanilla, charred poblano, hot corn oil, steamed cornhusk. She'd eaten nothing.

"Come stay with us in Xela," said Corísa. "You're here, why not? We can take Miguel Ángel awhile, he's such an easy baby."

She bounced him, discouraging his little mouth from seeking her breast through thick, faded fabric. He smiled at everybody.

Cristina felt a guilty glimmer of hope she didn't dare cling to, the prospect of a burden lifted. Simultaneously a fear. She felt alone among all these people, her family, but she also felt supported. When they were gone, if they took the baby too …

"A tight squeeze for us all, but it can work. You're family. Ours are grown enough to give us breathing room. Alizz is old enough to help a little."

"What about Francisco?"

"Tío Pancho? He's staying at Crescencia's, no?"

"Lencho," corrected Cristina. "He wants to be called Francisco now. I mean just look at him, he's so mature." Gangly and handsome, fuzzed upper lip, running and cackling about fireworks with the other boys. They both laughed. Laughing at a funeral — was there anything finer?

Corísa cupped a hand around Miguel Ángel's mango-soft skull and shook her head. "Poor Lencho."

Poor Lencho. His father, then his mother lost. How much of his brother's fate was already written? How much was his own?

And the tears came again.

She'd feared she wouldn't be able to cry, then that she would run dry before it was time. Tears came and went all through the reception crowd like storms — like sicknesses, contagious. She caught them too.

When this one passed, Great Aunt Crescencia and Mama's cousin Rosaría came to squeeze the baby. Round he went, a prince of prophecy, with praise and blubbering, Corísa to Crescencia to Rosa to Cristina: North, East, South, West. He was wet, Rosa said. The nappy bag was … but they were already handling it. *Now* everyone wanted to help. Miguel Ángel was lucky, luckier than Lencho; he wouldn't remember this.

"What's the latest from Teresa? Any news?" said Rosaría.

Not since three months ago, a phone call the details of which nobody knew. Mama said only that Teresa was safe across the border in the land of plenty where her lover and the father of her children had been lost — lost forever, as far as Cristina was concerned. Corísa agreed with this in a glance, the truest and most eloquent communication that had passed between them.

There was crying again. Even Miguel Ángel took the hint.

"Can we talk about Mama, please?" Corísa said, dabbing at her eyes with a spit-up cloth. "Tell us something about her we don't know. Tell us a story."

Hearing this, voices quieted, uneasy. Cristina and Corísa were the center after all, the daughters, the bereaved. But even here, at Mama's funeral, the past was dangerous. Especially here? A chair scraped. A bottle rocket whistled in the street outside.

Crescencia leaned back on the heels of her tiny white sneakers, clinging to her daughter's arm, to gaze up through the patchwork roof as though for inspiration. For something not about war or anyone else dying. "Rosacita, you remember you had a crush on that boy but Femia wouldn't let you chase him?"

"What boy?" said Rosaría, closing her eyes. An imperceptible shake of the head, no, please God no. "Abel, the barber's son?"

"No, no. That skinny boy who rode the motorbike, who wore shirts always open, to show off the ..." Tía gestured with a crooked finger between her breasts and bellybutton, a heart, a hook? "You remember? Who served at San Anselmo's in Piedras."

Tía Constancia was there, too. "Before they caught him with ...?"

"Yes, but that was later. This time I'm talking about ... maybe that was already happening, but nobody knew. Was it Dionisio, was that his name? Dino? Diego?"

Cristina, exhausted, freed from responsibility, felt her eyes droop. But there was something coming, she could sense it in her Tía's nervous tone. A story from when Mama was a girl. She pinched her own cheek a little, surreptitiously, and tried to listen.

"Dionisio Canselma." A resigned sigh from Rosaría.

"What happened?" Corísa prompted. A yawn. "Why didn't Tía want you seeing him?"

"He was bad news," Crescencia answered. "A rake." Great Aunt Crescencia had lived to be more than eighty; she might forget, but she didn't need to care what anybody thought.

"Oh, Mama," groaned her daughter Rosaría, who wasn't young either.

Corísa rendered up her half of the plastic chair to the storyteller, so Cristina did too, as was proper. But still unsteady after her ordeal with the angels, she sank into a heap on the cold cement at Crescencia's feet. Corísa with the baby joined her, then everyone else young enough to bear it — Pilar, Majo, all the kids not busy shooting rockets.

A scar, a sagging curtain of skin the width of a finger, ran from Crescencia's knee down her shin. Her shoes were hospital shoes of a kind no longer made. She was Abuela Nina's youngest sister, Rosaría's mother, Mama's aunt. "This boy Dino," she said, settling in, "he had all the girls' hearts, even the good ones. Even Eufemia's, I think, a little. You were what, Rosa, fifteen?"

"Older than that."

"But Eufemia was younger! She wasn't old enough to understand or know any better, but she had a sixth sense for this kind of thing. For when someone she loved was in danger, when their virtue was threatened. It was like she knew what to do. Like she saw it all unfolding. Ask any of the girls who worked at the comedor. Ask Cristina. It was a gift."

Pilar and Majo were giggling, perhaps about potential threats to their own virtue. Rosaría's fingers were already laced in her lap with resignation. Corísa, who had worked at the comedor too, though only briefly, played with the baby. Cristina sat up straighter.

A sixth sense. But no, it was just how people talked at funerals.

"It happened at the crossroads right outside this very market, on a Sunday morning after church when Dino was sure to pass on his bike. Rosa had it all planned out, very secretive. She snuck out early, ran home, changed out of her church clothes and got herself up like in a magazine, lipstick and a dress from the city she'd bought without anyone knowing. She didn't need it for this boy, but you know girls that age, trying so hard it hurts to watch. Now, where that big ocote still stands, there used to be a shrine, to San Isidore and Santa María de la Cabeza. At a crossroads, can you imagine? Before that, it was a stop on the fruit company railroad. But they tore up the tracks for a highway they left unfinished for years, so Eufemia's grandfather and his brothers built the shrine. Later the army bulldozed it and paved it over for the road the way it is now — they only left the ocote because we girls took turns linking arms around it for days — but never mind. So there's Rosa, all dressed for temptation, next to a shrine built in honor of a couple sacred for continence! And along up the hill comes Dino on his bike, shirt flapping open on his little chicken-chest, straight for the crossroads where he'll have to slow to cross the tracks anyway, where he can't help but stop for her. How Eufemia found out Rosa's plan, I couldn't say. She was so careful, weren't you, Rosa?"

Rosaría nodded curtly, a spinster still, older than Mama, getting older. Here came Pancho with a cup of punch for her.

"And they were both supposed to be at Sunday school! But she knew Rosa's heart, she'd watched her watching him go by that shrine every week, with a different girl behind him every time. Maybe she pined after Dino as much as Rosa did. But she was a good cousin, a good friend. She followed Rosa to that shrine, and of course then it was obvious what was going on. So Eufemia ran back up market street until she met Juan Tuyuc leading his family's sheep home from the mountain, and she made him turn round the way he'd come. What she promised him we'll never know, because poor Juan is with the dead too. But he came, and he drove his sheep ahead of him. Dangerous, because it was August, the rains had already come and the roads were slick, and before the traffic has to slow down at the bump there's that curve. Well, Dino comes roaring along, and here comes Juan Tuyuc with his sheep around the curve, and Dino slips, and over he goes right in among the sheep! Lucky no other girl was riding behind Dino that day! He comes up shouting, covered in hoofprints, and the handlebars have cut him, right where —" Crescencia made that hook again, the same as Tía had, over her heart. "— not really hurt except his ego, but Juan's beside himself, trying to stop the bleeding. Meanwhile Rosa has spied Eufemia hiding under her shawl at the back of the flock, and she's already running to me. 'Mamacita,' she says, bursting into the kitchen in her magazine getup all mussed with tears. 'Mama, Femia has murdered Dino!'"

Everybody but Rosa and Cristina gasped and tsked and laughed and clinked their cups and murmured about what a tragedy to have lost someone so good. Rosaría twisted her fingers. Cristina felt like throwing up, but she wasn't about to subject herself to any more attention, so wrapped arms around her belly.

Mama did have a sixth sense for these things. It didn't mean she was like Cristina, had been like Cristina all her life and had never said a word because she was afraid, afraid of the risks, afraid of the stonefaced angels following everyone, never saying a word.

Beyond the cracks in the patchwork roof, sunset had peaked and was fading. Someone turned on the lights, crisscrossed strings of bare CFLs buzzing. "Don't you know those are mercury?" Mama would have said. "Poison!"

"So what happened?" pressed Pilar, casually stepping just where Pancho had placed the cup Rosa had refused, hiding it imperfectly between her sandaled feet and Crescencia's hospital-booted ones. "Was Dino dead? Did Tía Femia pursue him?" Pilar was the same age now as Rosaría in the story. Whose shrewd vision would protect her from rakes, rapists, kidnappers, coyotes, mareros, cold-eyed angels?

"No, mija," said Great Aunt Crescencia, gratified, while Pilar scooped up the punch and guiltily sipped it, fooling no one. "Femia was much too smart for that!"

But she wasn't, not then. Cristina didn't need vision to see it. Mama had been shy, jealous, controlling, cowed and awed by God and His saints. She'd also been kind, solicitous, alone and terrified, perhaps, by a power she didn't understand and couldn't express — but not wise, no, not for a long time yet.

"I made Rosa change out of her dress and burn it. For a week I kept her out of school and sent them up the hill to say rosaries and help Juan with his sheep. This boy Dino should have been mortified and slunk off to die of shame, but he got his bike fixed up and the scratches painted over and was back, showing off his —" Again, Crescencia gestured. "— In time to get a bastard boy on poor Elisa Xaac and then run off to join the army.

"Eufemia came to me later that same day, very quiet. She knew she was in trouble, or she thought so. Not to say she was a flatterer. She wanted things up front. So mature, so in control, even then! I like to think I saw who she would grow to be. A strong woman. Who saw what was right and did what was needed, even when it was hard. Who took no nonsense. A teacher. A mother. What she did was dangerous, it could have cost that boy his life. If it had, God forgive her, I don't know. But it saved my Rosa's honor. And I'm not ashamed to say I let it go. 'Go home,' I told her, 'we won't speak of this again.' And we never did. Oh, of course I spoke to Nina, but she agreed with me, and that was that."

Abuela Nina was off at Crescencia's already; Francisco had taken her, worn out after the ceremony. She'd be napping, perhaps working at her needlepoint. She'd aged beyond remembering; even, if it were possible, beyond grief. Crescencia's story was the only version left. Cristina wanted nothing more of it. So what if Mama had visions, had said nothing of them to her daughter who desperately needed to know she wasn't alone? What did it matter if Mama had done nothing with them all her life but impose her moral judgment on people who depended on her?

Gradually the market plaza got loud again, the mayor, the chicken farmer and everyone else turning back to their punch and dulces and aguardiente. Interpreting, judging the story they'd heard. These were kind people, people she loved. Cristina couldn't bear it.

"How a woman like Eufemia could raise a child to make the same mistake," Crescencia was saying to Tía Constancia, "I'll never know." And then, to Cristina and Corísa on the hard, cold floor like supplicants at her feet, "Of course I'm talking about Teresa, dear, not you."

"I know," Cristina said, to drive their attention away. She was the spinster aunt now. But Mama *had* made the same mistake. She'd made it with Papi. Or where was Papi now?

Rosaría levered herself up out of her chair, patted her bunched huípil back into shape, and picked her way to the edge of the crowd, toward the market street.

Cristina left Corísa bouncing the baby and followed her, unsteady still, desperate to be free of them, of all of it. At a gap in the canvas, she touched Rosaría's arm. "I'm sorry. How could Mama have been so hardhearted?"

"She wasn't," Rosaría said wryly. "She was jealous. She wanted Dionisio too, she just didn't dare." She was digging for something inside her shawl. "Or maybe she was wiser, I don't know. It was a long time ago. Want to have a smoke?"

There was Hugo, hulking awkward against a canvas wall. His face lit when he saw her. Someone had brought him a churro and a cup of coffee. She yearned for his calm, recoiled from what he must think of her uneducated, uncultured rural family, their drinking and gossiping talk of sex.

"I'll catch up," Cristina told her cousin. Shrugging, Rosa ducked under the canvas into the darkened market, dusk beckoning through a rectangle beyond.

Cristina brushed sugar from Hugo's sleeve. "I'm glad you came. Thank you. But you don't have to stay. I know you don't know anyone but Lencho."

"And he hates my guts."

She smiled weakly. "He doesn't — he likes you. Too much, maybe ... but I'm serious, Hugo."

"It's odd to be the one not crying," he admitted, "But I'm not here for them." Hugo put the cup down, balanced the half-eaten churro across it and tried to wipe his hands.

Cristina knew where that was leading. She regretted touching him, encouraging him. She took a step back, raised her hands. "I'm not coming back with you. I can't. They need me here." They didn't. She'd done everything, as well as anyone could have asked. She'd worked herself to the bone, they all saw it. Her stomach wasn't settled yet. Nerves. Stress.

He started to protest, to argue. She interrupted. "There's no reason for you to stay."

Feeling cold, cruel, sick, and desperate, she fled from Hugo into the street.

Smoke trailed across the evening star, and Rosaría's bulky shape moved away from the shrieking children, down the street scored with the marks of roman candles, toward the shoulder of the hill. Her cigarette burned an orange trail.

There was no shrine at the crossroads, no sign there had ever been. Only a scarred pine, its trunk layered in dingy white paint, neither beautiful nor majestic. The ghosts of train tracks in tire marks on the pavement.

"It was San Cristofero carrying the child," said Rosa, "not María de la Cabeza. Not that needing more babies was anybody's problem. They paved it over in the nineties after someone hit it with a fruit truck." She blew smoke. "Maybe on purpose."

For years, Rosa had hand-rolled her own cigarettes with the ditch tobacco the local women grew along Tío Juan's remaining land up the hot springs road, ever since Great Aunt Crescencia's family had experienced a coming-down in the world. Cristina didn't know the details. When Rosa held the cigarette out to her, Cristina accepted it, took a hit, thinking it might calm her stomach. It was herbal and harsh and made her cough until her eyes watered.

"Sorry," said Rosa, smiling, rubbing reassuringly between Cristina's shoulder blades.

"I'm okay."

Rosa's hair was still mostly dark like Mama's had been, her face round, motherly, though not a mother's. It was very hard, now that Cristina was away from everyone, not to bury her face in Rosa's shawl and cry.

"Rosa, can I ask — are you lonely? You never — but it wasn't because of what happened with —"

She burst out laughing. "Of course not, Colocha! I never wanted a man, I just didn't know it then. It's not like what your mother did was a wake up call! But it didn't hurt. I was a very confused young woman. It took years before I made up my mind, and more for anyone else to accept it. Femia maybe last of all."

"Do you ever ... regret not trying it?"

"What, men? Not even a little! But why? You're not considering it, Colocha! Or is there something you want to tell me?"

If Mama ever had visions like Cristina, Rosaría, it was clear, had not. There was no point in confessing to them now, bursting out about how Mama was a mylar balloon on a broken string and angels were hovering everywhere waiting to make her one of them. But that wasn't the kind of secret she was asking for, Cristina realized. Not the jaguar's kind of secret, but Aníbal's. The kind clothes could hide.

"Oh! Rosa, no — it's not that. It's nothing," she blurted, embarrassed, confused. But that wasn't enough, it was standoffish, cold. Aníbal was the furthest thing from a spinster. That didn't mean Rosa was like her. Cristina wasn't even sure that's what they were talking about. "I mean ... I doubt I'll get married. I'm twenty-seven. It's not like I don't get catcalled in the street, but I haven't ..."

She was glad of the dark to hide the heat in her cheeks. But it must not have been dark enough, or she was just that easy to read. Rosaría's teeth shone around the cigarette. "Oh, you haven't?"

She had, once, with a boy from the market she hadn't been sure of — no Dionisio, but something like. He'd turned out all right, awkward, not what she'd expected. She hadn't known what she'd expected — maybe something not so messy. It had been an act of rebellion, of searching for herself. She'd never tried it again — at least, not yet — but not because she'd learned any great secret about herself.

"You don't want to talk about it, don't! Does it look like it matters to me?"

"But it does," said Cristina, flustered. This was not how she'd meant this conversation to go. How did she manage to feel so alone among all these people who loved her?

A streetlight clicked on, revealing the eyes of a pariah cat watching them from a doorstep.

"After the thing with Dionisio," Rosa said, "I barely spoke to your mother for months. Longer. We never really made up until after she married your father. It was stupid. He wouldn't have gone with either of us, we came from the wrong kind of family, thank God. We were both playing the wrong game. My mother tries to make her out like some old soul. That's what people do — make the dead into saints. I'm sorry, dear, I don't mean to bad-mouth her. Her intentions were good. You know she worked hard for you. But she didn't have anything figured out. Any more than the rest of us."

Cristina wasn't so sure. Rosa seemed content in who she was, immune to her mother's manipulations in a way Cristina had never been, and she was glad of that. But there was too much she didn't understand. "They all expect me to be like her."

"No, they don't. Crescencia, even Constancia? Maybe. But they're wrong. You think anybody expects me to be like my mother? You don't want to take over the comedor, don't. Take it from me. Romance, marriage, responsibility, whatever: if you don't live up to people's expectations, they're disappointed, and that hurts. But they don't stop loving you. Not the people that matter."

Cristina hugged her and tried not to think there was more to the story than even Rosaría knew.

The market street was a riot of fireworks spinning, spitting, ascending ten or twenty feet, then concussing echo on echo, first from the walls, then the roofs, the hills, the volcano, the sky. Cristina caught Francisco's eye as she ducked past.

Hugo was gone from his corner. The courtyard crowd had congealed; the vats of punch were empty, but the clear little bottles of aguardiente proliferated out of breast pockets, the smiling young woman on the label willfully oblivious to her deleterious effect on the men in her life. Next would come the cigars. Later, much later, there might be dice, gambling; by then most of the women would have gone to bed. Not Rosa.

The baby was no longer with Corísa; a man she didn't know held him, smiling, in a knot of strangers. She started toward them, then stopped, recognizing the pattern of Tía Constancia's head-scarf. It was all right. Miguel Ángel was safe, laughing. Aside from Papi, Teresa, and Mama, her whole family was in this courtyard or close by. Half the people in Zunil were related to her somehow. The other half had known her since she was born. They'd be disappointed. They'd survive. Mama hadn't been the first Yochi to die.

Cristina walked quickly to the corner and ducked through the side door into what had once been Abuela Nina's house, now Constancia's. Mama's room, like Cristina's room in the house in the city, only older, hadn't been Mama's in ages. Some of the things in it had been Mama's, according to Tía: one of the beds, one of the quinceañera dresses in the wardrobe, a set of bingo cards in a drawer, a wooden Santa Lucia with a hand held out for a candle, the paint flaked away with the wax so the hand was a stump. None of it correlated with the Mama she knew. Cristina collected her things, leaving the baby bag but taking her satchel. Impulsively, irrationally, she took the stub of a pencil that could have been anyone's, and a photo in a tarnished brass frame of a girl who looked a little like Teresa. She thought about taking the knob of the wardrobe, worn like Santa Lucia's hand, shiny like a tumbled stone. Mama had touched it, five generations of their family had touched it. There was a generation who needed to touch it now, to whom it would mean as little as it would to Cristina as soon as she got it out of this room. It wasn't like she wasn't coming back.

She needed to get away. That was all she knew. For that, she needed money for the bus and for food. There were paintings of hers in this house she could sell, but they were bulky, they would slow her down, no one would buy them. And she still had to run the gauntlet of the street to the bus stop. She could take some piece of jewelry of Mama's. Tía Constancia would regale her with the story of each earring and pendant, which suitor had offered it in exchange for which favor, how Mama had accepted it, whether rudely or gracefully, whether she forgave when forgiveness was called for, whether the gift enticed her to declare war or truce. But none of this would emerge until the late bright of morning, after the enormous breakfast, after yet another round of petitioners and tears.

In the water-and-clay-smelling kitchen, a bowl of change glinted in the flare of the fireworks from outside. All else was in shadow, but Cristina knew by heart the bowl's hand-painted pattern, the phases of the moon. If she scooped out every coin, there'd be a sun in the bottom.

Then the room filled with light. Lencho stood by the sink, ash burns on his fingers, digging in a drawer for more matches. The hairs on his upper lip were ridiculous. A thirteen-year-old man who knew how to work without complaining, who knew how to talk to people — even people his own age, of the opposite sex — who took the bus two hours to school sometimes by himself. With no father, no mother, he'd gone from four surrogate mothers down to three, one of whom bothered only when convenient. Now another was about to abandon him.

For a while.

She hugged him, squeezing while he squirmed. "Come with me?" she asked, sincerely if not seriously.

"Where?"

"To Comalapa."

He didn't ask. He didn't need to. "Hugo left. Like an hour ago. He looked mad."

He wriggled free, dug a blackened hand in a pocket, came up with a coin. A smirk as he tossed it in the bowl. "The guy's kind of a pushover." He wasn't going to try to stop her.

Already, she felt him falling away from her. No longer her responsibility. She felt giddy, guilty. "He doesn't understand kids. Be nice to him."

"I'm not a kid."

"I know you're not, Francisco, but he doesn't."

"You're going now?"

"The last bus leaves in twenty minutes."

"But it isn't over! The fireworks are just getting started. And later —"

"I don't want to know," said Cristina. Mama's death hadn't seemed to touch him. But that was wrong. Everybody's grief was different. "Stay. You'll have to go with Corísa — she's taking your brother for awhile — or else go home with Tía." She took a breath, trying not to let Mama's voice into her own. "I'd better not hear you've been gambling. Or drinking."

"Okay, okay." A firework exploded outside, rattling dishes. Francisco's sneakers squeaked on the linoleum and he was gone.

She stared into the change bowl, preparing herself to steal from it as though for a plunge into the cold volcano lake before sunset in the valley far from here, far from Comalapa, something she hadn't done since she wasn't much older than Lencho. She didn't know why she thought of it now. The water taxis would be moored for the night, the little girls with their swatches of bright cloth would be scampering among the restaurants along the pier below the apartment room she'd shared with Nati. Maybe a gaggle of foreigners would be paddling their kayaks desperately toward shore as the capricious night wind, Xocomil — the sin collector — stirred the once-glassy surface into clawlike waves.

The ayudante wore a backwards baseball cap embroidered with a fantastic northern cat-monster, its teeth bared above the brim, and a faded red t-shirt with a skull silkscreened at such an angle that the boy's head emerged from an eye socket. But he wasn't a marero, wasn't a killer. Killers, she presumed, were in demand; they didn't have to work real jobs.

The bus was full, though not to bursting, with people heading into Xela from distant villages to work night jobs, people coming from Retalhuleu to visit family, maybe to visit their dead, people just passing through, like Cristina. Maybe some of them were going north. Teresa had come this way, most likely. But she'd had money, more than enough, at least at this point in her journey. Getting as far as Huehue was easy; it was there people started looking for coyotes, or so Cristina had heard. She picked her way almost to the back, though there were open seats closer, to buy time to figure out how to approach the ayudante before he came asking for the fare. Regulars, of course, could ride on credit; if this were the bus from the lake to the city, or even from the lake to Comalapa, she might have been able to get by on a promise. She had almost enough to get as far as the bus station in Xela, where she might find a driver or an ayudante she knew. Even if she couldn't convince him to take her that far, she could get off in the park and walk. Xela wasn't the city. In the city she'd never have dared such a thing, not at night. Here, she could brave it. Or, if she couldn't, there was always Corísa's.

Except then she'd have to explain why she hadn't wanted to stay at Constancia's, why she'd taken a bus, why she wasn't coming to breakfast tomorrow back in Zunil. She'd almost rather sleep on a bench in the park.

He was coming. Nobody else had gotten on. He picked his way the same as she had though with less hurry, shimmying sideways between hips, using the luggage racks for support on the turns, which were constant.

She could make up some story. *My mother was murdered. She was murdered by the mining company for trying to protect our land. I have to get to her funeral.*

She dug out her sketchbook, stabbed herself on the spiral getting the pencil out, and drew furiously, elbow steadied against the top of the seat in front of her, the line jumping like a seismograph every few inches nevertheless.

"Where to?" said the ayudante, not curtly, just doing his job.

She cleared her throat. "Comalapa," she said, and passed him the sketchpad.

He looked at it blankly at first, saying nothing; the bus's running lights were dim, and the lines were thin, the best she could manage in a few seconds. He drew a flashlight from his belt and clicked it on.

It was an attempt at a design for a tribal tattoo, a shot in the dark, something she thought he might like based on the skull shirt and the hat — not Saint Death (that would be incredibly stupid if he actually was in a gang), just a woman's face she'd meant to be the Virgin's if she'd had more time. A face ribbed in bones and a few hints of geometric design. Worth the price of a two-hour bus ride? She doubted it.

The ayudante looked from the sketch to Cristina. He should be quoting her a price. Instead he just looked.

The sketchpad slipped from his hands back into hers, and he retreated up the aisle.

Squinting in the dimness, she looked for guns, angels, blood, but it was the same sketch she'd handed him. She could flesh out the face, not the Virgin's, but another woman's, even younger. But the bus's motion made her stomach clench and quiver and shove into the back of her throat, so she leaned back, squeezing her shoulders between those of the men on either side of her, and failed to sleep.

Instead she watched past them: her small, lonely reflection in the window and the lights of the valley turning somersaults with the switchbacks.

Nobody threw her off in Xela after the rest of the bus emptied past her. It filled again slowly, the ayudante shouting the names of the big towns on the way in one long roll like a livestock auctioneer. "Toto Toto Santa Cruz Chichi Chimal! Chimal Chimal Chimal!" A woman got on with chuchitos in a wicker basket. A man got on with cigarettes and chicle, a woman with fruit juice. Cristina slid over to the window and closed her eyes.

She opened them to the ayudante poking her with his flashlight. "Give it to me," he said.

She couldn't read him. "It isn't finished. If you wait I can —"

He just held out a hand.

She tore the sheet loose from the spiral, checking first to make sure there was nothing incriminating on the reverse.

When they stopped in Totonicapán, she saw him out on the side of the road setting fire to it with a lighter.

Comalapa was as she remembered. It had been years. Getting off the bus felt like stepping into a museum of herself after the curators had gone home. Murals covered almost every wall, though she glimpsed the colors now only in a half-moon splash of streetlight or headlight. It was, in a way, the place where she'd first been herself, away from Mama, away from responsibility. Pathetic, really: she'd lived here only six weeks. She felt jealous of Rosa having had a whole life to grow away from her mistakes.

Comalapa wasn't beautiful, not like the lake or even Zunil. The murals were beautiful and horrific. All the walls of Comalapa were fields, jungles, lakes, volcanoes, animals, people, blood, lava, pyroclastic mudflows, war, the underworld, the dead, the dying. They rewrote history, some of them. The rain of fire that destroyed Antigua the first time and drove the colonizers back to Kaminal had been the work of Maya sorcerers. The artists of Comalapa had been born from stalks of maize, like the first humans. Gaspar Ilóm lived on as the second coming of Tecún Uman, Kukulcan, Christ. But the murals had come too late.

The night here was colder than in Zunil, windier though no higher because Comalapa nestled in no mountain's arm. In the central park, men slept on benches, blanketed in wind thinly threaded with the scent of jasmine and night-blooming cactus. Bent trees born from seeds sewn by the conquerors raised arms scarred with the wounds of nails, the scars painted over in white, the paint splitting to reveal the scars. Outside the town, the hills — scored long and low like teeth beyond the rooftops — did the same with the scars of the earthquake. At the top of the main street, the church on its stepped platform had once been a temple, then a ruin, just a hill, now a temple again.

Hugo's house was at the east end of town, a long walk from the highway, near the cliff. It was a row house like Mama's, but older, smaller, with no guards or barbed wire, more like the house in Zunil. She leaned against its yellow walls, striking in that they were unadorned. She closed her eyes and didn't open them for a long time.

Across the narrow street, the walls that housed the gallery and the school were covered in the now-shadowed faces of artists. Cristina's was among them somewhere. She could get in through the metal security doors around back, if nobody'd fixed them, a stick through the gap to push up the latch. She could sleep in one of the hammocks strung around the courtyard, cold, but there would be blankets, and this way she wouldn't have to knock. She wished for Miguel Ángel's little body against her belly.

Picking her way through gravel and chicken-scratched weeds, she found a new lock. She could feel its ridged sides when she reached up through the gap. High, thready clouds tumbled over the hills. Zunil was that way, where there'd been a warm bed, if not her own. But no bed was her own.

She hugged herself upright and back across the empty street to Hugo's door.

He opened it after minutes during which she considered running back down to the central park to sleep huddled with the men on the benches. The light behind him made him huge. "Cristina?"

He was warm, but stiff.

Comalapa/The Ravine

Felipe spent that night curled on the rooftop, his tail over his nose, not cold, but hungry. The laughter from the streets of Zone Three, punctuated by the rare firecracker and more frequent gunfire, made him fantasize about hunting. Stalking the rooftops like so many seemed to hunt, El Bufo among them. But he couldn't; he didn't have the skills or the bloodthirst. Just the instinct, ghostly because unindulged. He could kill a chicken, maybe. Not a dog. He could fantasize about leaping onto El Bufo's shoulders from behind, breaking his spine.

Early in the night he heard them calling, El Bufo and the fortune teller, Lupita.

"Come back to us, please! I'm sorry you frightened me!" It sounded like she was crying.

"You can't get away from me! No one gets away! Believe it!" El Bufo was angry the way a storm is angry, drunk with rage and the rest of that bottle of rum from under her bed.

After their calls faded and they went back, presumably, to Lupita's — to fuck and to sleep while the night passed overhead like a great migration of shadow-bellied serpents — Felipe began to believe it. El Bufo couldn't be escaped.

He could hide up here a long time, if he had to. How hard could it be to kill a chicken? Or he could follow those delicious smells of chiles cooking in turkey fat to a courtyard somewhere nearby, feign inhumanness long enough to terrify away the inhabitants — or would they see him as human, pity him, and feed him?

But eventually he'd have to go back to Lupita's: to his clothes, his phone, his keys. Baby. The broken mask and the face that went with it were gone, but there were others.

It wasn't like he hadn't lurked on rooftops. When he first got the apartment with Aníbal and Luz — sometimes he only had to watch them together, circling to accommodate each other in the tiny kitchen, expecting him to adapt, requiring him, for the sake of not being alone, to pretend he'd adapted. Sometimes he couldn't. So he shimmied out through the pivot window of his room, scraping his belly on the latch, then scaled the sick vines and pitted steel beams of the ventilation shaft up and out. The pattern of his fur was perfect for tree shadows, less so for the angles and planes of the great anonymous city. He sought out trees. In the archaeological park, among the last crumbling fragments of ancient Kaminal, there were ancient, beautiful trees. Twelve feet of chain-link and barb wire surrounding the site couldn't stop him. What stopped him was everything in between. The zoo had trees; the zoo was closer, but he couldn't go to the zoo. So he'd wind up in the crown of a locust tree at one of the intersections along Montúfar, watching traffic, drug deals, night workers, perhaps a pair of lovers under a streetlight. It made him feel secret, powerless, and alone. The city kept his attention taut as a guitar string resonating to every truck or motorcycle that passed, every muffled conversation in a doorway, every siren, every plane overhead, every dog howl. Eventually he'd slink back to his room, overwrought.

Late in the long, damp, hungry night, he stalked to the roof of the Paradise. Head on paws he watched Baby waiting in the street below, unstolen. The masks — even the jaguar mask — were in her trunk; the dew-beaded windows enclosing that safe space where music soothing to his every mood — even this one — could be had from the speakers in digital hi-def at a touch of a button. Out of reach.

Dawn arrived with doves and roosters, and someone came around the corner, unlocked and half-unrolled the tienda's rusted, scarred, graffitied grate, got a warm orange soda, then leaned on one foot against the wall.

"Kid," said Felipe, keeping low as only a jaguar can at the corner of the roof. "Hey, kid. No, don't look, you can't see me. But it's me — that's my car, the Corolla. Remember?"

"You don't sound like him."

"I've been up all night. I've got a cold. Wait, he told me your name. Toby, right?"

"Everybody knows my name."

Felipe felt the growl coming up in his throat and swallowed it. "I paid you. You owe me."

"For keeping the car safe. It's still there."

"You weren't even here."

"You got lucky. Overnight costs extra."

"You talk back like this with him?"

"No."

"Fine. Whatever. Money well spent. Thank you. Now I need a favor, Toby. You know the fortune teller's? I left my clothes there, on the floor under the window. Can you get them? You can climb in the window." There was only the one window.

The kid slugged at his orange soda.

"I'll pay you. Afterward."

"I want to see you."

"What?"

"I'll get your things, but you have to let me see you."

This kid knew too.

"Fine," said Felipe. "Just get me my clothes first, please? Now."

The kid was gone and back again in under a minute. El Bufo, Lupita, Cristina Ramos, seventy people on a bus in Chichicastenango, and now some little hustler kid from El Gallito. What did it even matter? Felipe half-leapt, half-scrambled headfirst into another alley halfway down the block, paws onto gravel and broken glass. He peeked around the corner until he saw the kid coming, then stepped out on two legs into the empty street and walked to meet him, naked, calmly as he knew how.

The kid stopped a few feet from him, hugging the bundle of clothes to his chest. He looked disappointed. "Are you ... him?"

"Who else would I be?"

"I thought —"

It worked without the mask. It always had. The mask was about confidence. Believing his own bullshit. It always had been.

The kid bug-eyed him a minute, then seemed to shrug it off. He cracked a grin. "So what happened? That old witch magic you out of your clothes?"

"Shut up." Felipe lunged for the bundle. The kid let him have it, and Felipe ducked under the security gate into the store to get dressed, quickly identifying the lumps of his wallet, his keys, the two broken halves of the conquistador mask ... no phone.

A pull-chain CFL bulb ratcheted to life overhead. El Bufo sat on a stool in the cash register cage, sneering around a toothbrush, thick lips flecked with toothpaste like rabies froth. On the counter in front of him lay Felipe's phone, a pack of cigaritos and the gun.

The kid, Toby, pulled the security gate closed from outside with a clatter. "Sorry, man." Felipe could almost hear him counting his bribe.

El Bufo tossed something to the floor at Felipe's feet: a triple-pack of cupcakes featuring a deranged cartoon panda. "Put your fucking pants on and have some breakfast. Big day ahead of us.

Only place you can get those in Zone Three, by the way. Toby's favorite."

The cupcakes were chalky, sickeningly sweet; he washed them down with a coke from a crate on the floor, trembling from the sugar rush or from rage.

"You're paying for those," El Bufo said mildly. "You going to try to run away again? Or can we do this the easy way for once."

"Why wouldn't I run?" said Felipe, searching shelves of masa and canned lard and dried beans and rice and spaghetti and pork rinds for the door El Bufo must have come in by. From the alley behind Lupita's.

El Bufo spread his hands. "Because you want to do the right thing? Because you've seen me in my native habitat, you know who I really am. A good man. Not honest. But my heart's in the right place. You see that, right? If you'd prefer I can handcuff you, take back your keys and throw you in the trunk. That's how important you are to me, Félix. Four, you owe me."

Felipe gave him ten. El Bufo opened the register and counted the change like he'd been doing it every day of his life. The gun sat on the counter between them, but Felipe wasn't stupid enough to try. El Bufo didn't want to shoot him. The gun was there so he didn't have to.

What had happened at Lupita's had happened because he'd taken off the mask.

El Bufo closed the register, took the gun, the phone, the cigaritos, and came around and banged on the gate.

It slid open on Toby, grinning. He thrust out an open palm, then switched to a peace sign when Felipe brushed past him to dig the jaguar mask out of the trunk.

"So who the fuck is this, then?" said El Bufo when they were sitting in the car again.

In the mirror, a brown-eyed, statuesque-nosed, handsome face. Solid, kind. He'd been proud of it once, the face his parents would have given him if they hadn't given him whiskers and agate eyes that compressed to slits at noon. El Bufo should not be seeing this face. But the other was gone, maybe forever.

"Me," he said. "It's me." He started the car.

Toby lingered on the corner, big-eyed like any barrio kid meeting a hero for the first time. Felipe gunned it past him.

"Don't you want to know where we're going?"

"Can I have my phone back, please?" El Bufo was fiddling with it, trying to break in. He made a mental note to change the passcode. "I need music."

Too late. Somehow, he'd cracked it. Scrolling through albums, El Bufo zeroed in on Dub Side of the Moon. A heartbeat led into a dripping conga rhythm. Then there were coughs, bubbling bong rips, laughter, screams, and the opening bass riff of "Breathe."

"We're going to go talk to the men David Antonellis hired to kill him."

An enormous bowl of hot oatmeal with fruit, seeds, honey and cardamom: she ate shivering with the highland chill, wrapped in a coarse blanket from Hugo's guest room, at the far end of the same table where his students sat framed hazy-bright against a wall papered with sketches, watercolors, photos. She'd been the first awake, she and the rooster, then the curator, then the cook. It surprised her. She knew the routine, or she should have.

The students spilled into the room rubbing sleep from their eyes, babbling words she understood individually but whose significance she could not fathom. Chicks scurried after them in from the courtyard, pecking at the floor. Cristina kept her head down, her hair a curtain. She knew better than to try to insinuate herself into their giddy, too-temporary bonding; she remembered having been in their place, and it exhausted her. Six years. She looked over their heads at the work on the walls and tried to see promise in it.

Some of it was beautiful, some ugly — some of it deliberately, she didn't doubt. Hugo encouraged that. Nowhere could she detect a glibness or a pleasant lie. Here, an artist painted for themself or not at all. Then they left and found out the truth: none of them would become what Hugo was.

He appeared when they had cleared the plates and cleaned the kitchen, the same as ever in clothes worn but well cared-for: embroidered vest, wool slacks, and battered, handmade shoes. Addressing his students, but speaking to Cristina alone, he assigned tasks for the day.

"Be observant," he told them. "Be back for lunch with the subject you want to work on next. No one is to venture east of town into the hills, understand? Don't speak to any of the workmen or police. If you have to, be polite."

He carried a newspaper under his arm. She remembered the last one, with the news of Mama's murder. Why should there be police in the hills? She didn't want to know what had changed in the world; it could only be for the worse.

His students scattered. The paper remained under his arm. Was it there as a deterrent, to keep her from hugging him the way she had last night, the way he'd hugged her in the cemetery?

"What are you doing here, Cristina?"

What was happening between them? She didn't like it. "You said —"

"I did. And you're welcome. But when I asked, you said no. And now you're here. I need to know what you're expecting. Do you want me to be your teacher again, though I know you don't need it? Are you here to be told what to do?"

"No!" Was she? With her belly full of oatmeal, a blanket around her, she had only just begun to feel warm again.

Gingerly, as if she were a porcelain teacup or a very small child, Hugo took Cristina's elbow.

He led her next door to the office for two indestructible clay mugs of coffee the color of old charcoal and the taste of engine grease and fertile earth. Cristina had a sip and left hers on a desk. In the gallery, a huge, resin cast of an ancient lord — flowered scepter, feathered mantle, fanged mask — crowded to the high, angled ceiling three times larger than life. Surrounding him amid glass and white hung Hugo's stark scenes of the starkly everyday. Hands around the handles of tools, faces like those of the men she'd sat next to on the bus, bared teeth, too-open eyes, angry color: the art that kept this place open and put locks on the doors. It sold to unfathomably elite foreigners and the kind of rich ladinos you never saw in the street — not even behind black-tinted windows of spotless black SUVs. Not the kind who hired killers but the kind who didn't need to.

"I shouldn't need to tell you what to do." His voice echoed, and the echoes broke its gentleness.

He avoided this room as a matter of course. He wasn't a man who looked back. He worked on a piece until it was finished, then started another, though he understood his process wasn't everyone's. He'd learned from the man who'd made Comalapa into the tiny, muraled haven for independent vision it had become, dead now, whose own art school was still in operation on the other side of town. Hugo did not speak of this man.

They were here, now, she thought, so she could be reminded of this. And, possibly, so she could appreciate this fake-ancient monolith someone — not Hugo, probably the curator or his investors — had chosen as the school's centerpiece.

He sipped his coffee. "The guest room is yours. You'll be expected to do your part washing, shopping, feeding the birds. Take what materials you need. You'll paint what it occurs to you to paint, *as long as it's honest.* Insofar as you're able, you'll refrain from doubt or second-guessing. You don't have to prove it — you don't have to show anyone. Just do the work."

He was staring. She imagined him trying different framings and perspectives, deciding what wild hyperbole to apply in order to best make his point, to translate her into the brutal, vivid, unambiguous world of his art.

She wasn't naive enough to think it was how he actually saw the world.

After a moment, Hugo seemed to realize where he was. He headed for the gallery's main entrance, through the anteroom plastered with flyers for old showings scarred with thumbtacks and their rust. The door creaked. He left it open on the cold morning, dew covering half the street where the light had yet to touch.

Felipe parked by a hole in the fence at the edge of the ravine. El Bufo made him aim Baby back the way they'd come, toward where rutted dust turned back to pitted pavement. "Now it's the getaway car."

Then he made Felipe sit in the car listening to Dub Side — loud — while he got out and made a call. It was eerily like the first time they'd met. Felipe knew who he was calling, too. El Bufo's jaw clenched and unclenched. He paced, the wind rippling the cheap windbreaker. Gilberto did not pick up. Felipe quietly rolled down the window.

"Found the killers. Not that you care. Not much point asking for backup now. I couldn't trust whoever showed up not to shoot me in the back. Hope you're having a good time squandering all that influence and power I got you. Asshole."

He got back in the car. Felipe hastily rolled the window back up. El Bufo observed this without comment, then picked Felipe's phone out of the ashtray, unplugging it from the stereo. The music cut off.

"Give me the keys."

"Give me my phone."

"Take it."

El Bufo tossed it over the gearshift; Felipe fumbled, caught it.

The screen was on, playing a streaming video. A tree trunk jerked as someone bumped a camera. Leaves rustled, pixilated, froze, unfroze. Shitty signal. This must be the only place in Zone Three with service. The tail and hindquarters of a jaguar moved into view, followed by its shoulders, its forepaws, its teeth, and the bloody hulk of a fat brown creature as big as the jaguar itself: a deer, a peccary. The crackle and rip of claws on trunk. Buffering. Slowly, forcefully, tendons bunching in the jaguar's neck and shoulders, the trunk shuddering, digitized leaves quaking, the jaguar dragged the bloody weight out of the top of the frame.

"Get your other faces," said El Bufo. "All of them. You don't go into El Gallito half-cocked, understand? I was born here, trust me." This time Felipe registered the metal shank he slid from his sleeve to disengage the lock on the glove box: one smooth motion. He opened it, grunted at the absence of the revolver, shut it.

The calendars on the dashboard read Seven Water, San Bruno's Day. Not even a real saint. What would Lupita say? Her hands dripping dried corn and crystals. Nothing he could hope to reproduce, except the result: none of it meant anything. She'd said to run, and he had run, and El Bufo had caught him.

He'd ripped all the calendars off the dashboard and was balling them up when he remembered they served the secondary purpose of hiding Baby's very expensive stereo. Sheepishly, he smoothed them and put them back.

He popped the trunk, got out his rasta-colored backpack and stuffed into it hoodie, sunglasses, headphones, phone. The tire jack wouldn't fit; he wouldn't use it anyway.

El Bufo was at his shoulder, waiting to steal his secrets. Masks. Not the caiman — the Garífuna would stick out in the shantytown almost as badly as the Argentine, if the Argentine wasn't gone forever. In the jaguar mask, he could blend. El Bufo already had that secret. What were a thousand destitute and discarded shanty-dwellers on top of that? And what other option was there?

The skull. He drew it out, like pulling a bad tooth, from its hiding place under the spare tire. It was black, with a yellow smile and yellow eyes and across its brow a string of pearls — what he assumed the mask's sculptor had intended as pearls, not sugar.

He'd bought it in Antigua on Saints' Eve, in the craft market, the warren occupying the centuries-ruined cloisters of Santa María de Merced. It was only months since Luz had gone away to school, and he wanted to forget her. The mask was going to help him do it. He'd wanted it to be an actual mask, a mask everyone could see and know wasn't his real face. It hadn't worked. In the skull mask, he was someone he didn't like. Someone who danced with a violence that was exhilarating for awhile and then lost his way, who drank until he couldn't dance, who said things to women, who touched women and didn't care if it scared them. After his first night with the skull mask, he woke in the dawn still wearing it, lying half in the ruined church's cold shadow, half in sun, his clothes sticky, alone.

He had, on occasion, worn it again, when he felt like he had to remind himself. He stuffed the skull mask in the backpack and closed the trunk.

Through a jagged archway cut into a chain-link fence feathered in windblown plastic, a dust path beaten harder than concrete zigzagged a drunken seam down into a shanty city that seemed more the work of ants than people. Music thundered distant here as everywhere — heavy bass of the kind his hips were incapable of resisting even now. And the river thundered, gorged with toxic trash but hungry, arms of mist reaching into hollows as if seeking the tenacious root that, dislodged, would bring the whole precarious thing collapsing down. The wind smelled of chiltepes and fermented urine.

"The keys," said El Bufo.

Felipe held onto them, jangling them in his fingers, considering tossing them over the fence just to keep El Bufo from even thinking about getting behind Baby's wheel.

But El Bufo would get what he wanted; he always did.

"Here's how this works. You do what I say. If we get out of here with one of those stupid bastards in tow, alive so I can use him as a bargaining chip, I'll call my friend at Pavoncito, your friend gets released, and we're even. You can walk away. If that's what you want."

"Are you kidding?"

El Bufo kicked at the broken neck of a bottle. It skittered over the edge, raising dust. "Maybe. Or maybe, when you see what it's like down there, you'll learn something. You'll see I do what I do for a reason. Maybe, just maybe, you'll want to help me. We'll see. Or — you could take your keys and your phone and get in your piece of shit car and leave. Nobody's stopping you. But I guarantee you'll never see your friend again."

A sick, falling feeling in Felipe's stomach. Pavoncito prison. If Aníbal was already there, and El Bufo knew it ... But he could be bluffing. He was always bluffing. "You already called to get her released. I stood there while you did it. You said it would take time."

"That was bullshit. This isn't. This is fucking life and death. Killers are down there right now. They're not expecting us — got some bad news last night, found out they killed the wrong man, they're not getting paid. Probably sleeping it off. Do this right, we can take them by surprise. Do it wrong ..."

Felipe tried hard to believe it. How else could he do this?

He pictured Aníbal getting released. There was Luz in red lipstick, eyes running black down her cheeks. And here came Aníbal out of the ruinous, barbwire gate in blue hospital pants, a dirty t-shirt, her hair shaggy, her cheeks as smooth as ever except for the long, smashed-avocado bruises. Limping. Barefoot. Trailing blood from her right heel. They embraced. They kissed.

The sick feeling did not go away.

Felipe double-checked the doors were locked, patted Baby's fender goodbye and handed over the keys. Then he looked over the edge of the ravine, past rattling brown weeds, down and down into the foul mist that enveloped the shanty city. "How are we supposed find them in all this?"

"We work together. You do what you do best; keep out of sight. Place has a short memory — high mortality rate. But they remember me. I don't let them forget. I'll ask around. Soon as they find out what I want, somebody's going to rat me out. You follow the rat. Then you follow whoever they talk to. Something to understand about this place: it's a web. Spiders at the center pull the threads and everybody dances. Of course, there's bigger spiders." El Bufo jerked a thumb past the elevated highway to the city. Squinting, Felipe could make out the twin ancient-futuristic silhouettes of the Kaminal of Tomorrow Mall and Hotel, Atlantean colossi in the smog. "We missed our chance to squash them. Take what we can get." He leaned close, ashes on his breath. "This is a good thing we're doing. Understand? It wasn't their idea. Maybe they didn't have a choice. That doesn't matter. They're killers and they always will be. And if nobody stops them, they'll take after the men who made them and make more. We can't stop the cycle. But we can stop them, keep them from rising up the ranks. It's worth the risk. Because if we do, they won't have a chance to do any more harm to the people here. Like Toby. Or Lupita. Get it?"

She'd been twenty-one; she'd spent four years going crazy watching her friends start university or get married or both while she couldn't or didn't want to or know how. Here in Comalapa, it was Hugo who showed Cristina she had visions within her — not the kind Hugo meant. Her "eye," Hugo taught her, was no different from anybody else's. What set her apart wasn't what she saw, but what she did with it.

When the brief weeks of art school were over, she went home to Mama and resumed her routine, cleaning house, washing, delivering her sisters to school, collecting them again, watching them, inspecting chickens, plucking chickens, dismantling chickens, frying chickens, teaching Mama's comedor girls and her sisters how to clean house and watch and wash children and fry chickens. She tried to translate this domestic life through her artist's eye into something that was her own, but the painted-over canvases stacked in her room went to market, failed to sell, came back, gathered dust. She wiped them clean and painted over them, painting over herself, covering over the flaws of the past with the flaws of the new. Her work was changing, improving perhaps incrementally, but without the past to compare it to, what could she do but take it on faith? Papi had been able to afford art supplies. Then Papi was gone, so she started buying cheaper paints, then thinning them with water until the old images appeared through the new like the lake bottom through the water's surface, mingling with the clouded sky. She had trouble distinguishing between them.

Her friends Diego and Natalia — fellow students of Hugo's — tried to support her.

"Nobody pays for the truth," said Diego, bitterly at first, because like Cristina he had painted the truth and it didn't sell. Then he started painting like Natalia. Diego had both his parents. They had money.

"It's tradition," said Nati, who'd grown up at the lake selling foreigners the scarves her mother and father and grandfather wove. They expected a return on their investment. "It's beautiful," she said. And it sold.

Money meant more and better paint, which meant painting over those bad memories. This was what everyone did, which was why nobody paid for truth. It was easy. It raised no doubts whether she was "improving." When she came home with money, Mama met her with shocked praise. "Keep this up," she threatened, "we might have to learn to do without you."

"Don't be silly, Mama," said Cristina.

But it gave her an income like she'd never had, which let her let herself travel a little. Once Corísa was out of school, Cristina moved out of Mama's house to a room she and Nati rented from Nati's brother in one of the big towns on the lake, sending money home, visiting home once in awhile to fill in at the comedor or take Lencho for a few days or a week or more when Teresa disappeared and Mama couldn't. For the first months the rush of freedom was overwhelming; for awhile it was enough. She'd indulge a whim, get off the bus at the crossroads above the lake and get on a different bus just to see where it went. She drank pineapple and banana smoothies and ate pupusas in central parks in twenty different highland towns before they began to run together like diluted paint. In every one, she painted an oversaturated landscape tastefully unpopulated with flowering vines and faceless women.

Once in awhile she made something of her own just to know she could still do it.

Three months after Miguel Ángel was born, when Teresa left for good, Cristina dug out the five or six finished paintings that were hers. She lined them up on her rack at the artisans' market on a Sunday after church let out, then sat with Diego watching people pass, betting in whispers on who was only cutting through to the food stalls seeking Mama's chicken, who was rushing to beat the rest of the post-church traffic to the Ninth Ave valet lots, who were foreigners lost and terrified.

Her art made people stop; that much could be said for it. It scared them, she thought. Even some who weren't already scared. They tried to understand what they were seeing. Then, coming to no immediate conclusion, they shook themselves like dogs coming out of the rain and went on.

She laughed, and it felt good, bitter as the humor was. A good laugh was the best she could expect.

After nobody bought any, she painted over all but the one in which a coal-and-orange snake sinuated across a hurricane sky over a village square, fire rain falling from its scales onto a hunched and fleeing crowd. The stormfront had come out of nowhere; a triangle of fair sky remained, eggshell blue all the more fragile for the precipitous darkness at its flank. Only one face could be seen, foreground left, arms above his head; she'd meant it to be Lencho, but it didn't look like him, and she hadn't minded because of the expression, half in ecstasy and half in dread. She gave it to Hugo.

"You should concentrate more on your own work," Hugo said.

"Come back to Comalapa," Hugo never said, not once, until Mama died.

The footing was treacherous, the ground made as much of plastic as dust. Claws would make the way surer. Gulls wheeled overhead by the hundreds. In Felipe's mind's eye the jaguar dragged the peccary up the trunk of a tree. There were no trees here, just weeds, scraggly bushes and trash. Hulks shifted among wreckage: people, wearing trash on their backs and on their feet, carrying trash on their shoulders, dragging trash behind them, like they were made of it as well as its curators. And down it went like that, forever, down into mist. On the wind, the heavy scent of fertilizer.

Words came to him, lyrics, to match the muffled beats behind the river roar and the gulls' cries, words from within, from up out of this poison ground like roots, like the song had been waiting. He didn't need earbuds. They would shut out whatever doom was impending, whatever skull faces might lurch out from behind the next flap of sodden cardboard to mock him, then mow him down. But this music was in his body, in his head, reflected all around him. He fell into its rhythm, letting himself be buoyed by it, calmed. *You reap what you sow.*

El Bufo reached the first switchback and turned. Felipe hung back as he'd been told. A woman crouched over a fire, feeding it bottles and wrappers while the flames coughed oily smoke and toxic colors, the colors of huipiles, of Lupita's calendar seeds. A child looked on, fingers bunched over their mouth. Felipe didn't want to see their faces or the food they would cook over those flames.

El Bufo spoke to them. The woman pulled the child close. Their bodies, woman and child, were patterned dark and light: wrists and bare feet and the napes of necks brown with grime, palms and faces clean, shiny with color. Where did they get water? Bottled, if they were lucky. They weren't. The child ran from the mother, ducking down a skinny side path between blue plastic awning and citrus-patterned cloth.

He couldn't follow directly, the woman would see. That meant wreckage and weeds. From ugly soil between shanties sprung thorns, wild grasses, twists of wire, beans and squash climbing mutated corn. He plunged in, afraid of tetanus and who knew what else, of touching a single thing. Too late. He struggled to hold that calming beat in his head. Thorns and cornsilk caught in his clothes. He stumbled through a cinderblock living room. A tube television tuned to a telenovela fit imperfectly among the blocks. A ruinous couch, just fabric and springs, enveloped an unconscious person. Empty bottles crowded at their ankles. Woven mats made a floor, once-beautiful highland cloth faded to gray. A measure in 4/4 and the living room was behind him. Around a tarp that for a moment kept the beat in a breeze, the child was speaking to a man old or young, bent neck and shoulders like a vulture. The man questioned her sharply; she threw back her head and ran one way; the man moved in another. The man — her father, grandvulture, something worse? — would be easier to follow, but he didn't look a killer, just a garbage picker, a flightless carrion bird. Felipe couldn't see El Bufo anymore.

Should he have disobeyed, kept hidden? What was El Bufo's real plan? Was El Bufo following him, clumsy, half-drunk and overcaffeinated, invisible somehow? No.

He followed the child. But she'd been born here, like El Bufo, and she knew every drift of packing peanuts half-decomposed, every oil and sawdust mire. The arms of the ravine enveloped her.

He could barely keep up at a run, plunging, skidding, slipping. A skein of braided electrical wire flung up a tentacle to catch his ankle and he went down hard into something sticky-slick. His elbow came away dripping grease and blood. There was nothing he wanted to wipe it on.

He slung the backpack to one side, pulled off sunglasses, mask, and secured them inside. You reap what you sow. His eyes contracted to slits in the brightness. Sneakers fell away from paws; two bounding strides and his shorts slipped off too. Someone here would give them new life. The backpack hindered him; he struggled to keep it in place atop his bouncing shoulder blades. This was worth it, had to be worth it. He'd overcommitted already. Reggae rhythm rumbled in his throat. There — the girl reappeared, head and shoulders, through a plastic sheeting window in a refrigerator box house. Someone slouched to their feet, stooped, straightened, something angular and hard extending from their hand. Felipe dropped into the weeds. People could see him, had to have seen him. He lost the thread of the song.

A man emerged — no, just a kid, a couple years older than Toby, slinging the AK over one shoulder. He wore aviators, no shirt. His skin was a labyrinth of tattooed lines. Downhill he went, toward the river. This had to be one of them, the killers who'd sawed through Eufemia Ramos on their way to David Antonellis — to his doppelgänger. Felipe tried to work out if he should hate him. Passing the cardboard box where the murderer had emerged, he met the girl. He could have, should have shown her a human face as he had to Toby, a human finger pressed to human lips — but it was happening too fast. It was impulse, feeling. It wasn't under his control. Her eyes widened, but she didn't scream. A mouse scurried past under paw. He couldn't help the instinct. He broke its back with one soft blow.

He needed a face. For his own sake, he needed a face.

He sat down on the cardboard floor, shrugged off the backpack and dug out the jaguar mask again, not time for the skull, not yet. The girl stood transfixed. What did she see? What would this do to her, this fever dream? She had a harelip, huge eyes, hair that might have been trimmed with a machete. Felipe snapped his jaws. The girl fled.

He put on the jaguar mask, the sunglasses and hoodie, a pair of sandals made of plastic rope and old tire he found in a corner, tied a raggedy piece of cloth around himself with more of the rope. It stung. Was this what it felt like to belong here?

The tattooed kid, moving with the swagger of the gun on his shoulder, made for a gully where the ground was flatter, where runoff trickled brown between tires heaped sunken in drifts of dirty foam. An oily-vegetal miasma rose from the river finally visible below. Scavengers slogged through it, some in snorkeling masks and heavy gloves, some barefaced, barehanded. A gull struck the surface with a fleeting eruption and flew off dangling something snakelike. How could there be anything alive in there?

The river was El Gallito's heart. Or its liver. It sifted the trash, sublimated it, sluiced the most toxic of sludge down toward the toxic lake and the sea, but kept the heaviest treasures hidden. The city had garbage trucks, though whether they took your trash depended if your neighborhood could pay. What they took came here eventually, though first it was compacted and heaped into mountains upstream, where it collapsed sometimes, suffocating scavengers too desperate to let the river do its work. The *Diary* never talked about it. *Waking Dream* did. Felipe had averted his eyes as long as he could. He used to wonder how Luz could stand it, to take in all that grief. Now he couldn't look away.

The tattooed kid laid a hand on another kid's shoulder, this one a little older, sitting with a handful of others on overturned crates passing a bottle and a joint big as a cigar, puffing billows of smoke that couldn't possibly cover the smell. This one wore a red leather club jacket, the black figure eight on the back struck through with a lightning-bolt cut, the cut stitched shut with wire. Club jacket was drunk, stoned, lit. He staggered. He squinted up at the heights from which they'd come. Tattooed kid growled something in his ear.

Felipe strained to hear. He wanted to know what they thought of El Bufo.

In his scavenged clothes, his arm streaked in grease and blood, people stared. What would it take? He drew his arm across his wooden brow, smearing it with awfulness. Was it the sunglasses? With their orange iridescence, maybe they made him look marero. He took them off. From the wreckage at the side of the path, he grabbed a piece of driftwood plank, rust-stained with eroded screws. Hoisted to his shoulder, it could block the faces coming toward him up the path, another mask.

Before he got close, they were moving again, scavengers scrambling out of their way. Now he was close enough to hear, over the birds, the river, the beats.

"... hostages," said tattooed kid.

"Later," said club jacket. "If we have to. They'll slow us down."

"So we're running?"

"He's one old man. He should be running."

"Manacutli said —"

"We take *him* hostage. Ransom him. Make our money that way. Got to be worth something."

"Man, this is El Bufo. We go against him, people start turning on us. You know, I think maybe he used to be marero."

"Nobody *used to be* marero. *We're* the ones who protect El Gallito. We keep the cops out, we put food in people's mouths."

"You're fucking kidding me. We're not in yet, Josito. If we were in, we'd know. We're meat shields. Expendable, you said it yourself."

"Yeah." Club jacket shrugged. "Well, I want in. We killed for them. Five — and counting. I don't care who died or didn't die. They owe us. We'll show them."

"Show them what?"

"They can't push us around. We don't follow orders if they don't keep their word. I'm not out here hurting little girls for free." Stoned and high, club jacket couldn't hide that haunted look.

"They can push *me* around. You know what he said, he said if we don't —"

"Manacutli doesn't know shit. No better than we do. Look, you don't have to do anything. Leave it to me. Just go get El X. Meet at the dragon's head."

Not another one. How many machine guns did you need to murder a pretend diplomat, two bureaucrats and a cook? How many for one alcoholic ex-cop? He'd seen the autopsy report, the forensics. Felipe tried to remember. Sixty-six bullet holes? Five different guns. Four killers. Here were two, Tattooed and Josito Club Jacket. A third now, El X. Where was the fourth? Manacutli — was that the vulture?

Meat shields. Maybe these killers had trained the same way Felipe had, on laggy, pixelated team shooters at the internet cafes in Antigua. Staticky gunfire, flies, sour sweat. All you could see of yourself was a pair of gloved hands and a weapon. A knife if you were desperate, about to die. A pistol. Two pistols, if you'd killed somebody. A shotgun. An AK. A rifle. Kids with money to waste could rattle it all off in a second, debate the advantages of each. They'd hoot and laugh as somebody's avatar got blasted, flying from a twilit rooftop halfway across the map. You could fly, once you were dead. You could watch the others fight. Felipe liked that best. Being dead.

Tattooed was moving back the way he'd come, not swaggering because he no longer had the AK, but still a threat. He was coming straight at Felipe.

Felipe nearly clobbered someone with the plank. He dropped it and ducked away from the clatter of their dropped bundle of scrap, their shouting. Any second they might see, and he'd be fucked. He pushed out of the crowd to his right into a locust bush, thorns scratching. One stuck in the back of his hand. He fell. He crawled in under the thorns, kept crawling. He crouched, listening, terrified.

He couldn't just sit there bleeding.

He could follow Tattooed, who was unarmed. He could let Tattooed lead him almost to El X, then sneak up like a real jaguar, snap his spine, drag his body into one of these blighted trees to eat later. He could steal Tattooed's form — he could try — knock on El X's door and in all likelihood get murdered, and deserve it. But then he'd have lost Club Jacket, the one with the AK and the arrogance. *Meet at the dragon's head.*

He couldn't do any of that — the spine-snapping, the shape-stealing, the blood welling beneath his lips. Maybe if he were cornered, alone, life or death. If he were starving. Or protecting someone he loved? He hadn't been in the jungle, the real jungle, in a long, long time — not since that one school trip to Iximche. This place was as close as he was likely to get.

He took off the mask and everything else and shoved it in the pack.

He clawed up the garbage drifts, up the wall of the gully, scrabbling, slipping, soiling his blood-matted, ring-patterned coat. He saw a tree — one lone avocado, huge, its sprawling crown heavy with contaminated fruit. It had grown out of a fruit just like them. When? When this place had been something else entirely. When garbage had been cracked clay pots, corn and cacao husks, turkey feathers, eggshells, ashes, maybe once in a rare while a few human bones. He climbed high, to where waxen leaves shivered in a fetid breeze, and looked out over the devastation. Was it so different? Just a hundred thousand times more of the same.

Tattooed he lost quickly among the avocado leaves and the wreckage; the maze on Tattooed's skin helped him blend as effortlessly as Felipe's own camouflage. Club Jacket, on the other hand, had the swagger now, that hard implement of death lending credence to his convictions. By that swagger alone he'd have stuck out even without the target on his back.

The dragon's head was the broken-off prow of a fiberglass ship, the remains of some carnival ride, its garish paint flaked to soiled white, its eyes orange bulbs encased in car reflectors. It had feathers and scales. It was laughing. It surfaced out of the ravine as if it were riding a wave. Five paths met at its teeth. Club Jacket propped his foot against one of them, lit a joint and waited, looking almost like Toby but for the AK.

Felipe waited too, scanning the landscape for Tattooed and El X. And El Bufo.

And here he came, down one of those five paths, the broadest, most heavily trafficked. The people parted for El Bufo when they saw him coming with that thick gait, the ugly windbreaker flapping open at his chest, the cheap suit beneath it undoubtedly the only suit, cheap or otherwise, anywhere in El Gallito. He had the girl with the harelip by the ear.

He didn't even have his gun out.

Felipe knew a shouted warning would be worthless — it would only expose him. His phone was in his backpack, balanced precariously atop his jaguar spine as he hung from a branch high above the ground. If he traded claws for thumbs he'd break his neck.

Instead, he plunged out of the tree headfirst. Three bounds and he hit the ground at a run. Unmasked, he could move fast — he didn't know how fast or for how long — he'd never had reason to try. He tried, the ruinscape a blur of colors the palette of mold, rust, water-stain. Bits of junk kicked up beneath his paws like he was running on a wave, down along the curve of the gully, then up. He lost sight of the dragon behind the earth. Frustration rose in his throat, hot and deep. There was no way to keep out of sight. He didn't try. He was dodging handcarts, ducking between legs, the faces blissfully flooding past too fast to register. A grimy hand dragged against his coat, then slipped away. They saw him, these scavengers, these discarded people. Did it scare them? Did they think he was some magical being, a god? Did it matter? El Bufo knew. Lupita knew, Toby knew, Cristina knew, seventy people on a bus to Chichicastenango knew, his brother knew, his mother knew, his father knew. He wished suddenly he'd had the chance or the courage to tell Luz and Aníbal. Or his nephew.

He wondered how his life would have been different.

Gunshots. Protracted and sharp, almost musical, like a line of steel doors slammed one after another. The sound was nothing like in the computer game, but still he remembered those disembodied black gloves wrapped around the stubby black rifle, how it moved as you ran, how you had to aim low because the AK rode up in your hands as it fired, and if you did it right a zipper of bullets chewed your enemy apart from knees to neck. And then your enemy could fly.

When it hits, you feel no pain.

Felipe skidded into the intersection of the five paths, where the dragon leered and blood trickled from uphill, pooling in footprints. A shoulder of slate-gray cloud hung overhead. An acrid, metallic scent cut through the pervasive blend of roast corn, burned oil and sweet decay. Morning sun breaking the edge of the ravine sharpened everything to motes and points.

The girl lay on her back, El Bufo on his face a few steps behind her. Club Jacket stood between the dragon's teeth fiddling with the catch on the AK, trying to release the magazine, engrossed in what he was doing, seemingly not at all surprised by or even interested in the consequences of his actions.

Felipe didn't know how he closed what distance remained between himself and his prey.

His mouth closed around Club Jacket's collarbone, canines punching through leather into flesh. Blood welled around his teeth, and his lips pulled back involuntarily at the taste of it — iron, alcohol and salt — but the clench of his jaws did not relent. Bone snapped. The two of them tumbled together, awkwardly, thrashing, against the dragon's fiberglass jaw. Club Jacket made no sound Felipe could hear, and soon gave no more resistance than a letting-out of breath.

People were screaming, crying. The sounds seemed to come from a great distance. This, combined with the repeated, stabbing pain in his head, led him to conclude that the gunshots had been very close and very, very loud. In the periphery of his vision, people were running, but around him everything was still.

He'd never seen another jaguar. Nobody had taken him to the zoo; when he was old enough to take himself, he didn't want to. But he'd watched videos enough, read enough to know jaguars didn't roar. They didn't intimidate. They didn't challenge. They coughed, purred, or were silent. Invisible one moment, plunging deadly out of dappled light and shadow the next. They used stealth. And deception. He couldn't have warned El Bufo. But he could have stopped this. He'd had every chance to stop it.

He dragged Club Jacket's body up into the broken belly of the dragon out of sight, where he lay with it awhile as with a sleeping lover until his hearing and agency returned.

He dug out the skull mask and put it on, trusting, for the most part, it would cover the blood. He considered taking the club jacket — puncture wounds, blood, stapled scar — but thought better of it. He stepped out naked from the dragon's belly. Something sharp on the ground sliced into the arch of his human foot. He winced, but didn't cry out, nor did he limp as he crossed the meeting of paths, his thick, skull-man prick swinging against his thighs, past dumbstruck Tattooed and a squat, plastered-drunk teenager who must be El X, ignoring them both, to kneel at El Bufo's side.

"This was your fucking plan?"

El Bufo blinked at him, then looked at the sky.

"You said you'd get her out, you fucking bastard. You have to get her out." He fumbled inside El Bufo's ruined windbreaker for his phone, then the pockets of his cheap suit jacket. He found a wallet, then another, then the flimsy gun, his keys, then finally the phone, which he flipped open in bloody hands and was chanting, "The number. Tell me the number," before he realized that former Inspector of National Civil Police, former SAAS Operative of Unknown Rank Rodrigo Francisco Cuerva Zamora was dead.

He went back to the girl with the harelip long enough to see she too was dead and close her eyes.

Halfway back to the gap in the fence, he met the skinny vulture, Manacutli. He discovered he still had El Bufo's flimsy pistol in his hand. He found the safety, flicked it off and emptied the pistol into Manacutli's belly. After the roar of the AK, these gunshots sounded like firecrackers. Snap, snap, snap. Every time he pulled the trigger he expected the thing to explode in his hands, and he kept going anyway. When it was empty, he dropped it.

He climbed to the top of the ravine, passed through the gap in the fence, and found Baby still parked where he'd left her, unmolested.

The rearview mirror showed him a face he didn't know.

The Cathedral San Juan Bautista, on the highest of the worn-toothed hills of Comalapa, was an ancient thing besieged by the present, as much like a pagan temple as a church. Once-white stucco stained by rain and carbon monoxide rose against a brown sky. Cristina stumbled, climbing the scored steps with the first petitioners before mass, and stayed where she'd fallen, her back against a pillar, the cathedral façade rising above her. Electric and ethernet cables snaked through arrow-slit windows.

A man's hand on her. "Are you all right, miss?" Politeness not enough to counteract that touch.

She thanked him.

Visions boiled in her. The angels were ... but that was just a word for them. They looked so many different ways. Some had false faces made of feathers, paper, even food, some had no face at all. They were profuse. Everywhere. That there was one even behind this stranger's kind, intrusive hand made Cristina want to scream.

All she wanted was to be ignored, to be a stranger, alone in a remote highland town with a sketch pad, perhaps a pineapple and banana smoothie, and no obligations. Why had she come here? For Hugo? She needed to process. What had changed in her in Zunil, in that ring of angels, beside Rosaría in the incendiary-lit market street? She didn't want to be like Mama, to suppress the visions all her life until one of them killed her. She needed to let them out, to find out what was in her.

At the opposite pillar across the church steps, a woman was selling calla lilies, delicate ivory flutes brown at the edges, her face was covered with a starched-white shawl embroidered with red beetles. She sat cradling the flowers upright but bowed, almost a pietà. A subject for folk art that might even sell. Hugo's style would tell it truer.

She was not to second-guess, not to doubt. She opened her sketchbook; the blank page bore the faint lines of the masked jaguar's portrait.

The streets below filled with dresses and suitcoats crisp white and black, accented in beetle-shell ruby and aquamarine. Of dirt, not a speck was to be seen except in the creases. Sunday. In Zunil, too, they'd be lining up outside the churches: Tío Juan and his side of the family at the tiny tin evangelical church that doubled as a school out on the mountain's arm, Tía Crescencia and all of hers at the colonial church, as huge, old and eroded as this one. She would have had the front pew, by the pulpit. Father Eduardo would ask a prayer for her — for Mama, of course, but for Cristina too.

She still wore her funeral clothes, her corte and huipil in Zunil's colors, red, green, and blue with bees; everyone could see she wasn't from Comalapa. Her dress was sweaty, dusty from travel. The parishioners of Comalapa didn't care; they smiled, they were used to this. They bent to look. She hunched away, remembering the city plaza before the protests, the woman's voice accusing. *Blasphemy.*

She concentrated on the lily seller's hands.

She slipped the pencil through the spiral, grabbed the sheet and tugged. Rip. Rip. Rip.

She got up, shaking most of the graphite from her dress. What stayed would wash out. Service had begun; she crossed the steps between stragglers. She touched the woman's hands and they tightened around the flower stems. The woman stirred from sleep or daze, pushing back her shawl, shedding the illusion of divinity.

"I — drew this," said Cristina, holding out the drawing for the woman to see, to take. "I hope you don't mind. I wanted to buy one of your flowers, but —"

Instead of ragged lilies, in the graphite woman's lap reclined a graphite effigy: San Simón, the idol of the lake towns. Patron saint, patron demon, stiff and straight and emotionlessly laughing, swaddled in oversized, embroidered suitcoats. Christians hated that effigy. The most militant — like Mama — campaigned to eradicate it, to convert its worshippers back to true faith.

The lily seller recoiled from the image, and the sketch slid to the ground before the church doors. Battered, handmade shoes trampled it. Dismayed, Cristina fell on top of it before too many more boots pushed it out of reach. Then she followed them into mass.

Before the altar, she muttered her litany like a ward. "Mama, Miguel Ángel, Lencho — Francisco, Rosaría, Teresa, Corísa, Constancia ..." She lost the thread, mumbled, running through faces in her head, then recovered. "Luz, Aníbal. Félix?" She crossed herself emptily.

Hugo's right, she told herself, in that clamorous inner space of incense and ritual words. *You have to let it out. When you second-guess yourself, of course your ideas end up jumbled. People are a distraction, Mama is a distraction, God is a distraction. You can get away from everything but yourself, which is what you need to get away from most. But get away from everything else first.*

"Go in peace," said the bishop, a ladino in red vestments and a long gray beard, as much a stranger here as she. It must be a special occasion.

She ate lunch with the students. She avoided Hugo. She stole tortillas and fruit from the kitchen and filled a bottle from the solar purifier. She hovered in the supply closet: so many colors of paint and softnesses of pencil, creamy expanses of canvas and paper, broken easels repaired and repaired again. Pencils were easy to carry. Canvases were hard to hide. But she wanted paint. She needed color. She took brushes, two small canvases, pushed them into one of the old coffee sacks with shoulder-ropes sewn on by students long past. She balanced an easel on her shoulder.

She poked her head in at the office, thinking to leave a note, but the curator was there, bank-teller severe in heavy makeup and skirt suit. So instead Cristina covered her head with her shawl against the highland sun and walked east into the dry, eroded hills. There was a ruin she remembered.

Toiling up and downhill past steep milpas and concrete block farmsteads, she reached the highway. On the hillside above, big machines rumbled spreading a foul miasma. Police slept in their pickups. An opaque, stinking yellow liquid spilled down a distant slope and through a rusted corrugated pipe, eroding an ugly gully undermining the road. Nobody was fixing it. A sign in English and Spanish — many in the highlands spoke neither — warned not to come near, not to gather water from the stream. Foreign logos. A few dozen obviously local protesters in red-purple-black traje stood underneath it with their own signs, looking miserable. A Totonícapan waiting to happen? Or it had happened already. They called out to her in Maya Mam. She shook her head in incomprehension. She was in no condition to help anyone.

She turned off the highway and rounded the side of the hill. Noise fell away. Pavement turned to dirt with chunks of rubble, then just dirt. A boy with a plastic bag slung by the handles from his forehead smiled at her walking past. Three dogs chased her past an empty house. A path scored with hoofprints turned uphill. Dust on the breeze, the land overworked, the path crumbling. A trickle, not contaminated but muddy, ran alongside in a ditch. She saw a shepherd coming and hid from him in high honeysuckle.

Breathing hard, she reached the ruin, unmarked, overgrown, wind blowing over the walls. A disc of ashes smoked surrounded by wilted lilies and a bottle of orange soda like a cartoon tombstone.

She set up the easel beside the altar, then uncrumpled the sketch, smudging the architectural lines of the church facade and the flower-seller's clothes. Creases dissected San Simón's rigid figure like fractures in clay. "Is this what you wanted?" she asked him.

He laughed at her, and she knew why, and she knew what she had to do to shut him up.

She'd met him in the wooden flesh only once, in one of the towns on the far side of the lake, a water taxi ride from Nati's brother to a high wooden dock, up a ladder, then a steep path over roots worn smooth. The steepest parts were lined with stones equally worn, defining the way to a house almost hidden by brittle cornstalks, squash and castor bean. Nati greeted the mannequin San Simón with mock-reverence, laying a banana-wrapped tamal at its feet, wrapping a scrap of her mother's scarf material around its wooden throat and twenty other scraps like it. For Nati, this was a lark, a fortune-telling game like bingo at saint's day fairs. *Will I get the laughing death, the dancing temptress, the scorpion, the sword?* The family that lived in the house surrounded them, solemn, not joking, obscured by dark and smoke but for the sheen of eyes. Cristina passed out tamales and cigarettes, feeling lost in time. This was the ritual, descended from the ancients, mutated, threaded with Christianity, disguised to hide from it, but also the same.

For these people, she'd felt certain, she and Nati — strangers from the city — represented that influence, represented too vividly the armed men who in an entirely present past had come to take food and men and boys at gunpoint and gone again, upslope into the wilderness. The men and boys had not come back. Tamales and cigarettes were the least she could give.

Candle flames and smoke threads from the incense heaped on the altar guttered in the draft. Nati wanted San Símon to tell her who she would marry. Would it be Diego? She laughed. A nice businessman from the city, a foreigner, or a poor boy from home? The candles answered, or they didn't. "A poor boy," Nati said. "It figures." Then she asked on Cristina's behalf, while Cristina begged to go. The mannequin's mood was woodenly jovial. "He says you'll be a spinster forever!" she teased. "Just one more second, wait — it's not done, see?" And she took out a little clear bottle with the smiling woman on the label, broke the seal, poured a little among the incense, a few drops, a flare of blue, then sipped, coughed, wiped her mouth. "Come on, you have to or it won't be right. It's for him. Just a little. Then we'll go."

Cristina kissed the bottle. There was sweetness somewhere amid the chemical burning. Nati thanked the family, left them the aguardiente. As they picked their way steeply back down to the dock and the boat, wooden eyes burned into her back and laughter echoed.

What was inside her was the truth. The truth of the past, the truth of now, the truth no one spoke of: not the poor peasants on the slopes above the lake, not Mama, not even the jaguar, who lived this truth without understanding. San Símon, the terrifying little wooden demon, had been trying to tell her then. He was trying now.

She would go mad if she didn't listen.

Cristina sketched perspective lines: a room foreground right, a horizon line above. She peeled and ate an orange, green on the outside, pink within. She nibbled tortilla. The sun rolled across the hill of heaven, and a song surfaced in her head, accordion and tambourine and crooned, false longing, but she took what she could get. She couldn't hear the roar of the machines devouring the land, poisoning, or the incomprehensible cries of the protest, but every time a truck entered or left the construction site, she heard its engine howl and suspension hammer as it navigated the rotting gouge in the highway.

The room was a cell. The viewer was inside it looking out. There were two views: a door and a window. In the hallway, skeletons waited in line, green uniforms, black uniforms, berets, suits, rancher's hats, cummerbunds, huipiles, sabres, shawls. They looked happy, but that was the way with skeletons. In the window, clouds rolled, whole landscapes of them, mountains, valleys, canyons, plains. Way in the background by the horizon, a family sat at a table, so small their heads were dots. In the background left, down, down in the valleys, two more dot-headed people waved or danced or maybe cried or climbed, each alone, isolated. And in the cell, exaggerated in perspective though pressed in by the heaviest of clouds, a suit and tie were laid out on the cot. Two slashes of black on the pillow, a pair of loafers on the floor. From the high bars of the window hung a stripe of white. In the hall outside the cell, at the back of the line, one of the skeletons was naked.

She finished, or at least couldn't bring herself to paint another stroke, when the sun was rolling down heaven's far side, picking up speed.

San Simón sat by the extinguished altar, sated with offerings, no longer laughing.

Cristina had painted it, all of it. Maybe some had come not at her bidding, but she'd been watching, careful. She'd seen where it was going, she'd dreaded it, but she'd been compelled. She hated it, hated what it meant, what it foretold. She turned the easel into the wind so it would dry enough to carry home.

A hand shook her — Hugo's, she dreamed, but it was one of the students'. "Don't touch it," Cristina said through fog. "Don't look."

It was some unknown hour of morning — she couldn't turn her phone on or she'd see messages. She had returned to the school after dark and gone to bed hungry. Unable to sleep, she'd pulled the string of the overhead bulb, set the other canvas on the easel and started again. Her room wasn't bright enough, it hurt her eyes, and she was exhausted, sore, hungry, but it was better than seeing what she saw and doing nothing. It hulked at the end of the bed: a painted river of refuse, a phantasmagoria of plastic bags, plastic chairs, plastic toys, car parts, doll parts, human parts, pots, pans, banana peels, coconut husks, cornhusks, guns, knives, paintings, clothes, crosses, phones. On a choked sandbar in the center canvas, the corpse of María Elena lay prone.

Dead, Mael was dead. Cristina had known her for less than a day, but they'd plucked chickens together in Mama's kitchen. Of course she was dead, but Cristina couldn't admit it until she painted it, as surely as she knew Aníbal was in prison, in despair, or that she finally understood Eufemia Ramos's own visions had done nothing to prevent her death.

She saw it unfold, could not close the lids of inner eyes against it, now that they were opened: that morning in the market. She could have painted the look in Mael's eyes as she turned from the fence around the comedor, fled from the memory and that sneering soldier — who must have reported her, unknowing or not, to a conspirator. Mael had fled into the cathedral for a little peace, been followed, found, watched, snatched. Hurt, hesitated over, tormented with kindness, with frustration, hurt worse, and finally murdered, discarded among trash, by trash.

It was awful, unbearable, and she couldn't look away. She hated seeing, hated knowing. She wanted to forget the way Mama had undoubtedly and willingly made herself forget what she knew. It was the only answer that made sense.

Cristina felt what was forgotten boiling within her. She could raise it again with a touch. It would change her, ruin her. No way could she withstand it. What Mama had done — if she'd done it, her whole life through, until the last moment —

She zombied out of bed. She heeled her eyes until they focused. She still wore the huipil. She smelled sour, and the texture of the embroidery was pressed into her hip and the undersides of her arms. How many days was it? She pulled the painting from the easel and propped it facing the wall by the first, not bothering to check if it was dry.

The girl who had woken her stood waiting in the doorway. She couldn't have helped seeing the painting. Hugo waited in the hall with coffee. Cristina shut the curtain and waited for them both to go away.

The room was just the bed, the bright plastic skylight, a rug and a painting, not his but his master's: three chicleros in a grass-grown ruin, broad hats and sheathed machetes beside a fourth in dancer's costume, dragon mask, dyed feathers, all of them staring at the ground. She took it down and shoved it under the bed.

Now the room was a cell.

She borrowed clothes from the laundry line, remembering Aníbal's suit on the bed. She'd missed breakfast. She did everyone's dishes, then as much laundry as she could before she couldn't feel her arms. Exhaustion: that was the trick. That was how to shut out San Simón — or let him in, she didn't know. Work was how to shut herself off, how to let whatever was in there out and onto the page and let it hurt the least.

She sat awhile with the chickens. Then she got another canvas, a big one, and hiked back to the ruins.

Today there were fewer protesters by the poisoned creek, and she didn't stop to ask whether the rest had given up or been poisoned or run over with bulldozers or shot or just disappeared. She should stop. She should ask. She should set up beside them and work, be a warm body, a witness.

What she ought to ask was how to stop it. They didn't know, or they'd have stopped it. Who was to be asked? God or a blasphemous idol or herself, the bottomless black well of paved-over honesty erupting behind her ocular nerve.

She let it out onto the page. The nerve thrummed and she channeled agony through her fingers.

At a muddy river crossing, a crowd waited for the rickety, smoke-chugging ferry. A childless mother sat on a throne of arms in the back of a pickup truck bed framed in rusty bars, and other arms thrust money at her, rude gestures you couldn't read, miracle cures, fruit, aguardiente. God flung a sunbeam at her face. It was Teresa.

The far shore of the river was empty, cross-hatched with tire ruts.

"Don't look," she told Hugo that night when she returned. But he looked.

He insisted she eat with him, on the little porch that opened off his studio facing the cliff, where the hill with its ruins could be picked out if she hunted, one worn tooth among many beyond the bristling power poles and black lines that divided the sky, and then she could look nowhere else.

He couldn't ask what any of it meant. He couldn't ask how she was doing it, producing so much so quickly. So he asked after her health, was she eating, sleeping, was there anything he should know? "Have you spoken to your family? To let them know you're here."

If she opened her mouth she'd explode like a hundred punctured spray paint cans.

Alone again, she lay across the narrow guest bed, arms and legs dangling. Her whole body throbbed. She should sleep for days; she needed not to and could not. The canvases accumulated, turned to the wall. She'd done what Hugo asked. Now she was scaring him. Good. It was scary.

Night, darkness, roosters crowing, a bus pulling up, brakes hissing, then the engine howling as it pulled away. A mosquito by her ear. The rough wool of the blanket against her clammy skin.

In the morning, she limped down the line of tuktuk drivers on Comalapa's main drag below the cathedral, studying faces until she found one she thought she remembered from six years past. Exhausted, body and spirit, there was no way on earth she could make it back to the ruin under her own power. "I don't have anything to pay you." Not even art.

He drove her anyway, crammed into the plank seat with her easel hanging out the window. Of course, he had to stop at the washout.

She got out. There was only one protester left, a woman who looked Cristina's age, if not for the hollows and shadows. The driver hesitated. She thanked him, asked if he'd come back at dusk.

Mama in her mausoleum, old skeletons outside pounding to get in, a mirror for Aníbal's cell and Cristina's borrowed one. A riot presided over by heavenly hosts. Miguel Ángel in the womb. A botched execution. A jaguar and a quetzal fighting under the eyes of all the animals. There was too much in her head, no bottom.

She should step over the washout, hide from the goatherd, climb the hill. Her legs wouldn't move.

"Why do you stay?" Cristina asked, wanting anything but to stay and be subjected to the guilt of not helping, not being brave enough or caring enough or inconvenienced enough by injustice to stand up to it.

The protester frowned at the easel on Cristina's shoulder. Her small shrug was eloquent. "What am I supposed to do?" she sighed, in heavily accented Spanish.

"Give up," Cristina said awkwardly. "Someone you care about got sick? Go take care of your family. Or work, save money to get them away."

"There is no money except theirs," she said, looking at the enormous, toxic warning sign. "They pay for my kids' education. They own the house where we live. If I leave, if no one is here, someone could come along and drink this water and get sick. The goatherd boy could let his goat drink, and then his family could drink the milk and they would all get sick. You could get sick, or some other stupid artist."

"I can read," said Cristina.

"Good for you."

"Can I stay here?" Cristina asked. "I've been going up to the ruins every day. But I'm so tired."

The protestor shrugged.

She set up the easel. She stared at it, taking up a brush, unfolding a palette with trembling fingers.

"How do you spell 'don't drink' in Maya Mam?" she asked quietly.

"You don't." The protester's gaze was fixed on the road. "The written form of our language was lost for centuries. Most of us don't know it. I don't."

Wind and machinery roared, workers getting paid by some foreign corporation to do horrible things to the hills and their people that Hugo wouldn't let his students see. She could paint it, paint this scene, this woman, hang it at the head of the long breakfast table where they couldn't avoid it. But that wasn't what came out of her fingers either.

She painted the ruin. Night. A family kneeling with their gaudy offerings. Faces lit in the meager glow of candles, a lump of copal, a thread of smoke writing unreadable words. What was in the bottle wasn't orange soda, it was contaminated water, she knew it, but the viewer couldn't, except perhaps by reading their faces. If she was good enough. And the light — the faint orange light rising from behind the hills in east and west — it wasn't citylight or dawn. It was the vapor lights of the work sites, the kind of light that accompanied generators chugging, the shudder of land resisting the pressure of steel teeth. Cristina could feel the wind rise, smell the ammonium nitrate and cyanide, but there were no colors for such things. To read any hope in the situation at all, any sign those cheap offerings meant something or that there were people like Luz and Aníbal working in secret to change it, you had to rely on the faces.

By the time the tuktuk driver returned, Cristina's eyes had begun to water and her throat to swell from something in the air. Despite this, her eyelids kept drooping.

She propped the finished, still-wet painting against the corporate warning sign, not asking the protester's permission, not looking back as the tuktuk driver pulled away, not wanting to see the woman slap it down and trample it as soon as Cristina's back was turned.

She spoke no word to anyone at Hugo's school that night, though she wandered the rooms looking at art until late, so exhausted she couldn't sleep. The night was full of images, grief, recriminations. There was work to be done.

In the morning, she found the supply closet locked.

The message was clear. No more canvases, no more paint. She could have painted over some of what she'd already done, like she always had. But the paint would run out.

Hugo's office door was open.

He invited her, again, to join him for breakfast. She couldn't say no. He led her to the cafeteria, past all the rest of the students — who gave the clear impression they'd been talking about her — to the far end of the big table. She asked for milk and honey for her coffee, the addition of which was a spell to turn tongue-blistering tar to a delicious relief she couldn't help but drink in gulps, waiting for what was coming.

"When you came here as a student," Hugo was saying, loudly, for the benefit of all, "your work was unique. You lacked basic skills, perspective, blending, composition. You were impatient. You made it clear you didn't particularly care for my work." He didn't wait for her to argue. "Few do at first. They think they can do better. But you were honest about it. And you listened. You didn't think you knew everything. You wanted to learn." His face was the red of the clay he taught his students how to dig from riverbanks for pottery and pigment. "Teachers are supposed to be impartial. It's like asking a parent which child is their favorite. But you must know I thought you were special."

"Yes, I know all that," she said, with too much impatience. "And I still want to learn. 'An artist never stops learning,' isn't that what you tell them? But you're not —"

"Of course I'm not teaching you! Not now. Not that you've given me the slightest opportunity. But you're an adult. You know how to do this. And that's not why you're here, Cristina. You don't need me, you need my art supplies."

She stared at him. It was obvious she'd overstayed her welcome. But there was an enormous bowl of fruit and seed porridge and an equally ridiculous quantity of sweet coffee in front of her. She dug in. She sipped and swallowed and tried to savor it as her last.

"I know," he said. "I invited you. Over and over, I invited you here. You must understand my disappointment that it took your mother's death to bring you back."

The students tittered uneasily.

"I don't regret it. I'm not withdrawing the offer. Stay as long as you like. You've been under great pressure — from yourself above all. But you must see that I can't allow things to continue as they have. You disobey my simplest rules."

"Your rules?" She gummed the words around a mouthful, swallowed. "Because I've been going into the valley. How do you know where I've been?" She glanced at the students. The nearest had big, innocent eyes. They looked away.

"I tell them not to leave town because it's dangerous." He lowered his voice. "You know how my students are. They're like you. They've been protected from things like what's happening in the valley right now. It's for their own good."

"Is it to protect them, or to keep them from finding out?"

"Is there a difference? It's what their parents want. Believe me. And it's what I'd prefer for you. Your mother would throttle me."

"What my mother doesn't know," she said feebly.

He paled. "I'm sorry."

She shook her head. "Hugo, people are dying in that valley. People are getting shot and piled in ditches because of what's happening right outside Comalapa, and you — you send them to the park, to the bar, to the market —"

"And to the cathedral. Your lily seller ..." He gave a quick, grudging nod, a gesture of respect she knew he reserved for those who were no longer his students.

"But not to the ruins. Not to the roads, the neighborhood churches, the schools. Not to the mine."

"Nor do I send them off the cliffs. But that's not what this is about, is it?"

She ate in silence. Gradually the students resumed their conversation. What was it about? It was a dismissal. He'd offered her safety, time to herself, to work things through. She'd desperately needed it. Now she'd had it. Had it been enough? As much as she could expect. It would have to suffice.

Her spoon scraped the bottom of the bowl.

"Why did you ask me here, Hugo?"

He sat back, sipped coffee, studied her. "Anyone who knows you could have seen that tourist crap wasn't making you happy." Hugo didn't use vulgar language. He also didn't carry himself this way — it was subtle, a certain expansiveness in his gestures, but it was wrong. As though he'd forgotten himself.

He addressed the room. "Finished, everyone? Then follow me." He pushed back his chair, a shriek against the concrete.

Not to the gallery, but to the skylit, paint-splattered classroom studio, where out of harm's way hung an array of past students' best work. The students' easels and splatter of daily work had been cleared away. A lone easel, battered and multicolored like the rest, stood in position for a lecture, a demonstration, under the four cupola windows high above, with palette and paints arranged round the base of its three legs.

If he expected her to perform for them, she'd refuse. She closed her hands at her sides and prepared to suffer further reprimand.

He stopped halfway along the north wall. "That one. Your friend Diego Canselma's final work here, his best."

A bullfighter. Not quite "tourist crap," but close. The figure was rendered in detail, while everything around him, even the bull, was unfinished. He and his cape — his sword arm hidden from view by the turn of his body — were posed to make it unclear whether he'd delivered the coup de gras or received it.

She knew Diego, knew his heart, and she could see pathos in it. There was no sign of his bottled revolutionary aspirations or his bitter sense of humor. He'd gotten better before he gave up. But if you didn't know him, it was the work of an amateur who'd stumbled on a flash of compositional luck. She wondered if Hugo kept it up exactly for this purpose.

Hugo moved two steps and pointed again. "The first piece you painted here."

She remembered it: a subject she'd prepared in advance, in case she arrived at the prestigious art school and her mind went blank. A portrait, Papi's — or it was meant to be. She hadn't been the best at faces. He looked happy. He was meant to be listening. She couldn't help hearing quiet brass and castanets. If you could look beyond the frame as through a window, he'd be standing with one hand open on his chest, the thumb extended upward, the other moving in time. If she'd painted it now, Mama would be there somewhere she wasn't, a portrait on the wall, nested portraits — but she wouldn't paint this again. Not ever.

Hugo got a pole with a hook on the end from a corner and in two gestures like a knight wielding a long spear brought the painting down, laid it on the easel.

He indicated it to the crowd of students, then indicated them to her. "What does it make you feel?"

A semicircle of hushed scrutiny.

"Yes, it makes you feel something, doesn't it? You miss him. You miss what you thought he was before you found out, before it happened. Whatever it was."

"He's sad," ventured one girl, looking at the painting of Cristina's father. "Even though he's happy. He knows it won't last."

"You all feel that, don't you?" Hugo was a clouded mirror: unreadable, reflecting Cristina. "What's more, you feel you know this man and what he feels. Do you know why?"

Some of them thought they knew.

But he shook his head. "It's not anything I taught her. Her first work. She came with this inside her — we all have something like this inside us, otherwise it wouldn't work the way it does — but she came and put it onto canvas, just like you see it there, before I'd said a word to her. You all must see what that means. It means I am a fraud." He laughed, explosive and short. "Anyone can learn to paint proficiently. You all do it very skillfully, and in that your time here is not wasted. You may consider yourselves accomplished. But you won't do what she does."

He opened his mouth as if to say more, then closed it. "Class is canceled for the remainder of today." Thumbs tucked habitually into his vest, an uncharacteristic scowl fixed on his face, Hugo turned on a heel and was gone, leaving the gathered students in an offended uproar, those who didn't believe in talent or luck or fate arguing with those who did, and Cristina to bear the brunt. It had taken her all this time to figure out what he'd just given away to them in a few curt, infuriating words. They weren't ready to hear it. Of course they weren't; she hadn't been either. Which was why he hadn't articulated this to Cristina in all this time. She had to learn, to find it out for herself, to understand the nuance of it. That was suddenly obvious.

She'd thought of Hugo as a constant, someone who would persist in himself, thumbs in waistcoat, stubbornly, vaguely supportive, no matter what else changed.

She found him back in his office, taking rum from a drawer.

"Hugo, you don't drink."

"I don't drink around you. I know it destroys people. I know you disapprove."

It was the subject that had distinguished him from his own teacher. The worker drinking away his pain, drinking away his children's dinner, drinking away his wife. The charamilero, the poison drinker, who'd been a worker once, but for whom drinking had become a profession, who drank until he lost the power of speech, lost all but the memory of what made him human and could only shuffle across the cobblestones out in front of the cathedral, holding open a grimed palm for pity.

She sank into a chair, realizing he was already drunk, had been drunk.

He went to the gray metal wall of portfolio cabinets, opened doors, rifled through canvases.

"My father," he said, finding the portfolio he'd been seeking, folding it open, sliding it forward into her lap. "A landowner in El Peten. The man in your portrait … happy in the moment, and at the same time full of dread … I never saw that on this face. He was never satisfied. And he feared nothing, because nothing he had was worth enough to him to make him afraid of losing it."

A seated portrait, as stark as all of Hugo's work. The man's hair was plastered to his head, a cowboy hat perched on one knee, a drink on the other. He looked disappointed. He looked nothing like Papa.

"Do you remember Anja Pírenea?"

Her classmates, aside from Diego and Nati, were impressions she'd felt compelled to vie with only before she realized, at Hugo's prompting, that the one she had to vie with was herself.

"No reason you should. Anja lasted less than a week. She submitted only two pieces privately to me. Her family pushed her into coming before she was ready. The day she left — it was the day you submitted that portrait." The bottle clinked against the glass as he refilled it. "Anja saw her father, too."

"I shouldn't have come," Cristina said, her fingers worrying the edge of the portfolio.

"No," he agreed, without a moment's consideration. "You shouldn't have come. You turned me down so many times. I thought you understood. No, I don't mean that. You came, you're welcome. Was this what you needed? This isolation. You didn't need me, you'd have accepted refuge from anyone as long as they weren't family. As long as they didn't want anything from you. Did you get what you needed? Good. I'm glad."

The bitterness was unbearable, a mouthful of lemon rind, of black coffee, of lye.

She felt ashamed. He was right, she'd taken advantage. Of him, of his patronage, his … admiration? She would leave. She had to leave, now, she couldn't stand this anymore. In haste, she dumped the portfolio from her lap onto the desk. Rum sloshed from his glass.

"I'm in love with you," Hugo said. "I have been since … No, I'm in love with … her. I'm disappointed in you. I don't know how you could have painted that portrait of my father … whoever he is … how you could have been that person, that artist, and this artist you are now. You have a power, Cristina. In your vision, in what you see. I do not understand how you could have come here, learned what I had to teach — inadequate though it was — and then repressed that power for so long. I fooled myself I was doing it for you, for your benefit, asking you here. It was for me. I expected too much. You're not helping yourself. You're in mourning, Cristina. You're hurting my students, distracting them, undermining. I'm afraid I must ask you to leave."

The overpowering smell of rum — vanilla, and cloud forests burning — followed her out through the gallery. Somehow he'd spilled it on her.

She didn't know what to do, where to go. She went to the guest room and changed back into the huipil, which she'd spent hours scrubbing with handmade soap and now was blissfully clean. She stripped the cot and left the sheets in a pile with her borrowed, guilty-smelling clothes. Canvases were strewn all over the room. She wasn't ready to be free of them. They might be finished on the page, but the ideas, the process they represented was incomplete. But it was too late. There were no more paints, there would be no more release. It was over. The visions were out of her head, at least. She wasn't about to take them with her. Let Hugo sort through it all, if he thought she was such a genius.

She took her satchel and fled.

Straight down into the valley by the most direct route, Cristina took the road that was visible from half the rooms in the school, the one Hugo had forbidden.

There was no one by the sign, no indication anyone had been there protesting, warning people not to drink, except a few footprints in the yellow mud, and her painting, still leaning where she'd left it, unmolested. The police or the company probably hadn't carted the protesters off, or worse, left them piled in a ditch. They simply had to work that day, to afford medicine and bottled water for their families.

She would stay and protest awhile. She didn't have anywhere else to be.

A few construction vehicles and police trucks passed. The goatherd. "Don't drink the water. It's poisoned," she called to him timidly.

"I know," he said, looking at his goats. "But sometimes it's all there is."

After a few hours she gave up.

At the hilltop ruin, nothing was different except the way her legs ached and that someone had changed the offerings at the altar — the wilted flowers replaced with more ashes and new, fresh lilies, a candy bar, candles and a liquid-amber lump of smoldering copal. A photograph framed in old tin was propped against a stone: a yellow portrait of a girl in black leaning over a child wrapped in beetle-shell red and aquamarine. A memorial. For which one? Or both, it didn't matter. Whether they would speak the names in memory at next Sunday's service or not, here they were now on this hilltop, where ancient warlords had kept watch along the roads for Spaniards, and before that for their brothers.

She sank to her knees in the dust to conduct her own mourning. In her satchel she found the pietà, held the creased paper taut over the coal of copal until it darkened and the flame burst through. She found the portrait she'd taken from Mama's house in Zunil, the unknown ancestor, and set it beside the other before the altar. She crossed herself — why not, it didn't matter — and thought another litany of the names of everyone she cared about or missed or regretted or hoped for in the world. Mama Papi Miguel Ángel Teresa Mael Lencho Francisco Rosa Aníbal Luz Diego Nati Hugo the jaguar whose name she couldn't remember — if he had one it had been a lie — Pilar Majo Abuela Crescencia Constancia Pancho Cele Juan is that everybody? No, but she crossed herself again, not because she thought any gods or saints or angels, Christian or otherwise, were listening; her hand moved almost of its own accord. She turned a circle, east the sun, north hills, west Comalapa's cathedral spire and nest of wires, south the road into the valley lined with construction equipment and poisoned flowers and poisoned corn.

If she'd been allowed to paint one more picture, it would have been a close portrait, like the one of her father and of Hugo's. His face, his shirt collar and the top of his vest and nothing beyond. Outside the frame, he would be drinking something, coffee or rum, she couldn't decide. Clenching a fist around a brush. He would be proud and disappointed. He would not be in love.

I'm no prodigy, she told Hugo's unformed face in the blankness of her mourning. *I can't see into people's souls. My art isn't magic. So it affects people. Not the right people. Maybe I have talent. Not enough. Not the right kind. I have to face reality. I have Mama's business to worry about, my nephews' future.*

I have to go home.

She walked the ruins, saying goodbye to the foundations in their radiant crowns of dusk. She couldn't help wondering, like everyone who came to a ruin, foreigners in their sunhats and camera straps and locals alike: what must this place have looked like when it was new? She could guess, and her guesses were vivid. That was what drew people: guessing.

The sun rolled across the sky's vault and was replaced by the evening star.

The crowns on the ruins faded to slate. She considered again the imagined portrait of Hugo, but his unfocused form didn't resolve and she put it aside. Time to go.

Maybe the coffee existed only to counter the rum, though she supposed it didn't matter. He *was* proud of her. He believed in her art. He believed it was magic. Only because he loved her?

It had not been wrong to come. Standing in that ruin, painting, had been standing naked up to her knees in the sewage of her head, shoveling. Backbreaking and painful, but then her hands wore into blisters, the blisters burst and hardened into calluses. She hadn't found bottom. But it was possible to get there.

She left the photo. An offering.

She stumbled down the hill, goats bleating on the path ahead of her. Her exhausted muscles not answering, she got too close to them, too fast. She skidded off the trail and fell, biting her lip so she wouldn't cry out and bring back the goatherd. The crooked trunk of a skinny ocote broke her fall, and she lay folded against it, breathing its resin scent. She hauled herself up, ribs bruised, covered in dust. Down to the highway.

Still catching her breath, she leaned on the "don't drink the water" sign. A little tienda just before the bend was already closed for the night. She blotted her face with her shawl, then for the first time in a week got out her phone. Nine voicemails. Low battery. Low minutes. No money. Somewhere in her satchel was a slip of paper with a number on it.

When Felipe came back to himself, Baby was climbing out of the city, westbound on the Pan American Highway through late-morning traffic. Acrid exhaust poured from a chicken bus, clouding the windshield with soot. He pumped the accelerator, shifting from third to second to third, looking for an opening. Aside from wind and engine roar, there was silence. Even in his head, there was silence — and blood roaring in his ears.

The jungle. Thorns as long and thick as needles. Hummingbirds. Millions and millions of tiny leaves like fingernails on twenty-fingered hands. Palm fronds like parasols. Mud. Roots.

Mosquitoes. Blood. Deer. Howler monkeys. Toucans, trogons. Quetzals. Only as his heartbeat subsided to a shudder and his brain reengaged did he recognize this as a plan. He was naked but for a mask and four people's blood. He couldn't go back to the apartment, to where Luz was waiting. He wasn't about to go to his parents' or to Rubén's, though it was where this road led. He couldn't go home, whether that was Santa Catarina or the city. He was unfit for civilization. So what was he doing on this road? Getting away. Just like last time.

Nothing in the car to wipe off the blood. A rag in the trunk maybe, fast food napkins under a seat. El Bufo lying on his back with his guts in his hands in the bowels of the shantytown where he'd been born, alongside a dead marero and a little girl.

Felipe cut into oncoming traffic to pass the bus at the crest of the hill, narrowly missing a dirt bike coming the other way, barely flinching. At the fork in San Lucas he kept right, away from his parents, away from his brother. He got petrol at the hairpin in Sumpango, the usual routine: sunglasses, as few words as possible, rumpled stolen cash slipped through a hairline crack in the window.

El Bufo was dead, and there was no one to tell him what to do. Baby still had some other car's plates. If he got stopped by police, he was fucked, though that wasn't about to stop him pulling three g's through the mountain curves. When he realized he'd never get through the department border checkpoint into Chichicastenango, he stomped on the brake and pulled off the highway, north into patchwork farmland on the way to who knew where. In the rearview the volcano filled half the sky.

All that stuff on El Bufo's body — the wallets, the phone — there'd been a notebook. He'd had it in his hands at the hotel and never thought to flip through it. He could have taken it. Instead, he'd taken what? The gun. The fucking gun. He'd killed somebody.

Two people — one as a man, the other as a cat. With his teeth he'd ripped out the collarbone of a young, stupid, arrogant marero, Josito, who'd killed El Bufo and a little girl and probably Cristina's mother and how many other people and didn't care about anyone but himself. And with a half-dozen bullets from El Bufo's gun he'd murdered an old marero named Manacutli, a man with old motor oil eyes and white lightning aguardiente for blood and who used children, maybe even his own daughter, to do his dirty work.

Find someplace empty. Not a jungle; there were no jungles, not without driving half a day past cops and checkpoints. Just find somewhere to think. Or, preferably, not to think.

He drove until the farms fell into trees, the road rose into hills like slept-in sheets and the light turned them the color of skin, different colors of skin twined together. When the road dwindled to a rut, he pulled off upslope into leaves brushing like hands along Baby's sides.

He climbed out of the car, fought through growth to throw the skull mask in the trunk and hide the key under the wheel well. No one in sight, but in the distance, drums, and tortillas frying. He was hungry. Not for that. He dragged a huge downed branch to hide the car.

The woods were full of mosquitoes, crickets, sleepy birds, and one rabbit that rooted in place at the sight of him as much with surprise as fear. He ate it bones and all in seven bites, then curled himself around the crown of an ocote and dreamed of running, out of breath but running, his heartbeat the loudest thing in the world.

He woke to night, hungry. No moon. Dim stars vibrated amid shredded clouds. Clear, orange lights beyond the forest illuminated nothing. It didn't matter; he could see everything. Moths fluttered directionless. An owl perched in the pine across from his ocote, huge, yellow eyes missing nothing, reflecting his own. A meeting of minds, of peers — competitors. An agouti, nosing in the brush below, escaped neither's notice. The owl gathered itself on the branch, swelling with threat and intent. It dove, its wingbeat soft — silent to any ears but a jaguar's — but veered late from its prey, acknowledging the big rodent bigger than it could handle, acknowledging the prize was his.

Afterwards, he cleaned blood from his fur with his tongue. He stretched, then drank from a muddy trickle. Still hungry.

The jungle was quiet. It was still. It was escape. It was an illusion. No traffic, no horns, no music, no ads. No people — for now, but the pathways of the forest were scattered with trash, worn beneath human feet, bicycle tires, even an occasional motorcycle. There was no getting away from them. Not anywhere. If he could get away, there would still be himself. He'd been wearing their masks for so long.

It was easy, with heavy paws and hard black claws, to climb a tree and hide there. It was easy to stalk and kill prey — so easy only long after the fact did it occur to him to be surprised. But it was hard to stop the music from rising in his head. When the earworms came, he fought them. He tried to focus on the wind, the water, the footsteps of insects under leaves. But the music came again. And the faces: Luz, Aníbal, El Bufo. Little Juan Martín unsteadily meandering the jungle trails on their last family trip to visit the majestic ruins of Petén. The guilt came. He was too human.

He walked through the night. He followed the trickle to a torrent, then a stream, turned back when the stream ran through a cultivated field, between concrete shanties and under a road. He followed an incline until he reached the ridge, then followed that, roping in and out of ridges, a labyrinth; if he made his turns tight enough, he could walk forever, get nowhere. He curled up and napped when it occurred to him, never for long. When he closed his eyes, El Bufo blinked at him. Stars rolled in and out from clouds. Bats drew black squiggles across the sky. Dawn came, and with it campesinos passing through the woods on their way to the fields in straw fedoras, ratty baseball caps, too-large clothes, wearing their lunches in plastic shopping bags like backpacks, staring at their plodding feet, shadows long behind them. Exhausted before they'd begun. He followed them along the broad path between the fields to the road and thought about killing and eating them, and about what that meant to his humanity. For awhile he lingered at the edge of the trees, camouflaged, unmasked, unseen, watching them work and sweat. He got bored. The heat of the day came on and he slept and woke and slept again. The heat faded. The campesinos returned through the woods to their hovels high in the hills to cook their suppers and drink their aguardiente, and the sun oscillated, and the moon. The stars circled.

He came to no conclusions; nor did he come close to being caught or seen by man or woman, though he stalked and killed and ate creatures he thought of as neither lesser nor greater than himself: a turkey, a rooster that annoyed him with its cries and proved unpalatably tough, a small, malnourished cow that nonetheless was more than he could devour. He hid it in a tree exactly the way he'd seen it done in El Bufo's video, eliciting the realization that jaguars could smile, but could not laugh.

He found a place furthest from human encroachment where the forest had been devastated by storm, by the high, shearing winds that came more and more often and ripped the tops of trees right off, hundreds of them, like a blade out of the sky, and he knew that this too was human encroachment, like the heat, the drought, the floods. There was no escape.

He saw no other jaguar. He didn't expect it, but began to wish and pine for it before the campesinos trudged home again talking of football and the arrogant antics of the rancher's son. He was not, he was surprised to learn, a loner as jaguars were; he grew desperate for someone like him. Nothing came close, except the margay. After moonset on the third night, they both paused for a drink and came face to face across the trickle. A beautiful, tiny, jaguar-spotted creature the size of a housecat: his kin. Its eyes were deep, tawny-golden at the rims. The patterns that convoluted the fur of its cheekbones and brow were reflected in the forest shadow. It was wary of him, as he was. Of *her*. He wanted to ... he didn't know. Curl up with the margay in a cave somewhere and sleep, her warmth against his flank. He wanted to lick away the gunk that collected in her tear ducts, bowl her over with his tongue and the force of his love. More than love.

But more than love he felt regret that he hadn't spent his life in these woods and therefore they, and she, could never feel like his. That he and the humans he had chosen over her had confined her to this place, to this muddy trickle and these vanishing interstices of wild, bounded by highways, storm drains, hovels, fincas. Regret that he was only here with her now because of what he'd done. He'd done a thing which, to the margay, was as natural as breathing.

No. No, *killing* was natural. Not murder.

She, the margay, did not care.

The margay drank. He drank. They backed away from the trickle, from each other.

When the dawn came, his third dawn in these woods — that same dawn on which, in that book of myth Luz had gotten him to read not even a page of before phantasmagoria made the words swim, the gods grew frustrated with the wooden beings they'd created in their image, destroyed them in a rain of teeth and blood and started anew — Felipe slunk back to the car, ashamed.

His bare asscheeks adhered uncomfortably to the fissured fake-leather-actual-plastic seat, but he needed human shape to work the buttons on the phone. He needed to hear a human voice. Missed calls, texts: precious few. Four voicemails. Luz. He'd called so many times and she'd ignored him; before that, he'd done the same to her. He wasn't ready. Next, a client who somehow still hadn't taken the hint. Delete. And then El Bufo. Who was dead. But he'd had Felipe's phone all night while Felipe was on the rooftops failing to sleep. No fucking way was he listening to that. Last, an unknown number, a long message yesterday at sunset.

"Félix — Fe*lipe*." A hesitation, a wind gust breath into the phone. "You gave me your number. You said I could call if I needed a ride. I'm broke. I'm in Comalapa. You know where that is? Listen, my battery's hanging by a thread. I can't stay here. I'm just going to walk for awhile. I'll be on the main road south. If you can … if you get this, maybe you could meet me. I know we didn't end on the best note … but if you could just. You're the only one I can ask. I mean there's my family, but … Oh, it's Cristina? Cristina Ramos. From the protests. The girl with the baby? Only I don't have him now. I'm — my mother was murdered? You came to my —"

Another rush of wind or breath, and then nothing.

She sounded different. He wasn't sure how. Giddy. Was she drunk? He played it again.

Overhead, past the windshield, treetops moved in the faintest lowland morning wind. The campesinos passed along the trail, noticing nothing but the beginnings of their shadows where they lifted their feet.

Luz he could not help. Aníbal he could not help. El Bufo was dead. But Cristina. He remembered her in the seat next to him curled around a beat-up spiral notebook and a baby in a sling. Like a little kid in some ways, at least compared to Luz. Except he was pretty sure she was older.

He couldn't bring her mother back. He couldn't give her back the money he'd spent. There was absolutely zero chance her mother's killers would be brought to justice — the ones whose throats he hadn't already ripped out, whose bellies he hadn't pumped full of tinfoil. He was never going back to El Gallito. El Bufo was dead.

But he could give her a ride.

Cristina Ramos wouldn't care if he was naked. She wouldn't notice — she saw him as a jaguar all the time.

He scared the shit out of himself by laughing out loud. He hadn't heard his own voice in days.

Cristina and Felipe

She surfaced from visionary half-sleep freezing cold, curled in a knot hugging her knees some kilometers outside Comalapa, to the sound of a car pulling off the road beside her. For a pillow she had used her satchel; she snatched it to her stomach and wrested herself to a sitting position. She rubbed eyes with the backs of her hands, eliciting red lightning. Her calves ached. Gravel glued to her thigh and shoulder fell away piece by piece.

No one got out of the car. It was rust brown with a red racing stripe. The windows stayed closed, reflecting the sky and the tumbledown, board-windowed buildings of the outskirts.

Last night, after her phone battery died, after she'd walked for clouded hours berating herself for spending its last seconds on that stupid message, she had considered knocking on doors asking for shelter. They would have given it. Someone would have, someone in one of these half-shuttered houses with next to nothing for themselves. This wasn't the city. People were kind — they were Christian. Even the few who weren't. But she couldn't subject herself to their pity. Not after Hugo. Instead she endured a fitful penance of cold tiny stones digging into her hip.

She waited for feeling to return to her extremities, then staggered to the passenger door. She bleared at herself framed in the smoked window with Comalapa behind her. A thunk as the lock was released from inside. She opened it and there was the jaguar, almost exactly as she'd seen him — but hadn't had the strength nor light nor paints to capture — in the middle of the night: coat lustrous, eyes lustrous, body twisted to fit in the driver's seat of a '91 Corolla, head hanging, ears slicked against his head.

She dropped her satchel on the floor of the passenger seat, fell into the car and put her arms around him, her fingertips sinking up to the first knuckle in his fur, exactly as she'd imagined only more so. Beneath it, his body was stiff and unyielding.

She pulled back, the gearshift digging uncomfortably into her hip.

"Sorry it took so long." He reached past her, not touching her, to pull the door closed. She felt him sigh. "El Bufo's dead."

She recalled that "El Bufo" had been the bully of a police detective investigating Mama's case, threatening her family, the man who'd been hunting Mael. But the jaguar was abject; it was obvious. She sat back in the seat.

"Mael is dead," she said, in an attempt at the same careless tone, a dark-haired body in a grease-stained huipil floating half-submerged in a river more vivid than all the colors of pigment possible in the world.

"And Mama — we had Mama's funeral."

A balloon in the city sky, shrinking. Letting go of all those images was futile, they were replaced again almost immediately, redoubled. But letting Mama go, she had gained something. Permission.

She didn't know why she was telling him. She was talking to some ideal of him, to that feeling of fur, of something substantial she could hold that expected nothing of her, dangerous, like some stray cat.

"I killed one of her killers," said the jaguar.

"Which one?" she said. "Skull face?" As if this was all still a part of her dream.

The jaguar shuddered, stared, then seemed not to find the thing that scared him. "There were … there were four. I only saw three. This one had a red jacket. I bit through his collarbone. There was another with tattoos. El Bufo killed him. The others got away."

"What color were their feathers?" Cristina sighed almost before the question had left her mouth. It wasn't as if they could unkill Mama. "Never mind."

She reached into her satchel and compressed the sketchbook's covers between her hands, to keep its contents from bursting, staining the inside of the car with ink and graphite and acrylic, to keep herself from opening it up and drawing the jaguar in the act of ripping a man open and eating his heart. The weight of it grew until she couldn't stand it. She picked his phone out of the ashtray, plugged it into the stereo and encountered the lock screen. Two wrong guesses and he took it away, entered the code, gave it back. His touch, the pads of his paws against her fingers, was like a shock.

She scrolled through albums until she found it again. *Sketches of Spain*. She turned the stereo up loud.

"I don't know what to do," he said, paws on the wheel. "I don't know what I am."

"You're … a jaguar," she said. She still felt half-asleep. Maybe she'd never feel awake again.

He laughed. "I'm not. You see me that way, but I'm not. I'm not human either. All I do is run away, over and over, but I never get away, and I never get anywhere else. Tell me what to do, Cristina."

She'd spent the last she didn't know how many days trying to dig to the bottom of this drift of visions. It had felt like progress, but then Hugo.

"Drive, please," she said.

"Where?"

"Just ..." Not back to Comalapa.

He mumbled something. He pulled onto the highway south.

Under her nails, her thumbs were tingling from pressing the sketchbook so hard. She let go. She pulled the pencil from the book's coil binding and sharpened it with her penknife, shooing slivers out the window. She flipped through drawing after drawing until she got to a blank page.

Not many left.

Cristina dozed and woke and dozed against the headrest while the world wheeled, guided by the jaguar's paw. It was in odd ways not as comfortable as the bus, in other ways wonderful, luxurious. She could stretch out her legs, but didn't know what to do with her elbows. The ride was interminable and incredibly bumpy as he went all kinds of out of the way to avoid security checkpoints and cameras.

Not that she knew what the way was. Not for hours. At one point he made her drive, past some cops he couldn't get around, while he hid in the trunk. It didn't go well. She ground the gears, stalled out in the middle of the road, but the cops only laughed. Around the next hill, she stopped and let him out and he drove on again in shaken silence until the tension drained away and she fell to dozing again.

The answer came to her as they sailed over the shoulder of Santa María Volcano into the first curve of the downslope toward

Xela, the little city's layer of smog a gray line cutting the mountains off at their waists, making them look like the long dresses of the faceless women. A frog in her throat. "Dr. Ixchel," she managed to croak.

"What?" He turned down the music, which had shifted, inevitably, to reggae.

Cristina pulled herself up in her seat. She unstuck a strand of hair congealed to her cheek by drool, and her face warmed — Lencho and Miguel Ángel and no one else was allowed to see her so unguarded. But the jaguar had seen her asleep on the side of the road. The jaguar was some figment of her dreams, a pariah cat from her childhood she'd plied with morsels of fried chicken until he would collapse and render up his belly to be rubbed.

"Luz's friend. The keynote speaker from the protest. The old woman with all those degrees. Dr. Ixchel. That's who we need to find. You heard Luz talking about her. She — she has PhDs. She's ..." She rubbed ineffectually at the graphite stains on the heel of her hand, then used the same hand to rub sleep from her eyes. She didn't know how to articulate the feeling of meeting her, sitting beside her in Felipe's backseat that day at the protest. Ixchel was like an ancient seed: wizened and bursting with potential. "She didn't just live through the war — she lived through ... you know."

Trying to figure out what exactly she meant, Cristina hesitated long enough that the jaguar filled in. "Everything?"

"What do you mean?"

"History. The coup that ousted Árbenz — she'd have been, what, a teenager? Before that, the reforms. Land redistribution. The United Fruit strikes." He looked surprised at himself. "Though I mean, living through the war, the reconstruction, that's complicated enough."

"Of course, that's true," she said quickly.

She knew, vaguely, about all those things, that they'd happened not all that many years before she'd been born. But they weren't things her family talked about, any more than they talked about what had happened to Papi. Or Teresa.

Somehow, she would have to get them to talk. But not now, not yet.

"Live with Luz a little while," the jaguar said apologetically. "I guess you can't help picking stuff up."

"No, you're right," she said. "Everything, history." Dr. Ixchel was the opposite of the faceless women. She didn't exist outside of time — or if she did, she also had a past, a real past, longer and realer than anyone else's. She had a face, lined like a riverbed in drought. Cristina wanted to paint Dr. Ixchel's eyes the way she'd painted Mael's, but in reverse, with the world written on the skin, the world of war and disappearances, each hardship a wrinkle. Not a wrinkle but a feather. Each hardship one iridescent feather among thousands, until her face became a bird's. A quetzal's. Which was nothing she could explain, except in paint. Not even to a jaguar posing as a man.

Dr. Ixchel had wanted this: the two of them, Cristina and Felipe, together. It had come about without her having to do anything to make it happen. She didn't know whether to read into that. In the mirror, she looked ... awake, at least.

"All I'm saying is, if Dr. Ixchel doesn't know what you are — or what I am," she made herself add, "I don't know if anybody does."

"Okay. Sure," he said. "Except we don't know where she is."

"She's in Totonícapan."

The car hummed and shuddered as he downshifted through the curves. Over the stereo, a reedy-voiced Black man sang in English about revolution.

On the outskirts of Xela, that ancient city in the clouds, the city of Cristina's ancestors, there appeared out of fog the entrance to a brand-new, painfully modern shopping center: pristine pavement painted with neat white lines, private security vehicles, towering light posts sprouting humming halogens glaring even in daylight.

In the wilting little park at the center of the roundabout, a gleaming concrete statue of Tecún Úman brandished atlatl and jaguar shield, staring stonily aloft at the volcano. Proud, indomitable, the last king of their ancestors, he'd been killed defending this city — the last native city — in battle with the conquistador captain. According to the story, he didn't die, but was transformed into a quetzal; as the free spirit of his people, he lived on.

The car rolled through the roundabout, circling.

"Are we stopping?"

"Sorry, yeah. We'll go to Totonícapan. First, though, I need a favor." He pushed some grease-stained cash into her hands. "I need you to buy me some clothes."

She'd gotten him exactly what he wanted, without his having to say so. It was just a pair of red nylon shorts with an abundance of pockets and a digital camo t-shirt with a Jamaican flag decal on the chest, but it was eerie how much more like himself he felt sliding back into Baby's driver's seat and setting the car to purring.

He wasn't a jaguar. He was something else.

She slept again on the way, her cheek squashed against the window as the convoluted countryside of the highlands rolled past, until he screeched to a halt in the middle of a cornfield. "What is it?" she asked him, startled awake again. "What?"

He threw the car into reverse and pulled up alongside a small, dark brown sedan abandoned in the ditch. "Serendipity," he muttered. It wasn't a Corolla, but close enough. He didn't want to think how it had got there, so he just stole the plates and threw the old ones into the cornfield.

When she saw what he was doing, she made him leave money folded under a wiper.

Shielded once again by a lie, he went back to the main roads, where they could go faster. So they came to the crossing from Xela into Totonícapan department along the usual highway route and waited in line at the checkpoint. He flipped through fake IDs. But when their turn came, instead of the usual orange cones and armed officials, they found a double row of chains studded with spikes laid across the highway.

"Those aren't cops," he said. He double-checked that the windows were rolled up and the doors locked.

Cristina sat up straight and focused intently on the men approaching with machetes on their belts.

"Please don't," he said, but she rolled the window down anyway.

"There's a toll," one man said, his Spanish thickly accented with K'iche', his nose blistered from the sun. "For our cause."

As they watched, two women, one with a baby on her back, dragged a plastic banner, red, green, and black, into place covering the usual official sign. *THE COMPANY BOUGHT OUR LANDS. THEY GAVE US JOBS. THEY DIDN'T SAY THEY'D MAKE OUR CHILDREN SICK.* Only weeks ago, just down the road, police had killed a dozen protesters just like these, yet here they were.

WE ARE ALL TOTONÍCAPAN.

"Ask him what happened to the real cops," Felipe said in the quietest voice he could manage.

"They're calling it a 'police strike,'" the man said gruffly. "But what happened is we accused them too loudly of murder. Now they're punishing us."

"It's been three days," added the other man, thumbs in his belt like a rancher. "We've had all kinds of ruffians, private corporate security trying to assume control. So we decided to impose a little community self-government. Everything's fine. Pay the toll, and you can go on your way."

Cristina looked at Felipe.

He passed her some money, possibly too much again, because it was hers. He tried not to read the look she gave him as suspicious.

"We're looking for Dr. Ixchel," she said, handing it over calmly, even kindly.

The men's sternness might have softened. "The health clinic. North of the park, around the corner from the church." They dragged the chains aside. One of them tipped his straw hat.

The highway crossed a river — or what on one side of the bridge was a river, on the other side a waste where no living thing grew, strewn with ominous machines. What entered the jaundiced cornfields, the beanfields, the fields of dead lilies and squash beyond the town was the ghost of a river, a muddy rut glistening with yellow slick, streaked with red rust.

"It's just like in Comalapa," Cristina murmured, looking stricken.

Felipe was thinking of the photo in the Antonellises' kitchen, future generals and presidents smoking, plotting, next to a ditch full of dead campesinos. This was the land where the masks came off. "Silver mining," he said grimly. "These foreign conglomerates come in, the government sells them the rights for basically nothing in exchange for bribes, favors, prestige, and they clear cut and spray everything with ..." He drummed on the steering wheel, trying to remember the details, because it was easier than trying to take it all in. "… Some awful chemical that binds with a bunch of things that aren't silver, and it causes some even more awful chemical to form? And it uses up all the water they can possibly get their hands on, blasting it at a hillside to turn it to mud."

They were coming to the end of it now; here was a patch of green grass, and a locust tree that didn't look completely dead. He tried to resist stepping on the gas; there was no getting away from it, not really.

"See?" He was babbling now. "It's absurd, but I know these things because I absorb them against my will over breakfast with Luz and Aníbal. The land is just completely blasted afterward, useless, the soil is washed away. And the people. It's like this everywhere. I swear you can't possibly keep up with it all. It's like drops in the sea."

But someone could. And they could do something about it. Organize. Resist. Luz? Even now, without Aníbal? The cops and the private security forces would be back. And with more than machetes.

The fountains in the city square were silent. The clinic was a white concrete building with a faded logo suggesting it had once been a sub-branch of the ministry of agriculture. Inside, a pale nurse in cheerful clothes and a silver cross on a thin chain sat surrounded by papers. Behind windows, down a long corridor, locals lay in metal frame beds and on pallets on the floor. It was hard to make sense of their bodies: a stomach bulged oddly, an eye leaked yellow. Skin swelled with pustules and rash.

Felipe kept his sunglasses on.

Cristina cried. "Are they all people poisoned by the mining?" she asked, wiping her eye with the heel of her palm. Her fingers were black with ink or graphite.

"You don't have to worry about getting sick," the nurse said in a foreign accent. "Just don't drink the water." And she passed them each a clear plastic bottle from a shrinkwrapped pallet on the floor. Heavy, like bullets of light.

Dr. Ixchel was upstairs, standing before a transparency projector in front of a room full of women, children and old men. Teaching Spanish. Teaching them to read the mining company's warning signs. They asked questions he couldn't understand. She leaned with one hand on the desk.

Cristina hesitated in the doorway. A few curling strands of her hair haloed up from her face while the rest spiraled around it. If not for her, he wouldn't be here. He'd come looking for her because he wanted to help her — to help someone — to relieve his conscience for everything he'd done. And she needed help. She'd been sleeping by the side of the road. She still smelled sour — he should say something. But it felt good, being with her, beside her. Not easy, but right.

Dr. Ixchel looked up from her notes. She nodded. Her eyes invited them to sit. There were no empty chairs.

When the students' questions had been answered, when she'd squeezed the hands that were offered and was wringing her own hand as if in pain, she ushered Felipe and Cristina to seats in the classroom's front row and offered them stale dulces and bottled tea. "We have ceramic filters and solar pasteurization, but these methods work only to remove particulates and bacterial contamination. The poisons the company uses to leach precious metals from the soils are liquids in solution and therefore unaffected. So all our drinking water has to be brought in."

Dr. Ixchel was quick but careful, like a bird too aware of the hollowness of its bones.

Cristina clutched her sketchbook again. He still didn't get what that meant. Prophecy, he supposed with exhaustion. Forbidden truth. Jaguars. "You've been waiting for us?" she said.

"Sometimes it's obvious," said the doctor, with gravity, with an almost apologetic tightening and relaxing of her shoulders as she levered herself into the chair. "But there are no real answers, or I would have found them by now. It was all lost. It has all been lost for generations and generations. Sometimes — particularly when I've just returned here from the city — even I can hardly believe any of our children still speak Poquomam or Awakatek. We must make our own answers, remake them out of what remains: our bodies, what little is left of our lands. It doesn't matter if they're right or not. There are no right answers. What matters is whether they're the answers we need." Now she was shuffling through the jumbled teaching materials on the desk, searching.

He felt rather than understood the weight of what she wasn't saying. She wasn't talking about silver mines or private security.

A sentence, *Where is my father?* written out in five or six different languages, English, Spanish, K'iche', Q'eqchi', others he didn't recognize. A picture of the holy family arranged on the steps of the cathedral in Xela. A marketplace full of grain, fruit, spices. An ayudante making change on a crowded bus. A nurse administering a vaccine. An altar among ruins. A football pitch. A dance. A copy of one of the signs warning about the water. A flyer advertising Luz and Aníbal's protest, with instructions for where to get a free charter bus to the city. Dr. Ixchel threw up her hands and the papers settled across the desk.

Meeting their eyes seemed to extract from her some great effort. Felipe knew the feeling. "I'm sorry I'm not better prepared. Resources are thin, as you've seen. And we're so busy now, doing everything the government refuses to do. I simply haven't had the time — not that I knew what I could say. But I wanted to show you — ah!"

She opened a drawer and reached inside, almost disappearing into it she was so small. She reappeared holding a book full of clippings and handwritten notes, the covers worn white at the corners and spine. She thumped it on the desk facing them, letting it fall open where the spine had broken, to a full-spread illustration: an old, familiar copy of an older drawing of an unfathomably more ancient carved stone stela depicting a man in the mouth of a jaguar.

"I assume you've seen this drawing before. A foreign adventurer made this almost two centuries ago," the doctor said. "He took it home with him to the North, along with many others, and made a living reprinting them. They made him famous. And more came after him, searching for our lost treasures. But the stone itself, the stone this drawing depicts, stayed in the jungle where he'd found it. And eventually the image carved on it rotted away. The drawing is all that's left." She laughed ruefully, her eyes on Felipe.

It sent a shiver through him, as it always did, no matter how many times it happened. He hated it, feeling exposed, vulnerable, like being naked. What she meant by "our bodies" and "our lost treasures" was that *he* was as old as that stone stela, older, only he hadn't crumbled. Instead he'd died, been reborn, died and been reborn all through those intervening years, never any wiser but always just as alive, never human or animal, but something else. And still he needed some dead adventurer's preserving hand to show him what he had once been.

He saw why she wanted him to laugh. But he couldn't. "Why are you showing me this?"

"Because I'm the same," the doctor said. "Don't you see?"

She pushed a xeroxed drawing across at them; this one was of Tecún Úman. On top of that she placed a dog-eared travel pamphlet advertising guided hiking tours of the cloud forest in Sololá, foreigners smiling, drinking bottled water, an emerald green quetzal, with its blood-red breast, looking just like it did on the money.

This was a different feeling, new.

"And because so is she." Now the doctor indicated Cristina.

"What?" said Felipe.

"Me?"

Cristina looked so taken aback, suddenly he *was* laughing.

"You are like him. Like me."

"But I can't — I don't ..."

"Not yet." The doctor smiled so eloquently, with such awkward, embarrassed understanding, it made him glad again of his sunglasses, of his masks, of the layers between him and everything else. "For now," she told Cristina, "you're a woman who sees. I see the potential for you to be more. But if it weren't for you — if I hadn't met you both at once that day at the protest — I might not have said what I did."

Felipe had no trouble reading the doctor's averted eyes this time: she'd been afraid. Of *him*. Was she now? Yes, of course she was. But not of Cristina — never of Cristina. He understood this without rancor. He'd been afraid of Cristina at the beginning, because she saw the truth. But he'd been doing her an injustice. He hadn't known her. He still didn't know her.

"You must understand," the doctor went on, "that you are the only others like me I've met since what happened in my village."

Her face changed then. It became, briefly, a different face. An old man's face, thick, wrinkled like her own, with a broad nose and a disdainful, cynical expression — something like El Bufo's if he'd lived another forty, fifty years. Then it changed back. Felipe wasn't sure what he'd seen, if he'd seen it.

"There was a man in Uxun back then. I was only a child. He wasn't a good man or a kind man. But he showed me what I could do. Not to teach me, not to pass anything on, but to use me, control me, make me his. I used it to escape him and to survive — when the army came, I took my master's form. That was so long ago. It doesn't mean no others exist. I wasn't out looking, I was hiding. I've been hiding ever since. It was luck — and your friend Luz — that brought the three of us together. But that only makes this — you, us, together — more important."

They sat and stared at each other, all three of them.

"Luck," repeated Felipe, thinking of the abandoned brown sedan in the cornfield, and then of everything, of El Bufo laying in wait for him outside the airport, taking him to Cristina at her mother's house, then to Lupita. He thought resentfully of the calendars taped to Baby's dashboard, and of the days, the seeds, falling. "Not fate?"

The doctor levered herself upright in the chair, and he realized her feet didn't even touch the floor. "In my experience, fate isn't inevitable. It's something you live up to. My fate was to save my people, the day the army came to San Rafael. I knew they were coming. I didn't know what they would do, but I could guess. They'd done it before. It's why I fled. But I could have stayed, I could have warned people, I could have used what I knew. I could have used what I am. Maybe I could have — but I didn't. I survived — but I was the only one. I've had to live with that. Now maybe I get to make a different choice."

"I don't understand." Cristina touched the picture of Tecún Úman. "You took your master's form? You mean — the way he does?" She shot a glance at Felipe.

"Yes," said Dr. Ixchel simply.

"What *are* you, doctor?" asked Cristina, then blushed. "I mean, what are ... we? I can see Felipe, that he's ... but I always could, even though he looks normal to everyone else. To me, you seem like a very wise, intelligent, very kind old woman."

"That's what I want everyone to see." Ixchel opened the book to a different illustration, this time a reproduction of a handwritten manuscript page, the left column in K'iche', the right in Spanish. He recognized some of it from Luz's library: the *Popol Vuh*. She pointed at a word. "*Wayob*. Animal souls, or literally, 'sleepers.' That's K'iche', and also Yucatec. In Nahuatl, *nagual*. In Qu'cab, we would have said *wayna ah ik*. Are they words for what we are? I don't know. But since I'm the only one left who speaks Qu'cab, I guess I decide what the words mean. So I say it means us. If you want me to guess, I'd say it means we're old souls, souls who once were other."

She held still a moment, hands in her lap, taking in both of them. She turned to Felipe. "Close the door, please? And the shade."

He did as she asked, locking it, peeling free and folding down over the square of glass a paper shade made of old teaching handouts taped together.

When he turned back, the old woman was gone.

On the back of Dr. Ixchel's chair perched a sapphire-and-emerald bird, rings of scarlet circling its eyes like bruises, a long, long, green tail curving gracefully to the floor where it ended in whorl after whorl the blue of thundercloud, crater lake, lagoon, sky after hurricane. Breathtaking. Fragile. Not like the coins or the pamphlets at all.

Cristina's eyes had welled up again in tears that she didn't brush away or try to hide.

It didn't even surprise him, somehow. He didn't know how he should feel. He took off his sunglasses to watch the colors iridesce in Dr. Ixchel's feathers and tried to puzzle out whether he should feel less alone or more sure of his place in the world.

"Why do you hide it," he said, not a question because he knew the answer, wanting Cristina to hear. Wanting to hear it said aloud. He took a step toward her, and at this slightest movement the quetzal startled. Her wings flared, pine-dark and midnight on the undersides, and she strained toward the louvered windows that opened out on the square with its dry fountain — Felipe felt her panic, her longing in his stomach, his chest.

Cristina cried out and half-rose from her seat, reaching. "No, don't go! Please —"

A moment later, the doctor sat placidly human again before the desk, straight-spined, not remotely filling the chair, fingers knitted in her lap.

"I hide it," she said, "because I'm afraid. Afraid of breaking people's hearts. Afraid of failing them, like I failed the people of San Rafael. And of course I'm afraid of what people would do, if they knew. You know what they say about the quetzal in captivity?"

"They die," Cristina whispered.

"It's a long, long time since our people were free, yet the men who rule this country chose the quetzal for a symbol. People have every right to be afraid. But we can't afford to let fear defeat us. What happened to Qu'cab — it was my fault as much as anyone's. I think about it every day. What happened to Chicomuceltec, to Itza', what's happening to Lacandon — I never want it to happen again. It's why I'm here now, why I teach. It's why I came to the city to speak. It's why I met you. I hid when the army came to San Rafael because I didn't want my story to end like Tecún Úman's. But I can't accept that those are the only options: to fight and die or hide and live. And I don't want either of you to make that mistake. Or you'll regret it the rest of your lives."

She was afraid even to say it.

Felipe felt suddenly, irrepressibly restless. Like he'd felt in Lupita's house just before El Bufo pulled the gun. Captivity, control — fate, making your own fate — he hated being told what he had to do. Lupita had told him to run. Now the doctor was telling him to fight. Which was what El Bufo had been telling him all along.

Had Tecún Úman's death looked like El Bufo's?

He thought of the margay, alone and isolated, the soft fur between her brows fine enough to reveal the wary tautness of the skin beneath. Her little stretch of woods would shrink, closer every moment to a cage at the zoo. Eventually, the water in her little trickle would turn to poison.

He prowled the circuit of the classroom. A long bulletin board at the back was scaled thick with photos of townspeople, babies, students, adults smiling, learning, singing, protesting, celebrating, not a single photo of the sick or dying, no photos of protests broken up by police, no funerals, no empty streets, no dry fountains, no dead crops. It was a mask, for when they needed it, like all the others — the way Tecún Úman was for Xela, the way San Simón was for the lake people — a mask this town used to fool itself out of giving up.

While he prowled, Cristina rose and moved close to the doctor, tentative, birdlike herself, taking her hand.

"Why can I only see him as a jaguar, not a man?" he heard Cristina ask.

"He won't let you."

He stopped short. "You don't know that," he said, and he pulled off the mask, the jaguar mask that let him see himself the way his parents saw him, the way Luz saw him. Just like at Lupita's — only it was easier this time. Because of Cristina. "I don't control what Cristina sees. I barely control it at all. Without a mask —"

"You're wrong," said the doctor. "We're the same, can't you feel it? Look at me. This is my mask."

Her mask — her face — was so expressive, with its wrinkles, so easy to read. There was so much expectation in it. He couldn't stand her gaze. "But you're —"

"An old woman? You don't know how old. I was already old when the army came to Uxun. What little I know took a long, long time to learn. The old man in Uxun when I was a girl could do what we do." Her face became his again as she spoke, thick and cruel, and Felipe couldn't deny this time that he'd seen it. Could she make her face whatever she wanted? "He spoke no Spanish, he had never seen the city. A cloud of cigar smoke followed wherever he went. It masked the alcohol fumes, as long as you didn't get too close. I wasn't so lucky. But I learned from him — in spite of him — to trust in myself, even if I trusted no one else. In the end, I used him. I beat him. I survived, I escaped, and he's gone. Maybe, if you'll let me, I can make it easier for you. I can teach you. Is there anyone you trust, Felipe?"

His eyes strayed involuntarily to Cristina, who had opened her notebook and was sketching, the pencil hissing as it wore itself out against the page. "No," he said, too forcefully.

The doctor smiled — she saw right through him. Like Cristina.

He prowled to the windows. It was past noon; out in the square, vendors by the silent fountain hawked chiltepes and contaminated fruit. In the beds a floor below, children were dying. Aníbal languished in a jail cell at Pavoncito. El Bufo lay rotting in El Gallito, his body returning to the refuse from which it had sprung. David Antonellis was holed up somewhere plotting his next move, his wife hiding in her suite staring into smog, sipping the best coffee in the world. And Luz ... he wondered where Luz was now. Not hiding, that much was certain. Luz, he thought, would take Tecún Úman's path every time.

He wanted to deny everything she'd said; he couldn't. Luz was right to love this woman, to worship her. She'd made mistakes. She was quick to admit them. She'd done everything she could to live them down. Even though she was afraid of all the same things he was.

Voices in the hallway, outside the locked door.

The doctor stood. "I'm afraid I have another class coming in. There's a volunteer hostel around the corner; they have bunks and clean water. You're tired. You could go there and rest. Later, if you decide you want my help, I could show you the ruins of Uxun. I could show you —"

But the truth had already fallen on him, with a finality breathtaking in its suddenness. He couldn't believe it had taken him this long. He had to do something. Luz. Aníbal. El Bufo. Eufemia Ramos and her daughter. He felt it like an itch. "No," he said. "I'm sorry. But I can't wait. You're right. I've been running away. But … I'm not going to do that anymore. I'm going to … fight.

"It's not that hard," he told her, told himself. "I already fucking killed two people, how hard can it be?"

The doctor didn't seem surprised. Relieved, maybe. Vindicated? But she had another class coming in. She collected scattered pages and put them away.

Cristina's eyes were wide, her pencil frozen above the page. "What are you going to do?" she asked.

"I have no idea," he admitted. The jaguar mask was in his hand. "Go back to the city, I guess. Maybe I can sneak into the prison. I'll —"

"I'll go with you," Cristina said in a rush.

"You should stay," he found himself saying, not meaning it. "Coming here was your idea. You could learn from her, you could

…" He was ashamed at the relief he felt — at not having to do it alone.

Cristina closed the sketchbook. She slid the pencil through the spiral. Her hands were smeared with tears and graphite. She brushed at her eyes with a corner of her shawl. She hugged the doctor. "Thank you. For everything you do. We'll come back. I promise."

The doctor let go of Cristina's hands, took one of Felipe's paws in both of hers. His head swam sorting through the permutations, wings, fingers, even as he began to understand that, to Ixchel at least, it didn't matter.

He put the mask on.

Outside, the streets were emptying for siesta. A dead pigeon lay on the rim of the fountain. Eroded stone saints stood in alcoves on the church facade, hands and faces worn away, just empty robes.

By unspoken agreement, they went to the hostel and paid for scant showers in solar-heated rainwater that felt to Cristina like she'd been given new skin.

The host told them of a truckload of uncontaminated produce arriving from out of town, but at the sight of the hungry crowd waiting despite the heat when it arrived, they backed quietly away.

The car's engine gasped to life with the hot scent of burnt oil, overtaxed from too many hours in the arms of mountains.

"You don't have to do this," the jaguar said. "I don't even know where I'm going."

She hugged him, impulsively and hard. "If what she said is true … if we're really the only ones … we can't just ignore it."

It still made her want to laugh out loud: this beautiful, wild creature, long and lean, with huge eyes so green, hiding himself behind a tiny wooden mask that didn't even cover his whiskers. But, she supposed, it meant he looked human. To everybody else.

A deep breath, a quietly guttural sigh against her chest. He reached under his seat and passed her a giant wad of greasy cash. "We're going to need fluid. And petrol. And food."

"Where did it all come from?" she asked in amazement, a moment before she saw in her head the four angels with their submachine guns, the narrow table under Mama's silly altar and Cristina's terrible art. The single, hollow plaster saint: Antonio, patron of lost things. She lifted the sheaf of rumpled bills to her face and inhaled the faint, familiar scent of fryer grease.

He shifted into gear. The car crawled across the empty square, bouncing over cobbles. "El Bufo. He took it from the crime scene."

"My mother's money."

The jaguar winced, but spoke with determination. "The police would have kept it if he hadn't. And he tried to give it back to your family. As a bribe. So they'd give up that girl, the witness."

"María Elena," said Cristina flatly. Here again was proof that what she'd painted in Comalapa was not out of her head, and she would be free neither of the vision nor the guilt of María Elena's death. And a reminder that El Bufo — and Felipe — had been among those hunting for her.

"He's an asshole, a bully," the jaguar blurted. "I mean, he was. But he was doing it for a reason. He was actually trying to help people, to protect them. In his way. I didn't think so at first, not for a long time. But you should have seen —"

"Do *not* compare him to Dr. Ixchel."

"I'm not," he protested. "Listen. I'm telling you this because — it's like you said. Like she said. We're the same. We have to trust each other."

She remembered how afraid she'd been. Of both of them. Her instincts, she'd learned, were worth trusting. "You haven't told me how you got the money. Did you … find it after he was dead?"

No, that wasn't it. He didn't have a human face, he didn't blush, he didn't smile or frown in ways she could read — but it got easier to read his body language, the cant of his ears, the swell and sliver of his pupils, the way he blinked. "It was before that," he confessed. "Nobody took the bribe, so El Bufo just … left it. He didn't care. He wanted power — secrets — not money. I knew your family wouldn't accept it. I *needed* it. Luz and Aníbal never had enough for the rent. Everything they had they spent funding the campaign. So I took it … but I didn't actually use it," he added hastily. "I mean … not much. I thought I'd keep it for you, give it back when I had a chance to explain. I didn't even spend any of it until —"

"Shut up," she said. A jaguar in a man mask. What did she expect? Of course he was a liar, a thief. She was only figuring out how to read him now, after all this. Even though she could already see through him. She was like him. With everyone else, lying must come easy.

They made it off the cobblestones onto smooth, newly-paved mining company road. The car sighed; Cristina let go of the door handle, but she wasn't about to relax.

He pulled into the petrol station. Past the lights was the highway. When he turned to face her, the penitence written in the droop of his whiskers and ears was impossible to miss. For a second she thought she saw herself in his eyes: pale, exhausted, angry. Different from how she thought of herself, how she looked in the mirror. More adult. She straightened half-consciously, resisted brushing at her hair.

"The money's yours. I'm sorry I didn't tell you before. I understand if it means you can't trust me. I wouldn't, if I were you.

Anywhere you want to go, anytime. I'll take you. I don't expect that to make it up to you. I'll pay you back. Everything I spent — these clothes, the gas. Two simcards. A shitty cup of coffee. I paid a kid to watch the car. I paid a witch to read my fortune — it's a long story. I'll make a list. I left enough for the rent in one of Luz's books in my apartment — we can stop there when we get back, I'll get it for you. And if there's something else I can do to make it up to you, Cristina, tell me. Please. You're the last person I want to hurt. But … right now, Baby needs gas, to get us back to the city or anywhere. She needs oil and fluid. And a good night's rest, though she can't have that yet. What you're holding is everything I had. If you don't want to help me, I get it. I can take you back to the doctor, right now if you want. I can make money. I can try to find a fare. I can sell Baby if I have to. I'll take a fucking bus."

She remembered suddenly what he'd told her that morning when he'd picked her up by the side of the highway outside Comalapa. He'd said it again with Ixchel. He was a killer. A killer of killers. And yet she'd never seen him haunted by any angel. Could she hold him accountable for stealing and lies but forgive him for murder?

Could she ignore what they'd found out about each other, when they barely knew what it meant?

"Take off the mask," she said. And he did it — without a word, without even hesitating, with the attendant approaching beyond the tinted glass. He offered it, then dropped it in her lap when she wouldn't take it.

She touched it: warm, smooth, heavy, threaded with an orange ribbon. She saw herself again in his eyes — eyes the green of every living thing in the evening after a wet season downpour. She wasn't going to get lost in them.

"You're not getting off that easy," she said, and paid for the petrol.

He drove to the lake with his phone on infinite shuffle, keeping to the highway, detouring only to avoid police and the places where last year's flash flooding had eaten the roads. Cristina could skip the dubstep and hardcore if she had to. But she didn't. She didn't say anything at all, for hours. Just listened. A few times she reached for her sketchbook, then seemed to catch herself.

He knew there was nothing more he could say. So instead, he tried to plan.

He could climb prison walls past midnight, rip out the throats of guards, of inmates. But how could he find Aníbal, how could he get her out safe? Pavoncito was huge, sprawling, not merely corrupt but ruled by corruption. The guards served at the pleasure of the narcos and mareros who used it as a base; behind its walls they were immune to prosecution, to retaliation. At least according to Luz and *Waking Dream.*

Cristina fell asleep as they were passing the lake, her feet tucked underneath her, hugging the satchel to her chest. Her eyes moved behind her eyelids. The volcanoes — Santa María, Tolimán, Atitlán — rose and pendulumed and shrank again, and the shadow of the car's roof and the sun warred across her sleeping shape like night and day. A few twisting strands of her dark hair seemed to reach for the light.

He listened to Luz's voicemail, finally. The one from after the protest.

"You probably guessed she's in jail. I was too, for a hot second. There must have been hundreds of us, in a drunk tank. She wasn't with me — I couldn't get to her. They couldn't keep us all. I think they released anybody they could ID."

Her voice was clipped, cold at first, then angry. Furious. Then at last she was sobbing.

"But Aníbal — you know, she never takes her passport unless she has to. She cares so much. They won't even admit they have her. It's like she doesn't exist. Why am I telling you this. You fucking asshole, I need you. How could you just leave us?"

He called Aníbal. Six rings, voicemail.

He could not bring himself to call Luz. He called Luz. This time it wasn't voicemail but a busy signal. Or else the number had been disconnected. He dropped the phone in the ashtray.

He glanced at Cristina's sleeping form for the thousandth time in an hour and found her eyes upon him, wide and dark, half-full of sleep but unwavering.

"Hey," he said. "Hey, what is it? You awake?"

"I'm awake," she said. She didn't sound sure.

"What are you looking at?" He laughed, nervously. "I'm a jaguar, I know." He hesitated, then tipped up the mask and bared his teeth, a yawn, a grimace, the awkwardest of jokes.

He was so busy trying to assimilate that sleepy, trusting expression, trying to accept that it was meant for him, that he nearly slammed into the wall of stalled traffic when it appeared over the crest of the hill, the last hill before the descent into the city, into Babylon.

He couldn't stop fast enough. He knew exactly the moment when the wheels would lock and he would lose control, and it was too close. It wasn't even four by the dashboard clock — and they were going into the city, the wrong way for rush hour traffic. This wasn't normal traffic. At the bottom of the hill, past hundreds of stopped cars curving in and out of sight along the mountain, a barricade blocked the eastbound highway: half a dozen green and black official vehicles from three different departments angled across the road. A tripod-mounted machine gun hulked in the bed of a pickup. Beyond them into smog, he thought he imagined smoke rising in columns from the city.

There were more cars coming fast behind him. This would be the end. A pileup, nowhere to run. Trapped in a toxic river of twisted metal. If they survived.

Cristina had her seatbelt on. A few feet to her right, the flimsy guardrail and a steep, steep drop.

Then there was no longer time to think.

The moment before the wheels locked and he lost control, he turned: just a hair to the left. They skidded. The tires shrieked. He warned Cristina to hold on, but he couldn't hear himself, didn't know if she'd heard. Baby spun counterclockwise. Her rear fender scraped the guardrail above the abyss; the rail pushed them away. They spun toward oncoming cars, all trying desperately to stop. The motorcycle in front screamed, its rider twisted, deliberately went down. It wouldn't help, he had to know he was dead.

Baby's rear right taillight crunched into the back of an ancient Range Rover. Felipe's body was slammed back against the seat and to the right, Cristina's mirroring his in his periphery, soft curls rising around her head, then falling. Cristina was alive, unharmed, her eyes unclouded. The motorcycle's wheels bounced off the driver's side door, and Felipe did not watch to see the rider's neck snap or his body be flung under the Range Rover's wheels. For an instant, everything was still. A terrible, deadly illusion.

Cristina reached for the door latch. She was going to get out and see if the rider was safe. But he wasn't.

"No," said Felipe.

He shifted into first.

"Wait," she said. "That man on the motorcycle —"

The burned wheels caught and the car moved, leaving bits of itself crushed into the Range Rover, inching across the median and out into oncoming traffic.

From his right came city traffic, slow, slowing. From his left, an official taxi that wouldn't stop fast enough not to crush the motorcycle and rider. But Baby would not be there.

Second gear. Baby roared back up the hill the way they'd come, horns honking behind them.

Cristina was rigid, gripping her satchel and the door — but alive. He put out an arm to reassure himself this vision was real. She was warm, sticky — sweat not blood — and the world went on dangerously for too many beats before he could pull his hand away. She blinked at him.

"You're okay," he said. Reassuring her, himself. She didn't answer.

The jaguar mask was askew in the rearview. He adjusted it.

Also in the rearview, far away, two tiny police motorcycles pulled out from the roadblock, red lights oscillating.

"Shit."

"What?"

"Behind us." Third gear. His favorite. "Listen," he said. "There's — things you need to know." He dodged around an empty farm truck, the steering a little mushy, half the tread burned off the tires. "El Bufo wasn't really with the police. He worked for the SAAS. A spy organization. He was in disgrace, for something he did before I met him — taking bribes, not taking enough bribes, I couldn't figure it out. But he still had connections. That's how he found out David Antonellis wasn't dead."

"The other murder victim? He's alive?"

"I'm sorry. I should have told you."

She bit her lip, shaken. "I — think I knew," she mustered finally. "I already knew Mama died for nothing." She took more deep breaths, glanced over her shoulder. " There's things I need to tell you, too." She gestured with the satchel. "To show you."

"Can it wait?" The speedometer crept upward as they crested the hill, coming off the cliffside and into the long, straight slope through Sacatepequez.

Cristina shrank still further into her seat. "Okay."

"The point is, I'm in their system. This car — one just like it, anyway — is in their system. I'm in trouble. I don't know how much. More, soon. Those weren't even my plates I threw in the cornfield. El Bufo switched mine with one of my neighbors'. Maybe he'd have put them back after this blew over, when he got back in. But he's dead. And it doesn't look like it's blowing over. If they found me in that pileup ... I don't know if they know he's dead. But when they do, they're going to have questions."

He was not just being paranoid. The two police motorcycles rocketed over the hill behind them.

"Can you slow down? Please."

She was right. He was running out of room; the bus station ahead would be thick with pedestrians, taxis, tuktuks. *What would El Bufo do.* Cackling at the insanity of this proposition, he waited for the last curve to put the cops out of sight, then cut left onto a narrow, hillside street, away from the apartment buildings and box stores along the highway, in among trees and private villas. Ignoring NO TRESPASSING signs and a camera he couldn't avoid, he banged through a closed but unlocked gate, into deep chicozapote shade, and pulled up next to a car concealed under a canvas cover.

He wanted her to trust him. He imagined this wasn't helping. "Help," he said.

They scrambled to pull the cover off the other car and over Baby, unveiling a tiny red Japanese roadster that looked like it had never been driven. Fucking rich people. His pulse was exploding.

He pulled her behind a tree trunk by the gate, the earth springy and dry underfoot, thick with waxy leaves lost to drought. The villa glowed through the trees.

The two motorcycles wailed by out on the highway, shrill sirens and bruise-colored lights.

Her breathing was quick and shallow.

"Cristina. Hey." He touched her arm, the hair there softer than his own fur. He pulled his hand back.

"This is crazy."

"I know. Believe me. I'm sorry. You can still back out, you know."

"No, I can't," she said, too loudly. "Stop it. I'm not backing out, and neither are you."

"Okay," he said quietly. "I just — what the fuck are we supposed to do now?"

"We need to go to Antigua. To the artisans' market."

"What? Why?"

"You need a new mask. I — saw it. In a vision, in Totonicapán. Come on, we can't stay here. I'll explain on the way."

They were pulling the cover back over the ugly sportscar when a black, mirror-windowed SUV came down the driveway. The doors swung open, emitting dense men in dark suits, but Felipe was already starting the car. The mangled rear bumper scraped the SUV's as he pulled out. Wincing, he went left, further down the narrow side street, which narrowed further. "Burning bridges, everywhere I go."

Looking back, she saw one of the suits close the gate. They didn't care. They had their own problems. Like everyone.

He passed her the phone. "Help me navigate, please. Back roads. I used to come this way all the time, but it's been awhile."

Cristina thumbed the screen until it showed a nest of roads twisting, reorienting to their movement. Switchbacks, down and down. In the world beyond the dark glass, hillsides rose past them, green and gray through haze.

When he'd touched her arm, hiding among the trees outside the rich people's house, she'd felt a human hand. Calluses. Dirt under fingernails. And his jaguar paw too. It had been the same when Ixchel let down her guard: a bird and a woman, in the same chair, occupying the same space.

Sitting beside him now, trying to calm her breathing, trying to think of a way to get him to see everything she'd seen, she thought of hiding from him with María Elena on the roof of her mother's house. How afraid they'd all been. Of him, of everything.

Life isn't fair, Colocha. Mama had said it many times, but Cristina would always remember best when she'd said it after Papi hadn't come home all those nights in a row, more nights than ever before, and Mama had to explain to her daughters why she still wasn't calling the police.

"I know why you keep running," Cristina said. "Everybody keeps their head down. That's how my Mama raised us all safe in the city, without Papi's help or anybody else's. You keep your head down, you survive. Or you don't. Maybe you starve, maybe you can't feed your family, maybe you get gunned down by angels in broad daylight. My sister Teresa couldn't bear it, so she left. Now she's lying in a ditch in the desert." No use trying not to see that scene in all its surreality. There wasn't time to paint it, and it wouldn't change anything. "Even Mama could only take it so far. She walked into those bullets. If she hadn't tried to warn the other victims, if she'd had the sense to hide herself like Mael, she might be alive. She did the right thing, and she died."

"That's why nobody talks about the war." He slowed to dodge around a tuktuk struggling up the hill. "They think not talking is keeping it from happening again. We all keep our heads down, and people like Molinero keep on like always."

"And it doesn't protect you." She was still pressed against the seat back, gripping the armrest. She tried to relax. "Mael hid, and they found her anyway. My Papi wasn't out agitating in the street, and they disappeared him. That was three years after the peace accords. It doesn't matter if you keep your head down — they let you live until you're in the way. After that — you might as well do the right thing." She wondered if this was what Mama had been thinking. If she'd had time. Again she saw the mareros, the angels, and Mama, wiping her hands on her apron, stepping out to meet them.

"But it still gets you killed." He hunched over the wheel, angry. Yet she could still see him: human, jaguar. She knew what that meant. "Look at Aníbal," he said. "Running into a wall of riot cops? What did she think was going to happen?"

"She was standing up for what she believed. Dr. Ixchel —"

"— is smart enough to pick her battles. You heard her. The quetzal dies in captivity."

And Anibál, Cristina knew, was no different. "So we'll be smart," she said.

Down, down. They passed little stores where brown-edged fruit spilled over the narrow sidewalk onto paving-stones. Bouganvillea cascaded over a weathered aluminum privacy fence three times as high as a person. Someone walked bent under a backpack.

Agua Volcano appeared above rooftops to their right, dormant for five hundred years, its cold crater concealed in cloud. She'd painted it more often than she could count, so often it had become an abstraction, its flanks lit by morning or afternoon light, clouds a royal torque around its neck. A dappling of fair-weather shadows played on the green quilt drawn over its flank — or, like now, a gray ceiling, making the chain of towns in the valley at the mountain's feet seem comfortable and close, the pollution and lights and crime and corruption of the city far away.

"Turn here," she said.

"I remember."

She put the phone aside and got out her sketchbook.

"You know I've never seen a single piece of your art?"

She let out a hissing breath. "It's not about me trusting you, it's about you trusting me."

She fought against an urge to draw the lahar, the avalanche of boiling mud that long ago had roiled down the volcano's flanks to bury the old city. Ash clouds, lightning-lit. A church tower struck by a black wave. Tiny figures fleeing in the foreground. Not every terrible thing that had ever happened was caused by people hurting people.

She flipped through pages: details done in stolen moments, compositional studies from her binge in Comalapa. "I draw because it helps me feel better," she said, "not because it's always true. I found out a long time ago the only way I can make a living at it is painting beautiful things — beautiful lies. So I stopped telling the truth. For so long I forgot it. That day at the protest, I knew you were coming before I saw you." She found that page, the first time she'd drawn him. She made herself hold it to the light. "This one, look — no, don't, you're driving." She kept flipping. "I saw Mama die. In a dream. The killers — I know what they looked like. They killed Mael because she'd seen them, and *I'd* seen them, and I knew it, the whole time I was trying to protect her. Only I didn't believe it."

"You're saying you ... can see the future? Without magic seeds or anything."

"Seeds?"

"Never mind."

"I don't know. Not the future. I see the present, the past — things about me, things I care about, my family … people I love."

"What else have you seen? What have you painted lately?"

"Not much since yesterday. I haven't had a chance. Before that … a lot about death. Mael's death. Mama's. Aníbal — I painted her in prison." There was no sketch, just the canvas. She'd left it in Comalapa. Cristina opened her mouth, closed it again, unsure of how to translate the images into language. "She's in a room by herself. There's a high window, with bars. And I think a lot of people have died in that room. I think she knows it. And maybe she expects to die there herself. There was … there was a noose."

"Jesus," said Felipe. "Are you fucking serious?"

"I'm sorry," she said. "It's just —"

"No." He blinked rapidly under his sunglasses. There was a wrong rumble in his throat. "I get it. I believe you. I'm a jaguar in board shorts, you're … like Ixchel. Like me. It's not your fault, it's just what you see. What else?"

"There's a lot. About you," she admitted, feeling her face flush. "Not your death," she added hastily. "Just … jaguars." She watched his human face change as he took that in. She didn't want him to read too much into it. She didn't know what there was for him to read. But she liked watching his face. Wary. Uncertain. But it suited him, the Felipe she had come to know. She wanted to tell him it would be okay.

"Nothing about El Bufo?"

"No — I mean, I didn't know him. Except." She skipped to the next-to-last marked page. "It's just a doodle. I did in Dr. Ixchel's office, when she was talking about masks. Here." She held it just below the rearview, just for a second, so he could look without killing them. In the bottom left corner, she'd drawn a cartoon of a squat, balding man in a windbreaker and a cheap suit, wearing a frog mask.

He laughed. "Wait. Is that —?"

"I think it's you."

At the market in Antigua half an hour before closing, the crowd was thin, the produce picked-over. Flocks of flies fought over smashed annonas and mangoes ripe past bursting. It was cold in the shadows, still hot and blinding in the sun. He wore the Garifuna mask, afraid of running into anyone he knew. His mother would be five aisles over, wrapping unsold textiles in a stained tablecloth to sell another day. His father might be stepping off a bus a block to the west, slipping his bad arm back out of sight inside a pinned sweatshirt-sleeve. He hadn't seen them in months. It wasn't that he didn't want to. If they saw him, he'd have to explain. They wouldn't let him leave. Later, he could come back and explain everything.

From the corner of his eye, he looked to see if Cristina would catch him lying to himself and instead found her trying not to laugh at his long, skinny face, his longer, skinnier limbs. "Doesn't this mask eat?"

"Garifuna food is the best food in the world," he said seriously. "On the right day, at the right place in the city, this mask gets me a feast. But it can't teach me to cook. I could ask … but then they'd see right through me."

"I can teach you to cook. My mother's fried chicken and rice." She smiled, and he thought of them together in his tiny apartment kitchen. A fantasy, warm and illusory. He shook his head. No time for that now.

They found the mask-seller deep in the market's cloth-walled warrens, between a sea of carved wooden cooking implements and a waterfall of hammocks. She was packing up too, folding masks carefully into a bolt of night-blue cloth. "Wait," he said.

Hard-faced and unsmiling, the mask-seller needed no mask of her own. She had what they wanted, at a price double what they could afford with all that remained of Eufemia's fried chicken money. *Fuck you,* said the frog mask, leering. Her masks, said her expression and her price, weren't for ladino city dwellers with halfway-steady jobs. They were for the poor highlanders who still spoke the ancient tongues, who before remote, ruined altars still danced the ritual dances which were masks for even more ancient traditions. Or else they were for tourists who could pay. That all-saints' eve when she'd sold him the skull mask, when he was the richest he'd ever been or would be, it had taken half an hour's bartering to talk her down enough he could get drunk on what was left. Her masks evoked something when he looked at them — inspiring, frightening. In Cristina too, he could tell.

"You don't need them, you know. Dr. Ixchel doesn't need them, remember? You never did."

He remembered all three of her faces: the quetzal's, emerald-iridsescent, the old woman's, wrinkled and kind, and the old man's, wrinkled and cruel.

"Yes, I do," he said. "You're the one who drew the sketch."

He knew. They'd been carved and painted into likenesses that had evolved over a hundred generations; they absorbed oils and salt from skin, moisture, dust and soot out of the air; time and use smoothed hard edges into curves. But they were wood, inert. What significance they had, he'd invested in them. It was something he'd let himself forget. Because it was easy. They'd begun as gifts from his bewildered parents, who understood no more about their youngest infant son's true nature than he did. Rubén had been terrified of the masks; they'd given him nightmares. His mother and father hadn't found the evangelical church that turned his father into a panhandling preacher until after their sons started school. What they'd believed before that, he didn't know. She had given birth to a jaguar. That they hadn't left him in the wilderness to die or taken him to some priest to be exorcised was miracle enough. That he'd grown into a passable human being, not in jail, not a monster? He'd been lucky. Incredibly lucky. He owed the masks for some of that, at least. Anyway, this was no time to fuck with what worked.

"Then show her," said Cristina patiently.

"Show her what? No. Are you crazy?"

But she was right. The spoon-seller was already gone. The market warrens were deserted; no one was looking. Cloth walls rippled in evening wind. And the mask-seller already knew. She must, or why had she sold him the skull mask? Or the jaguar mask to his parents, for that matter? She glowered, hovering over her bolt of night-blue cloth, impatient to be away. The frog mask laughed in warty, bug-eyed benevolence.

El Bufo was dead, but nobody knew it, except in El Gallito, and whoever the people in El Gallito passed their whispers up to. Everyone, maybe. Or maybe he'd already ripped the throat out of anyone who would have whispered. In Pavoncito, Aníbal would be looking out a high, barred window at a sunset-lit cloud. Somewhere else, Luz would be fomenting revolution. Cristina was right there, waiting.

He wasn't going to hide anymore. He wouldn't run. He was supposed to be doing something heroic. Might as well start small.

He slid finger and thumb through the eyeholes of the caiman mask, pulled the ribbon over his ears and set it down beside the frog mask. He followed with the skull mask from his bag. Then the jaguar mask. Among the mask-seller's other wares, he'd noticed another conquistador, this one green-eyed, the moustache drooping instead of upturned. But she'd already folded it away.

The mask-seller rose abruptly to her feet, mouth gaping.

"It's okay," Cristina told her.

She gave them the frog mask for free.

He stopped at a megastore on the ridge outside Villa Nueva to buy the cheapest suit they had, two steps down from polyester, textured like fiberglass. He got dressed in the parking lot, at that fleeting moment before sunset when the light was that orange-golden bright that made even stained concrete beautiful, when a host of sparrows crossing the highway cast a shadow like a rain of ash and the waters of the polluted reservoir glowed molten, fed by the river of sludge that ran with El Bufo's blood.

There was no mistaking it now: three columns of oily smoke rose from the skyline.

"Where's it coming from?"

"Palace of Justice?" he guessed. The Presidential Palace was too much to hope for. Unless … "But I guess you'd tell me if you knew already."

She made a face at him. "It's not magic," she said, then made a different face, because it was. They got back in the car. Without asking, she picked his phone out of the ashtray where he put it down. She waggled the passcode screen at him.

"Oh-six-oh-two-four-five." He cleared his throat, a jaguar's deep cough. "Bob Marley's birthday."

She didn't laugh. She concentrated on the phone, her fingertip moving slowly over the keyboard. He wished he could read her better. She was, after all, an older woman, an adult. Not a mother, but she took care of two kids. Had she ever run away from responsibility? He wanted to know her well enough to understand, without asking, what it meant when the little crease formed between her brows.

"Oh my god."

"What?"

"It's ... a lot. Let me go back." She read out headlines. "'Antonellis Alive, Implicates Administration in Murder Conspiracy.' 'Administration Dismisses Conspiracy Allegations.' 'Fugitive NGO Treasurer Embezzled Donor Funds.' 'Antonellis Sex Scandal Revealed.' 'Riot Crowds Shut Down Old City, Citizens Advised to Shelter Indoors.'"

Felipe unrolled the window and thrust out an elbow, still watching the columns of smoke. "Well, I guess that answers that question."

She kept reading.

He started the engine, had the car in gear, then shut it off again. He had to think. "So he's in hiding somewhere, and they got close, forced him to go public. And now they're digging up all this dirt about him, trying to discredit him. And meanwhile ..."

The crease between Cristina's eyebrows deepened. "He's accusing the president himself of ordering the assassination. Though it doesn't sound like he has any proof."

"There is no proof, or El Bufo would have found it. These guys are pros, they've been disappearing people for decades. What happened in Totonícapan was just stupid, mean cops overreacting. Molinero, Sonriente, they're smarter than that." He tapped out the start of a rhythm against Baby's flank. "But maybe there doesn't have to be proof. Maybe everybody feels the way you do — we do — tired of keeping their heads down — and they've just been waiting for an excuse. Still, there had to be a spark, a catalyst. When did it start?"

She scrolled back. "It looks like ... yesterday morning, they announced he was alive?"

"Can I look, please?"

She flushed. "Of course." He leaned in, and they stared at the little screen together, shoulder to shoulder over the gearshift.

There was so little information, so much noise. Enough to get lost in. Articles, opinion pieces, comments, accusations. He scanned the timestamps, tried to sort through the spin. It was impossible. He sat back in his seat.

"So El Bufo stopped returning their calls. Whatever murder squad they put on finding Antonellis didn't have any luck either. They get impatient, figure they have to get out in front of the story. That forces his hand — now it's not just the SAAS and the mareros looking for him, it's everybody. So he plays the only card he has."

"You sound like a detective."

"I'm just thinking out loud." The cheap suit itched. "El Bufo was a fucking miserable person. He hated everybody. But he was smart, and he knew how the world works. I guess I do know how he thinks. Antonellis, on the other hand — I don't have a clue. That part doesn't matter anyway — it could just as soon have happened the other way around: he caught wind the murder squad was coming for him, and he figured the truth could protect him."

He kept scrolling, kept reading. Looking for a leverage point. The smoke columns scrolled into the sky.

"Oh, no. Felipe. Is that ...?" She shaded the screen with her hand.

And there was Aníbal, in a dirty white t-shirt, her hair frizzy and unkempt, her face sheared into digital artifacts, a gray play button hovering over her chest. The headline was more of the same. He read it out loud, his stomach dropping. "New Testimony Implicates Antonellis."

He turned up the sound, opened the video to fullscreen, and hit play.

Aníbal's face resolved, softened, then animated. She looked so tired. She didn't look heroic. A muffled question was put to her from off screen. The answer she gave, it was obvious, had been rehearsed.

"My name is Annabelle Jane Trieste. I'm assistant director of Indigenous outreach for Kaminal Reborn, an NGO. It's a volunteer position — I'm unpaid."

Another prompt from offscreen.

"We have offices in Antigua, but ... No, it's foreign owned."

In the same exhausted tone, she acknowledged the obvious, her status as a foreign national, the terms of her temporary visa. The voice offscreen said something else, more strident.

Aníbal hesitated, took a breath. "David Antonellis allocated LNCF funds to us in the explicit understanding we were to use those resources in the interest of furthering civil unrest." Then, for just a moment before the video cut away to a blathering news anchor, her demeanor changed. She half rose from the chair. The news anchor cut in; Felipe started the clip over again. He watched her face, closer.

"She gets angry at the end. Isn't that what it looks like?"

She hadn't lost herself completely.

Cristina nodded mutely. Her eyes slid away from the video, focused out across the highway into the sunset.

"She tried to cut some kind of deal. That has to be it."

"What kind?"

"To let her out of jail. To let her stay in the country. It would be so easy for them to revoke her visa. Luz talked about it like it would be the end of the world. Her parents don't care. They haven't since they found out what she does here — who she is.

Aníbal … she acted macho about it, but she doesn't want to go back. Maybe ever. Only it didn't work."

"What do you mean?"

"Whatever deal she made, they didn't hold up their end. Her phone's still off. They're still holding her. They still think they can use her." He muted the sound and started the clip again.

"I can see it," said Cristina numbly.

"What?"

"Pavoncito. Right there, look." She let him sight along her pointing arm, and there it was: a sprawling complex of brickwork and barb wire beyond the lake, half-hidden among trees, except for the towers. "That's it, isn't it?"

He nodded tightly.

He was thinking of the way Aníbal had been with Luz that night at Forty Doors. Slick, confident. Unflappable. She even danced like a boy. Only better. Except then, at the end, not so confident anymore. She'd said something about love, about loving Luz but still not knowing her.

Two things occurred to him. First, he'd always thought Aníbal's macho act was a mask, like his own. It wasn't. It wasn't an act. Second: you could love someone you didn't really know. In fact, you had to. Luz and Aníbal were the model: they were what love looked like, the ideal. If they could do it, be together and that much in love after two years and still not know each other, then that *was* love. Not knowing.

On the tiny phone screen, the exhausted Aníbal found again a scrap of fight left in her. She showed her teeth, she half-rose from her chair.

"Hey," said Cristina. "We're going to help her. We're here to help her, right? There's got to be something we can do."

"Yeah." He swallowed. He wasn't about to storm the prison gates tearing out throats. It would be suicide. But there was one play he could make.

Aníbal had survived behind those walls a week. Another few hours wasn't going to kill her. He hoped.

It was a bluff worthy of El Bufo, but it had too many holes. "I need to show up with something to offer. A gift. Or they won't even let me in the door. Then I need something to hold back, something I can bargain with. It might be different if I had his badge — or his phone — but they're sewage by now. Like he is." He'd had every chance to take them, to loot El Bufo's body, he just hadn't been thinking straight. A jaguar was not a scavenger. Nothing to be done about it now.

"Wait. Who are we bargaining with?"

"The SAAS. El Bufo's old bosses."

"You mean the spies? You were afraid to try tricking a Garifuna cook out of her spice rub recipe. Now you want to go up against people who lie for a living?"

"It's what he would have done. It's what he *did*. If anybody can get her released, it's them. They're at the center of the web, as close as we're ever going to get. Pulling the strings. Are you saying it isn't going to work?"

"I don't know! That's not how the visions work."

He touched the frog mask where it sat on the console between them. "You saw this."

"I know. But I don't know how. I'm sorry."

He shook himself uncomfortably inside the cheap suit. " We just need to think it through."

He thought best while he was driving.

"Put your seatbelt on, please?"

Cristina had thought the eerie columns of smoke rising from the city would fade with the sunset, but city light reflected off the clouds, outlining the smoke from above. She could almost see the revolution happening, now, again, like that day in the plaza when she'd lost Mael and found Felipe: people taking risks and getting hurt for what they believed in. Thousands and thousands of people. Huge, reckless risks. Permanent, life-changing hurt.

"Where are we going?"

"Home," he said. "I keep trying to get in touch with Luz, she keeps not answering. I need to know what she's thinking. I think she's involved in all this."

"Involved?"

"In whatever's going on. That." He nodded at the smoke. "She knew about Antonellis. She was working with him before all this started. She has to know what's going on with Aníbal. The whole time I've been running around, running *away*, she's been here. You met her. She wouldn't just sit on her hands."

He sat hunched over the wheel. He nodded his head to a beat she couldn't hear. He pushed his phone on her again. "Music, please?"

She scrolled through albums, recognizing only a few. Now that he was human — now that he trusted her — he suddenly made her feel old. She'd sacrificed her childhood — music, cars, clothes, technology — to her sister's kids. A smartphone: music, internet, a camera. She wondered how he could justify the expense. *Stealing,* she thought, then regretted it. Trying to be adventurous, she picked an album of reggae remixes, was pleasantly surprised by handclaps, crisp drums, and a woman's warbling voice singing about revolution, tables turning, turntables. It seemed to be the right choice, because he relaxed a bit.

She tried letting herself relax too. But he was driving like a maniac, even though he didn't have a plan — not a whole one. She was supposed to be helping. She was supposed to be able to see what he couldn't — she'd promised him that.

Then she remembered. Struggling, doubting, trying to force it only made things worse. Everything that had come to her on the hilltop outside Comalapa had come not because she was searching for it, but because she'd shut it all away.

She let out a breath.

She went back to the news feeds, reading about arson, looting, people barricading highways with their bodies. In her mind's eye Luz marched in front of a crowd, dressed like a revolutionary: the same leather jacket, but fatigues underneath instead of a dress, red lipstick smeared, eyeliner apocalyptic black, her hair tied in a red bandanna, brandishing a flag Cristina didn't recognize. In one of the gated neighborhoods they sped past, a banner was stretched between buildings, unreadable in the dark. She tried to imagine what could possibly happen to make her family take to the streets with picket signs, or worse, set anything on fire. Mama's murder hadn't done it.

Police lights flared ahead. Felipe turned abruptly down a dark side street, passing barred and boarded windows, turning again, the headlights panning across a tamarind tree with its trunk scarred from getting in the way of cars. He stopped and killed the lights at the end of the block to watch the police vehicles go by — three of them, heading north toward the city, taking the intersection in a screeching turn. Then he pulled across Calle Real into another darkened neighborhood and stepped on the gas again.

Dogs volleyed challenges back and forth across the ridges. More sirens doppelered in the distance like the trills of birds. His whiskers glowed faint green in the dashboard lights, trembling in exhaust-scented wind.

Cristina got out her own phone. She called Lencho, who surprised her by picking up right away. "Tía?"

"I don't have much time to talk. I just wanted you to know I'm okay."

"Where are you?"

"I can't talk now, Francisco. But ... will you do something for me? Tell everybody to stay away from the city."

"They're already there. Tío Juan took Pilar and Majo and Tía Constancia, they're going to clean up the comedor and try to reopen."

Her heart fell into her stomach. "But not you?"

"I'm in Xela. With Corísa." He didn't sound happy.

"Good, you stay there please."

"Tía, when are you coming? I want to go home. I'm missing school."

She laughed, a little hysterically. "Since when do you care about missing school?" But he was trying to be good. "Soon, okay? And promise you'll tell everyone what I said? Stay away from downtown. There's too much going on. It's not worth getting hurt over."

"I promise," he said.

"I love you. Listen to Corísa. Give your brother a kiss for me."

In the parking garage, the security camera was no longer turned to the wall, so Felipe put on the Garifuna mask. No point taking stupid risks, not now. The stupid risks were all ahead of them. He pointed out the camera to Cristina. She wrapped her shawl around her head.

On the way to the stairs, he noticed Baby's license plate, screwed onto a rust-black '92 Civic. In the shadows, it and Baby looked almost identical. He glowered at it a minute — but what was the point now?

Upstairs, one of the apartment doors — not his — had been kicked in, then crossed with police tape. Outside his own door, his and Luz and Aníbal's, stood a stranger, a dense guy in jeans and a WE ARE ALL TOTONÍCAPAN t-shirt. He folded his arms, looking determined and ever so slightly out of his depth.

"I live here," said Felipe. "Look, I have the —" He didn't. All his keys but the spare were with El Bufo. " Is she here?"

The bouncer shook his head.

"Well, can you let us in? I'm her roommate. Felipe K'icab. Maybe she mentioned me?"

"Sorry," said the bouncer, not budging.

Felipe swallowed the growl that rose in the back of his throat. He could just take the keys. The guy didn't even have a gun. Of course he didn't. It was Luz. Nonviolent resistance.

Cristina's fingertips on his arm, her dark, calm eyes. *The mask.* He wasn't Felipe K'icab, he was a nonexistent rasta of Afro-Caribbean descent who couldn't cook.

"He's just worried," she said to the bouncer. Her brow knit as she studied him. "Angry and scared," she added, carefully. "She's his best friend. We know she's in trouble. We were in Totonícapan this afternoon, meeting with Dr. Ixchel. We want to help."

Felipe stepped back, chastised. He needed the anger, needed it to be able to function at all, to do this. But this guy didn't deserve it any more than Cristina.

The bouncer relented. "Yeah, she is in trouble. We all are. Look, I'm sorry, but I couldn't let you in if I wanted. I'm just here to try and keep *that* from happening." The smashed door down the hall.

"Stay here," Felipe told Cristina. "I'll be right back."

He ducked under the police tape. The other apartment mirrored theirs, only with slightly fancier furniture, no maps, no books, no campesinos above the sink. And it had been torn apart.

Were they looking for Luz, or El Bufo? Not much he could do about it now.

He went into one of the bedrooms, cranked open the window, took off the mask and put it in the backpack with the others. He squeezed through into the airshaft, dropped the two stories to the ground at the base of the shaft, and looked up at his own bedroom window. Shut tight.

From among weeds, broken glass and gravel, he dug up the pawnshop revolver. He cleaned it on his shirt, made sure the moving parts still moved, blew hard into the barrel. The police, he hoped, were busy elsewhere. So much for his security deposit. So much for stealth. He flicked off the safety, then pointed the gun with an anticipatory wince at his window and pulled the trigger.

He opened the cylinder. Empty. Well, duh.

He threw it. It bounced off the concrete to the left of the window and fell back clattering into gravel and weeds.

He picked it up and threw it again, harder. And again, until he was rewarded with a rain of shattered glass. Lights came on in one of the upstairs apartments, then another. Not caring who saw or didn't, he clawed his way up and in past the broken glass. He fished the jaguar mask from his backpack and went to get the door.

"Come on in," he said, ignoring the bouncer's astonished stare. "Excuse the clutter."

The main room looked like a print shop had exploded. It looked the way her childhood bedroom had, back home in Santa Caterina, only worse. Without Aníbal — or Felipe — to keep her in check, the contents of her brain had spilled over and filled every available space. Books and stacks of flyers lay on top of photos on top of torn pages on top of newspapers on top of maps, all over the table and floor, the kitchen countertop, the couch. On top of those, takeout containers, coffee mugs, coffee rings, crumbs. Crabbed notes filled margins, inside covers, napkins, notebooks: phone numbers, email addresses, names, dates, scribbled snatches of conversation, websites, locations, highlighted quotations, black marks, places where she'd pressed so hard the pencil had ripped through the page, ghost script where the pen had run out of ink and she'd kept writing. Pathways of bare floor led from the door to the empty fridge to the crammed-full sink to the bedroom to the bathroom. Cristina stood in one of them, awkward, unsure where to step.

He cleared a spot on the couch for her, then made another so he could sink into it.

While he'd been off playing detective with El Bufo, getting his fortune told, murdering mareros, digging himself a pit of self-pity to wallow in, digging himself out again with Cristina's help, meeting Dr. Ixchel — falling in love with Cristina — all that time, Luz had been here. Doing this.

Fomenting revolution?

The answer was here somewhere. A way to help her. To save Aníbal.

He made coffee. He brought out a portable speaker, set it atop a pile of books, sat down amid a pile of scattered notebook pages and started reading. The bouncer, Mynor, still confused, accepted some coffee and went back outside. For maybe the first time ever, Felipe found he couldn't concentrate with the music and had to shut it off. Cristina helped, or tried. She tidied, filling the trash bin and the compost, washing dishes. Later, he caught her doodling, embellishing Luz's circled faces and names and notes until they looked more like illuminated texts. "No — don't stop," he told her.

He found the old university edition of *Men of Maize* face-down on the floor, open to the page where he'd slotted the rent money. In place of the money, there was a note. *Fuck you,* it said. *I spent it on bribes.* He couldn't believe that things would ever go so far back in the direction of normal that they'd need to worry about rent. It had been Cristina's money anyway.

Hours later — hours spent nursing his own coffee at his own kitchen table for the first time in what felt like a year, poring over highlighted passages in revolutionary pamphlets, newspaper photos bearded in blue ink, illegible notes in the margins of everything until his eyes burned with fatigue — he was staring at a heavily annotated, months-old copy of *Waking Dream.* The headline announced an LNCF fundraiser had been canceled due to "political instability." Felipe read and reread the headline for the fifth time, gave up, tried to toss it across the kitchen table onto a pile of copies just like it, and instead knocked a full carafe of coffee and grounds all over everything. Scrambling to get potential clues out of the path of the spill, his legs cramped from sitting too long, and he fell over. He lay there, laughing.

Cristina rushed to help. As they scooped up sodden newspapers, Felipe tried to hide the past-due notices in the trash. On her way back to the sink, she froze, spoiled coffee dripping on the tiles.

"What?" he asked.

"I just noticed that painting." The campesinos. "It's one of Hugo's. My mentor."

"Luz bought it," he said. "On one of her NGO trips."

"I remember. I mean, I think I sold it to her?"

"I used to hate that painting." Seeing those workers in the flesh, passing through his tiny scrap of forest on their way to the fields, wasn't what had changed his opinion. What he'd seen in Totonícapan … They were slaves to poverty, but at least they had livelihoods, families, stories to laugh about on the long walk home. All that could be taken away.

His head swam with Luz's handwriting.

"Your mentor — do you think he's out there now? Marching with a picket sign? Setting shit on fire?"

"No," she said, decisively. "He's always told the truth in his art, but he keeps his head down like everybody else."

"Not everybody," he said. "Not anymore. That's what all this means. Look." An article about the police strike in Totonícapan, a list of phone numbers scrawled in the margin, crossed out, checked, circled. "She's … trying to understand people. So she can get through to them. She always has been. To show them that what they do matters. And I guess she did it. She convinced them. Not all of them, but enough to bring the city to a standstill. I don't know how. I can't see it. I lived with her two years and she never convinced me. But that has to be it."

"She did convince you," said Cristina. "You're here, aren't you?"

He stared at her.

A hand in his fur — fingertips, hesitant, the way you stroke a feral cat at first unless you want to lose a finger. "You need to take a break."

She hadn't had even a drop of coffee. He tried to think what this would have been like without her. His head hurt. Faint lightning bolts danced on the walls. It was long past midnight. "You're right. We all need sleep. He opened the door into the hallway. "Go home," he told Mynor. "Go to bed."

Mynor shook his head. "The rasta said he'd be back. Anyway, Luz would kill me. Is there any more coffee?"

Cristina sat at the table amid wreckage, drawing.

Felipe sank into a chair across from her. He'd sat with Luz and Aníbal this way, the handful of mornings he'd been up early enough.

Luz was in danger, putting herself at risk trying to save the people from their oppressors. Aníbal was in jail. He couldn't help either of them. He still didn't have a plan. All he had was a cheap suit, a frog mask, and this woman, in her rumpled huipil with its pattern of dancing quetzals, red, blue and green, strands of dark hair curling in front of her face, on her cheek what looked like a pencil smudge or maybe a bit of coffee grounds. He had the impulse to brush it away with his thumb.

Her pencil paused above the page, and she looked up.

"Tell me what to do, Cristina. Please." It wasn't what he'd wanted to say.

"You're exhausted. You should sleep. In the morning, we'll go see El Bufo's spies." She went back to drawing.

But if she wasn't going to sleep, he wasn't either. He shook his head. He knuckled his eyes open. He tried to make his way through the permutations, one more time. "We don't have anything to offer them. Antonellis, that's who they want. They can't kill him; he's already done his damage. But they could still arrest him, put him on trial for corruption, make him responsible for all this. I thought something here might tell us where he was. Mynor said Luz has been in touch with him — I'm not sure I believe it. Maybe she knows where he is — but she's not picking up her phone. The only other person who might know is his wife. And believe me, she's not telling. If she's even still in this country. I wouldn't be, if I was her."

"She doesn't love him?"

"I think she does, actually. I just don't think that's enough."

Cristina cleared her throat. She held a red colored pencil stub almost by the tip. Her fingers and the heel of her left hand were bruised in ink and wax, red, blue and black. "What about me?" she said.

"I —" He caught himself, barely. What was she asking? He was tired.

"I mean ... I could be your bargaining chip."

"What?"

"I'm an eyewitness to my mother's murder. Like Mael. I saw what happened. The killers' faces. The green ring. Everything. It was like I was there."

"Cristina. They killed Mael. Maybe not the SAAS, but somebody. Right?"

She nodded, tight-lipped.

"So you can't turn yourself in. They'll kill you."

"You've got a better idea?"

"No! But I can't —" He couldn't even think it. Risk the only person who was like him? Cristina, who'd remained quiet, calm, through all of this, who had only just appeared in his life?

But he didn't have a better idea. Only worse ones.

He could bluff. He could go in with El Bufo's face, pretend he had something, get as far as he could get by lying, take a hostage, demand Aníbal's release, demand Molinero's resignation, keep making demands until they stopped humoring him, then start ripping out throats. Until he was dead.

It would be better than doing nothing. It would be better than putting Cristina at risk.

Cristina put the pencil stub down and turned the sketchbook so he could see. A self-portrait. Her curls defied gravity, wave-patterned, circling her face like a lion's mane. She had two human limbs: an arm, a leg. The other arm was a wing. The other leg was a serpent's tail.

"This is real," she said. "I don't know what it means, but it's real. Understand?"

He didn't. He looked close. What was the expression on her face? The line of the mouth. Giddy determination?

She rested her chin in her hands, smudging more of that dark ink across her cheek. She was just as tired as he was. That was bad. Because he was so tired he was delirious. So tired he'd started thinking she might just feel about him the way he'd begun to feel about her.

So tired he wanted to touch her and find out.

"Cristina, we need to sleep."

They brushed their teeth hip-to-hip in the tiny bathroom with its scents of rust and lemongrass, staring at each other in the smeared mirror. He offered her — without authority — Luz and Aníbal's bed. She refused.

"I'll take the couch," he said. While she showered, he made effort to clean his room, sweeping up broken glass, gathering dirty laundry by the armload, dumping empty beer bottles and coffee cups in the already overflowing kitchen sink. Under the bed he found a little cash, crumpled, smelling of fried chicken. He left it by the lamp. His tiny portable speaker played an old delta soul spiritual, "Sinnerman." He stripped the sheets — full of cat hair — and remade the bed. Orange citylight filtered through the shattered window from the airshaft.

He struggled awake on the couch sometime before dawn, hearing voices in the hall. No dreams, just fog. Mynor was arguing with someone. A key in the lock, and the door swung open.

"I don't have time for this, Mynor, I have to get —"

Luz.

She looked as strung out and exhausted as he felt, impeccable makeup unable to hide the creases under her eyes and around her mouth. She'd aged ten years since he'd seen her. It hadn't even been a week. She wore ripped jeans, high-heeled boots and a WE ARE ALL TOTONÍCAPAN t-shirt — not the same one, it couldn't be, though this one was wrecked enough — which she was already stripping off over her head as she came in the door.

He felt his face for a mask. There wasn't one. He felt around on the floor for it, for the backpack. Nothing.

She stopped stock-still in the middle of the room. She reached blindly behind her for the light switch.

He rolled off the couch to his feet — paws, at first, but then he rose further, stood, human legs, human shoulders, human face, his own face, the one she knew. Ixchel didn't need a mask. She could be anyone, and so could he.

Luz flicked the light on.

"Luz, he's back," said Mynor, framed in the doorway. "Felipe. I tried to tell you —"

"Get out," she said.

Mynor backed out discreetly and shut the door.

They stood staring at each other, she haggard and unbelievably sexy, disheveled in a black lace bra, he out of his mind with exhaustion, looking like — what, he didn't even know.

"Felipe. You fucking asshole. Now, you show up? Fuck you."

"Luz —"

She swept past him, boots kicking aside papers, books, coffee cups, into her room and out again a moment later, pulling on a clean top, the white peasant blouse with embroidered hibiscus flowers. By then, he'd found the jaguar mask on the counter by the sink and put it on. She hadn't noticed. It was time she knew, past time, but not now. Not like this.

"Where the fuck have you been. No, I don't even care. You left us. You left me, and I did fine by myself. I worked my ass off. I didn't need you. They're probably kicking us out of here any second, and it's fine, they can have it, what even is the point without Aníbal. But I'm going to burn all this shit before they do. Come on. None of it matters after tomorrow anyway. All the important stuff is in my head. Pick it up. The books, the maps, everything." She flung open the door. "Mynor, get back in here and help."

"I can save her," said Felipe. "Luz, listen. Aníbal — I can get her out. I've got a plan."

Silence. He thought he could hear Cristina's sleeping breath, uninterrupted, through the bedroom door.

"Bullshit." She balled up a copy of the *Diary* and threw it at his chest. "How dare you say that? Nobody's getting her out. You don't think I tried? Haven't you seen the video? They manipulated her. They lied to extract a false confession. She went to jail thinking I betrayed her. She ran into that crowd to prove to me she didn't care, to prove she believed in the cause as much as I did. Now she's never getting out. Never. Not until we burn Pavoncito to the ground."

The despair in her voice, the abandon, made him want to crumble from the inside. But he wouldn't. He clenched his whole self around his heart, trying to keep it together.

"No. Seriously. I really think we've got a chance. I've got cards to play. It's risky. But it can work. I swear. Please, just let me explain."

"Are you fucking kidding me?" She looked at Mynor, who nodded eagerly, clueless. He came in and shut the door.

She dropped onto the couch, flung out her arms, crossed one leg over the other. "Fine. Go ahead, tell me." She got a cigarette out of her purse — Aníbal's brand. Luz hadn't smoked since they were kids.

Felipe wiped his mouth. "Okay. Thank you. I'm — going to need a little coffee." He reached for the carafe, tipped out a last few drops. "Coffee?"

She laughed. Her eyes were red. "These days I need a little more than coffee."

He searched the cupboards. Not finding any immediately, he took a moment to run water into Aníbal's ceramic filter, which began its slow, soothing drip into the tank below. With his back to her, he placed a hand on the jaguar mask. He didn't have a choice. It was the only way to convince her. She'd known him as long as anyone. She'd understand. She had to.

But as he was turning around, Luz gave up fumbling with Aníbal's pearl-handled lighter, flinging it and the cigarette across the room.

Felipe ducked away, and the mask stayed on.

"I don't have time for this!" She surged up from the couch. "I've got to go. Now. You want to help me? Burn all this, get out of here and don't come back. This place isn't safe anymore. Mynor, make sure there isn't a single piece of paper left in this apartment with my handwriting on it, understand?" She flung an accusing finger at Felipe. "And make sure he doesn't follow me. Okay? Are you listening, Mynor? Say yes if you understand."

Mynor glanced at Felipe, then back at Luz, like someone afraid to take his eyes off a wild animal lest it attack. "Yes, Luz. Okay. I hear you."

"Felipe, I'm sure you really want to make it up to me." He tried to ignore the dripping sarcasm. "Maybe you even believe you can save her, the same way I believe I can make it up to her. But things are already in motion. We're both already fucked. I can't stop it now. Nothing can stop it. I've got to go. I'm sorry. Really."

She kissed him hurriedly on the cheek, and grabbing one of the dog-eared spiral notebooks Felipe had stared at until the letters swam, stuffing it in her purse, she swept out the door and was gone.

Mynor gave Felipe a mortified, apologetic look and stooped to gather papers off the floor.

Cristina, thank god, had slept through all of it. Felipe stood numb for a minute until exhaustion crashed down on him again. He flung himself on the couch and closed his eyes.

The Quetzal

She woke to the sound of him practicing El Bufo in the bathroom. Cruel laughter. She lay in his bed, smelling him despite the clean sheets, looking at the ceiling, imagining him mugging with that face in the mirror, until it got quiet again.

When she came out into the main room she found it disorientingly clean. Not knowing what else to do, she moved into an awkward domesticity that felt simultaneously excruciatingly normal and like she'd fallen into some mirror universe. After coffee, migas, and refried beans with Felipe looking at her across the little table as if she might disappear or go up in flames, he explained what had happened with Luz while she slept. After a lot of loud dubstep she managed to withstand because he promised it was getting him psyched up — today, of all days, he needed psyching up — she hugged Mynor where they found him propped in the hallway, told him goodbye and go home — he wouldn't — and they piled into Baby and drove to Zone Three.

"We're not going to the plaza?" She had to shout over the music.

"We are," he shouted. "But there's people I need to see first. I never told them what happened to him. And — maybe they can tell me something about him. Something I can bargain with."

Instead of your life, he meant.

Zone Three looked like any other half-decayed barrio she'd glimpsed from bus windows. Mama had warned her daughters against places like this: bad people, narcos, murderers, rapists, monsters who kill babies and drink their blood. It was cruel, paranoid. But the city *was* dangerous.

The dubstep must have been working, because Felipe rolled in like he owned the place, the bass making the dust dance on the dashboard.

He stopped outside the burned-out ruin of a corner store. Mandalas of shattered glass decorated the pavement. *The Paradise*, read the blistered, fire-black, hand-painted sign. He said something that was drowned utterly as the "music" shifted from robotic pounding to a rattling keen like a chainsaw being murdered.

"WHAT?" she screamed, hands over her ears.

He switched off the stereo. Her ears kept ringing.

"I said, 'Jesus. They must have really hated him.'"

"Who?"

"The mareros? Everyone, I guess." He rolled the window down. Everything smelled like burning gas and melted plastic.

From the alley, a boy Lencho's age stepped out of a doorway.

"You're alive," the boy and Felipe said to each other.

"Nice suit," said the boy.

"Is she —" Felipe started.

"She's inside."

"I'm going in," Felipe told Cristina. "You can stay if you want. This is Toby. He's okay." He got out of the car and went down the alley, into the same ruined door the boy had come out of. The fire must have burned the whole block. She was afraid to find out who could still be alive in there.

"You know what he is?" the boy asked, staring at her, as if it was written on her skin. He was too much like Lencho. "He showed *you*?"

She cleared her throat. "He didn't have to."

She followed Felipe through the door, Toby trailing behind her, into a ruined shrine. Among fragments on the floor, she recognized pieces of plaster saints like Mama's: a disembodied hand raised in benediction, a fragmentary lamb, a crook, a sandaled foot. A scarred poster of a robed young woman in a skull mask, holding a rose, had survived somehow, and someone had lit a little lump of copal on the floor beneath it amidst a tangle of flowers — weeds from the street.

In the wreck of the next room, Felipe had taken off his mask and appeared as a jaguar, sitting on his haunches in the sunbeam from the broken window, golden and dark, while the woman embraced him.

She could see him all at once. That kind, open face, the broad nose not so different from Tecún Úman's — but without its tragic pride — the labyrinth-patterned fur, the slick yellow canines, the enormous eyes like Caribbean pools full of terror, the boyish clothes: it made Cristina wonder what she'd look like if she could see herself this way, if she could really look. The way she'd looked to Dr. Ixchel. Like in the drawing from last night, jumbled parts of different monsters?

"I can't stay," he murmured. "I just needed to make sure you knew."

"We knew. Didn't we, Toby? Even before all this."

"Will you leave here? Go back to the highlands?"

"Everyone I care about is here."

"Lupita," Felipe asked, "you don't … have anything of his? Notebooks? Clothes, or anything?"

"Not anymore." She pulled away. "But let me cast for you."

He stiffened. "They didn't take your seeds?"

"There are always more seeds." She drew a plastic bag from around her neck, inside her faded blouse, and brushed a space on the floor.

"I don't have any money," he said awkwardly.

Cristina had spent her life pretending to be comforted by plaster saints, running through memorized words in unison with everyone she knew. And it did help. She couldn't deny that. Anyway, she wasn't qualified to protect him from himself. And it wasn't about him, but this woman who'd lost everything.

Again and again San Simón had appeared in her paintings, laughing in the background of a peasant scene, laughing in the arms of a dying lily-seller outside the cathedral in Comalapa, laughing with the town drunk in front of the Church of San Martín at sunset. She kept painting him out, and he kept coming back. And she thought, *What do I know about it?* Jaguars posed as men driving taxis. Ancient quetzal shapeshifters taught Spanish to children. Angels went around wearing the bodies of murderers. Boys, abandoned by their mothers, grew up happy and strong. Kaqik stew made from the same recipe, with the same ingredients, in the same kitchen, tasted different if a mother made it, or a sister, or a daughter.

She gave Lupita the money she'd found that morning by the bed.

Lupita knelt down on the floor, picking weed seeds, little bits of gravel and broken glass from the bag, arranging them carefully. Click, click, click, click. She believed; it was obvious. Deeply enough it could bring her comfort even now.

"You want to know if it's enough," she said. "It's never enough. Rodrigo knew that. You do what you can. Until you can't. Death hasn't left you, Felipe. You brought it to him. You carry it wherever you go. But you don't have to let it control you."

He took the old woman's hands, letting the rest of the seeds fall where they may. "What can you tell me about him? About Gilberto, his partner? Or the people he worked for?"

She shook her head. "He never talked about his work. You know that."

"Anything, please. I'm going to try to be him, Lupita. To fool some people he worked with. To save someone I love." And he showed her the frog mask.

She sat back on her heels. "They — loved the same woman, once," she admitted. "Rodrigo's wife. A ladino woman, from a rich family. It went badly. For all of them. But they also loved each other, in their way. That's why they hurt each other so much. Toby can tell you."

Toby stood beside Cristina. He looked stricken. He shook his head no.

"It's all right," said Lupita.

He went to her, and she wrapped the boy in her arms until he pushed her away.

"I saw them fighting once," he told Felipe. "In the street. They were drunk. They'd won some case, gotten a bonus, or a bribe, so they went out together. He paid me to make sure they didn't do anything too stupid. But I couldn't stop them. All I could do was make sure they didn't end up sleeping in the street. It was ... gross. Like they were trying to kill each other. Anyway, they wore themselves out — they were both bloody and red in the face, and finally they just sat there leaning on each other. Holding hands."

As Felipe took this in, and Toby recovered from having to tell it, Cristina watched Lupita, trying to understand how she could incorporate a worldview which allowed her to so calmly, securely pile away kernels of trash into a plastic bag amid the burned-out husk of her personal shrine and the fact of her lover's inevitable murder. Cristina saw all at once what this place had been before the fire — how it had been a home for all three of them sometimes, Lupita, Toby, and El Bufo. She stepped over melted plastic furniture and heat-shattered concrete to a corner where the hearth had been. She worked her fingers under a clay tile, into a crevice concealed by ashes, and it came up with a scrape of protest, and underneath was a dark cubbyhole in the floor.

Lupita looked up. "Oh! I forgot all about that."

And then she was making Cristina uncomfortable with her scrutiny while Felipe accepted each of El Bufo's treasures Cristina lifted from the cubby. An unopened bottle of aguardiente. A gun. He ejected the magazine — empty. A passport — expired. A pack of cigaritos, the plastic film all melted into the packaging. A wallet — nothing in it but a little money and a badge. "Fake," he said, and he started laughing.

"Let me read for you," Lupita said, and Cristina, brushing ashes from her hands, understood that Felipe's discomfort in this woman's presence wasn't about her unshakeable faith in the future, in fate, but that she expected him to be its agent. And now Cristina too.

There was no escaping it. So she knelt with Lupita over the cleared circle on the floor and closed her eyes and imagined a brush in her hands and the broken-toothed skyline of Comalapa, and her mind painted a sky while the words of portent washed over her like wind.

As they were leaving, Lupita grasped Cristina's arm. She winked. "Don't let him get away."

Felipe lifted the mask to his face again as they passed Santa Muerte and stepped out into the street.

Toby followed them to the car. "Are you going downtown?" he asked, gesturing to the east, where the smoke had been.

"What do you know about it?" said Felipe.

"Nothing. What everybody knows. The mareros, the narcos, the police, the president — they're on one side. We're on the other. You can't always do what you're told."

"You learn that from El Bufo?"

"Take me with you," said Toby.

"Absolutely not," said Cristina, thinking of Lencho.

"We're … not exactly going to the protests," Felipe said. "Anyway, doesn't Lupita need you?"

"She's fine," the boy said, waving a hand. "The mareros already took what they wanted." And he darted past Felipe, clambered over the driver's seat into the back. "Come on, let's go."

The sky, where no trickle of smoke remained of the fires of the night before, was the same one she'd imagined inside. It could mean everything was over, that the embers were fading and going out. The scent of melted plastic and scorch in the air said otherwise.

Hands. Cristina didn't need to close her eyes to see the hands. She saw hands holding banners, holding other hands, truncheons, firecrackers, hands covered in masa, washing clothes, hands wearing wedding bands, diamonds, thick dark rings with green stones, hands plucking at marimba, hands passing money, hands that were paws, hands that were birds' feet, hands that were roots, children's hands, old hands, hands with odd numbers of fingers, hands opening doors, closing them, holding mangoes, avocadoes, annonas, limes, lilies, wooden spoons, holding babies, holding cats, chickens, turkeys, canaries, hands holding elaborate ritual objects patterned from flaked obsidian, holding bottles of aguardiente, rum, tequila, mescal, cigars.

She steadied herself against the car.

Felipe didn't know what he'd expected — empty streets? Bodies? Tanks patrolling Avenida Elena? There were blockades, police in riot gear, banners. There were flags everywhere, national and local like in the days before a football game, and the same giddiness in the air, energy like atmospheric pressure. But there were also people going about their lives. Kids sold fruit on street corners, scampering out in front of traffic to juggle limes and avocados when the lights changed.

Toby rode with his nose pressed to the window.

Morning mist lifted, and the plaza's cobbled surface had been transformed by fallen flags and threads of colored bunting, scorch marks and the white residue of chemical weapons. Rats and pigeons rutted in a pile of forgotten fruit. The plexiglass masks of the knot of riot cops on the corner by the cathedral seemed to track Baby's passage.

He had the badge, the suit, a whole bottle of aguardiente, El Bufo's face in the mirror, and the false confidence instilled by the dense waves of industrial soundscape issuing from the stereo. He wasn't ready.

"Where is everybody?" Toby was saying.

In jail. Dead.

"They're coming," said Cristina, and Felipe believed her.

He stopped at the corner of Ninth Ave and Sixth, out of sight of the cops, where those concrete reliefs of ancient pyramids and gods had been defaced in sky-blue paint. He tilted the mirror, curled his lip like El Bufo. "You're getting out here."

"You're not him," said Toby.

He threw up his hands. "Fuck's sake, could you pretend like I am, please?"

Cristina's laughter cut through the tension, beautiful, not cruel. But scared.

"Sorry." Smiling, Toby clapped his shoulder from behind, exactly the way El Bufo might. "You can do it, boss. I believe in you."

"Thank you." He attempted an impervious scowl, but his mouth broke into mirth.

Toby got out, and Felipe rolled down the window. "Look. That's where we'll be." The Presidential Palace, with its arches, its flags, its imperial crests imposing, imported belle epoque marble rising out of another time. "Anything happens, you'll see. But this is as close as you're getting, understand? Stick around the artisans' market — should be plenty of people, foreigners with money. Whatever happens, they won't let anything happen to the foreigners." Except in extraordinary circumstances.

A woman passed in shawl and huipil, head bent and hurrying, trailing a knee-high boy by a tether. Toby looked small, surrounded by the city. Absurdly confident. Gawking at the cathedral, the pigeons, the stained sidewalk, the drab concrete and bright graffiti like he'd never seen any of it before. Maybe he hadn't.

"Be safe," Cristina told him. "Go see my aunt Crescencia if you need help. The Comedor Santa Rosa de Lima, ask anyone. They'll take care of you."

Toby went around to her side and hugged her quickly through the window.

The plan was running through his head again. Such as it was. Circling around a sticking point he couldn't get away from. Luz's whirlwind visit hadn't changed a thing. He owed her. He owed Aníbal. The suit itched.

"Kid. Hey, kid. Wait a minute." He unplugged his phone from the stereo, and in the sudden absence of music, pulled the backpack full of masks from under the seat and held out both. "Here. Keep these for me."

Toby glanced furtively up and down the street. He took the phone first, studied it. He looked up, questioning.

"Bob Marley's birthday," said Felipe.

Toby grinned. He tried it, then nodded, satisfied, and dropped the phone in a pocket. Then he opened the backpack — carefully, almost reverently, as if it contained some secret power. "You sure?"

They were only masks. "Think I'm going to let them fall into the wrong hands?"

Toby pulled out the jaguar mask, turned it and raised it to his own face. Nothing happened. Still, it was eerie. Felipe had never seen it on anyone's face but his own.

El Bufo sneered at him from the mirror. The jowls, the pox scars. The gummy eyes. The nicotine-yellowed teeth. Where had this face come from? Inside him, somewhere. Same place as all the rest.

He gunned the engine, and the jaguar on the sidewalk threw a peace sign as he slid away behind them.

Left on Tenth Ave, left on Fourth Street, the long way around. There was still time. Time to catch his breath. Get his bearings. Psych himself up. Tamp down his jitters. He turned on the radio and scanned for music, but no, El Bufo hated music. He shut it off. El Bufo's comforts were a bottle, a cigarillo, a cup of coffee.

Eyes on the road, he unplugged the phone charger by feel, fumbled the electric lighter plug out of the dashboard tray.

From the breast pocket of the itchy suit, he passed Cristina the ancient pack of cigarillos from the cubbyhole in Lupita's floor. "Can you get these open?"

He lit one at a red light, inhaled acrid and bitter smoke. *Relax,* he told himself.

He glanced over at Cristina, found her pressed against the passenger door, knees to her chest, the way she'd sat when they'd first been in the car together, when she'd still had her baby nephew wrapped in her shawl.

"I'm sorry," he said. "I'll put it out."

"No, no, it's fine. Do what you need to do." She closed her eyes.

He started to reach out to her, realized it wouldn't help. "Just until we get there," he said. "So they can see it." The plan was barely half a plan, but it was what he had. He had to stick to it, as far as it went. "I'm not him, I don't know what he knows. Anyone questions me, they're going to figure it out. The only way this works is if we drive right up to the gate where he took me the first time, and I bullshit them as hard as he did."

"What if it doesn't work?"

Confidence, arrogance, beyond all reason — that was El Bufo's secret. Toby knew it too. Felipe didn't have it. So he'd just have to stop being Felipe. "It'll work."

He studied El Bufo's face in the mirror, contorting it experimentally: a leer, a frown, beetled brows, bug eyes. "That was bullshit," he said experimentally, faking El Bufo's thick consonants, his deep tone. "This isn't." Except it was. "Spiders at the center pull the strings. Everybody dances."

"What?"

Against the protestations of his knotted stomach, he told himself she needed to look afraid. It was working. He remembered, in drunken, stoned fragments, the night he'd worn the skull mask. He'd been an asshole then. He hated it, but he could do this. He had to.

"Just practicing. You okay? You ready for this?"

She couldn't be. She nodded, tightly.

And he took the left onto Fifth Street, that narrow one-way that ran into the cold of the Palace's shadow. Today the sleek, mirror-black SUVs and men in dark glasses seemed quaintly civilian next to the display of military force that surrounded them: ranks of submachine-gun-toting soldiers in jackboots and digital camo, armored personnel carriers — even a tank, a huge, squat, senseless lump of metal. A helicopter thudded somewhere in the sky.

Felipe parked in the middle of the street. He threw the e-brake on hard and patted Baby's steering wheel goodbye. He understood, with sudden finality, that if anything went wrong, he would lose her. Even if everything went right, there was every chance he would lose her. It was why he'd given Toby the masks. There was no exit strategy beyond this bluff, and blind, stupid confidence could get him only so far. El Bufo's death had taught him that. Baby would end up in an impound lot. When they couldn't get any evidence out of her — he'd wiped her for prints, cleaned everything out but Cristina and the key, but there was DNA, if they cared that much — they'd sell her on police auction or for scrap. She could end up mouldering in the ravine with El Bufo.

Which was to say nothing of what could happen to Cristina.

She sat hunched in on herself, like she was going to her death. Why had she agreed to this? What did she know that he didn't?

Too late now.

As before, guards approached at either window. This time, they were rather more heavily armed. He blew smoke and tried on El Bufo's leer. "Morning, gentlemen. Little present here for Gilberto, if everything goes right." Not looking at Cristina, afraid of his reaction if he did.

As before, the guard stepped back at the sight of him. This time, he pulled off his glasses, his human eyes narrow and suspicious, his trigger finger never straying from the well.

"Thought I was dead?" Felipe barked a laugh, pushed open the door and stepped out, remembering El Bufo's superiority, his nonchalance. He looked at the other guard. "Have her gift-wrapped, if you would. Carefully. Wouldn't want her damaged." The keys were in his hand; he dropped them in the street. "Leave it with the valet, would you?"

He wasn't Felipe K'icab, he wasn't Félix Orellano. He didn't care about the car. It wasn't his Baby.

The other guard opened the passenger door. He couldn't watch — so he took a last, heavy pull at the cigarito and threw that away too, blowing smoke from his nostrils, managing not to cough as he swept toward the gated entrance, past the rows of armed men, just leaving her there in their custody like it was easy. Hands in pockets? In front of all those assault rifles? Would El Bufo give them an excuse to search him? No, he would not. Even if he had nothing to hide. Which he didn't. Except the obvious. The brand new, itching suit jacket: he'd kicked it, trampled it a bit. He had the fake badge, the wallet, the empty gun, and the bottle of aguardiente sticking out of his suit pocket; he'd broken the seal and splashed a little on the lapel for verisimilitude.

Nobody stopped him.

Plastic zip handcuffs. A black bag over her head, rough and scratching. At least it was clean. Her satchel was taken from her. She'd emptied it of all but her government-issued ID and the sketchbook, emptied that of all but the most telling sketches. It was all in her head. All of it. Cool morning breeze played over her bare calves as she was led over uneven pavement, past a high curb — she stumbled, was caught — onto smooth cement, through a quietly rattling chainlink gate. She was wearing the huipil —

unwashed since she'd left Comalapa — and her embroidered shawl. Luz's clothes wouldn't have fit, and Cristina wouldn't have known how to wear them, to act so sophisticated and free. She was just a few blocks from the market and Mama's comedor. If she concentrated on the breeze, it might be any other morning, a month or a year ago: Mama alive, Teresa alive, Mael alive and knowing nothing of political murder or the city. Cristina could be on the way to meet her for the first time, to be kind to her, to ease Mama's hardness.

Then she was inside. The wind died and was replaced by tile echoes. She knew exactly the palette she'd use: cold-hued pastels, a sickly green.

She thought she heard El Bufo cough. The click of metal, the clink of glass against a molded countertop. Then she heard him laughing. "It's worthless, remember? Null and void. Where is he? Who do you think? Gilberto. *Inspector Ayora.*" The insolence in his voice, in his bearing. She couldn't see him, but she could. The jaguar's posture and the man's: the one so much more startling than the other. The jaguar's lips half-drawn from his teeth, all his weight on his toes, gathered to pounce, he looked fierce and desperate — as fierce and desperate as a jaguar in a frog mask could look. El Bufo, belly thrust out, eyes on the ceiling, couldn't care less, and he hated these people with a passion that oozed from his pores to slick the scuffed floor. El Bufo scared her the way she'd been scared that first night at Mama's house — of both the inspector and the jaguar. This frog-masked jaguar wasn't Felipe anymore — it was nothing like the jaguar she had learned to trust, who was doing this to redeem himself, to save his friend. She had come here for him, to support him, to prove she trusted him and was worthy of his trust. But she knew she should stop thinking of this sneering, hateful man as the jaguar at all — for now — but rather as El Bufo's vengeful ghost.

"I want a private audience," said El Bufo's voice, receding as she was led away. "This witness is under my protection. He'll get nothing from her without me."

The bag came off. She was processed, fingerprinted — as if she were a suspect, not a witness, no doubt just to humiliate her — and photographed. She saw herself in the black-and-white photos they took: a dead expression, like Mama's at the wake. She saw, in her own face, Mama, Papa, and Teresa. She was what remained of them. It had never been about trying to carry on with what they'd done, perpetuating the lives they'd led. She couldn't. Nobody could. It was about carrying them with her. If all this went horribly wrong, a part of them would be lost all over again.

The officials asking the dull questions, ordering her to look here, then there, did not wear raptor-plumed angels like overcoats. They weren't monsters, they were distracted, exhausted office workers in drab-colored clothes, surrounded by drab-colored machines. When it was over, she was led past cubicles to a featureless door. Down a corridor to her right, she glimpsed potted greenery, a corbeled ceiling, sumptuous carpet, a chandelier. Then she was ushered through the featureless door into a windowless room, her restraints secured to a table. The door was locked behind her.

Nothing happened. No one came.

Trying not to think of this void as a cell, she grasped at details: a black square of one-way glass, a light switch, a plastic bubble in the ceiling to hide a camera. In the camera, again, she imagined she could see herself, fisheye-distorted. Besides that, blankness.

She knew what to do with blankness. She didn't need a pencil, or paints. It was all there within her, death and life, ready at a moment's notice.

She sat in the cold metal chair at the square plastic table, her zip-tied hands folded at its center, and drenched the bare walls in color.

Blood. Families sitting down to dinner, first in open, dirt-floored courtyards over steel drum tables, then in open courtyards tiled in labyrinth-mosaic yellow on tables made from thousand-year-old trees, then in open fields of lava rock and weeds, then in open wounds. A traffic jam of buses, taxis, pickups, bicycles, skateboards, beetles, fish, bees, huge babies crawling. A cemetery of graves unfathomably deep, one stacked body after another, monuments and mausolea tall as clouds. A jungle from the roof of a ruin, extending into mist. Jaguars, quetzals, trogons, herons, hummingbirds, parrots, canaries, feral cats, housecats, dogs, coyotes, coydogs, snakes, bird-snakes, dragons, bats, deer, crabs, scorpions, cows, chickens, turkeys, dolphins, manatees, crocodiles, caimans, rats, mice, mosquitoes, roaches, flies, maggots, butterflies. A movie theater packed with skeletons all in elaborate hats that blocked each other's view, except they weren't looking at a screen, but at the viewer. A crater lake hosting races between demon-filled canoes. Ruins, temples, churches, angels, saints, demons, kings, godkings, bishops, sinners, witches, priests. A heap of burning books. A heap of burning bodies. A crowd of everyone she'd ever met or seen, everyone in the world, all looking up. Ixchel. Miguel Ángel. A navel. A mouth. A vagina. A placenta. A tree of blood. The Tree of Life. Tecún Úman. Pacal. Christ. Cortés. A river. A river of refuse, of lava, of gold, of cacao, of honey, of blood.

The door opened. El Bufo came in and sat down, Gilberto came in, closed the door behind him and took the other chair. The ventilation system clicked on, making the blank room seem even emptier.

"I missed this, you know." Gilberto's body language was cool, relaxed. Disingenuous. He was good at this. He barely had eyes for Cristina. "What are you trying to do here? Who is she really?"

Implication stormed in the recirculated air over the three of them. A deepening intimacy between two of them, the closeness of shared past — but it was the wrong two, and they were supposed to pretend it didn't exist.

"She's a key eyewitness to a botched political murder, and she's going to bring down this administration. You with it, if you're not careful. Just watch."

"You can lay off the grift now, Rigo. I sent the security monitor for coffee and atól. You know the drill. Ought to give us half an hour, at least."

El Bufo was silent, scowling. Afraid he'd been seen through already? She couldn't let him do this on his own. Cristina stood up, awkwardly, chained to the table. "We want everyone arrested at the protests set free, all charges dropped."

"'We?'" returned Gilberto flatly. "Is she your lover?"

Cristina blushed. But she didn't need magic to read something in the way he said it. A ghost map unfolded on the table beneath her hands, full of gray areas, but also connections.

Meanwhile El Bufo was scowling even harder.

She stretched the plastic chains, bending awkwardly so she could whisper in Felipe's ear, "He's not your enemy. Don't you see? He cares about him. About —"

"The hell he's not," said El Bufo. "Tell her, Gilberto. Nobody's listening? Then tell her how you fucked over my career for yours. Tell her ..." He was fishing. He didn't know enough to play this role, so he was easing around the gaps.

But she was forgetting how much time they'd spent together, El Bufo and Felipe.

"How I fucked your wife?" Gilberto snapped. "You weren't using her."

El Bufo's thick face didn't register surprise, just rage. If Cristina and the table hadn't been between them …

She shrank back into her seat.

"Honestly, Rigo. I thought I was doing you a favor. She was getting desperate, you wouldn't talk to her. I thought if I gave her something else to think about, she'd ease up on you and you'd relax. But also …"

The map took on detail, color, old blood brown and coffee black. She saw his wife's face. Not beautiful, but human, vulnerable. Nobody deserved to be used like this. It had been years ago, but they had never spoken of it, just let it fester until they hated each other. Why bring it up now? Gilberto was lonely here, without his partner, without allies. Desperate.

It wasn't like she was reading their minds. She didn't need to. She hadn't known the visions could work like this, feeding her puzzle pieces, letting her fill in the gaps.

"Say it," she told Gilberto. "This is the only chance you're going to get."

Gilberto looked at her, and she saw herself. Dirty huipil. Soft black curls. Small, round-shouldered, humble because still grieving. Someone who knew about last chances.

"But also," he began again, quietly, coldly, far from the words, "it was a way for me to feel closer to you, Rigo. You wouldn't let anyone in."

Except Lupita, Cristina realized. Now El Bufo's face was slack. The map grew one more node, rebalanced. She wished he could see it. She could see him — Felipe — trying to take this in. What could he say? This was supposed to be an interrogation, it gave every outward indication of being an interrogation, and here she was mediating between repressed lovers who couldn't bear to speak their hearts.

"Look, I'm sorry," said Gilberto. "You're right. People died because of what we did, and I let you take the fall. But I wasn't the one who'd been deliberately sabotaging every relationship I could touch — including with the man who pulls the strings. You checked out, Rigo. By the time it happened, I figured you were off playing some other game because you'd lost your taste for this one. Because you'd finally seen the cost. You wanted me to take the fall with you?

"It was a way I could salvage something. Otherwise we were both fucked."

"You think I didn't know the cost?" El Bufo said quietly, dangerously.

But it was wrong, too much and not enough. Felipe wasn't El Bufo. She didn't need magic to know he was thinking of Luz and Aníbal and what a monster he'd have to be to react the way El Bufo would react. There was no way he could keep this up.

But Cristina saw. Not everything that had happened between them, Gilberto and El Bufo, or what they'd done. But she saw the pattern. She saw it everywhere. In this blank room, a void in a hurricane, her eyes were open, and everything poured in. She saw Mael's humanity dissolving into the river of garbage, she saw the same happening to the real El Bufo. She saw the poison river outside Totonícapan, the curving bands of sulphur yellow in the dry riverbed. She saw the old photo, Monterríos and the men lined up at the edge of the ditch. She saw a young mother and father buying a mask for a baby. She saw Aníbal in prison. She saw Tecún Úman fall. The chain of consequences had no beginning and no end.

"Who died? What did you do?" she asked them both, though only one could possibly answer. "The massacre in Totonícapan, was that — because of you?"

Gilberto sat back. "You told her?"

A hollow, frightened laugh. "I didn't have to."

They were both looking at her. She fought the impulse to rip the mask off the jaguar's face just so she could have one face she could read. But she was chained to the table. His hand was all she could reach. She didn't touch it.

"Now you see why I wanted you to meet her."

"You didn't kill anyone," she told El Bufo, willing it to be true — then immediately regretted it.

He laughed. Because he had. El Bufo and Felipe both.

"We didn't murder any farmers," said Gilberto.

"But we set the blade swinging," El Bufo confirmed.

Now Cristina saw the old, incriminating photo crowded with angels. Angels everywhere there weren't men. She shouldered among them, flinging them off, the way she hadn't been able to that day when they danced at her mother's grave.

"They were hunting a dissident. A 'terrorist'. But they sent the wrong men. Or the right ones. It was just like during the war. Shelter the rebels, protect them, that makes you one of them. Scorched earth." Gilberto looked at his watch. It was heavy, showy, fake. On the same hand, he wore a ring with a green stone. "Time's ticking. Soon we'll have coffee and atól. If there was something you wanted to say ..."

"What about my mother?" Cristina demanded. "Did you send them after her, too?"

"Her mother," said El Bufo, "was Eufemia Ramos."

Gilberto's adams apple bobbed. He looked between them. At least he didn't bother feigning ignorance. "That was just another crime. It was only coincidence they turned out to be connected."

"Coincidence?" Her plastic restraints clicked and scraped against the plastic table. Was it possible to lie so often and so much you forgot what truth was? Did that explain El Bufo? But

Felipe had been lying all his life. "Your boss ordered that killing to cover up what happened in Totonícapan!"

"And you hired me to investigate," said El Bufo, "because your boss needed it swept under the rug. You didn't want me back. You were setting me up to fall. Again."

"No." Gilberto's calm had crumbled. He was seeing what kind of interrogation this really was. "That's what I wanted him to think."

"Bullshit." And El Bufo was out of his chair and rounding the table, and Gilberto was too, in the other direction, his chair falling with a clatter, putting Cristina between them.

"Stop it!" she shouted, unable to move. They circled, then slowed. "Don't you see? He was in love with you. And you're such an amazing detective, you never even saw it. Or did you? And you couldn't deal with it, so you ignored it. You retreated from him. You took it out on him, like bullies do. Like you do to everyone. Like you did to Felipe. You forced yourself into his life. And into Lupita's. You obsessed about magic, about fate. Why? Because you needed to feel like you were in control of something. But that was never Gilberto's fault. It's this place, this world. Working here, for Monterríos and Sonriente. It made you feel powerful, but you were their pawn like everyone else, and you couldn't stand that. But that's how life is. Nobody's in control. My mother died, my father and sister disappeared, and it's like wind. Like rain and rivers. Everything dies, nothing ends."

She wrung her hands in their restraints.

El Bufo and Gilberto both stood limp, the fight run out of them.

"Let her out of those," said El Bufo. "She's not the threat."

Gilberto took out a knife, and the zip ties ceased cutting into her wrists and slithered down the table to the floor. She rubbed the ridges where the plastic had left its mark.

"Sit down, both of you. If they come back, they'll notice something's wrong."

They sat.

"You're going to free all the protestors. All of them."

"I can't," said Gilberto.

"If you don't, we'll tell everyone what really happened. How Sonriente ordered a hit on a foreign diplomat to cover up his responsibility for the massacre. It might not destroy him. But I'm sure it'll be enough to get you fired."

"You can't know that. I don't even know that. You think if that was his plan he'd tell anyone?"

"I saw it happen. I see everything." A lie.

"She's not lying," El Bufo muttered. "She knew about us. God knows I didn't tell her. What more proof do you need?"

"You're telling me magic is real? Fate is real. And this —" Gilberto gestured faintly at Cristina, and she felt the insult. This *girl*. "This is what you've been doing all this time? Instead of your job."

"This is how I did my job," said El Bufo. He didn't mean Cristina, but Lupita. Lupita counting seeds and shards of glass in her squalor, determining who should live or die, for El Bufo to make it so. Only it wasn't El Bufo, it was Felipe. She needed him to be Felipe. She needed to see his face, and not this mask. She imagined for a moment, giddily, that it was working, that they'd pull off this impossible bluff, save their friends. They'd live, he'd get to be Felipe again. Instead of this.

"I remember how you used to be, Rigo," Gilberto was saying. "When I pulled you up out of the rank and file. Remember? When we thought we could change things from the inside?"

"Not really," El Bufo grunted.

"You hated Sonriente. Hated him so hard it looked like love. There were days I thought you'd kill him, right out in the open in front of twenty recruits. You wanted so badly for things to change, for a while I believed it."

"They still can," Cristina said. "You can help us."

"'Us?'" Gilberto rounded on her. "You think this asshole cares about a bunch of protesters? Maybe once, but no more. You think you see everything? You don't even know him. He gave up working for change a long time ago. He wants to be Sonriente. He wants revenge."

Felipe cracked El Bufo's knuckles, scowling.

"You're the one who doesn't know him," said Cristina. "He cares. He's here, isn't he? He's protecting the people he loves."

"There's no such thing as love," Gilberto snapped.

El Bufo let out an impatient breath. "I've had enough of this." He got up and went to the door.

"No one's coming," said Cristina. She didn't even have to look.

Gilberto checked his watch again. "I give them five minutes. If you're planning on beating me to death, you better get cracking."

El Bufo ignored this, looking up at the bubble in the ceiling that failed to hide the camera. "You'll be deleting this recording."

Gilberto narrowed his eyes. "Don't do anything stupid, and I won't have to. Come on, it hasn't been that long. Nobody flags it, footage gets overwritten after a week. We used to do this all the time."

El Bufo thrilled and terrified Cristina with a look that said he was indeed contemplating something stupid. "This time is different. Surely you see that? Make a decision, Gilberto. Are you going to prop up this regime so you can keep lording it over me? Because I didn't fall in love with you?"

Gilberto coughed a laugh. "This regime isn't under threat, Rigo. There's nothing you, or anyone, can do to hurt Monterríos, or to stop Sonriente from succeeding him. It's fate," he added, mocking.

"So you're not going to help us." She didn't know why she was even pretending surprise. "You're not even going to try?"

"Your threat has no teeth. I can't order a hundred political prisoners released and keep my job."

"We can discredit David Antonellis," said El Bufo. "He hired an actor to die in his place. To martyr himself without really dying. He's a coward. Like you, Gilberto."

"No," said Cristina. "We can't ..." She didn't understand Luz's plan or how she'd accomplished what she had. She certainly didn't care about Antonellis. Somewhere amid coastal humidity he was ashing a cigarette over a rusted balcony railing, slapping at mosquitoes, obsessively hitting refresh on a cheap laptop, while in entirely different surroundings his wife did the same, right down to the way she sat, blood coffee curling steam at her right hand. Missing and hating each other, pitying themselves. They'd played their hand and failed. But giving them away would risk derailing whatever was happening outside in the streets. It would undermine what Luz and Aníbal and Ixchel had worked so hard for. Wouldn't it?

"I have to try everything," Felipe told her, in his own voice, from behind El Bufo's face. "We need Anibál. Luz needs her."

"You won't 'bring down this administration' that way," sneered Gilberto.

"Of course not," El Bufo admitted. "It'll make them stronger. And you'll keep getting more like them. But tell me how to stop that, Gilberto, and I'll do it."

Gilberto studied him. "You would."

"Anything. As long as our friend goes free."

And Cristina believed him, and it scared her.

"But you can't, can you?" said El Bufo. "If there was a way, we'd have found it years ago. And now, if you could, you wouldn't even try. Because that's what it means to be part of this." He gestured angrily at the blank surroundings. There were boot scuffs on the walls, the door, coffee stains on the floor, a stale cigarette smell, and no other sign of humanity. "You've got your fingers on the threads now. Even if a fly does tear the web, you'll build it back again exactly the same. You firing me was the best thing that could have happened. Otherwise I'd have never got away."

Cristina's vision showed her the drab tiled corridor outside, and a man approaching in a cheap suit just like El Bufo's — squat, clean-cut and placid-faced, with coffee and atól, the bright light of the outside world slipping away behind a closing door.

"He's coming," she warned.

She could smell the atól. And it took her back to the last time she'd sat among those women, hip to hip to hip to hip around the warmth of the simmering pot. It took her further down the market aisle to the Comedor Santa Rosa de Líma, where Pilar and Tía Constancia served plantains and tortilla-wrapped eggs in front of the sad banner they'd rearranged again to camouflage the bullet holes.

Terrified, knowing they were out of time, she touched Felipe's hand. "Whatever you're going to do, do it now."

Gilberto sat splay-legged, fingers drumming on his rooster thighs. He had no idea what was coming.

"We were playing the wrong game all this time," El Bufo told Gilberto gently. He took off the frog mask. He became the jaguar. "He's been dead for days," the jaguar told Gilberto's blank, open-mouthed stare. "But he figured it out, before the end. That's why he left you. And it's why we're here now. To show you what was lost."

"Holy shit," said Gilberto. His adam's apple rose and plunged, rose and plunged. His chair clattered out from under him. He stood, wild-eyed, like a rooster faced with the ax. The jaguar was between him and the door. He looked to Cristina, who couldn't help him. There wasn't a soothing word she could say. Her mind could show her visions for days, and she wouldn't understand him well enough to know what this could mean to him.

Felipe had been born into this world a jaguar. He'd had his whole life to learn to cope. Cristina didn't know the first time she'd been shown a vision — the first time she'd shown one to herself. It faded together the way childhoods do. She was remembering the carpeted stairs of the townhouse in Mixco, how she, Corísa and Teresa made their dolls climb them, imagining the volcano. Had she been imagining? If she and her sisters and their dolls had somehow climbed the great dead cinder cone of Agua, would the crater lake under its ring of cloud in morning light have looked exactly as she told them?

But it wasn't the same for Gilberto. He didn't have a lifetime in which to try to understand. They were asking too much. And time was up.

"He's right outside the door," she warned.

The jaguar put the mask back on and became El Bufo. He retrieved Gilberto's chair from where it had fallen. Gilberto flinched.

The door opened, and the cheap-suited government stooge was preceded into the room by the comforting, warm, awakening smells of coffee and atól. Cristina's stomach rolled.

Then the stooge saw Gilberto's face, and what was there caused him to let the cardboard tray full of reprieve slip forward out of his hands and splatter sickly to the floor.

"Don't —" said Gilberto, uselessly, as the stooge backed out of the room.

"He'll look at the tape," growled El Bufo. He caught the door before it slammed, was after him and gone.

Cristina saw the jaguar ripping out the throats of mareros. But she had to trust him. She was poised at the crest of a wave, imagined she could direct its fall however she chose. Outside in the plaza, protestors were gathering again. Luz was on her way to join them, pedaling down Montufar on a borrowed bike. In the alley, heavily armed police and SAAS were forming up for another day of arrests and brutal repression. Aníbal languished in a kind of stasis, trapped in a cloud, battering herself against the walls of her own head. Upstairs, Sonriente sat at a big mahogany desk gazing out a window at the plaza, sucking coffee from his ugly mustache. Ixchel taught Spanish.

Gilberto looked lost. Like he'd gone away, outside himself — the opposite of Aníbal. "I haven't seen one of those since my son was a baby. There was one at the zoo — did you ever go? It was always asleep. They used to have it in this depressing little cage. Like something out of a cartoon. Or a dream — we were all so sleep-deprived. Then she found out who I was. When she left, she took my son with her. And I was relieved. And I thought, Who was dreaming who?"

Bitter coffee and sweet mush mingled on the institutional tile. Gilberto nudged the puddle with a battered leather shoe. He looked at her imploringly. "He used to talk about them. We'd be in the office late, going over paperwork, we'd hit a wall, and he'd be going on about their bite strength in kPa, how they could pierce a human skull like cracking an egg. Or making up some bullshit story about how a jaguar challenged a bat to a race under the full moon. What do I know, maybe every word of it was true. Maybe I'm in some kind of fugue state from overwork and none of this is happening. Maybe I'm talking to myself."

"It's happening," she assured him, with nowhere near the reassurance those words should have implied. She had nothing for him that would reorient his concept of the world, its hierarchy. She thought about touching his hand the way she had Felipe's. She didn't have the slightest desire to hug him, though she felt it was called for. "It shocked me too, at first," she said.

"But you're like him," he said.

"Yes," she admitted. A fierce rush of pride.

"Then that means —"

She didn't know what it meant.

Gilberto stepped across the puddle, not quite managing to avoid it, leaving the imprint of a heel in squashed pudding. Roughly, he took Cristina's arm.

Cristina said a hasty goodbye to the blank room whose walls dripped with the world. She took the world with her.

Gilberto rooster-walked her to the security console in the corridor, thrusting El Bufo and the stooge aside mid-argument. "Get someone to clean up that mess," he told the stooge, a dismissal.

Then he ran back the recording.

And there was the jaguar, for just a moment. That a camera registered it proved it was real. It could be shared on the internet. On the first page of the *Diary*. Exploited. Felipe — a kind of ancient being lost in the real world — had the power to shapeshift, to impersonate men. Cristina was just such a being. And this information could be shared, and the whole world could undergo the same psychotic break that gripped Gilberto.

He ran it back again.

"It's not going to change," said El Bufo.

Gilberto's adam's apple bobbed. "No," he said. But he ran the footage back one more time, got out his phone and recorded it, screen to screen. The scratched security monitor reflected his face, the industrial fluorescents, and was reflected in his glasses in turn.

He selected those few seconds' span of security footage and hit delete. Then he turned and regarded El Bufo as he placed a call on his phone. "Zotz, is that you? Fucking awful reception in here ...

The arrests from yesterday, last week. All of them. Want all charges dropped. That's right. Yeah, yeah, you can put it on me."

He disconnected. At El Bufo's incredulous look, he turned the phone to show he'd actually been on a call.

"You could have called your mother."

Gilberto shook his head. "Trying to give you what you want. So you'll give me what I want."

They both looked at Cristina.

"I can't read minds," she told their waiting glances. "I can't see the future." Nothing had changed that she could see. Pavoncito wasn't ruled by the guards or the SAAS. Whatever clemency came, for Aníbal, it might be too late. The long line of dead men still waited at her cell door. How much could anyone take?

"Fine," said Gilberto. He reconnected the call. "Zotz. Can you hear me? Tell the people what you told me."

A pause, a cough. Then a fragment of a voice, dry and cold, filtered through the fortified walls of the Presidential Palace. "*He's not going to like this one bit.*"

"Thank you, Zotz." Gilberto closed the phone, put it in his pocket with his hand wrapped tight around it. "Now come on. We're going upstairs."

On the elevator, she stood between them. Felipe texted at Luz, trying to warn her, prepare her, confirm what Gilberto wanted them to believe. But this was a leap of faith. Desperation. Gilberto was wearing a gun; Cristina could see it through his coat.

It was like they were already dead. That was why she felt so free.

The doors opened.

Just past the landing, concrete and industrial tile gave way to imported white marble and thick, red carpet that silenced their steps. On the walls, gilt mirrors and vases of somehow-pristine calla lilies alternated with colonial landscapes where doll-like peasants worked steep slopes hung with haze. Even the suits on the armed stooges were less cheap. Cristina felt the impulse to hide her unmanacled hands as they passed between two of them, but El Bufo swaggered.

Gilberto's hand in his pocket was on his phone, not his gun. "In his office, I presume," he said blandly to one of them, who nodded curtly, impassive.

The pressure was too much. She had to let it out. She didn't care.

Giddily, not giving herself the chance to hesitate, Cristina indulged the first impulse that came to her. She pulled one of the paintings off the wall — staggered under the weight of the frame — and carried it to the t-junction ahead, where a row of white marble busts stood in spheres of creamy light. The nearest was of ousted President Jacopo Arbenz. She let the heavy frame fall forward out of her hands, impaling the canvas on his oddly triangular head with the most satisfying ripping sound.

She laughed, delighted.

"Stop right there!" The stooges drew their weapons. "What the hell do you think you're doing?"

The white marble under her feet exuded a deep cool that penetrated all the way to her bones.

Gilberto stepped between her and the guns. "Relax," he said, his jangling, taut body anything but. "Lower your weapons. She's with us."

El Bufo's eyes were laughing with her.

The stooges did as they were told, but followed behind them.

Left at the junction, and down to the corner office on the right: a window — the first window she'd seen in this place. Immediately, she could see this window from the outside, from the plaza below, an anonymous, black rectangle among rows of them, below the cornice with its carvings of conquerors, above the wrought-iron fence surmounted with spikes. This was only the third floor. Above them was another office — the president's? Above that, the roof, with its helicopter pad and barbed wire, bathed in sun fierce despite the pollution. In the plaza, the people were gathering. The fountain spouted mist. She searched for Luz and Mynor.

El Bufo cleared his throat and knocked. "Special Agents Zamora and Ayora," he called, deadpan. "Here to introduce his majesty to a person of interest, in a matter of the utmost urgency."

The stooges were right behind them, at a discreet few paces' distance, weapons out.

"Put those away," El Bufo scolded them.

They ignored him. One had a hand to an earpiece.

Cristina opened and closed her fingers, trying to work out the tingles, unsure if she wanted them filled with a brush and palette, Felipe's hand, a jaguar's paw or a cheap submachine gun set to empty itself at a touch. It was all so silly, so far beyond reasonable for the three of them to be here — here. What were they supposed to do when the door opened? What did Gilberto expect to happen?

He met Cristina's eyes, drew them across the corridor, to where an exit sign glowed above a service stairwell. He made sure El Bufo saw it too.

The door opened. "Enter," said a voice from within.

Sonriente sat at the big mahogany desk in front of a map of Zone One, surrounded by paste-faced advisors. In person, his features were exaggerated and sharp, like the nightmare some endangered trogon might describe to terrify another bird of the remote highlands who'd never encountered a human being. She wanted to tell Felipe this, to laugh with him about it, so hard they'd lean against each other for support.

El Bufo leaned in, flung an arm around Gilberto. Showed all his teeth.

Sonriente wasn't smiling. "Well, Special Agent Ayora?" said the voice hideously devoid of anything that could be trusted or believed in. "What's important enough to interrupt this emergency tactical briefing? The safety of our streets is at stake."

"This can't wait, Director. It has the potential to quell these protests at once." El Bufo maneuvered the rigid Gilberto through the doorway, drawing Cristina creeping in their wake, away from the men with the guns.

On the walls flanking the desk hung reproductions of two pages from the Madrid Codex, enormous snaked and tentacled deities of death and rain, char-black and bloodless white, surrounded by their worshippers, the days. She fought an impulse to genuflect.

No regime in history, the frozen Gilberto was probably reminding himself, had ever been changed by the surgical removal of a single head. Nor even by the bloody purging of a room full of conspirators. Real change came through attrition. The CIA-backed coup that sent Arbenz into exile had been an exception — even Cristina knew that, and she'd been sheltered by force from current events all her life. Of course, Arbenz had been removed to restore a bloody status quo.

But the swelling crowd outside the windows made it impossible to ignore that they were only the crest of a great wave of resistance. Waves crashed and receded, and the beach was unchanged, Eufemia's ghost might insist, had she not already become one with the volcanic vapors and pollution. But Cristina couldn't deny anymore how they were all part of the ocean.

El Bufo's face confirmed it. The mask was coming off. No more deception. Their plan, their bluff, whether it had succeeded or failed, must hurtle along under its own momentum until it struck a wall of bullets. Aníbal was sprinting headlong into the gas cloud, and Luz had no choice but to follow.

What was called for now was a gesture of defiance.

She pushed between the two detectives — one all stretched skin, the other solid as clay — and stepped up to the massive desk. She took a pen from the hand of the nearest advisor — her breath mingling momentarily with his breath, his face a politician's mask, bemused and disapproving, oblivious to the very real danger. On the map of the city, with heavy strokes as though the pen were a dagger, Cristina tore through the paper but failed to scar the dense, impervious wood beneath as she inscribed a pair of facing glyphs. She wasn't practiced in this style, but she wasn't going for polish or perfection. It was like the graffiti she'd seen in the plaza that day. Had her ancient ancestors, her mother's mother's mothers, ever made art this way — spray-paint hiss, a brutal point made in haste? She couldn't know. She couldn't know.

Before she could complete the stroke, Sonriente pushed back his chair and ripped the pen out of her fist. He wasn't a large man, but as dense as El Bufo. The deadly incongruous smile, his namesake, was sliver-thin. He gestured over the heads of his seated advisors at the two stooges behind them in the corridor. "I want this woman removed."

The stooges shouldered their way in. Polyester rustled like bats' wings as the advisors tried to get out of the way, but the desk was too big, there was no room. K'awiil and Camazotz leered from the walls. El Bufo tripped one of the stooges as he elbowed past, shoved him.

"Please excuse the interruption," said Gilberto, and then Cristina couldn't hold in the laughter anymore.

The expensive fountain pen had left rust-colored ink all over her hand. Kneeling on the desk, she reached and smeared it across Sonriente's face. His skin felt like crepe.

Then El Bufo pulled off the frog mask, letting it fall to the floor. And there, in the middle of the office of the chief of the national secret police, stood the jaguar. A jaguar in a cheap suit. The ghost of a washed-up detective in a cheap suit. A handsome, frightened young man with a strong K'iche' nose in a cheap suit that was too big for him. Resplendent, nonetheless, in his shadow-patterned coat that made the eye ache and slide away, he growled a faint question. The advisors pressed back against the walls. Sonriente held the pen like a blade.

Cristina wanted the people in the plaza to see.

The jaguar wheeled and bounded, planting two heavy paws on the chest of the other stooge, knocking him into the arms of the advisors, sending the gun flying.

The way was open. Cristina needed no further invitation to jump down off the desk and run, between Gilberto and the jaguar, back out into the corridor lined with the busts of dead robber barons. She made for the exit sign, the service stairwell. She hit the door running, it slammed open and an alarm sounded. She hesitated on the landing.

The jaguar's head materialized against her hand, shocking her with its rightness. There were shouts, and there, when she glanced back, was Gilberto.

"Up to the roof," he yelled over the siren wail, dazed and breathless. "Or else down to the street. Guards everywhere." It was clear he wasn't about to make the decision. It was horrible what they'd done to him, she understood distantly. He thought she and Felipe were gods, or demons. He thought he was damned. It was hard to feel any sympathy.

In the street in Cristina's mind, shock troops massed for battle with protestors. If the alarm weren't sounding in her ear, she could have heard the crowd in the plaza. She could see them. Through a long, narrow, black cylinder that passed its eye across them like a needle sewing thread. Through the eyes of snipers hunting someone in that crowd, or several someones, from above.

She went up, ears ringing.

As the door opened out onto the Presidential Palace roof, revealing the morning, the light on the cathedral spire and the rooftops of the city, the breeze, the noise of the crowd, Cristina found that she was crying.

The jaguar's tail lashed, curving like a question mark at either extreme of its sway. "Lock it," said El Bufo's voice.

Gilberto got out his keys.

A rooftop patio, ceramic-tiled, patterned like the plaza that remained invisible beyond parapets. Awnings bulged like sails, white canvas pulled taut on steel cables. Across the patio, up half a flight of stairs, a black helicopter hunched atop its pad like an overfed fly.

"Snipers," gasped Cristina. "Three of them. There, and there, and ..."

The jaguar growled an acknowledgment and was gone.

"No," she protested, boneless at the loss of his head under her hand.

She could see everything, like never before. Something was happening inside her. Something was being revealed, being born. Was it like pregnancy? New life within her, growing more insistent by the moment, waiting to come out. Teresa could have told her. Even Corísa. Ixchel had warned her. She wasn't ready.

She could see the crowd in the plaza waiting with bated breath to be chastised, more people flooding in from the streets beyond. Gulls wheeled overhead; she could see the crowd through their eyes, until they scattered at the approach of another helicopter, a news helicopter with its own impenetrable eyes. She could see the armed men flooding up the stairwells. She could see the man who'd been on the other end of Gilberto's phone, Zotz, scratching his nose at a metal table, a green-jeweled ring on his hand, surrounded by papers and the ash-dark walls of Pavoncito. She could see herself, as she had in the security camera and in the mugshots, only this time she was framed in the crosshairs of a sniper scope that held steady as death. She could see angels.

The insistence of the visions were dizzying, and she had to cling to Gilberto's arm to be sure which way was up, to remind herself which visions came from her own senses.

But Gilberto wasn't steady either.

He dropped the keys and, with the toe of his battered shoe, jammed them under the crack in the door as far as they would go. "They've got keys too," he said. "We need to get away from here."

There was no place to go.

Then the sniper eye on her was gone. A scarlet-winged angel, beautiful because its face had never once adopted a human expression, dissipated like vapor.

The jaguar was an angel for angels.

"Come on," Cristina said to Gilberto, and just to be moving, to not be paralyzed, she pulled him across the patio, into the awning's shadow and out of the sun. It didn't matter. The snipers would find them, or the guards. The first of them were already at the top of the stairs.

Down in the street, at some signal from Sonriente, the click of a ring on a desk, the riot cops opened a gate in the fence and poured into the plaza three ranks deep. The tank rolled behind them. The crowd recoiled, compressed. Banners sagged, then came taut again. WE ARE ALL TOTONICAPÁN.

The door to the stairwell was unlocked from within. Struck by a polyester-suited shoulder, it scraped open. As the first guard appeared before her real, human eyes, Cristina pulled Gilberto around to the other side of the awning, out of his sight, back into the sun. Armed SAAS operatives poured onto the patio. The first shouted inconsequential demands that they turn themselves in, addressing each of them by name. "Special Agents Zamora and Ayora. Dissident Cristina Yochi Ramos. Show yourselves. Now."

Gilberto was clutching his phone again as if it were a talisman, a ward. His power had been stripped away along with his sense of purpose, of order in the world. Losing El Bufo like this — losing him and not losing him, being haunted by him — had done something to him she couldn't comprehend.

She didn't pity him, but felt as though she should. "Give yourself up," she offered. "You can tell them we held you hostage."

Gilberto shook his head, his mouth slack. "They'll know I deleted the footage. They'll find out I ordered the prisoners released. I'm a traitor. They'll know."

"Then you might as well use that footage for something." The news helicopter banked over the plaza, rotors beating. She pulled him further away from the door and the armed agents, down against the parapet at the rooftop's edge. "Send it to the *Diary*. Send it to *Waking Dream*. Isn't that why you recorded it?" She could see it: a few seconds' pixellated phone camera recording of grainy security footage of a man becoming a jaguar under bleach-white fluorescents. Would anyone understand what it meant?

Gilberto looked at his phone as though it could tell him what to do.

Cristina saw the face of a second sniper slam into the rooftop and go out like a light. Now only one black angel eye remained, not searching for her, not aware of the jaguar, but scanning the crowd below.

There was no beauty to what she saw — not individually — and yet the impulse was there to assign beauty to it, collectively. A way to distance herself from the pain of it, the sacrifice and fear, grief, suffering, the agonizing hope. And she could do it. She imagined the texture of the brush between her fingers, the gentle resistance of canvas. She could put it all together into something she could share, that others could see, bright and dramatic and overwhelming. At least it wouldn't be only hers anymore.

It was too bright. Beside her, Gilberto slid down into the shadow of the parapet, shading his phone screen from the sun with his hand.

Luz's head and shoulders appeared in the last sniper's scope, slid past and were gone. Then she reappeared.

She looked beautiful. Red lipstick, glossy black hair, makeup to hide exhaustion. She'd changed clothes again, the black shirt she wore was brand new, and the rainbow face on it was Ixchel's. She was riding on someone's broad shoulders — it was Mynor; he'd found her! — shouting into a bullhorn. Orders for retreat, a song of solidarity or defiance, Cristina couldn't hear. She could only see. But she could see in the fierceness with which she held the bullhorn to her lips how losing Aníbal and then Felipe had taken from Luz the last shreds of possible excuse to look away from injustice, to relax and simply live; all she had left was the cause, the people.

Not with her mind's eye but her eye, Cristina saw that the last sniper knelt at the far southwest corner of the palace rooftop, the rifle steadied against the parapet. She left Gilberto where he was and ran, an impossible distance to cover in the space of a trigger pull.

But the jaguar reached him first, swift and quiet on heavy velvet paws. A slash of blood on white imported stone, and the rifle fell, clattering, over the side. In the crowd, Luz went on leading, blissfully unaware of the angel averted, of what a different kind of protest this could have been. But it still could be — there were angels more than enough. This time, Cristina was certain, Luz would be the last to run, and her own portrait could take its place next to Berta Cáceres in the gallery of martyrs on Felipe's apartment wall, unless —

Balanced atop the parapet, the jaguar sank onto his haunches. The news helicopter banked again and came back; its camera panned, zoomed. A sleek black and golden blur on the edge of the palace rooftop shrugged out of a cheap suitcoat, pulled a sweat-stained shirt over its head. A woman stumbled and caught herself at the jaguar's side, curls whirling in the wind from the rotors.

At the back corner of the crowd nearest the artisans' market, by the barred cathedral gate, Pilar held Tía Constancia's hand so hard the knuckles stood out white. Mama stood by the oven, turning the rotisserie spit herself because the motor was broken. Papi danced stiffly in the living room to the stereo turned low, alone after everyone else had gone to bed. Sparrows with sunrise-gold streaks above their brows built a nest in the crook of Tecún Úman's elbow out of plastic mesh and dry grass. Francisco sat on a park bench in Xela, Miguel Ángel dribbling on his shoulder, glumly watching his cousins throw pebbles in a fountain. Hugo painted a stark portrait of an angry girl who could have been Cristina, who could have been anyone. Rosaría lit a cigar. David Antonellis lay in a cheap hotel room, long legs hanging over the bedframe, a laptop on his chest, scrolling the feeds, when the door burst open and jackbooted angels poured into the room. Aníbal sat on a bed alone in a cell. She looked up as a key turned in the lock. Toby pulled the ribbon of the jaguar mask tight behind his head and ran to join the crowd.

The jaguar was naked, tail lashing, defiant in his puzzle-patterned coat. Cristina buried her hand in it and felt the pulse beneath.

She put her lips to his ear. She wanted to tell him it hadn't been in vain, that Aníbal would be released, was being ushered out the doors of Pavoncito even now, a hero's return, battered, traumatized, but not broken. Still herself. Alive. And because of what they'd done, the world would change for the better.

But she couldn't be sure. And she couldn't lie. Not now.

Instead, she kissed the jaguar's ear and told him something true, and together they waited, gazing out beyond the parapet at the crowd and police in the plaza surging against each other like a pent sea. They were so many, and the conviction welled up inside her that if these hundred thousand could only know, if the firing squad assembling behind her could see, if she could give them all the same revelation — not a grainy clip of security footage or a shuddering helicopter newsfeed but the vivid, incontrovertible truth — it could all change in an instant.

It wasn't like it had been on his brother's bus at all.

How many were looking at him this time, seeing his true self, at least his true shape? Not just here in the crowd. They saw him on the cameras in bars and bus stations, on the big screens at the mall, the ancient tube tvs propped on rotten cardboard in El Gallito. His parents — *we interrupt this telenovela to bring you a special report* — his brother, his little nephew Juan Martín? But not Luz; Luz was busy.

What did they see? A jaguar, perched atop the Presidential Palace with a once-quiet girl in red-green-black traje at his side, her soft curls moving in the breeze, moments before bullets would transform them into a fireworks display of blood-red streamers shooting out over the helmeted heads of the riot cops. The crowd could not see the semicircle of security forces closing in on the rooftop behind them, AKs at the ready, Gilberto Ayora standing slack-faced behind them cradling his phone. Did it matter? They saw him.

The eyes were more terrifying than the guns. The masks were gone. El Bufo was gone. The frog mask lay on the floor in Sonriente's office where he'd discarded it; all the others were with Toby. That horrible itchy suit was pooled on the rooftop behind him, never to darken his shoulders again. He was himself, only himself.

He'd miss El Bufo. He felt strangely grateful to have been him. But even more so to be himself again. At least for a moment.

Don't bring this trouble on us, his brother Rubén's eyes had said. Felipe's parents had bought him his first mask, hiding all of him but his own green eyes. He'd never registered the fear in theirs, only love and forbearance, yet they had extinguished the light in his brother Martín's eyes for nothing but being what he was. But Cristina's were the eyes that mattered to him now, and though in this moment they were glazed, unfocused, darting as though she was dreaming awake, he knew she saw him for what he was. Her hand in his fur was light, the barest touch, electric. An umbilical connecting him to everything that was in her. Which, he somehow knew, was everything.

The helicopter thundered overhead. The volcano slept beyond the smog, a shade darker than the sky, a shade lighter than the fishscale domes of the cathedral. Mist rose and fell from the fountain. The arrayed police and soldiers had yet to fire a shot. That would change, any moment it would change — but for now, there was exhaust, pollution, rot, death, but also wind, the green and whispering life of trees. He thought he could smell someone cooking atól, and a faint, resiny wisp of copal.

Directly below them, between the crowd, the riot fencing and the palace wall, a row of scraggly locust trees grew in stone boxes, only the tips of their crowns reaching into the early sun. Their foliage was yellowed, desiccated by the dry season; they provided no cover. But they offered him escape. He could leap from the parapet, and one of those trees could catch him. He could scramble down behind the fencing; the cops were focused on the crowd. Baby might still be parked around the corner, waiting, ready with her dark glass and bass-boosted digital soundsystem. He could escape.

But he couldn't take her with him. He couldn't carry her, couldn't save her. Cristina had placed herself in his care, put her trust in him, forgiven him, followed him all the way here. To this. Had she known? She couldn't have. Had she suspected? It would have been hard not to. Why, then? What had she seen in him? What Ixchel had seen. Together, they'd saved him. From isolation, from himself. It couldn't have happened without El Bufo, but El Bufo had only broken him down; Cristina and Ixchel had built him back up.

The crowd were pointing upwards, exclaiming. Swelling up with hope and expectation he couldn't fulfill.

He felt her fingertips tighten against his fur. So he looked at Cristina, and that was when he saw and understood: the feathers, the scales, bursting from beneath her dirty, worn huipil in colors just as bright and brighter. When she fell from the parapet, she wouldn't fall. She would soar.

Afterword

The year my sister moved to Guatemala City, it was the place with the most murders per capita in the world. Guatemala (Iximulew in K'iche) consistently ranks with El Salvador, Nicaragua, Haiti, and Honduras among the poorest countries in the Western Hemisphere. Guatemala's Indigenous population numbers in the millions, among the largest concentrations of Indigenous peoples in the world. Beginning in the early 2000s, thanks to the Canadian mining firm Goldcorp, Guatemala became the proving ground for the now internationally reviled state tactic of criminalizing environmental defenders.[1] Murdering them is a tactic far older, but gaining momentum all the time. In the last ten years, more than 1300 land activists were killed in Mesoamerica — more than anywhere else in the world.[2]

When I fell in love with ancient Maya monumental architecture and sculpture, growing up in the affluent Northeastern US, I believed the Maya were an extinct culture, like the ancient Egyptians or Babylonians. I read accounts by dead, English-speaking white men of the "discovery" of their "lost" cities. I went

---

1 https://www.theguardian.com/environment/2023/aug/18/fighting-huge-monster-mine-battle-guatemala-playbook-polluters

2 https://www.theguardian.com/global-development/2024/jan/22/he-had-a-machete-in-his-cheek-how-guatemalas-hydropower-dream-turned-deadly

to see their artifacts in museums and didn't think about how they'd got there.

The reasons for all of the above are in no way distinct.

The policies that led Colón, Cortés and de Alvarado to plunder and incinerate the great cultures of Mesoamerica have continued unabated from those days to these, with only the tactics and the players changing. Foreign powers groom local collaborators, making them complicit in the subjugation of their own peoples in order to avoid blame. Resources of every kind — mineral, animal, vegetable, human — are drained from colonized nations the world over to perpetuate and solidify the dominance of the colonizers.

I'm not telling you anything new. But it was new to me once, because it is in the interest of colonizers to obfuscate, indoctrinate, and discredit.

Every awful thing depicted in this novel and worse has been perpetrated against the Indigenous Maya, Garífuna, and Ladino peoples of Guatemala in the name of the economic exploitation of its natural resources by the Global North. Every valiant act of self-sacrifice, too, is real. I've taken unaccountable joy in rendering all this in vivid prose, but there's little here I've invented.

In 1954, the CIA under US President Eisenhower orchestrated a coup ousting Guatemalan president Jacobo Árbenz, the country's second ever democratically elected leader, replacing him with military dictator Carlos Castillo Armas in only one of numerous such interventions in Central and South America and the Caribbean, which continue to the present day.[3]

The writer O. Henry coined the term "banana republic" in 1904 to connote the means by which the North kept Guatemala and Honduras in a state of political instability in order to enable unchecked exploitation of those countries' natural resources,

---

[3] https://nsarchive2.gwu.edu/NSAEBB/NSAEBB4/index.html

notably fruit.[4] For most of the 20th century, the United Fruit Company operated a transportation monopoly in Guatemala; it owned outright all of Guatemala's railroads and international ports, employed its considerable political clout in discouraging the construction of highways that would lessen that monopoly, and was the country's single largest landowner. Its corporate entity lives on, and continues to exploit Indigenous people and resources, as Chiquita Brands International, now based in Switzerland.

Perhaps the most comprehensive and devastating argument I've encountered for all this is still Eduardo Galeano's *Open Veins of Latin America*, first published in 1970 — a banned book in many of the countries whose exploitation it discusses — in which Galeano lays out an exhaustive, compelling case against the systematic strip-mining of Central and South America by colonial powers over five centuries.

As I write this early in 2024, nothing I'm seeing makes me think any of this is going to stop. And it's going to become harder and harder to track as the massive disinformation machine that is generative AI ramps up, journalists get murdered and laid off, and regulation is dismantled. Currently, the US and Canada are competing to catch up with China in control of rare earth metals, considered strategic assets for things like solar panel manufacture, which has engendered a renewed effort to mine the wealth out from under the ancestral and sacred lands of Indigenous peoples in Mesoamerica.[5]

The good news is, the resistance isn't going anywhere.

Intensive and prolonged local activism and international human rights oversight in Guatemala since the peace accords in

---

4 https://interestingliterature.com/2023/06/banana-republic-phrase-meaning-origin/

5 https://www.newsweek.com/newsweek-exclusive-us-bid-help-secure-sanctioned-1bn-nickel-mine-guatemala-fenix-1792282

1992 have brought about positive and meaningful change. In 2019, for the first time, Guatemala's highest court acknowledged local community objection and ordered the Fénix nickel mine to cease operations. "Phoenix," what an awful name, evoking the regenerative myth of Tecún Uman's rebirth over a project that will render Indigenous lands toxic or outright uninhabitable for centuries to come. The mine has continued to operate illegally, forcing local Q'eqchi authorities in 2021 to institute a road blockade, to which Guatemala's president in turn responded by imposing a state of siege amounting to martial law.[6] All of which will sound devastatingly familiar. And this is only one example of many.

What are any of us to do? Anything. Whatever you can.

There are enough worthy causes out there in a world beset by engineered ecological and climate collapse; likely you don't need another one. But if you bought this book, you're already helping to make a difference. I'm donating all my income from sales of *The Jaguar Mask* to environmental justice charities including Cultural Survival.[7] If you've got the bandwidth to learn more, please check them out and subscribe to their newsletter.

Thank you very much for caring.

---

6 https://www.culturalsurvival.org/news/guatemalan-president-suspends-civil-rights-facilitate-nickel-mine-demand-battery-minerals

7 https://www.culturalsurvival.org/

Acknowledgements

This book is the product of years of research and travel, but more than that, a ton of deep, revelatory introspection, psychic enema, emotional wringer, the whole thing and the kitchen sink, too. I must first and foremost thank my intrepid, brave, generous sister Danielle and her wise, dedicated, patient partner Erick for providing me the excuse to spend time in Guatemala, hosting me, teaching me, traveling with me, bearing with my bubbling enthusiasm, mistakes, and misapprehensions. Also, perhaps even moreso, I must thank Erick's family, who welcomed a weird, oversized, gangly stranger and gave me so much of my understanding of that astonishingly beautiful, heart-wrenching place and its long-suffering and generous people.

Profound thanks also to everyone who read and listened to and advised and encouraged me in persisting with the many drafts and pieces of *The Jaguar Mask*: Danielle DeLuca, Erick Colop, Bonnie Jo Stufflebeam, Marissa Lingen, Terra LeMay, Barbara Krasnoff, Mercurio D. Rivera, Grá Linnea, Jennifer Linnea, Molly Tanzer, Desirina Boskovich, Robert Levy, Christopher M. Cevasco, Scott H. Andrews, Jason Ridler, Justin Howe, Erin Hoffman, Andrea Pawley, Andrew Kozma, Gavin Grant, Christopher Brown, Cameron McClure, and Lauren Bajek. And to the others I have no doubt forgotten. Writing is hard. It takes a village.

Love in memory to the people I lost while writing this: Patty Simmonds, Dina DeLuca, Peggy Bordewieck.

Special thanks to the editorial staff of *Reckoning* for providing such uniquely supportive community, creative context, and inspiration.

Finally, to Selena Middleton, editor, fixer, peer, tireless advocate and booster of two of my books now: thanks to your persistence, this is a better, kinder, truer book I can be proud of. I'm in your debt.

About the Author

Michael J. DeLuca's novella *Night Roll* was a finalist for the Crawford Award in 2020. He is the publisher of *Reckoning*, a journal of creative writing on environmental justice. He also runs the indie ebook site *Weightless Books*, and his short fiction has been appearing since 2005 in places such as *Beneath Ceaseless Skies*, *Apex*, *Mythic Delirium*, *Fusion Fragment*, and *Three-Lobed Burning Eye*. He lives in suburbified post-industrial woodlands north of Detroit with partner, kid, cats, and microbes. The only mask he owns, for better or worse, is the conquistador.

MORE BY MICHAEL J. DELUCA

Don't miss Michael J. DeLuca's dreamy urban fantasy retelling of Tam Lin. This novella, a Crawford Award finalist, is a quiet revolution of perseverance, love, and a touch of magic.

EBOOKS ARE ALWAYS ON SALE AT WWW.STELLIFORM.PRESS

YOU MAY ALSO LIKE

these Stelliform Press titles by Indigenous authors.

Lush worldbuilding and humor buoy this Hawaiian best-friends-save-the-world underwater fantasy novella.

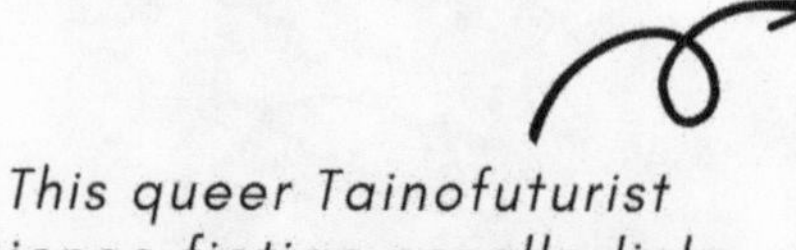

This queer Tainofuturist science fiction novella links climate and colonization and underscores the importance of Indigenous solidarity. A breathless read, packed with feeling.

EBOOKS ARE ALWAYS ON SALE AT WWW.STELLIFORM.PRESS

Earth-focused fiction. Stellar stories.
Stelliform.press.

Stelliform Press is shaping conversations about nature and our place within it. We invite you to join the conversation by leaving a comment or review on your favorite social media platform. Find us on the web at www.stelliform.press and on Bluesky, Threads, Twitter, Instagram and Facebook @StelliformPress and on Mastodon at mastodon.online/@StelliformPress.

Printed in the USA
CPSIA information can be obtained
at www.ICGtesting.com
JSHW081809060824
67461JS00006B/18